t4

PERIDOT FLIGHT

ALSO BY DORIS LESLIE

PERIDOT FLIGHT

a novel
reconstructed from the memoirs
of
Peridot, Lady Mulvarnie
(1872–1955)
by

DORIS LESLIE

Decorations *by* PHILIP GOUGH

THE BOOK CLUB
121 CHARING CROSS ROAD
LONDON WC2

MADE AND PRINTED IN GREAT BRITAIN BY
EBENEZER BAYLIS AND SON, LIMITED, THE
TRINITY PRESS, WORCESTER, AND LONDON

For
Mr. and Mrs. William Foyle
who
also remember

I am most grateful for Counsel's advice and that of other legal friends who have helped me in the reconstruction of the Court scenes of fifty years ago.

D.L.

PROLOGUE

I FIRST came to know her in the spring of 1950. She must then have been nearing her eightieth year, though none to see her would have guessed it. Despite her frailty and lack of height she was an outstanding personality with a forthright commanding manner, a dry sense of humour, and eyes of a surprisingly unfaded green. Her dress was more suitable to eighteen than eighty, and she wore a blonde, unmistakable wig.

At that first meeting she informed me she had been 'quite a person' in her day, had figured in a *cause celèbre*, and made a fortune from a face cream. 'It is not used or heard of now, yet it was very popular in my time. They had no beauty parlours then.'

But not until I visited her at her charming seventeenth-century house in Hertfordshire did she tell me she had written her reminiscences, based on a journal she kept in her youth. Her memory was extraordinarily retentive, and in our talks together she brought vividly before me that period 'so nostalgically near to yet so remote from this vulgar, noisy, atomic age of yours, that it may justly be called history'.

Signed photographs of bygone celebrities littered the piano in her drawing-room, furnished in the fashion of half a century ago. On the wall above the mantelpiece was a conspicuous portrait of an officer of the first World War; and, on an occasional table, supported by a miniature easel, the framed crayon drawing of a bulldog's head. 'That's Jasper,' she explained, 'my best beloved. I've not been without a bulldog for almost sixty years until this summer when the last of them died, to live again in the past,' her eyes strayed to the portrait on the wall, 'which at my age is the present.'

When I left her she handed me a bulky parcel: the reminiscences. 'You have,' she said, 'my full permission to make a book of this, should you care to do so. Every word of it is true, but as none of whom I write is alive today you can't be sued for libel. You may alter the names if you wish, but not mine, for that is too good to be true!'

9

1*

It was no easy task to decipher that spidery crabbed writing, nor to piece together the yellow dog-eared pages, many of which were unnumbered, some missing. This made it impossible to publish the memoirs in their entirety and with no supplementary narrative as was my original intention. Certain excerpts from the journal, kept intermittently for fifteen years, have been included, but the memoirs were written several decades later, and I have only the word of Lady Mulvarnie to vouch for their authenticity.

ONE

'My last night under this roof. Tomorrow I leave here for ever but if Milly thinks I'll serve in a shop she is mightily mistaken. No thank you. Never again. I wonder what will happen to me now. All that is certain is my two weeks' board and lodging at Mrs. P.'s and after that who knows? Tomorrow is an end or a beginning. . . .'

THE end of a life that for eighteen years had been centred in Tamar Street, Finsbury Park. Today Tamar Street is a bombed site, but much of its earlier environment remains to offer reconstruction of that age, 'so nostalgically near to, yet so remote from ours'. Parallel with that which once was Tamar Street lies a dismal terrace of two-storeyed houses, euphemistically styled Eden Crescent, bearing evidence of damage wrought in paneless windows and battered front doors topping broken steps where squalling children sit and play or hideously bang with tins. A corner house of more pretensions than its neighbours, in that it boasts a bay window, still bears the legend 'Bed and Board', and was, as inquiry elicited, the property of Mrs. Popham, 'Mrs. P.', as we later come to know her. No trace of the premises in Tamar Street, owned by one Roger Cheke, 'Chymist', can be found, unless it were in resurrected grimy chips of coloured glass, red, yellow, green, glinting jaggedly amid the tall wine-tinted weeds sprung from the rubble.

As Mr. Cheke, 'Chymist' [qualified] emerges from the memoirs, we see him as the hub round which the early youth of Peridot revolves. He was tall, meagre-chested, and he had an Adam's apple—she draws him lucidly enough—protruding from a scraggy neck above a Gladstonian collar. A walrus moustache concealed his upper lip but not his teeth, for they also protruded. In addition to these alluring features Mr. Cheke suffered from a laryngeal weakness of his vocal cords, which, we are told, caused his voice 'to squeak like a door that needed oiling'; and, as if to challenge remark on this minor affliction, he was wont to emphasize his utterance in capitals. He had, in fact, missed his vocation, since but for this chronic disability of speech, he would, he said, have taken Holy Orders.

Of her mother, Peridot, or 'Perry' as they called her, can remember nothing more than a little blurred face bent above her cot and a song of 'White Wings' at bedtime. Perry was barely four years old when her mother died of the dead son she bore to Mr. Cheke.

She was the daughter of a missionary, the Reverend James Flight, who, leaving his only child, Mabel, in the care of an aunt at Ealing, went with his wife to serve God among the cannibals. When from this expedition they did not return it was generally assumed they had succumbed to yellow fever, but Mr. Cheke had it firmly they were 'Eaten'.

The Reverend Mr. Flight left worldly wealth to the extent of fifty pounds, with which the orphaned Mabel was endowed; this, supplemented by the aunt at Ealing, sufficed to educate her at Miss Genn's select Academy in Camden Town. At seventeen she was promoted to the post of pupil teacher in exchange for her board and keep. Two years later she obtained a situation as a nursery governess—to her ultimate undoing.

'She would never give the name of her Employers, nor the Locality of the House,' recounted Mr. Cheke, 'where she was Wronged.' But he guessed it could not have been far from 'Here', meaning Tamar Street, for he first made her acquaintance 'in this Very Shop when she came to buy a Cold Cure.'

That casual acquaintanceship rapidly ripened, on the part of Mr. Cheke, to something warmer. She was lovely enough to have turned the head of any man, even one less susceptible than he. What though he were her senior by five and twenty years, she was desperate—'had Erred'—thus Mr. Cheke again, 'been Betrayed by the Scoundrelly Son,' he surmised, 'of Those she Served.' Discovery was followed by dismissal. She was penniless, and, the chivalry of Mr. Cheke aroused by her plight, he rescued her, he said, from 'Worse than Death'.

It is not suggested that these intimacies concerning her dead mother were divulged to Perry in one confidential flow. Indeed it is likely that judicious probing extracted more than was intended to be told; and had he not been driven to it, as she was frequently reminded, by her behaviour on a certain regrettable occasion, he might possibly have waited to reveal 'the Shameful Truth' until she 'Came of Age'. But, 'Since that you have Turned on me. . . .'

She had.

An intensely cold spell marked the end of the year 1889, when Peridot, shivering up in the attic at twenty-five Tamar Street, Finsbury Park, went on strike.

Mr. Cheke had ambition. He had enterprise; he would not solely depend on chance custom, nor on the dispensary. No.

The less important members of the medical profession who patronized Mr. Cheke, Chymist, did not suffice, he said, to pay the Overheads. If Doctors This and That, whose charges per visit ranged from five shillings to seven and six, had called on Mr. Cheke's pharmaceutical assistance, well and good. But they did not. Those whose practices extended from Camden Town to Highgate—in carriages—were more snobbishly inclined to favour Bobberts of Bond Street, Quires, or Messrs. Croy and Belldon. Only the Shillings and Half Crowners who walked to their cases bought their patent medicines of Mr. Cheke, and most of these made up their own prescriptions. It was incumbent on him, therefore, that he should expand. In a Sideline; for Ladies.

They, his chief source of custom, were not, save in female pills, supplied with any personal accessory. If, for example, a toilet cream were required, it would be served to them unattractively labelled 'Eradicates Blemishes, Blackheads, and Spots', and 'Equally Beneficial for the Chaps'; which succinct phraseology might have been misconstrued. 'There was no Discrimination, no Sarvwah Fair in these Proprietary Brands,' said Mr. Cheke. So why should he not produce and launch on the market a Proprietary Brand of his own?

And thus it came about that Perry was called on to pound with a pestle and mix in a mortar a concoction devised by Mr. Cheke. The formula, basically simple, had for its chief ingredients castor oil and zinc ointment with a dash of rose wate. or Eau de Cologne. This mixture named, according to its perfume, Lotus Flower Cream and Mecca Balm, was sold at sixpence the small jar, a shilling the large, at a profit of eighty per cent.

And no cost for labour. . . .

'. . . I was the labour, up there in the attic, pounding
the stuff half the night and dead beat at the end of the day.
For besides that I assisted him behind the counter, serving
out cough mixtures, corn cures and blue pills, and pink
pills and what-not, I had most of the house-work to do.
Then, so soon as supper was over, off I would be sent to
fill five dozen jars, the minimum ordered by him.

He had fixed up a trestle table in the attic with a wobbly
three-legged stool for me to sit on. There was no fireplace,
no warmth, no gas, only the light of one tallow candle to
work by. I used to wrap myself in blankets from my bed and
wear thick woollen mittens, and yet went in torment from
chilblains. Much he cared! As for Milly, it was pretty
obvious she loathed me. She may have had reason enough.
When she shouted at and bullied me I smiled. When she
beat me I stood there uncowed to give her back as good as
I was given. Not in blows for I was little, she was large, but
I knew how to make her see red. . . . "One of these days,"
I would tell her with that smile, "my father'll hear of those
empties in the dustbin. Six of them this week—my word!
Won't you go off with a bang when you're carried below
for hell's burning with all that whisky inside you." And
then she would grab at my hair to wrench it from my scalp—
that did hurt, too!—and call me a mealy-mouthed stinking
little bitch, and God alone knew what she'd done to have
me stuck on her—"Like a plaster on a boil," I agreed, and
would ask: "Milly, do you shave?"—"Do I what?" "Shave,"
I said, smiling. "Because if you don't you ought to. You're
growing a beard." She was a dark woman with heavy black
eyebrows and a sprouting of hairs on her upper lip and chin.
She sprang at me again but I dodged that one and went out
to answer the shop-bell and serve Epsom Salts to a woman
with a wart.

"That should be taken in time," I said, "or it'll be too
late." "D'you mean this?" she said, touching it. "Yes," I
said. "There was a lady used to come here with one on her
nose just like yours, and it got so big she had to have it cut
off, her nose, I mean, not the wart. And she looked so awful
she had to wear a mask, but if she'd have used our Mecca
Balm it would have been cured in a month." "Really?" she
said, frightened. "Yes," I said, "and it's wonderful for

everything. You'd not think to look at me now that a few weeks ago you couldn't see my face for pimples, would you?" She said no. "Well, believe me," I said, "I was ever such a sight and the doctor, he couldn't cure me so I cured myself with Mecca Balm."

She said she would try the small size for sixpence. "Better try the shilling one," I said, "while you're about it. You'll need to lay it on thick. You may find your nose gets a bit sore while the stuff's working, but our Lotus Flower Cream will soon get rid of that. You just smear it on in the daytime under a dab of rice powder. It won't show."

So I sold her a jar of the Lotus Flower and a box of rice powder as well because she said she hadn't any; and I took 3d. from the till as my commission which I didn't think was stealing as I'd earned it—and about all I did earn, too!'

There is no conscious sense of martyrdom in these recollections of her life at Tamar Street. Disdaining self-pity she returns a reciprocal hate to Milly, her bane, sparing a whimsical commiseration for Mr. Cheke's compliance to gynocracy. But while Milly reigned supreme above the shop Mr. Cheke maintained seigneurity within it; not because his wife had no right of entry there; had she so wished, she would have ousted Perry from those precincts, or Mr. Cheke himself, and taken over paramount command. Pharmacy, however, held no interest for her more than as a source of supply for cachous or essence of cloves.

It was after the death of the first Mrs. Cheke that Milly came as housekeeper to Tamar Street, recommended by the local veterinary surgeon as devoted to children and of highest moral tone. Mr. Cheke may well have believed himself blessed. Her solicitude in his sorrow was touching. She would offer him cheer in the form of hot toddy to 'liven you up', though Mr. Cheke much preferred tea; or, 'a blow on the top of a bus, poor dear, to take you out of yourself'—which took him out of himself so far as to end at the Methodist chapel.

That her vows to honour and obey him were ignored within an hour of their marriage, did not disturb Mr. Cheke. He was in love. To be sure he had been in love with Milly's predecessor, but this all-absorbing passion was quite beyond his ken; and he had qualms. Her excessive response to connubial raptures delighted, exhausted, dismayed him. He was fifty, and she gave him palpitations. Disillusionment was swift; and those qualities vaunted by the vet., and so engaging in the days of their earlier acquaintance, were found to be conspicuously absent. She was lazy, and to Mr. Cheke's fastidious taste, 'not Very Nice in her Person'. She seldom, he regretted to remark it, changed her under-clothes, and would lie in bed all the morning reading penny novelettes and smelling strong of 'Spirituous Cachous'. A daily char performed the household duties until Peridot, on leaving school, replaced her.

His wife, as Mr. Cheke unhappily discovered, was a woman of violent temper and words. Where she learned them he could not conceive and had never dared inquire, but that she cultivated 'Undesirable Friends', of both sexes, who would troop into the house at all hours of the night with boisterous song and, shockingly, in liquor, was only too apparent. Yes, life at Tamar Street for Mr. Cheke, no less than for Peridot, was scarcely what he might have called 'Felicitous'.

Through veils of distance Milly is presented as apple-cheeked, aggressive-bosomed, not unhandsome, and in her choice of language not particular. With approaching middle-age she had grown stouter, lazier, her voice more strident, her antipathy to Perry more pronounced. She was, in fact, the prototype of every murderous stepmother devised by the brothers Grimm, whose tales for the curdling of youthful blood Perry voraciously devoured.

Mr. Cheke, on the contrary, did not greatly differ from other children's fathers, resignedly accepted as superior beings who extracted a slavish obedience, attended church on Sundays in frock-coats and black top-hats—though Mr. Cheke attended chapel in a bowler—and were second only in their daughters' sight to the Universal Father of them all.

Yet, sharpened by ill-usage, a child's perspicacity was quick to discern Milly as a dominant factor and Mr. Cheke the merest cypher in his house; of which is given ample demonstration. One incident particularly lights a beacon-flare, pointing to later understanding.

'I was poring over homework in the kitchen. They were in the parlour adjoining it. The door stood ajar and I could hear Milly letting forth in a torrent of abuse. As this was not uncommon I paid no attention until, "As for that dirty little brat," I heard, "why couldn't you have put it in an orphanage? A pretty penny it has cost you all these years—paying for its schooling and its dinners at Miss Genn's."

"Her mother's dying wish," he croaked.

"Mother be damned! God knows you did enough without taking in her bastard—and a lot o' thanks you'll get from her, I'll say. She's a wrong 'un through an' through, sly as they make 'em. You've only to look at her eyes—green as a cat's—to know what she is and where she'll end. On the streets, I wouldn't wonder. And the sauce of it! I'll have the hide off her back before I've done with her, I promise you. And if I'd 'a known I'd be saddled with another woman's bastard passed off as your own I'd 'a seen meself further before I'd 'a tied up with a fusty old josser like you. . . ." '

'Only she didn't say "fusty" or "josser",' adds Lady Mulvarnie, 'but something else a great deal less restrained.'

And though much of this discourse passed unheeded, the gist of it rankled to sink deep. Milly believed her a wrong 'un and sly. Meaning deceitful. A liar. And everything bad. The word 'bastard', however, had left her unmoved. Having noted it often as a form of address by cabmen to their horses or by dustmen to each other, she took it to be a term of endearment, or, as used by Milly, a synonym for 'brat'. But 'sly' and a 'wrong 'un' was a different thing entirely.

A tear rolled down her nose and dropped on her essay, a summary of *Ivanhoe*, and blotted it to lose her marks for neatness.

She was reminded of that incident on a cold and foggy night in November '89. She was now nearing eighteen and her school days at Miss Genn's were almost two years behind her, since when she had become Mr. Cheke's general assistant, and, as she calls herself, Mrs. Cheke's 'general slut'. For besides that she must spend half the day in the shop behind the counter when not hauling up coals, lighting fires, and doing the cooking and chores, there were Mr. Cheke's two Proprietary Brands to be mixed, filled into jars and respectively labelled; and this must be done at night.

The attic, lit by one candle, was murky with the fog that

crept in through a broken window-pane to send icy shivers down her spine and smart the eyes and rasp the throat and set her coughing. Chilled to the bone she sat at the trestle board dutifully pounding, mixing, filling, while the feeble candle-light flickered on the mildewed walls from which the paper peeled in dank, lank strips. A gnawing and a scuttling behind the wainscot betokened what she hoped were only mice but feared were rats. From two storeys below Milly's nagging voice rose up in harsh crescendo, loud enough for Perry to distinguish the repetition of her name and to guess herself the cause of fresh complaint.

She could picture the two of them seated by the fire: Milly lolling in an armchair with a bottle at her elbow and a glass of hot grog in her hand; and her father on the horse-hair sofa going over his accounts and sipping peppermint water to allay the effects of the Welsh rarebit he had fancied for his supper. It was Saturday and the shop had stayed open until half-past ten, which meant that Perry would not get to bed until long after midnight, with five dozen more jars to be filled.

The contrast between the cold of the attic above and the visualized warmth of the parlour below, the crackling fire, the kettle on the hob, and Milly with her skirts pulled back to her knees, toasting her legs at the blaze while her voice aired repetitive grievance, proved too much for Perry. She seethed; and the realization of injustice suffered, and hitherto patiently borne, surged within her to swell in volcanic eruption.

"I'm sick of it! Sick of it! *Sick!*" The breath of her words steamed out in treble gusts, as, seizing the pestle, she brought it down with all her might on the mortar. It chipped but did not break; and, unappeased, she hurled the basin to the ground and watched it bounce.

"Beasts! God'll punish you!" Again her breath gushed forth like smoke; she was possessed, her face distorted with the fury that consumed her. Although small she felt herself growing in stature; a giantess, whose crazy shadow in the candle-light flickered on the walls in fearsome mimicry.

Savagely she kicked at the mortar as if it were Milly's posterior; its contents, frozen solid, had not spilled in transit from the table to the floor. "Beasts of hell!" shrieked Perry, and her double on the wall mocked her with raised impassioned arms.

"Wass'er row up there?"

Milly's voice, accompanied by a lurching on the stairs, announced that Mrs. Cheke, in her cups, was off to bed.

At the door Perry meekly answered: "I only dropped something."

"Don't forget to put out the cat," Milly bade her through a yawn, "it messed in the kitchen last night."

"Which I had to clear up, thank you," muttered Perry; then hearing the steps of Mr. Cheke along the passage to the shop, she bit her fingers, less to soothe the itch of chilblains than to relieve the tumult of her mind; and, with a final kick at the placid mortar, she snatched up the candle, wrenched open the door—it had slammed itself shut in the draught—groped her way down the crooked stairs, and burst in on Mr. Cheke.

He, having shuttered the shop, had turned down the gas, leaving one jet low burning. In that half light the blue, green, red, and yellow carboys that guarded Mr. Cheke's plate glass shop window illumined with fantasy the fog-thickened gloom. Brilliantly coloured, filled with magic waters, these gargantuan flasks had always held for Perry a secret magnetism. The fleeting impressions of her childhood and early adolescence were multiplied in hopeful expectancy to see leap from those bright-hued depths a genie, or a Prospero, perhaps. In her last term at Miss Genn's, the school had been taken to witness Mr. Irving's production of *The Tempest*, an unforgettable experience. And even in maturer years, at near upon eighteen, with her hair put up and her skirts let down, she was half persuaded that those spherical containers were linked with occultism, wizardry—or what?

Through the dim transparency of shadows, shelves, holding bottles of potions and poisons, receded; glass cases, reflecting prismatic points of light, threw into fervent relief the black-coated shape of Mr. Cheke, his leathery lean face, the moustache, the Adam's apple. And in that necromantic moment when all things had undergone bewitchment, when, cold no longer but burning in the frenzy of her wrongs, Peridot was moved to utter the unutterable.

"I've had enough of this! Sick to death of doing servant's work—that's all I am—a servant. Stuck up there in that freezing attic in this weather with no fire, not even a paraffin stove. What sort of life have I had since I left school, I'd like to know? Serving out corn plasters and cough cures to slum women and dirty old men, and selling your face stuff at six-pence and a shilling when it costs you no more than a farthing a pot—a rank swindle!" She was beside herself, exulting in the storm that overswept her to extinguish Mr. Cheke.

He stood aghast.

"Yes!" shouted Perry. "*And* I don't mind telling you I've helped myself to commission from the till—tuppence, some-times thrippence. Haven't I a right to it when you're making all that profit out of me—slave-driving? You're a beast!"

From Mr. Cheke's sagging lips issued the feeblest of squawks; his hand crept to his chest as if to quell the turbulent behaviour of his heart, while he strove for self-assertion in the teeth of this apocalypse.

"Are you Mad?" he managed to articulate; but such weakly remonstrance was lost in the avalanche of words that poured from Perry.

"Both of you are beasts—you and Milly. She's the worst. She's got you, like *that*"—she ground her heel into the boards as if to crush a beetle—"but she won't get me. I'm off! I'll go and earn my living as a teacher. I could any day. Wasn't I top girl at Miss Genn's for a whole year? I'm not to be trampled on and made to do the dirty work in this house for Milly—her general slut, that's what I am. And look here"—she held out her small swollen hands to him, pitiful in mittens —"I've got chilblains." A sob tore at her throat, but no tears fell; her eyes, a fiery green, blazed, as the demons of passion swooped to fall upon and savage Mr. Cheke.

"You're a horrid mean man," yelled Perry, "not to pay me for the work I do. You'd have to pay anyone else. I want a winter coat, and I won't have Milly's old one cut down for me. I won't! You should be ashamed to see me go shabby—dirty old clothes"—tears were rising now. She bit them back to sling a David's challenge at this trembling Goliath. "You're a cruel unnatural father and I hate you!"

It was mutiny, unique and terrible, the like of which in his most awful nightmares of hydra-headed harridans identified with Milly, Mr. Cheke had never dreamed, much less imagined. And to think that he had nursed beneath his roof this unsus-pected criminal, a fire-breathing revolutionary who ranted, raved—to Turn on him. "Bad Blood, Bad Blood," mouthed Mr. Cheke.

"Don't you swear at me!" threatened Perry.

"I didn't—I said——" Again Mr. Cheke pressed a hand to his chest and gasped, "you've given me a Pain."

"Pain?" repeated Perry in some faint alarm; he certainly looked pale; and less as a sop to him than to her conscience, she added: "Indigestion. That Welsh rabbit."

Swift to seize upon this temporary lull from horrifying violence, Mr. Cheke, gathering the scattered remnants of his dignity, adjusted the shake in his voice to retort:

"Unnatural Father, am I? Well, now that you have Turned on me you shall know the Truth about yourself. I am Not your Father."

The uncertain light of the lowered gas made a halo of her hair in the whiteness of her face.

"Not," she breathed, "my father!"

The battle was won and Mr. Cheke the victor; for, as visibly she seemed to shrink, so did he, recovered from cataclysmic shock, expand.

"Sharper than the Serpent's Tooth," quoth Mr. Cheke, "is your Ingratitude," and placing his hands on the counter as if it were a pulpit: "You have Turned on me with Words that rend my Heart. You have likened me unto a Beast of the Field. Me! Your Benefactor. Hear now, Wretched Girl, the Shameful Secret of your Birth. You have no Name. I gave you Mine having married your Mother, who came by you in Sin. And may God forgive you this Outrage to my Charity, for as He sits Above"—Mr. Cheke pointed to the ceiling—"I Never Will. Now go to bed."

She did not stir; nor did her smile's incredulity convey to Mr. Cheke that this 'Truth' about herself was only semi-understood, for:

"If you are not," she said, "my father"—and saying it she simpered—'yes, she Positively Simpered', thus Mr. Cheke's interpretation of that smile—"if you are not my father," and her eyes were wide open upon him, "who," demanded Perry, "*is* my father . . . Mr. Cheke?"

* * *

That he could not satisfy her curiosity was no deterrent to

reiterated question. With the pertinacity of a virulent mosquito she hovered round him persistently to probe. And the more he evaded direct answer, so did she return to the attack. She had the *right* to know who was her father. And what did he mean by 'shameful truth'? Why was it shameful not to have a father? Lots of the girls at school had no fathers. And all this talk—which later she dragged out of him—of her mother's 'Sin'—what had she done? She hadn't been stealing, had she?

"Then why did she lose her situation? And why was the son of the house a scoundrel?"

". . . Anyway it's only guesswork that there *was* a son of the house who betrayed her."

"Well, that's what you *said*. I suppose you mean he sneaked about something or other she shouldn't have done and got her the sack."

"Well, then, why do you keep on about 'Sin'? Was she divorced?"

"All right! I was only asking. . . ."

"At least you can tell me this. What was her name before she married you?"

"Then if her name was Flight my father's name was Flight. So why do you say I have no name?"

"Why can't you *answer*?"

"Look. If I'm not your daughter I'm some other man's daughter. So my mother must have been a widow when she married you. There's no sin in being a widow, is there?"

"Well, if she wasn't a widow and wasn't divorced——"

"—I shall go barmy!"

So it seemed would Mr. Cheke. Had he known that the girl was so Completely Unaware of the Facts of Life, he confessed to Milly, he would not have been so Hasty. It was a Grievous Mistake to have sprung this Truth upon an Innocent——"

"Innercent my——!" exploded Milly. "She's about as innercent as them perishin' cats up there on the tiles." An amorous miaowing from the roof gave ear-splitting point to that remark. "Go on! She's only kiddin' you, but she can't kid me. I'll let her have it!"

Milly did.

"Now then, Innercent—you bloomin' little 'umbug. Of course the pore old [josser] don't know who your father was.

Nor I'll bet my bottom dollar did your Ma know either. She
was anybody's fancy, see? And if you want the facts of *your*
life, here they are. Cheke took and married your mother in her
disgrace and out of charity, so *he* says. Coo!" Milly sniggered. "Charity! Them come-ter-Jesus sort are always the
worst—'ll go after any pair o' garters. I should know! You'd
be surprised. *I* was—I don't mind tellin' you. As for that
Mabel, your Ma, she wasn't arf artful, I'll say. Nabbed 'im
quick on the nail, trust her! Featherin' a nice little nest for
herself and her byblow. Yes, that's what you are, my girl—a
byblow, or if you like it better, a *bar*stard. And if you don't
know what that means, go and look it up in your school dic-
tionary or go ask your teacher Miss Genn and give her kittens!
And now pr'aps you'll see why I didn't fall over myself to
have you here in my house passed orf as his daughter—and
paying for your schoolin' and your keep, when he don't know
from Adam who begot you—some lowdown tyke, or other,
I'll be bound. And if Cheke 'adn't been sersoft, he'd 'ave put
you in one of them foundlin' 'omes what takes in the likes o'
you till they're fourteen when they 'ave to go out to work as a
scivvy or factory 'and at five pound a year, which is all you're
fit for and a damn sight more than you're worth—you dirty
little gutter-snipe. *Bar*stard!"

Milly spat.

And the storage of her venom thus, temporarily, depleted,
Milly paused; while her silent victim, on whom the 'Shameful
Truth' had at last obtruded, bowed her head beneath it—for
a moment. Then her chin lifted; her eyes met those of her
tormentor squarely, and, if we may believe her:

'I didn't answer back. Though all my instinct clamoured
to flay her with my tongue as she flayed me I just stood there
and smiled, and, strangely, knew that I no longer hated her.
Perhaps I felt she wasn't worthy of my hatred for those
who inspire hate may equally, I think, inspire love. . . . I
can see her now as I saw her then, red-faced, blowsy, in her
soiled dressing-gown, uncorseted, with flabby dropping
breasts, her hair in curlers and an ooze of spittle on her
loosened lip. . . . And so I left her.'

To go in search of Mr. Cheke; for this revelation, although shattering, did not stay inquisitorial pursuit.

At her entrance Mr. Cheke emerged from his dispensary holding a bottle filled with pink fluid in one hand and in the other a label. He licked it, attached it, and standing at his counter dipped a pen in the inkstand that stood there and wrote: '*One tablespoonful to be taken thrice daily after meals.*' "Run round with this at once," he said, "to Mrs. Popham."

"Run round with it," Perry answered inexcusably, "yourself."

As one who doubts his senses, Mr. Cheke looked up, agape, to ask: "What's This? What has Come Over You?"

"Your black-bearded wife," smiled Perry, "has come over me. I am not going to stay in this house any longer with her. It won't hold us both, and that's flat. You see, I understand now what I didn't understand before. I'm not ungrateful for all you've done for me—paying for my schooling and giving me your name. But I'd rather be called by my mother's name in future if it's all the same to you. And I know now what it means to be a bastard. There are bastards in history, but I never—sort of—connected them with me. What about Charles the Second? He had lots of bastards and he made his sons dukes, though one never hears much of his daughters. I must have been a fool when you talked about the 'Shameful Truth' not to have tumbled to it that I am illegitimate. Isn't that the word? Which is obviously why I've been treated like a servant. So I'm leaving like a servant. And I give you," Perry said, "a month's notice. From today."

Then, with the bottle still in his hand, his face swept clear of all expression save that of horrified amaze, something 'came over' Mr. Cheke. Something swift and terrible that stabbed him in the heart and caused him to drop what he was holding. And, as mechanically he stooped to retrieve it, he emitted a groan and doubled, writhing, feebly to gesture at the row of blue-black jars high upon a shelf, with the names of their contents lettered in gilt. "Ca-ca-camphor" uttered Mr. Cheke. "Give—fetch—quick."

He had slithered to the floor; he was violently retching, and his face, a ghastly yellow, shone with the sweat of his excruciation.

"Drops—three—wa-ter," he ejaculated, "camph——"

Panic-stricken, Perry climbed upon a chair, procured the camphor, measured in a phial the three desired drops and diluted them with water; and, as she knelt to support that lolling head upon her arm, an awful sound came from him.

"Father!" Force of habit in this fear-gripping crisis rose uppermost to call him by the name she had renounced. "Father! You're ill—I'll fetch the doctor!"

The phial in her shaking hand knocked against his teeth; in the act of swallowing he belched. Camphor spurted; his mouth stayed open, his eyes were glazed and staring. Dreadfully he gurgled, made as if to speak again, and died.

* * *

During the week succeeding Mr. Cheke's departure to eternity, 'Miss Flight', as henceforth she names herself, suffered—we have her word for it—'agonies of self-reproach'.

Had she not been so outspoken, had she known that his heart, thus the doctor's verdict, was 'gravely affected', and the recurrent pain in his chest, diagnosed by Mr. Cheke as 'Indigestion', was symptomatic of something much worse, she would never have 'Turned' on him to bring about that fatal seizure, disclosed by the autopsy as angina.

Remorse stalked beside her, bitter, unrelenting, nothing lessened by Milly's alcoholic outbursts that rang the changes from copious tears to the shrieking accusation: "It's that Perry—yes, you! You was with him at the end. You killed him—murdered him—or as near as dammit—for his money. Well, you won't get a ha'penny. I'll see you hanged first, s'elp me God!"

She was got to bed, given an emetic and lay torpid for twelve hours.

"Will she die too?" Perry hopefully inquired of the doctor.

"Die? Bless my soul, no! That good lady's condition, my dear, is the result of too frequent resort to strong waters. Let her rest undisturbed. She'll come round."

And with remarkable resilience Milly did come round, to busy herself with the buying of mourning and to prepare for what she called a 'slap-up' funeral, attended by her cronies and a few expectant tearful relatives of Mr. Cheke.

And when, with grisly pomp, the mortal remains of Mr. Cheke had been duly interred at Kensal Green, and the mourners returned to Tamar Street to partake of port and sherry wine and cracknel biscuits; and when one Mr. Todd, a portly gentleman in spectacles, solicitor to the deceased, had read the Will to the satisfaction of all save the expectant relatives and Perry, who was out of the room at the time, washing up; and when the company in general, and the disappointed relatives, had gone upon their ways, the doctor came to visit Mrs. Cheke.

Perry, who admitted him at the side door, asked, if he pleased, to spare a word with her alone.

Into the shuttered shop she led him, pale as a primrose in her shabby black, an old dress of Milly's cut down for the occasion. The fringe of ash-blonde hair emphasized those strangely coloured eyes set wide apart under faintly surprised eyebrows.

Could any sudden shock have killed him? That's what she must know.

It would depend, was the answer, on what kind of shock.

"If one had said—something to upset him? I was with him, you see, at the end, and I said—what I shouldn't have said."

Reassurance was prompt. She must not give it a thought. The post-mortem had revealed an advanced case of *angina pectoris*, a condition of the heart in which death can occur at any moment.

"Then you don't think my saying I would leave him—that's what I said—could have brought it on?"

"He might have died," the doctor said evasively, "walking up the stairs. You have nothing whatsoever with which to reproach yourself." A shrewd professional eye marked the swollen eyelids, the dark stains under. "How are you sleeping?"

"I dream." She shuddered. "And I wake—and I see him" —her glance sped away and she pointed—"just there. He toppled down. I can't stop dreaming of it."

"I'll make you up something that will soon dispense with dreams," was the brisk reply; and to Milly, the doctor reported: "Miss Cheke needs change of air and scene. Her nerves are shattered by the shock. I am sending her a tonic. She is feeling the death of her father very keenly."

"Her father!" We may well believe how Milly pounced on that. "*He* weren't her father. I could tell you—but I won't

And if you ask me, I'd like to know what went on in the shop when he was took. She'd been pesterin' and botherin' him—givin' him no peace for this last month. She killed him as sure as if she'd knifed him and I'd say so with me dyin' breath. I'll never forgive her as long as I live. And if it's change she needs then she can go and welcome. I don't want her here."

And, covering her face with a black-edged handkerchief, Milly, loudly sobbing, left the room.

Of the portly gentleman who was sorting papers at a table: "What provision," asked the doctor, "has been made for that poor child?"

Not very much, it appeared. The Will was produced and there likely followed some talk between the two.

In the original Will the deceased had left to his daughter— "Daughter, mark you," Mr. Todd pushed his spectacles up to his forehead, leaned back in his chair and said—"for she was his daughter in the legal sense, since her mother bore her after her marriage with the deceased."

The doctor nodded. "So? And this Will——?"

The lawyer readjusted his spectacles, gazed on the document, and mumbled—"bequeaths to his daughter Peridot Cheke the sum of three hundred pounds in trust until she shall attain her majority—h'm." He turned over a page. "But in this codicil, dated—let me see—four weeks ago—yes, here we have it—that—um—um—'revoke the previous etcetera—and bequeath to Peridot daughter of Mabel my first wife the sum of fifty pounds in addition to which bequest I leave to the said Peridot should she be a spinster and still living under my roof at the time of my death the sum of one pound per week only for two weeks' board and lodging at a suitable establishment to be paid for in advance out of my estate . . .' It appears that the deceased drew up this codicil himself, but it is duly witnessed and appears to be in order."

"Ah, well," said the doctor glumly, "at least she'll have fifty pounds." He took his bag and hat from a chair and added: "I brought her into the world . . . And I suggest you pack her off to a suitable establishment as soon as may be. She's better away from that woman."

Mr. Todd absently agreed. "Yes. . . . There's something else here. 'The black japanned box to be opened in the presence of——' Yes, indeed, as you say, she should certainly

be placed in some more—um—salubrious environment. I will
see what I can do or suggest. A post as governess, perhaps.
She is very young, but, I believe, has been passably well edu-
cated. A much superior type to the widow. Well, good day
to you, doctor. Very pleased to have met you. Good day."

*   *   *

On a morning in the New Year, 1890, Perry, in answer to a
letter from Mr. Todd requesting her attendance at his office,
boarded a westbound omnibus. It was a day of fitful sun and a
scurry of cloud with more of March than January in the breeze
that, like a mischievous urchin, tore bowlers from men's
heads, dragged at the manes of horses, and sent gusts of grit
and dried manure whirling in the gutters.

Finding the bus to be full inside, Perry climbed to the top;
this, as one of the latest omnibuses, boasted a gangway and
side-seats instead of the old-fashioned 'knife-board'. Skewer-
ing her hat more firmly on her head, she dived into the pocket
of her skirt and took from it Mr. Todd's letter. Although she
knew it by heart she read it again to assure herself that Mr.
Todd would be obliged if Miss Cheke would call upon him at
above address on the morning of January 30th, at eleven
o'clock, or alternatively to suggest another date or time at her
convenience.

So here she was, very much at her convenience, since Milly
had gone to Brighton for a month pending her removal from
Tamar Street.

The premises and good will of the business had been sold
for some nine hundred pounds at what was understood by the
widowed Mrs. Cheke to be a damn sight more than she had
hoped for. Mr. Cheke's successor, having taken possession so
soon as the title deeds were signed and the money paid over,
had politely indicated that the service of Miss Cheke as
general assistant would no longer be required.

Milly, who expressed herself 'well shut o' the lousy old
shop and that hovel above it with its rot and its rats and the
damp from the roof', announced her intention of visiting a
friend of hers at Brighton. It was on the cards, she confided
to Perry, and not to be spoken of outside these walls, that this
same 'friend', whose sex was not revealed but to whom Milly
obscurely referred in the plural, might be buying an hotel—'a

small one, see—six to eight beds on the main road from London to the coast',—and that 'they' might want her to 'go in'
with them.

Perry rejoiced. For if Milly 'went in' with whoever 'they'
were, she might never come out again.

And now, left at Tamar Street to await the final exodus
fixed for the second week in February, she found herself free,
her own mistress, for the first time in her life.

Milly had grudgingly doled her a pittance, five shillings a
week to be repaid when Mr. Todd released the legacy of fifty
pounds, which, Mr. Cheke's widow declared, should by rights
be hers. And a crying shame it was to leave so much away
from his lawful wife to one who had no claim on him beyond
his charity. But that five shillings' loaned allowance sufficed to
feed Perry on sausages, kippers, sardines, with a chop or rump
steak on a Sunday. There was plenty of coal in the cellar with
which to build a fire in the parlour where she sat in Milly's
armchair munching apples, roasting chestnuts, and reading
books discovered in the attic that she had never had the time
or opportunity to read before.

Among dry-as-dust treatises on chemistry, discarded, she
retained *Jane Eyre*, *Fox's Book of Martyrs*, *What a Woman of
Forty Ought to Know*, Gibbon's *Decline and Fall*—heavy going
this—and a paper-backed novel translated from the French
and of startling obscenity, which conveyed to her, however,
no instruction more than that it was 'completely daft'. She
had now, besides these relaxations, the leisure to play on the
rusty old harmonium that, though sadly out of tune, served
its purpose in those early days to indicate her not unexcep-
tional musical gift. At Miss Genn's earnest request Mr.
Cheke had reluctantly allowed her to take music lessons for
six months, until Milly, we hear, 'put her foot down' against
any such 'wasteful tomfoolery'. We have it that on Sunday
evenings Mr. Cheke, if Milly were out visiting her 'friends',
would be moved to sing hymns, in his cracked voice to Perry's
accompaniment. And, now that she was alone in the house,
the dingy parlour blossomed with 'Flowers that bloom in the
Spring', or other tuneful melodies heard on barrel-organs
but for the most part improvised.

Then came the letter from Messrs. Todd and Son and Todd,
Solicitors, to put her in a state.

Why should Mr. Todd, Solicitor, request her attendance at his office? Why not write and tell her what he had to say? Could it be that Milly's repeated accusations had at last drawn suspicion to herself? One could never tell with lawyers, nosing round. One read in the newspapers of awful things happening to bodies that were buried and dug up again to be examined, and innocent persons sent to trial, committed for murder. . . . And how could she, who had no witnesses to speak for her, prove that she had nothing to do with the death of poor Fa— of Mr. Cheke? But—if she had not spoken as she did on that last fatal night, if she had not been so 'high' with him, or waited till the morning to tell him she was going—which of course she didn't mean, for where would she have gone?—he might have been alive now. Still, 'Never cross a Bridge', as he so often used to say, 'until you come to it. Sufficient for the Day . . .'

And what a day! Almost spring-like. Sniffing the air she thought she could detect—above the smell of dung and horse, and the clay-bespattered corduroys of a man who had flopped into the seat beside her with a bag of tools at his feet—the scent of open spaces and green country ways where violets grew wild under hedges, not packed into painfully tight little bunches as offered by a woman down there at the kerb.

Peering over the side of the bus Perry read the news-placard announcements: 'Lord Randolph Churchill's Speech', and 'Influenza Epidemic Latest Death Roll. . . .' Although she had no notion who Lord Randolph Churchill might be, she knew all about the influenza. According to popular belief this scourge, which for the past few weeks had devastated Britain to dislocate business, close factories and strike at its victims from the Household of the Queen to the coal mines of the North, had been imported from Russia, and was colloquially known as 'Russian Flu'. None the less, the streets were crowded, and at Oxford Circus loiterers were gathered round a fallen cab-horse.

In a welter of pity Perry watched the attempts of the cabby and two policemen to raise the poor struggling beast. "It's cruel to overload him!" she cried to no one in particular. "Just look at all the luggage on top of that four-wheeler——"

"Ar," was the guttural assent from the man in corduroys. "Allus see somethin' o' that sort at the Suckuss. They slip on them flags. 'E's up now."

A heaving of lean, sweating ribs, a stamping and a blowing and a backing to the shafts, a buckling of leather straps, the return of the cabman to his seat, and of two stout men, a stouter lady and a boy to the cab, a general dispersal, and the traffic moved on.

Dismissing, with a tug at her heart, a last glimpse of the horse's lowered head, the glint of white in a terrified eye, and those patient straining efforts to obey the crack of a whip, the jerk of a rein, Perry turned her attention to Jay's shop window, displaying wax models of wasp-waisted ladies dressed in the 'Latest Spring Modes'—so early in the year, too!—and such wonderful gowns. Silks and satins, high-sleeved, shimmering, a kaleidoscope of apricot, emerald, cerise, to captivate and dazzle; and, in another window, as the bus rolled on, 'Tailored Jacket, Seasonable Chic', in steel grey velvet and tomato coloured cloth, trimmed, with rows and rows of braid and stitching—and the hats! Boaters, bonnets, and a thing called 'The Aureole' in white with an upturned brim in fluted heliotrope, priced boldly twelve and six. Just imagine! marvelled Perry, and wondered would she ever be rich enough to pay twelve and six—would you believe it!—for a hat.

Regent Street was a crawling cavalcade of omnibuses, red, yellow, chocolate, green; hansoms, four-wheelers, one-horse broughams, carriages and pairs driven by coachmen in great fur capes to their chins, with a footman similarly smothered, on the seat beside them. At the next halt outside Liberty's, a closed carriage drawn by a spanking pair of greys caused among the passers-by considerable stir when from it stepped a lady, very lovely, in a sealskin edged with sable. Her hair was a sheen of gold beneath a purple velvet bonnet—and Perry felt an elbow in her ribs.

"See 'er?" a hoarse voice queried.

"See who?" asked Perry, dodging an overpowering whiff of beer and onions.

" 'Er. Lily Langtry. Bit of orlright, ain't she?"

Not caring to confess that she had never heard of Lily Langtry, Perry nodded assent and turned her head away to avoid her fellow-passenger's effluvium.

"Don' 'arf give you the sick, eh?" continued the gentleman in corduroys, "ter see them liv'ries and 'orses gallivantin' up and dahn spendin' money like water—and 'oo pyes?" From somewhere on his evil-smelling person he produced a shred of shag, conveyed it to his mouth and meditatively chewing, announced: "Us. *We* pyes. Nose-grindin'. Tuppence overtime. Talk abaht them strikes—ruddy lot o' good they done. Wot price the gas-stokers' Union, eh? Free fahsand of 'em aht in the Sahth Metr'polt'n an' this 'ere Livesey tykin' over unskilled workers to undercut the old 'ands. Yerss! An' them dockers with their march past in 'Yde Park—all them dr'ectors lickin' at the tanner, crawlin' on their bellies full o' promises. Not arf! An' that there Card'nal Oo-is-it tykin' up the Cause to let 'em dahn agyne. An' where'd it get 'em, eh? A bloomin' deadlock. No surrender. Gahn!" The beery man leaned aside to shoot from his mouth a juicy gob. "Wot I sye is let them bleedin' capt'lists wot keeps their kerridges and Lily Langtrys—Prince o' Wyles or nothin'—try wot it's like to keep a wife an' arf a dozen kids on fifteen bob a week. I'd larf!"

And to Perry's relief her communicative neighbour, whose discourse might have been in Hindustani for all she understood of it, rose from where he sat, shouldered his bag, and cheerily whistling clattered down the steps of the bus.

"Fez, pliz. En'more fez?"

"Would you," Perry asked of the conductor, "kindly tell me when we come to Filbert Street?"

" 'Ere y'are, Missy. Pic'dee Circ's for Filbert Street. Firs' on lef', sick'n on righ'. Min' 'ow yer go."

Filbert Street, a dreary street on the skirts of Soho, was composed of blackened brick houses interspersed with questionable byways; a narrow street where vendors of roast chestnuts, hot potatoes, and hawkers with barrows of oranges and vegetables, unconcernedly held up Her Majesty's mail van, a donkey-cart, a brewer's dray, a cab, a private hansom. Barefooted urchins, grouped around the warm glow of braziers, begged "a 'apenny, Miss, to buy a 'ot p'tater".

Seeking in her purse for two ha'pennies to scatter, Perry collided with a cluster of gesticulating foreigners, slipped on an orange peel, and recovered her balance to be accosted by a seedy top-hatted individual in a clerical collar who asked if she were saved? And away from whom, in some alarm, she hurried: a street of noisome alleys where barred windows, bolted doors, guarded the activities of those who snatched a livelihood beyond the limitations of the law; thieves, harlots, counterfeit coiners, tenanted shops that sold delicatessen, theatrical gewgaws, ballet shoes, grease-paint, masking a less innocuous trade. But certain business houses, including that of Messrs. Todd, Solicitors, still retained the dignity of long establishment. The newly pointed brick-work, the gold lettering on windows either side the door, betokened that Todd and Son and Todd stood immune from and impervious to equivocal surroundings.

The private hansom, previously noted, was now stationary at the kerb outside the entrance. Prepared for the worst Perry mounted the steps and went in. A door on the right of the oak panelled hall, marked 'Enquiries', led her to inquire of a pimply youth seated on a stool before a desk, with ink on his fingers and a pen behind his ear, if Mr. Todd could see her if he pleased?

Had she an appointment?

Yes.

Detaching himself from the stool, the youth, truculently bidding her to 'step this way', conducted her along a passage to a room containing a table, some several chairs and a tall dark gentleman with a trim little beard, who testily demanded of Perry's pimply guide: "How much longer am I to be kept waiting?"

"Any minute now, sir. Mr. Todd is very busy, sir, this morning. Won't keep you a minute, sir," fawningly replied the youth, and vanished.

Perry sat, and taking from the table a copy of *Punch* dated August 11, 1889, was subjected to the scrutiny of the gentleman who straddled the hearthrug before a blazing fire with his hands beneath the tails of his dapper grey frock-coat. Carelessly flung upon a chair against the wall was another coat —an overcoat—lined with astrakhan.

A glossy high hat, a pair of grey gloves and an ivory handled ebony cane reposed upon the table. All this, and the gentleman's eyes of a startling blue, unswervingly fixed on herself, Perry, in one comprehensive glance from under lowered lids, observed. And when, placing a chair, he addressed her politely: "Madam, will you take a seat nearer to the fire? Pray forgive me for keeping the warmth to myself," she, flattered at the 'madam', answered, equally polite, "Thank you, sir. I am not cold."

2

He bowed, and under his moustache his small mouth twitched. His hair, as black and glossy as his hat, receded from a broad dome-shaped forehead. She judged him to be elderly—thirty-five, at least—and noted the tone of his voice, very different from those to which she was accustomed, for:

'. . . He pronounced nearer as "nearah" and fire as "fyah", in a lazy sort of drawl as if it were too tiring to speak. His next remark, however, made me doubt his sanity, when, to my dismay he said, "You're like a bottled chili." Or that is what I thought he said, which seemed to me offensive. I glared at him. He laughed, a silent laugh, to show his teeth, very white in his face which was tanned as if by the sun of hot climates. "Absolutleh chinkwechento——" I could make no sense at all of it; and then the boy came in to say that Mr. Todd would see him now.

With another bow to me this singular dark gentleman, leaving behind him his overcoat, his hat, his cane, his gloves, and a dainty scent of lilies, went out.

I confess curiosity prompted me to touch and examine that rich fur-lined coat, those gloves of grey suède, also smelling of lilies, and his hat, gold-initialled on the inside of the crown, A.G.H.-W. Steps at the door returned me in haste to my seat at the table, absorbed in that five months old copy of *Punch*.

"Pray excuse me," he took from the floor a moroccan leather case, which I had overlooked in exploration of his property. "I trust," said Mr. A.G.H.-W., "that I do not unduly detain you from your business with friend Todd. Mine will soon be despatched." And within ten minutes he was back again, followed by the pimply boy who held open the door for me to pass. And with that twist of a smile which was not quite a smile, Mr. A.G.H.-W. said: "I have seen you before, and I'll see you again sometime or other in —Frenzy. Good day to you, prim Vera," or that is what it sounded like to convince me more than ever he was mad.'

But the following interview with Mr. Todd drove all thought of this encounter from her mind. Rising from a massive mahogany desk he greeted her formally, bade her be seated and without further parley came straight to the point.

Miss Cheke must realize that, although a minor, she was virtually alone in the world, but as sole executor of Mr. Cheke's Will he would take upon himself to keep—a—ah—a watching brief upon her, as it were. Had she made any plans for her future? Apart from a legacy of fifty pounds her father had arranged that she be boarded and lodged at a suitable establishment for two weeks only to be paid for in advance, of which Miss Cheke was doubtless aware.

Miss Cheke was aware of nothing at the moment other than immense relief. No hint or suggestion in Mr. Todd's ponderous statement that his request for her attendance at his office indicated a more sinister intent.

Had Miss Cheke a choice, Mr. Todd pursued, of any such establishment as mentioned in the Will?

Yes, Miss Cheke admitted, she had thought of Mrs. Popham's.

And who, Mr. Todd wished loftily to know, was Mrs. Popham?

A lady, he was told, who lived in Eden Crescent and took in lodgers, mostly shop-girls, she believed.

Taking from a drawer a memorandum book Mr. Todd asked for and jotted down the number of the house in Eden Crescent. "But, Mr. Todd," Perry earnestly assured him. "I don't want to work in a shop, you understand? Milly—Mrs. Cheke—is always at me to serve behind a counter and live in. I'd sooner starve."

With a slight inclination of his head Mr. Todd made another memorandum and inquired if Miss Cheke had considered an alternative.

Yes, at one time she had thought she might like to be a governess because her mother was a governess, but after what she'd heard from her fa—from Mr. Cheke she didn't much care for the idea.

"Do you know," questioned Mr. Todd, "by whom your mother was employed?"

Perry shook her head. "She would never say." And in a tone of urgency she added: "I think I ought to tell you—Mr. Cheke was not—my father."

Mr. Todd leaned back in his chair, placed his finger-tips together and weightily replied:

"In every legal sense he *was* your father. He acknowledged you his daughter and registered your birth in his name."

So you know that, do you? These lawyers know too much, Perry silently commented, and, with a touch of defiance, she said: "But that doesn't make him my father. He told me——"

"My dear young lady," was the bland interruption, "the law is not concerned with what your father told you. I repeat that, although not of his blood, you are legally the daughter of Roger Cheke, deceased."

The faint surprised curve of her eyebrows was lost in the straw-pale fringe of her hair, and:

"Mr. Todd," she rejoined, "don't you think it's rather hard on me to be landed with the name of a father I don't want? And I may be very stupid but I really cannot see how I can be the daughter of a man who was no blood-relation to me, whatever the law," the least little smile came upon her lips, "may say."

Despite its gentle utterance this retort from one so insignificant and, to the taste of Mr. Todd, so plain, caused his fleshy face to redden, while with the utmost disfavour he gazed at his young client in her shabby black, who sat regarding her hands demurely folded in her lap.

Mr. Todd cleared his throat. "I have explained your case, Miss Cheke, and time," he glanced at a clock on the wall, "is getting on. We now come to the purport of your visit here today. In his Will your father expressed the desire that this," he laid a podgy finger on a black japanned tin box that stood on his desk, "should be opened and its contents examined by you in my presence. It is locked and it has no key." And with what would appear to be unnecessary violence, he rang a brass bell on his desk to summon the pimply boy.

"Bring," commanded Mr. Todd, "a screw-driver and a hammer."

The return of his underling with the required implements restored to instant action Mr. Todd, who, pending their arrival, had sat in heavy silence, withdrawn into himself. After some fruitless attempt to unscrew the lock which resulted in considerable business with the hammer, and a hitting of his thumb to draw from him forcible mutters, he succeeded in lifting the lid of the box.

"Pray examine the contents, Miss—ah—Cheke. This box and all it contains is bequeathed to you. It belonged to your mother and has not been opened since her death."

Her mother! Whose face from a faded photograph gazed up at her, so young, scarcely older than herself. . . . A girl with a soft half-smiling mouth, and hair coiled round her head in braids. No name of a photographer, no date, other than that suggested by the dress of twenty years earlier, a tight-fitting bodice buttoned to the throat, and the draped apron skirt with a bustle.

"So this is my mother," she whispered, "my little young mother."

Tears dimmed her sight as she looked at those childish features, striving to see in them some likeness to her own, and could see none; for her mother's hair and her eyes were dark, long-lashed, "not small silly pig's eyes like mine. . . ." She spoke aloud and to herself, for Mr. Todd had risen and was standing at the window impatiently pulling at the tassel of the blind. "My mother," Perry told his unresponsive back, "must have been ever so pretty."

She took up a bundle tied with pink ribbon, super-inscribed: 'From my dear parents to me'. These she set aside to be read later. Another photograph claimed her attention; this of a bewhiskered clergyman with his hand on the back of a chair on which sat a crinolined lady wearing a stony smile and her hair in a large chenille net. On the back was written:

'To our beloved little Mabel.

May God bless and preserve you and if it be His Will that we see you not again on this earthly plane may we humbly bow to the Call of Duty and our service to Him Who watcheth over you that our dear one may walk in Righteousness and rejoin us through Jesus Christ, Our Lord, in that Happy Land where there is no parting of the ways.

Presented to our darling child on the eve of our departure for the Fiji Islands, December 10, 1857.

Marion and James Flight.'

Her grandparents!

"Look, Mr. Todd, my grandparents. He was a clergyman."

"Quite so," said Mr. Todd, wheeling round. "Is there any-thing more?"

The hands of the clock pointed to a quarter past twelve. He took out a cumbrous watch, compared it, rewound it, and hemmed. Ignoring his evident impatience to be quit of her, Perry had discovered a third photograph, of a slender young man with fair smooth hair brushed back from his forehead, and faintly surprised eyebrows arched above a pair of light wide-set eyes. His clean-shaven lips were blunt-cornered, upward tilted, and he stood, full length, one hand on a photographer's artificial barricade in a daniacal pose; but the shape of the face, too oval and feminine, surely for manhood, struck a fleeting chord of recognition.

"Mr. Todd!" exclaimed Perry, "who's this?"—he had returned to the window. "I seem to know—who is he?" A name was scrawled across the back. "Why, what does this mean? There's a girl's name here. Jean Marie. Mr. Todd," she called to him, "do look."

Resignedly he came to look—and look again from the imprint of a boy's face to that of the girl, who, lips apart, eagerly watched him. Although Mr. Todd might not have discerned in those same wide-set eyes, those same oval contours and delicate articulation of bone structure, a Botticellian reminder, the resemblance was compelling, unmistakable, astounding! "But the name," he observed, "is not necessarily that of a girl. This photograph," and he peered closer, "was taken in Paris."

"Paris?" ejaculated Perry. "How can you tell?"

"Although the photographer's name," pronounced Mr. Todd, "is illegible, you will see, if you examine it carefully, that the address is the Rue de la Paix, and the signature here" —he turned it over—"is dated August, 1870. At that time refugees from the Franco-Prussian war were flocking to England from Paris." He brought his gaze to bear, with renewed interest, on Perry. "In what year were you born?"

"January the twenty-sixth, 1872." She answered him absently; her scrabbling fingers had found something else. "Just look at this funny old ring with the crest of a cock perched on a crown holding in its beak some kind of a flower. . . . Here! Let me have that photograph again." She fairly snatched it from him. "Do you see?" she cried, excited, "he wears a square ring on his finger—just like this. It's a much clearer picture than those others. Who ever can it be? Mr. Todd, do I imagine it, or am I at all . . . like him?"

At his desk Mr. Todd was examining the ring with the aid of a magnifying glass.

"This stone," he told her, "is a peridot."

"My name!" The colour had fled from her cheeks.

"And the crest engraved upon it," he continued, "is not a crown but a coronet, indubitably French, possibly eighteenth century, with the chanticleer holding in its beak the clover—the trefoil. Yes," mused Mr. Todd. "I should say that this is the crest of some aristocratic French family." And as he returned her the ring his manner had noticeably altered; it was almost deferential. "Extraordinary," reflected Mr. Todd; again he took the photograph to gaze from it to her. "The likeness is quite extraordinary. Remarkable."

"Yes," she panted slightly. "Even I can see it. One can't always see the likeness of another to oneself. Mr. Todd," she asked him in a tremble, "is he . . . do you think he's . . . my father?"

The lawyer got up from his chair. "It is possible, but on the other hand, no photograph, especially one so early, before the modern method was perfected, can be relied upon, and does, in fact, prove nothing. Will you take the box with you, Miss Cheke? Or shall I send it by the parcel's post?"

She said she would take it; and with it she took the resolve, as recorded, 'to reshape my life from the crest on a peridot ring'.

TWO

Eden Crescent
March 6th, 1890

'Have been here two weeks almost. Still looking for a situation. Agencies round here no good. Mrs. Kent's is the best. Sent me to three ladies' houses all said I was too young. Mrs. Kent advises me do away with fringe and wear a veil to my hat. Bought one with black chenille spots three three a yd. makes me look like the spotted dog pudding Mrs. P. gives us on Sundays. Other days its prunes and rice. Don't care for myself without a fringe too bald but more like the photo of Jean Marie than ever. . . .

Later. Evening post brings letter from Mr. Todd. Will I kindly let him know if I have found a situation if not has suggestion to make which he trusts will meet with my approval. Not much hope that I shall approve of any suggestion from him but shall have to get something soon. Can't afford to stay on here must look for cheaper lodgings. Have 55 shillings in money box saved out of commission taken from the till and after all I did tell him on that last awful night but don't suppose he took it in. Shan't be sorry to go from here except for leaving Phyllis.

N.B. Have written to tell Mr. Todd am open to offer of place.'

AND in due course came Mr. Todd's reply to the effect that one of his clients required a young lady companion for his ward and niece. The duties would not be onerous and the salary of fifty pounds per annum was, in Mr. Todd's opinion, more than adequate. If Miss Cheke were prepared to consider such a post he would make an appointment for her to wait upon his client at his office to be interviewed. An early reply would oblige.

To which Miss Cheke early and obligingly replied that she would be pleased to wait upon Mr. Todd's client at his office if he would tell her when, and she wished to inform Mr. Todd that in future her name would be Miss Flight.

Among the eight or nine boarders at 'Mrs. P.'s', only two are mentioned: Miss Hubbard, a spinster of uncertain age, and one Florrie Jenkins, much younger, to whom Miss Hubbard scathingly referred as 'Fast'. Of the others Perry saw little or nothing, since their divers employments as factory hands, seamstresses, laundresses, demanded an early morning exodus from the house in Eden Crescent to which they did not return until late at night. The two laundresses, who, with regard to the dangers of their calling due to unprotected machinery, received the munificent wage of half a crown to three shillings a day for a minimum of sixteen hours' work, were not seen by Perry at all.

Miss Hubbard, by virtue of her status in the Gloves at a West End drapery establishment, topped the social scale at 'Mrs. P.'s', from which height she looked down upon the laundresses, factory hands, and seamstresses as 'low life'. But Miss Cheke as the daughter of a chemist, and, since Mrs. Popham knew her by that name, must while there in residence retain it, was accepted without question by Miss Hubbard as her equal and on very short acquaintance as her confidante.

Miss Hubbard, to whom the privilege of 'living out' had been accorded as result of twenty-five years' service at Taylor and Mantell's, earned the maximum sum of forty pounds per annum from which was deducted twenty pounds allowance for her board and keep.

On the first Sunday after her arrival we find Perry alone with Miss Hubbard at tea in the boarders' basement parlour, for which, with a fire, Mrs. Popham charged sixpence, inclusive of muffins and jam.

"Don't, whatever you do," was Miss Hubbard's advice, "take up shop work. Of course if you're smart at the job as I am, though I say it as shouldn't, it has its good points, and to be in the Gloves is always well thought of. Many's the time—a muffin, Miss Cheke? She'll make you pay for it whether you eat it or not—I was saying that many's the time I've fitted titled ladies with twenty-button lengths for Her Majesty's Court."

Miss Hubbard had, we are told, 'a perpetual sniff as if her complaints were stored in her nose'—to be ejected in a catalogue of fines for offences, such as absence for illness or passing bad money to send up on pulleys to the cashier's deck. "And

in the rush of the sales, I ask you"—Miss Hubbard sipped tea
with genteel relish, her little finger curved aloft—"how can
you examine every coin to see if it is counterfeit or not? But
that's what you're supposed to do, and a shilling off your wages
if you don't. If I could have the shillings I've paid out in fines
as a beginner for sending up bad half crowns, I'd have had a
tidy sum laid by me now, to say nothing of standing on a
chair."

"Why, whatever's wrong with standing on a chair?" inquired Perry.

"Only that it's all against the rules." Spitefully Miss Hubbard bit into a muffin. "If you can't reach a shelf you must
wait for the steps which someone else is using, and if the customer is in a hurry and goes off without buying you're fined
for that too if Sign happens to spot it, and so in the long run—
these are last Sunday's I'm sure, toasted up—so in the long
run no matter how careful you are, you can reckon on a loss
of two ten a year just in fines."

And worse than fines, instant dismissal should an assistant
omit to credit a customer's account on the return or exchange
of goods. "And let me tell you," Miss Hubbard concluded
with sniffs, and resort to a very starched handkerchief leaving
her nose somewhat red at the tip, "let me tell you that any
young lady who thinks of serving in a shop, even such as
Mantell's what holds the Royal Warrant, should think twice."

Perry said that she hadn't thought, even once, of serving in
a shop. No fear.

Florrie, however, enlarged and at length on the life of a
shop assistant. "Look. Don't take no notice of that dried-up
old haddock. Why has she stuck it so long, then? She needn't
have. I'm blowed if I would, only that there's other ways and
means," Florrie winked an eye, "of earning here and there a
bit of extra."

"Such as?" prompted Perry.

"Well . . ." a titter and a sidelong glance. "There's always
after hours and your evenings off."

"I see." Perry nodded. "Taking night work you mean, to
earn that bit of extra."

"You bet!" Florrie gave a loud guffaw. "And quite a big
bit of extra too, not to mention late dinners and a bottle of fizz
thrown in with a coupla quid, if you're lucky."

"Two pounds!" Perry's eyes widened. "I'd no idea one could earn so much working after hours. Is it something special? And where would one apply for such a post? At Mrs. Kent's?"

"Listen to her!" spluttered Florrie. "Don't make me die!"

Perry stared at her coldly. "I can't see why you're laughing."

"You'll be laughing too, ducks—on the other side of your face," Florrie straightened her own, "if you go asking Mrs. Kent for something special after hours. And don't," Florrie rounded on her sharply, "go mentioning to Mrs. P. or Miss Hubbard that I've put you wise about that bit of extra. It's done on the quiet so to speak, in me spare time."

This conversation took place in Florrie's bedroom, a top attic lit by two candles in saucers. The stench from a paraffin lamp mingled with the smell of perspiration and patchouli exuding from a collection of tawdry dresses, hanging on pegs along a wall, and partially concealed by a tattered red curtain. A cardboard box with the lid half off exposed a black hat trimmed with scarlet ostrich tips, which Perry decided, inwardly, was common; but with flattering enthusiasm, pointing to the box; "I like your hat," she said. "Very stylish. You didn't buy *that* from your wages as a shop girl, I'll be bound."

Florrie, seated on the bed, mending a pair of lace-frilled drawers, shot a look, sharp as knives, at her demure young guest who, uninvited, had taken to herself the only chair the room contained. "Either you're a dark horse—or I'm a bloomin' cherub," she muttered; and viciously she snapped her teeth upon a cotton thread.

Unheedful of this remark. "Those drawers," ventured Perry, not without some envy for their Valenciennes lace, "are ever so pretty. Did you make them yourself? Don't tell me if you don't want to, but," she glanced aside at the row of dresses on the wall, "I can guess now what it is you do in your spare time."

"Oh, you can guess, can you?" Florrie retorted with vigour, and red in the face. "Been at the same game yourself—I thought as much. Up to every dodge, you are!"

"I wouldn't say that," Perry hastened to assure her, offering to Florrie's scowl her most persuasive smile. "I've never done it for money, of course. But if you want any help with this extra work of yours, which I'm sure must keep you at it till all hours of the night, I'd be willing to oblige. We could get through quite a lot together, couldn't we? Two pairs of hands are better than one. You'd find me very useful."

"What the hell!" exploded Florrie.

"No, but look," besought Perry, "I'm not suggesting we go shares. I'd never expect to earn as much as you do at it— two pounds with late dinners thrown in at your customers' houses and all—but I could do the odd jobs like pressing and that. I've always made my own underwear and nightgowns."

Florrie who during this recital had sat agape and in the giggles, now sprang to her feet. Casting aside the enviable garment on which she was engaged, she burst into laughter, harsh and uncontrollable. Perry amazedly stared.

"Pressing and—Gawd!" Florrie's voice cracked on a note of hysteria. "Get through quite a lot togeth——" She clutched her side. "Help! You've given me a stitch—keeping on at me as if you didn't know. Or *don't* you know?" She seized the startled Perry by the shoulders, gazing down into her face. "S'truth!" she half whispered it, "what's a kid like you goin' to do with its life? Where will you end? D'you think you can live on ten bob a week on the straight? Never in this world! Look at that scrag of a Hubbard, always moaning, selling gloves—and where will *she* end? Selling matches. How can you or me or any one of us put by for our old age? Oh, yes, find a chap and marry him and what then? Half a dozen kids and starvation wages. Twenty-five bob a week at most—skilled labour. I could'a married on that. Not me! I let him go." She swallowed painfully. "What hope is there for us, slaving our guts out in order to live, and no one to care if we die? Why shouldn't we take what we can get and chance it—while the going's good? We'll be old and crabbed and sour soon enough and then—the workhouse. But I'm putting by, I am. I'm thirty now and when I've saved a coupla hundred quid I'm going to 'op it, see? It'll take me another ten years, but I can live for the rest of me life on that—if this sort o' life don't kill me."

"Why should it kill you?" At a loss to understand the reason for this outburst, Perry added earnestly: "I think you're doing too much, if you ask me. It must be a great strain to work both day *and* night. I should give it up if I were you."

"I wish to Christ I could." Florrie steadied her lips to a smile, "but I can't. Nem'mind." She nodded brightly, avoiding Perry's troubled look. "It'll all be the same a hundred years hence, so why worry?"

'It is not yet a hundred years hence,' recalls Lady Mulvarnie, 'but conditions endured by women who worked for their living when I was a girl are by no means the same, thank God.' For the time was to come when she would have cause to remember and, within her province, to allay the wretched existence accepted by these unfortunates as alternative or supplementary to a life of prostitution.

Her first introduction to Mrs. Popham's household did not, however, include her fellow boarders, for she arrived in the afternoon when they were all engaged at their respective drudgeries.

Mrs. Popham received her at the door in a soiled flannel dressing gown with egg stains down the front for which she apologized, saying, 'she had just got out of bed with the sick headache'. Perry's tin trunk, containing all she possessed in the world including the black japanned box, had already been delivered by the coal man for sixpence, and was standing in the hall. With Mrs. Popham's assistance she dragged it up the stairs to a room on the second floor that, though poky, sparsely furnished with an uninspiring view of chimney-pots, appeared to be, in her new-found independence, a charming habitation.

Mrs. Popham must at this time have been in her sixties. She was short, chubby, highly-coloured, garrulous. Her hair, which if washed would have been white, was approximately grey as were also her ill-fitting teeth. Perry was asked would she like a cup of tea, and in Mrs. Popham's parlour on the first floor front divided from her bedroom by a pair of folding doors, they sat before the fire with the tea-table between them.

We are given a glimpse of that parlour. The wall-paper, a dingy brown which may once have been yellow, was wreathed with blue roses and peeling in patches. The carpet, grease-spotted, covered boards that creaked to every step. Dust lay thick in the folds of green velvet draping the mantelshelf over which hung a fly-blown mirror. A coloured print of the Queen was pinned above the chiffonier where stood a bottle of stout, half a loaf, a limp aspidistra in a red china pot, and the remains, on a plate, of a bloater. From this noisome skeleton Perry averted her eyes. There was a prevalent odour, not only of fish but of mice, of boiled cabbage and of air that had never been renewed by ventilation; and although the table offered quite a spread of squashed-fly biscuits, seed-cake, and currant bread and butter, the smell of the bloater and other things, unseen, was scarcely conducive to an appetite.

Mrs. Popham, pouring tea from a pot with a rubber spout, evinced a lively curiosity concerning the recent upheaval at Tamar Street.

'. . . She had heard that my stepma had gone for a pick-me-up to Brighton. She must have got a good price for the freehold of that business. She supposed I would come in for my fair share of it. Was my stepma going to have me live with her? I said I hoped not. "You don't get on with her, do you, dear?" "Who would?" I said. "I believe you," she said, looking down at her cup with her lips tucked in. "I should have thought your poor Pa could have done better for himself than her. Not a patch on your poor Ma, that one wasn't." "Oh——" I said, and swallowed a crumb the wrong way. "Hold your breath, dear, and count ten," said Mrs. P.

I couldn't hold my breath, and I couldn't count ten, but I managed at last to blurt between squawks, "Did you—did you know my mother, then?" "Know her? I should think so," said Mrs. P. "She lodged here."

I had never heard that before.

"In fact it was through me, in a way," said Mrs. P., "that she first met your Pa. She was wanting a bed-sitter and couldn't pay much, being out of work, so I let her have the top attic for five bob a week. She come here with a shockin' cold and I sent her round to Mr. Cheke's to give her something for it. So that's how it was, you see." Mrs. Popham cut a slice of seed-cake, very thin, and put it on my plate. I left it untouched to ask, "Did she ever tell you where she worked?" "No, dear, only that they was French people." I felt my fingers go numb at the tips as I heard myself say, "What was the name of these French people? Do you know?" "She may," said Mrs. P., "have mentioned the name, but being foreign I shouldn't have remembered it. And I make it a rule never to ask my girls questions, so I don't hear no lies."

I sat in silence.

"But I do know this," Mrs. P. said suddenly. "There was quite a lot of French people round about here at that time when the Germans sieged Paris. The papers was full of it, how they was starving, and eating cats and rats and things, and those who could get away, did. And I remember your mother telling me she'd been teaching English to a little French boy."

A little French boy. . . . Jean Marie's brother could it be? "It's coming back to me now," said Mrs. P. "Your Ma told me the lady was a widow. A Countess or something. Very high class."

And this time I did hold my breath.

"You're not much like your Ma," Mrs. P. was saying. "She was darker than what you are, and not meaning it personal, dear, a great deal better looking." "Yes," I said, and smiled. "She was pretty and I'm plain." "Well, we can't none of us help our looks," Mrs. P. said kindly. "You're young yet. You may improve as you get older." Her tone suggested doubt. "Your Ma," she continued, "was in mourning, too, when she come here—for her Auntie." "Yes," I said, "there was an aunt. I didn't know she died." And I went into a trance again. Mrs. P. was still talking, but I didn't hear a word until—"So when they brought him home on a stretcher——" "Stretcher?" I came to with a jerk. "Yes, dear, I was telling you. He slipped on a banana skin outside the Masons' Arms and broke his skull. Between you, me and the gatepost he wasn't himself. Yes," sighed Mrs. P., "I've had my cross to bear. We used to let to gentlemen—commercials and that— but when my poor hubby was took I felt it wouldn't do for a lady on her own to have men about the place, so I put an advert in the local paper for ladies only and had dozens of replies. Your Ma saw the advert and that's how she come here, and since then I've never had a man inside the house. One," said Mrs. P., "with all respect to the dead, was quite enough for me if not too many."

And just at that moment, from Mrs. Popham's bedroom,

came the sound of a snore, or rather a long succession of snores, sonorous, dreadful and—drunken.

Mrs. P., unabashed—I wondered at her nerve—offered me a squashed-fly biscuit. Staring her straight in the face I refused it. No man in the house, indeed! And one snoring his head off, dead drunk, in her bedroom. This, I decided, was no place for me. I must ask for my money back—two weeks' board and lodging paid for in advance—and go.

I got up.

"Mrs. Popham," I said, very quiet, "whether you know it or whether you don't, and I'm not deaf either, there's a man in the house now, this minute."

"A man!" If I had said a man-eater she couldn't have been more startled, looking round about her and under the table as if to find him sitting there. "You're seeing things, dear." "No," I said, "I'm hearing them." And I pointed to the folding doors.

Then Mrs. Popham laughed—and how she laughed!— till her top teeth dropped out and fell into the cup splashing tea all over the cloth. "You didn't half give me a turn," she said, fishing up her teeth to replace them with a click. "It's only Phyllis." And rising from her chair she opened the door to her bedroom and called, "Come on, Phyllis, come and have your tea, dear."

I cannot say that I was much relieved. A drunken woman, as I knew to my cost, could be worse than a drunken man. The snores had redoubled in volume to end on a snort and the sound of a heavy flop. Phyllis had evidently fallen out of bed.

Returning to the fireside, Mrs. P. refilled the teapot from a kettle balanced on the coals. She had left the door ajar and in the aperture appeared a frightful face, heavily wrinkled, hideous, white, with glaring pink-rimmed eyes and a yawning great cavern of a mouth. The face was followed by a body, also white, barrel-shaped, broad-chested—"A bull-dog!" I cried, quaking. "She won't hurt you," said Mrs. P. "Come in, Phyllis, and say how d'ye do to the lady."

It didn't walk it waddled up to offer me a paw. "She's taken a fancy to you, dear," said Mrs. P. "She don't to everyone. I named her Phyllis after a book by Mrs. Hunger-ford. A lovely book that was. Have you read it?"

No, I hadn't.

"I sat up all night reading that book," said Mrs. P., "when I was whelping this one's mother—a lovely bitch—but I lost her with that litter, the heads, you see, dear, being such a size. Phyllis was the best of six. I reared them on mare's milk and sold the other five. I kept this one but she's not a patch on her mother—worth a mint o' money and if I tell you there was a gent round here offered me twenty pound for. . . ."

So now it was all of the mother of Phyllis and not another word of mine.'

And but for the favour of Phyllis Perry might have found herself the least bit homesick in those first few days at Mrs. P.'s; homesick for a home that had never been a home, yet the one remaining link, now severed, with her childhood. As Mr. Todd had been at pains to remind her, she was virtually alone in the world; a world as far remote from the life that she had known as this planet is from Mars.

Fin-de-siècle! The close of a century sinking to rest in the sunset of an age that had emerged from the storms of industrial revolution to intellectual freedom and progression unexampled in the annals of British achievement. Immortal names, ringing down the darkened years to come, were dedicated to the service of a homely old lady in a widow's cap, emblem of monarchy mighty and lasting, of an Empire solidly great.

Yet we, of another and perhaps a lesser age, who look back on the end of a century, see, in those years of its dying, a febrile restlessness, herald, not of death but of birth: a Renaissance.

The new age had come before its time. Everything was new; art was new, brought over from France as *l'art nouveau*. Past favourites in gilded frames depicting stags at bay or Roman maidens at their baths, that hitherto had decorated drawing-rooms, were replaced by extravaganzas of curious design, and the lavender twilights of Whistler. Colours faded to 'greenery-yallery', resuscitated from the 'eighties and the aesthetes. It was an age of preciosity, 'New Culture', 'New Hedonism', denounced by Jeremiahs as the 'Decadence'. But for all its manner posturing and artificiality, that last decade, flinging to the winds its Nonconformist conscience, was marching toward a social and spiritual reform, the 'New Democracy', as preached by Edward Carpenter.

Led by that paradoxical master of sensation, Oscar Wilde, the 'New Decadence', translating life into epigrams, shocked while it delighted. Individual expression was the order of the day. All strata of society were imbued with the prevalent urge for release from the shibboleths of mid-Victorian convention.

The least expected most suburban quarters harboured pale youths with poetic aspirations and long hair. In Belgravia young women were demanding of papas to be allowed to take a University degree. Marriage was not now the Alpha and Omega of feminine existence. Spinsterhood might find its compensations. Strictly masculine professions were compelled, by urgent clamour, to throw open their doors to petti-coat invasion. The Women's Franchise League, headed by Mrs. Pankhurst, had declared that no person, by reason of sex alone, should be disqualified for appointment to any chosen office or position.

The 'New Woman' had arrived.

But this new world, beyond the drab precincts of Tamar Street and 'Mrs. P.'s' establishment, was yet by Miss Flight to be explored.

On that first evening of her arrival we find her—she admits it—'very low'. A second survey of her room had disclosed, in corners, the accumulated dirt of other occupants. Perry's passion for cleanliness revolted. She would turn out this room in the morning, even if she had to buy a scrubbing-brush herself. And she unpacked; then, after one glance inside the chest of drawers, she stowed her clothes away into her trunk again. Those drawers too, would have to be scrubbed.

With her handkerchief she dusted the mantelpiece and placed her mother's photograph upon it, but not that of Jean Marie. He must remain in the black japanned box, locked in her trunk, since Mrs. P.'s avowal of 'No questions ever asked' belied her avid curiosity. . . . And so we find her at the window on this wintry afternoon, watching the shadowy figure of the lamp-lighter pass from post to post. The gas-jets bloomed beneath the magic of his wand like great golden tulips in the dusk. Below in the street four or five bearded Germans were playing the 'Blue Danube'. The blank and dreary outlook of houses opposite melted in a vision of things unseen, unguessed; of life unimagined, of songs unsung. . . . "I don't think I can bear it," whispered Perry.

Bear what? Her freedom, her loneliness? But she had known loneliness enough at Tamar Street; yet at least she had been certain of a roof above her head. What if she should find no employment within these next two weeks? Still, she had that fifty pounds. She wouldn't starve.

Rhythmic waves of sound floated upward; involuntarily her body swayed; all her blood was turned to music with a tingling in her toes, as wheeling from the window she, who had never danced, was dancing to a German band, arms floating, silent-footed, while delicious little shudders crept up and down her spine. . . . "I'm going barmy," she said, and stopped to light a candle and hunt in her pocket for her purse. Taking from it the few coppers it contained, she unfastened the window, flinging down pennies. She heard the tinkle of their fall on the pavement, and guttural thanks intermingled with a final brassy blare.

There was a scratching and a snuffling at the door; her face broke into smiles; she lifted the latch. Phyllis entered sedately, made for the bed, clambered up, and with a sigh of satisfaction, enthroned herself upon it like a queen.

The band had ceased to play; the room was silent. Kneeling by the bedside Perry wound her arms about those massive shoulders and put her lips to that heavy wrinkled cheek. "You're perfectly hideous," she whispered, "but I love you. . . ." Nor did it strike her as strange that the first consciousness of love in her life was for a dog.

*　　　*　　　*

Mr. Todd had made an appointment for her to meet her prospective employer at his office the following Friday. Mrs. Popham, who, by dint of perseverance, had managed to extract from Perry the purpose of this visit, was full of dark forebodings.

According to the oracle, a certain battered book which Mrs. Popham constantly consulted, Friday was not a lucky day for those born, as was Perry, under Aquarius, when—'Business Transactions,' Mrs. Popham read, 'should be avoided'. From that same Delphic source Mrs. Popham had been initiated in the art of fortune-telling by the cards and in the tea leaves; by which tokens had appeared in Perry's teacup an ominous dark stranger, substantiated further by the cards and 'Mrs. P.' as: "Up to no good, with the nine of spades to crown you, and three gossiping queens for mischief. There's sorrow, dear, for you in this lay out, and disappointment. Shuffle them and have another go."

But the other 'go' proved even more depressing than the first; and with hope deferred if not entirely deflated, Perry set forth, on that Friday morning, for her interview. Nor was she reassured by Mr. Todd's summary of the proposed situation.

The young lady for whom Mr. Todd's client desired a companion had been hampered from birth with 'a disability'.

"You mean," suggested Perry, "that she's not quite—right?"

Mr. Todd, glancing up from over his spectacles, coldly replied that the young lady's misfortune was physical, not mental; and referring to his notes: "She is in fact," he said, "a cripple, who has hitherto been consigned to the care of governesses, but in accordance with medical opinion her uncle, who is also her guardian, has decided she would benefit better from younger companionship." He leaned back in his chair to enlarge upon that. "There is some slight similarity of circumstance between yourself and this young lady—whose name by the way is Miss Curran—for she, too, is an orphan."

"We don't know," Perry dared to remind him, "that I *am* an orphan, Mr. Todd."

With another crushing look, Mr. Todd proceeded, "I was about to say that Miss Curran's disability prevents her from leading the normal life her position in Society demands; and again, like yourself"—his smile was a little sideways as if comparison between the two were a mere polite concession—"she has few, if any, relatives of her age. Would you, therefore, be prepared to consider this post, that, I need hardly remind you, would be much to your advantage, Miss—er—Flight?"

Miss Flight said doubtfully yes, she might consider it, on a month's trial, perhaps.

Certainly a month's trial, Mr. Todd agreed, always providing his client would be prepared to consider Miss Flight. His tone implied that such consideration was most unlikely; and ringing the bell to summon his minion he asked had Mr. Hope-Winter arrived?

Mr. Hope-Winter had arrived, and, as it seemed, in a taking. Scarcely waiting for the pimply boy's announcement, he made his presence known before he could be seen by Perry, whose back was to the door. "Well, really, Todd! I have a luncheon appointment in ten minutes and you've kept me in there half an hour. Is this the young person?"

Mr. Todd, with obsequious apologies and bows, was on his feet. The young person crossed hers, in the flutters. She had recognized that voice and the vague scent of lilies emanating from its owner, introduced by Mr. Todd as Mr. Hope-Winter, Miss—um—Flight.

"But that," said Mr. Hope-Winter, seating himself, "is not her name."

The blood rushed to her face. She glanced daggers at the traitor Todd, who, full of urbane smiles, had gone back to his chair. Without turning her head she turned her eyes to look round at the gentleman, to see him quizzically looking round at her.

"We have met before," he said, "but never until recently in London, I believe."

"You have met Miss—Flight," Mr. Todd's porkish countenance expressed profound amaze, "before?"

"I protest," Mr. Hope-Winter airily objected, "to the repetition of that name. Obeying the laws of recurrence she has outwitted time and space and comes to us, re-born, as she was in the beginning, as she is and ever will be—but not in those dreadful black clothes. Surely, Todd, you see it? She's the Primavera."

Mr. Todd, who could see nothing of the sort and had as little conception of his client's meaning as had the subject of this oblique address, received it with smiling indulgence for the vagaries of leisured wealth.

The property owned by Mr. Hope-Winter in the neighbourhood of Soho and lately bequeathed to him by a great-uncle, had brought Mr. Todd into contact with a personality unlike any he had heretofore been called on to advise. Messrs. Todd and Son and Todd, though of impeccable repute, did not aspire to deal with those whom the senior partner reverentially described as the 'Upper Ten'. The clientèle of Messrs. Todd were drawn chiefly from the shop-keeping and lower middle-lasses and with doubtless more lucrative results, in that their fees, however modest, were paid on demand. But the great-uncle of Mr. Hope-Winter, having died at the age of ninety, was a relic of those days when Mr. Todd's grandfather, then head of the firm, had taken snuff in his office with the nobility whose distinguished patronage had somewhat atoned for their long outstanding credit. The passage of years, while increasing the income of the present representative, had sunk it sadly down the social scale. Thus, Mr. Hope-Winter, essentially of the élite, must, despite his eccentricities or because of them, be humoured.

"But isn't she?" Mr. Hope-Winter insisted. "Drape her in diaphanous starry-blossomed muslin and".—he shrugged a shoulder—"there you have it. The same colourless transparency. Not cadaverous, but warm as any of Sandro's poutingly peevish Madonnas. I must go." He got up. "Engage her temporarily, Todd, with a view to a permanency. She must come as soon as possible—at the latest a week from to-day." At the door he turned. "And for heaven's sake, Miss—ah—whatever your name is—wear anything grey, but not black. One would think you were in mourning for your future. You're too young to be in mourning for your past. *Arrivederci*."

He was gone.

Perry wetted her lips. If this poor crippled girl were quite right in the head, her uncle most certainly wasn't.

"Mr. Todd," she said firmly, "will you please to tell the gentleman that I refuse the place."

"You refuse!" incredulously echoed Mr. Todd. A dark flush unbecomingly mottled his dewlaps. "And may I ask why?"

Mysteriously smiling to herself she submitted no answer to that.

"Miss Cheke——" Mr. Todd, manufacturing patience, cleared his throat, "I beg you to consider the advantages offered by this situation, which no young woman placed as you are without a penny and alone in the world, has any reason nor right to refuse."

And with the utmost contumely he gazed at her whose lips were moving in voiceless calculation, to achieve: "Fifty pounds is—let me see—noughts and five twos are ten—twelve thousand pennies, Mr. Todd."

"You cannot live indefinitely," rejoined the vexed Todd, "on fifty pounds."

"I don't intend to"—her smile still tinctured with mystery stayed—"indefinitely, Mr. Todd."

Only by an effort of supreme restraint did he withhold his hand from assault upon his client's ear. "I can always," said Perry, casting down her eyes, "be a governess, or read newspapers to old ladies and take their pugs out walking. I like dogs. There's a bulldog at Mrs. Popham's. Her name's Phyllis."

This information was received in a silence charged with high explosive.

"Mr. Todd," she meekly queried, "when am I to have that fifty pounds?"

"As your legal adviser," he pronounced, with marked hostility, "I am bound to urge you to accept this situation, on a temporary basis, as suggested by Mr. Hope-Winter, with a view to a permanency which can, of course, be terminated by a month's notice on either side."

"I see," Perry was examining a hole in her glove. "And what about my clothes? I know they're dreadful, but his manners are worse to tell me so." The green eyes were dreamily uplifted. "And if Mr. Hope-Winter doesn't like black he can buy me what he does like, for I can't, unless you care to give me, Mr. Todd, that fifty pounds, or perhaps a little something—in advance?"

Thus Perry found herself possessed of an entirely new wardrobe supplied by that Universal Provider, William Whiteley. We believe Mr. Todd could not have been too agreeably surprised to receive from Mr. Whiteley a detailed account of purchases bought by Miss Cheke, much in excess of the sum as agreed to be deducted from her legacy, less his legal fees, and debited to the account of Messrs. Todd. A copy of this communication, enclosing the details of the account, accompanied Mr. Todd's letter inquiring if the list of goods ordered by Miss Cheke were correct, and if so on whose authority she had exceeded the sum approved by himself as for strictly necessary purchases.

We have her reply, of which she also kept a copy, to the following effect:

Mr. Todd.

Dear Sir,

I did not know I had to have anyone's authority to buy anything I like with my own money as I had to have some decent clothes and may I also ask on whose authority you are keeping my legacy from me as it is now four months since Mr. Cheke died and I haven't had a penny of it yet so will be obliged if you will please to let me have what is left of that £50 (fifty pounds) after you have paid Whiteley's bill and what you want for your fees which I didn't think I would have to pay and don't see why you can't take them out of what you are charging for everything else which his wife ought to pay and not me. And please to let me have Mr. Hope-Winter's address which you never told me and what time I am expected there on Friday next

Yrs Truly
Peridot Cheke
(known as Peridot Flight)

By return of post came Mr. Todd's reply expressing pained astonishment at the ungracious and ungrateful tone of Miss Cheke's letter. It was evident that Miss Cheke did not appreciate that in placing a limit of ten pounds to her expenditure, he had acted solely in her interest. But since it appeared she had wilfully disregarded his advice, he sent her herewith his firm's cheque for nineteen pounds and sixpence which he had instructed Mr. Cheke's bank in Finsbury Park to cash on presentation, being the balance of her legacy of fifty pounds made up as follows:

To William Whiteley	.	.	£20 17 6
To Mrs. Millicent Cheke in payment of a loan of 5s. per week for seven weeks	.	.	£1 15 0
To Messrs. Todd & Son & Todd, legal fees and attendance	.		£8 8 0

Would Miss Cheke kindly acknowledge the receipt of the cheque?

The address of Mr. Hope-Winter, who would expect her at four o'clock on Friday the 29th instant, was 111, Brook Street, Mayfair.

*   *   *

Mayfair meant nothing to Perry. Her knowledge of that fashionable district extended no further than impressions of Park Lane seen from the windows of a cab on occasional visits to Margate, via Victoria Station. But Mrs. Popham, whose thirst for information had been by no means slaked on the arrival of sundry cardboard boxes delivered by William Whiteley's van, had come to know as much as, or even more than Perry knew herself, of her prospective situation.

"Very classy," was 'Mrs. P.'s' verdict, "with a double-barrelled name and all. You can take it from me, dear, Brook Street, Mayfair, is tip-top."

Mrs. Popham, it seems, had an intimate association with Mayfair in that before her marriage to Popham, who was a butler in the same place as herself, she had served a Lord and Lady in Grosvenor Square. From this and other connexions with similar noble establishments, Mrs. Popham had gleaned knowledge enough of life that was 'tip-top and classy' to suggest that Perry should buy a new trunk. "There's sure to be a lady's maid in a house like that, dear, and you wouldn't like her telling them in the servants' 'all that you've brought nothing better than an old tin box. I know what ladies' maids are—Nosy Parkers, always making trouble. The first thing they do is to look at the luggage and never mind whose it is."

How much, Perry queried with caution, would a new trunk cost?

A really good one to last a lifetime, she was told, would cost anything from two to five pound, but, if she liked, Mrs. Popham would pop in on Mr. Marks's and see if he had any second-hand. "Only that he'll want the cash down, dear, if you've any by you."

Perry, having paid Mr. Todd's cheque into the bank and on the manager's advice placed fifteen pounds on deposit, had by her also a secret hoard of sixpences, threepenny bits and pennies extracted as commission from the till at Tamar Street. These she exchanged for two sovereigns and some surplus silver. As a result, therefore, of Mrs. Popham's popping in on Mr. Marks, Perry found herself the owner of a shiny black dress-basket brought by Mr. Marks to Mrs. Popham's door. "So if you can oblige, dear," hinted Mrs. P., "with what I've just paid him, dirt cheap at the price and good as new——"

Perry obliged with the inward reflection that thirty-five

shillings for a trunk far from new and certainly not good, was anything but dirt cheap at the price. Nor could she help wondering if 'Mrs. P.' had herself taken commission from the deal. However, she still had in hand sufficient for immediate necessities, besides the assurance of a capital sum to her credit in the bank that made her the proud possessor of a cheque book.

The day before her departure from Finsbury Park was spent in exploration of the neighbourhood. Accompanied, or more correctly dragged along by Phyllis on a chain, she took up her stance beside a pillar-box in Woodberry Down, that wide tree-bordered road of Regency villas standing in their grounds of half an acre.

Of the postman collecting the mid-day letters she inquired if he knew of any French people living hereabouts. With one eye on her and the other, warily, on Phyllis, he replied not that he knew of and did he bite?

"She," Perry frostily corrected, "does not bite."

"Cor!" He backed from the unamiable interest of Phyllis in his ankles. "I wouldn't like to take your word for it." And shouldering his sack of letters off he went.

Returning to Eden Crescent Perry ate her dinner of shepherd's pie and prunes and, again chained to Phyllis, waited by that same pillar box for the afternoon collection. This was made by a grey-bearded postman who offered to her question a tantalizing clue. He had done this round, he said, for more than twenty years, and he had an idea that there used to be a French lady—a Countess Somebody—living in one of these houses at that time.

"Had she a little boy?" asked Perry, palpitating.

He couldn't say, but he remembered her coming to the door one Christmas Eve to give him half a sovereign as a Christmas Box—more than he had ever had before.

"Her name," urged Perry, "can you remember that?"

He shook his head. "You're askin' something now, Missy. Too long ago."

"Was there—did you know of a Miss Mabel Flight living with this French lady?"

Again he couldn't say as he did. There was no such name around here now, at any rate.

Perry's heart that had leapt sank to her boots. While Phyllis, gingerly sniffing at the pillar-box, impatiently jerked at her lead.

"That's a nasty bit o' goods you got there," remarked the postman. "Does he bite?"

"No," said Perry wearily, "she doesn't."

One last hope was left to her: Miss Genn. And leaving Phyllis with her owner she took the omnibus to Camden Town.

Miss Genn was a small, bustling, pigeon-chested virgin of fifty, with quick birdlike eyes and a precision of speech that caused her to pronounce her A's as E's, an infective tendency imparted to her pupils. In a lapse of two years from Miss Genn's propinquity Perry had lost this refinement of accent, immediately recovered in the ensuing conversation with Miss Genn.

That lady's Academy, as the prospectus proclaimed, catered for the Daughters of Gentlemen, on the tacit understanding that the daughters of trade were not permitted entry to those exclusive cloisters. An exception had been made in Perry's case since, not only was the defunct Mr. Cheke an Apothecary bearing the letters M.P.S. after his name, but that the maternal connexions of his daughter Peridot, being of the clergy, were beyond reproach. Mr. Cheke's second marriage, 'a sad may-salliance', Miss Genn called it, and of which the least said the better, could not, in all justice, reflect on his poor child; and with due regard for these fine distinctions, Miss Genn offered to her former pupil a welcome of modified gush.

"My dear Peridot!" Never did Miss Genn permit the solecism, not infrequent among persons less cultured, of pronouncing Peridot as Peridott. "This is indeed an unexpected pleasure. Pray sit down."

Perry sat down on the edge of a chair facing Miss Genn at the fireside. How often in the past had she and her schoolmates been called to that chair which, according to the possible extent of misdemeanours, presented to its victims all the horrors of the dock.

"You have been much in my thoughts of late," said Miss Genn, a polite and excusable fiction, "and Ai have wondered what plans you have made for your future. Your stepmother——?" Miss Genn delicately paused.

"She has gone to live at Brighton, Miss Genn "

"Brighton?" The echo of that word was a model of discreet insinuation, evinced by a disparaging pursing of the lips, an inflation of a maidenly bosom. "Ai see."

"Ai came to tell you, Miss Genn," continued Perry with an imitative narrowing of vowels, "that Ai have found a situation."

Miss Genn expressed reserved delight.

"But this is excellent news, my dear Peridot. May I ask with whom and where?"

"In Brook Street, Mayfair, Miss Genn." Perry allowed a second's pause before she supplemented with faintest braggadocio, "Park Lane."

Miss Genn received this intelligence with unimpressed restraint; a slight inclination of her head indicated that Mayfair, or indeed Park Lane, were the natural destinations of any pupil schooled at her Academy.

"I am to be companion to a young leydy," Perry proceeded, "who unfortunately suffers from a disabilitee."

"Dear me—not——?" Miss Genn tactfully suggested.

"Oh, no, the young leydy's misfortune," quoted Perry, "is physical, not mental. My father's solicitor, Mr. Todd, recommended me to a cleyent of his for the post. A Mr. Hope-Winter. The young leydy is his niece."

"*Mr.* Hope-Winter?" A quick sparrow-like glance accompanied the query, "is there not a *Mrs.* Hope-Winter?"

"I didn't ask, Miss Genn," said Perry simply. "He interviewed me in Mr. Todd's office and engeyged me on the spot."

"Then I am sure," Miss Genn graciously conceded, "that all is quaite correct. And if Mr. Hope-Winter—a hyphenated neame, I presume?—should desire a more personal reference I will gladly submit it."

Perry thanked her and resourcefully seized upon that opening to ask, with apparent inconsequence: "Miss Genn, did you ever give a reference to my mother when she went as governess with French people?"

"French people!" Miss Genn elevated her eyebrows. Although French, as a necessary part of the curriculum, was taught at her Academy by an aged Mademoiselle, Miss Genn associated all things French, and Paris in particular, with Beelzebub. "Never to my knowledge," declared Miss Genn, "was your dear Mamma employed by French people."

"I had heard," persisted Perry, "that my mother was employed by a French Countess."

"French teytles," Miss Genn rejoined, in professional manner, "are not considered of much consequence in England. The French Revolution swept away most of the great families of France. I am confident that if your dear mother had ever thought of taking a post with"—she gave a little cough—"a French Countess she would have told me. The only reference I gave her, that I can recall, was as companion to an elderly lady in Regent's Park who was certainly not French. I lost sight of your mother for some time after that until she brought you to see me after her marriage to your poor Papa, when you were about five months old. I think you must have been a particularly well-grown infant for your eage, for I distinctly remember remarking that you already had two teeth."

"Is that young," Perry innocently asked, "for teeth?"

Miss Genn enshrined herself behind a vestal blush. "One day I hope you will be better instructed to answer that question than Ai. And now, my dear Peridot," she rose briskly from her chair, "Ai fear I must bid you good-bay. I am giving a lecture on bees to the parlour-boarders, at six o'clock—so if you will excuse me—and pray let me know how you progress."

She was dismissed, her search fruitless; her last hope had gone. She would never find Jean Marie.

THREE

'Geraldine's birthday. Telegram from Mr. H.-W. in Florence wishing her Happy Returns. Says Sending present by registered post Benvenuto Cellini ring glorious sunshine here Firenze at her loveliest dined last night with Spanish Art critic Alvarez go to Seville with him next week via Paris much love Uncle remember me to Peridot—and all that in a wire I ask you! I gave G. a Russian leather bound diary with silver clasps. Didn't know what to give her as she seems to have everything but I know she has almost used up her old one. She says everybody ought to keep a diary. Didn't tell her I've kept one on and off for 3 yrs. or she would have asked to read it. She is always reading bits of hers to me. Yesterday she read what she wrote the first day I arrived here. Has possibilities. Quaint little creature, slightly cockney and very re*feened*. She couldn't say that of me now. Look at the hours—beg pardon—*ahrs*—I spend in my room practising to speak as they do with their voices coming out of the backs of their throats. I still make mistakes calling a table-napkin a serviette and blouse blowse and girl gurl and county cownty. They say cahnteh and blooze and gairl and are never pleased to meet you when they meet you or shake hands when they are introduced. Find it a bit of a strain to say nothing of G.'s hellish tempers, which if I want to stay here and I certainly do I must bear with and smile and smile. She is mad on Shakespeare at the moment. We're reading Othello this week. I'm Desdemona she's the Moor and Iago and everybody else. It used to be Omar Khayyam in between Gilbert and Sullivan. We've done the Mikado and Pinafore and Patience and seen the Gondoliers three times. I play she sings if you can call it singing. She's tone deaf but thinks herself as good as Jessie Bond. She says if the hand of the potter hadn't shaken she would have gone on the stage. She says thing like that to tear the heart out of you one minute and the next is yelling the house down in one of her rages till honestly I don't know how I stand it, but I do, must always stand it because—well, just because she's Geraldine. . . .'

FROM these artless confessions we infer that Miss Flight has made some use of her time and opportunity as a well-established resident in Mayfair. When a few months earlier, having sent her trunk in advance by Carter Paterson, she presented herself at Mr. Hope-Winter's door: 'It was opened,' we are told, 'by a tall young man in blue swallow tails and a yellow waistcoat, his hair plastered flat to his head with a sticky white powder.'

Concealing astonishment at this superb apparition, who gazed through her as if she were a window, Perry, returning his look with one equally as distant, summoned academic dignity to say: "Ai am Miss Flight. Ai am expected."

"Yes, Miss."

She was admitted.

At the foot of a wide oaken staircase another personage received her, a silver-haired stately old gentleman, whom Perry, primed by Mrs. P., presumed to be the butler. At his heels she followed up the stairs; her feet sank in carpet soft as moss. On the first landing, under a window curtained in rose-coloured gauze, stood a cream-painted coffin-shaped box filled with hydrangeas and palms. More stairs and a glimpse through a half-opened door of a room with rugs on polished floors, pictures and tapestries on walls, and gilded furniture. This, Perry inwardly commented, isn't a house, it's a palace. . . . At a door on the third landing from which at right angles ran a corridor, the white-haired old gentleman paused, and, as befitting the announcement of a menial, uttered in suitably deprecating tones: "Miss Flight."

She was given a confused impression of tall windows, lace-curtained and draped in peach satin; of a grand piano covered with a silken shawl; of long rows of bookshelves, much blue and white china, and everywhere flowers in vases and bowls. On a chesterfield couch, a young girl, reclining, turned her head to say languidly: "Tea, Larkin. Now."

"Very good, Miss."

The door reverentially closed.

"Come here, Miss Flight," the languid voice continued. "I

am dreadfully short-sighted and cannot see you clear from this distance. Do come to the fire. I am sure you must be freezing. Such typically English spring weather."

Far from freezing, but in a gentle perspiration due to fright, Perry threaded her way through a maze of occasional tables and small chairs and armchairs, upholstered in chintz, to the couch.

"Bring," Miss Curran gestured vaguely, "that stool and sit beside me."

She obeyed in speechless wonder, for:

'Never,' raves Lady Mulvarnie, 'have I seen before or since so lovely a creature as Geraldine Curran. Her hair, a dark chestnut, fell about her shoulders like a burnished cloud —the strangest hair, wiry, electric, springing back from a forehead smooth and ivory pale. To me, in my ignorance of the aesthetic movement, she was hideously dressed in olive green velvet close fitting the figure, untrimmed and cut square at the throat. She had narrow restless hands, and her eyes were tawny-golden like a tiger's, with eyelashes half an inch long.'

This lyrical description, although written forty years after that first meeting, does not unduly exaggerate if we may take as testimony Whistler's portrait, 'Geraldine'. Hers was the beauty, so often complementary to, or, as it were, nature's compensation for, those afflicted with that same incurable infirmity.

"Take off your hat," commanded Miss Curran, "and let me look at you."

Perry unpinned the new hat bought of Mr. Whiteley, and nursed it on her knee.

"Yes," myopically Geraldine narrowed eyes. "Uncle Adrian was right. You *are* Botticellian. What is your name?"

"My——?" stammered Perry. "Miss Flight."

"Don't be silly. Your Christian name."

"Peridot."

Geraldine lifted her head from the cushions. "How enchanting! I could have 'loved you for that name of yours long ere we met. . . .' Are you making it up?"

"No." Perry moistened her lips. "It is my name."

"I can't believe it. You look very young. How old are you?"

"Eighteen."

"I shall be eighteen in October. Peridot." Softly she
savoured it. " 'The sweetest name that ever love waxed
weary of.' You read your Swinburne, of course?"

"Yes, indeed," lied Perry, who had never heard of him.
"He is mai feyvourite author."

"Poet," corrected Geraldine.

"All poets," Perry dared in Gennish accents, "are authors,
surelee, Miss Curran?"

"Oh, dear me," sighed Geraldine, sinking back on her
pillows, "I do hope you are not argumentative." Her long
fingers were for ever moving, picking at her thumb-nail, pulling at her dress. "Your predecessor, Miss Marchant, a
sprightly thirty-five with a giggle and pince-nez, was argumentative. 'Really, Miss Curran, I don't wish to quibble but
since we're splitting hairs——' She was always so tiresomely
platitudinous. Don't *you* be platitudinous. I shall call you
Peridot and you may call me Geraldine, only you mustn't
speak so mincingly. You are putting on a voice. . . . You
look quite pretty when you blush. Tell me some more about
yourself."

"There isn't"—Perry's face was scarlet—"much to tell.
Ai—I am an orphan. My father was—French." The shock of
Miss Curran's accusation had almost banished from her mind
her noble ancestry, founded on Miss Genn's assertion con-
cerning the great families of France. "He deyed—died before
I was born, swept away in the French Revolution."

Geraldine, who had closed her eyes, opened them again,
to ask: "Which revolution? I suppose you mean in 1870, but
he couldn't possibly have died then or you wouldn't have been
born at all if you are only eighteen. And anyway I understood
your father kept a chemist's shop in some rather awful suburb
in North London."

"That was—my stepfather. My real father——" Her
breath dwindled.

Geraldine was watching her amusedly.

"What," came the inevitable question, "was his name? It
could hardly have been Flight if he were French."

A second's frantic pause, then: "Flight was my mother's
name." Desperation rose to the emergency. "It is difficult to
find employment with a French name. The French are so—so

3

disliked." Why, oh why, had she not prepared herself for this?
"My schoolmistress——" No, best leave it at that.

But Geraldine would not leave it at that.

"Your schoolmistress?"

"Miss Genn. She advised me to——"

"Change your name? How absurd! Only the bourgeoisie
and Radicals are anti-French and make caricatures of them as
'Froggies' with Napoleonic moustaches and imperials."

The crisis was over; Perry sat exhausted.

"So you are half French." Geraldine regarded her with
interest renewed. "And I am half Irish, but I have a soupçon
of French in me, too. One of my great-great-grands, a de
Tournay, married into us under the Restoration. She was a
mistress of Charles the Second. Yes." Her eyes were narrowing again. "You could easily be French, though you're more
like Sandro's Simonetta, and she was supposed to be English.
It is quite a mistake to imagine that all Latin races are swarthy
and dark as mulattos. Denys l'Auxerrois was blond, or as
Pater describes him 'flaxen and flowery', which"—her gaze
lingered—"might well describe you. Denys has always been
for me a very real person, as he was to Pater. You remember
how he says: 'I seemed to have seen the tortured figure there,
to have met Denys l'Auxerrois in the street.' You know his
'Imaginary Portraits'? Don't you adore Pater?"

Thankfully the arrival of tea circumvented an answer to that.

A silver tray loaded with a silver tea service and porcelain
cups was placed by a footman on a table near the couch. The
butler brought a cake-stand, and arranged the cushions for
Miss Curran to sit up.

"You need not wait, Larkin."

"Very good, Miss."

Noiselessly treading, the butler withdrew. The footman
shovelled coal on the fire from a gleaming brass scuttle, swept
the hearth and as noiselessly followed him.

"Pour the tea, Peridot, and pass me a cucumber sandwich."

Perry glanced at the cake-stand. On one tier, sandwiches;
on another bread and butter, wafer thin; an assortment of little
cakes below; after that an iced cake, and finally a plum cake.
She passed the plate of sandwiches, three-cornered and
nothing but a mouthful, and poured tea from the heavy silver
pot.

"Help yourself, you dear little thing," said Geraldine munching. "You are like a white mouse. You have exactly the hands of a mouse. I think you're sweet. So awfully prim. But you aren't eating anything. Have one of those." She pointed to the dish of cakes.

"I will have one of these, please, if I may. Thank you."

Perry took a sandwich. Her tongue clove to the roof of her mouth. It was agony to eat with Geraldine peering at her with those half-closed inquisitive eyes. The tea was undrinkable, pale and tasting of scent. Geraldine sipped, made a face and set down her cup.

"You haven't put sugar in this, have you?"

"Yes—I——"

"Stupid! Why didn't you ask? I don't take sugar in tea. Pour it away."

Perry poured it away in a porcelain bowl and refilled the cup without sugar. She was just about to add milk from a silver jug when—"Cream," snapped Geraldine, "not milk." Cream! Perry searched and found a smaller silver jug and passed the cup, replenished.

"Cut me a slice of that iced cake," was Miss Curran's next command. "And do eat something. Have another sandwich."

"No more, thank you. I've done very nicely, thank you."

The slice of cake was dutifully offered. Geraldine's fingers fluttered; again she grimaced. "Ugh! No! There's jam in it. The cook knows I loathe jam, yet she will keep on sending jammy things up to me." She flung herself back against her cushions. "Well, if you've finished, you may ring."

Ring? . . . Perry looked about her.

"There." Geraldine petulantly pointed. "Next to the mantelpiece."

Perry got up, pulled a china bell attached to the wall and went back to her seat. Hate was in her heart, and a smile on her lips. "May I give you another cup of tea?"

"Noo more, thank you." Geraldine was staring at the ceiling. "Ai've done very naicely, thank you."

All right, Miss High-and-Mighty, said Perry, smiling still. You may be rich as Croesus and a howling beauty, but I'm not dirt for you to tread on, and if there's one month's notice to be given either side it won't be *you* who gives it, see? But this she did not say aloud. What she did say, gazing at the sky framed in the lace-curtained window, was: "It looks as if we'll have a storm."

"Yes, Miss?"

The footman at the door.

"You can take the tea-things, Charles, and tell Mrs. Smith her cake is horrid—full of jam."

"Very good, Miss."

The footman carried out the tray and came back for the cake-stand. Geraldine, scowling at him, said: "Send Bowler to me."

"Yes, Miss."

He left the room.

Geraldine was restlessly picking at her thumb. Her dark level brows almost met above her nose that still retained a wrinkle of disgust. Perry's hat slid from her knee. She stooped to pick it up, glancing furtively at Geraldine. Any more remarks? Not one. Miss Curran seemed to have forgotten her existence; and, watching those thin unquiet fingers, that long graceful body, helplessly stretched, Perry was reminded of some wild creature, caged. Her heart twisted. She lowered her head.

"You wanted me, Miss?"

Another of them at the door; a sallow sour-visaged person this, in black, relieved with white at throat and wrists.

"Yes, Bowler. You can take Miss Flight to her room. Go with Bowler, Peridot. We dine at eight." Geraldine's eyes had not stirred from the ceiling. "See that Miss Flight has everything she needs."

To her room she was conducted by the long-faced Bowler, whose manner suggested that of a wardress about to admit her to a cell.

"I've unpacked your clothes," Bowler said, with truculence, "and put everything away except that black tin box"—conspicuously placed upon the dressing-table; for which Perry thanked her, privately regretting that she had omitted to provide her trunk and tin box with a key.

"It was Miss Geraldine's idea," continued Bowler, "to put you in here what has always been kept as a spare room. The governesses was on the floor above. I didn't have to wait on them."

"And you won't," said Perry gently, "have to wait on me. I prefer to wait upon myself."

"So long as we know where we are," agreed Bowler, "to begin as we mean to go on. I don't mind for this once to un-pack you, but it's not my place to maid companions." One of the dresses, recently acquired, a juvenile grey 'demi-toilette', lay on the bed. Lifting a nostril Bowler glanced at it aggres-sively. "And as that's the only thing you seem to have fit for evenings I've put it out for you to wear tonight. It's not real decollty but it will have to do. I suppose you're not used to dress for dinner."

"Where I came from," Perry carelessly replied, "it is usual to *un*dress for dinner."

This remark, digested and discarded with a toss of the head, was followed by the query: "Who was you with last?"

"If you really want to know," said Perry confidentially, "I was with Siamese twins."

"Go on!" ejaculated Bowler.

"I will," Perry fluttered her eyelids, "go on, if you can keep it to yourself. They were the daughters of the Sultan of Turkey. It must never be mentioned, of course. The Sultan wouldn't wish it to be known. I wouldn't have left," she sighed, "only that they married."

"Married!" gasped Bowler, pop-eyed. "You don't mean to say they was married?"

"Yes." Dreamily Perry surveyed the middle distance. "To another pair of Siamese twins."

"Look here! What," demanded Bowler, "do you take me for?"

Perry gazed at her. "I'm looking—and I hardly like to say."

"Well," snorted Bowler, "there's one thing, you won't be here long."

"Prepare yourself," said Perry, "for a shock. I've come to stay."

Bowler's lemon-tinted face turned salmon pink.

"So did the governesses come to stay. Six of them in my time, and out within the month. You wait."

Perry smiled.

"I will."

"I've been here the longest," Bowler heatedly pursued, "ever since the old nurse died, and that's getting on these two years. Spoilt her, that nurse did, something chronic. Talk about a Tartar. I wouldn't like," she said, "to be in your shoes."

Perry's eyes reverted to Bowler's outsize feet.

"And I wouldn't like," she said, "to be in yours."

"You may think you're funny," Bowler's voice was slightly raised, "but I don't take sauce from no one, not even paid companions. Now you know!"

Complacently Perry watched her somewhat noisy exit and turned to a tour of inspection.

The bedroom, which henceforth would be hers, is described as 'large and lofty with a glass-shaded chandelier and wall-brackets for lights. The wall-paper was patterned in a design of red and yellow crocuses . . .' The William Morris influence, at that time unrecognized by her. 'There were arm-chairs and an ottoman upholstered in yellow brocade with curtains to match at the windows. A red carpet covered the whole of the floor, and the brass bedstead had a lace counter-pane lined with yellow satin. I turned it back to examine the sheets, of finest linen, hand-embroidered. The wardrobe, of inlaid satinwood, had double doors with a full-length mirror in each and drawers in the middle. The dressing-table was of the same satinwood, with a looking-glass draped in white muslin and tied with yellow bows.' . . . But the fact of a fire burning in the grate seems to have impressed her more than any of this, for: 'At Tamar Street a fire in a bedroom—but never in mine—was allowed only in case of illness. . . .'

There came a tap at the door followed by the entry of a little maid in starched cap and apron carrying a can of hot water. Perry watched her take the ewer from the wash-stand, place the can in the basin and cover it with towels. Then she brought a pair of steps, and mounted them to light the gas in the chandelier and wall-brackets. When she had finished she said: "Will you please to ring, Miss, if there is anything else you'll be wanting?"

Perry asked her name. "I'm Annie, Miss, the under-house-maid. Your bathroom is the first door on the right. Shall I turn on your bath for you now, Miss?"

A bathroom! Just imagine! . . . Perry had never seen a bathroom in her life. 'We had a hip-bath at Tamar Street which Mr. Cheke used on Saturday nights in front of the kitchen fire, which Milly to my knowledge never used at all, and that I could only use when they were out. . . . And believe me how I wallowed in that huge marble bath framed in mahogany, and the lovely scented soap! No wonder cleanliness, they say, is next to godliness. . . .' She was a little perturbed about dinner. 'Eight o'clock. What a time to have their dinner, and having to wear your best dress for it too. But I was glad I stood up to that Bowler.'

There were silver-backed brushes on the dressing-table. As these she did not dare to use, she used her own. . . . 'It had lost some of its bristles and was bald in parts, so I hid it in a drawer. What Mrs. P. had said of ladies' maids was right. I didn't want that Bowler nosy-parkering around.'

Then she struggled into the grey 'demi-toilette', found the hooks and eyes unmanageable and pulled the bell, a long red rope hanging from the ceiling with a tassel at the end. After a few moments the same little maid answered it.

"Yes, Miss?"

"If you would please," Perry said apologetically, "to hook me up behind."

She was hooked up behind. The full-length mirror returned a reflection of pale hair gleaming under the gaslight, of a face, faintly coloured, and the unexpected whiteness of bare throat and arms against the grey.

"Oh, Miss," Annie stepped back to admire. "You do look nice."

"Yes, I was thinking I look rather nice myself—up to here." And Perry put her hand before her face to hide it.

The little maid giggled. "Oh, no, Miss!"

"Oh, yes. Plain as the back of a cab. Where do they have their dinner?"

"In the dinin'-room, Miss." A look of surprise had supplanted the giggles.

"Where is it?"

"You don't have to go to the dinin'-room, Miss, until dinner is served. They'll be in the drorin'-room." And, going to the coal-scuttle, Annie peeped inside. "I'll fetch some more, and then if you're ready, Miss, I'll take you down."

"That'll be nice of you, Annie, but please don't trouble."

"It's no trouble at all, Miss. I'll just fill this up——"

She carried out the scuttle and presently returned with it, breathless and rosier than ever; and as Perry went to help her take the scuttle to the hearth, "I say!" she exclaimed, "what a weight. Do you have to lug this great heavy thing up and down those stairs all day and half the night? Why can't that

stuffed image with flour on his hair bring it up for you? He
doesn't seem to have anything to do but open doors and carry
trays."

"Oh!" Annie's mouth crumpled into laughter. "Stuffed——"
But she sobered in a second to say: "The footmen don't bring
up the coals, Miss—not to the bedrooms."

"Do you," Perry asked her, "have a fire in your bedroom?"

"Me?" Annie knelt at the grate to busy herself with poker
and tongs. "No, Miss, we don't have no fires."

"Where do you sleep?"

"Sleep, Miss?" Annie sat back on her heels anxiously
watching the flicker of a flame spring up between the smoke
wreaths. "Me and the scullery maid share a top attic. It's
ever so hot in the summer with the skylight overhead."

"And ever so cold in the winter, I suppose?"

"Not so bad, Miss. We turn in together when it's freezing."
But there had been no one to turn in with at Tamar Street
when it was freezing.

Annie rose to her feet.

"That's better, though it didn't ought to smoke. I'll be back
to see to it again before you go to bed. And now, Miss, if you'd
like to come down——"

Perry followed her down two flights of stairs to the drawing-
room. The door was half open.

"In there, Miss."

'. . . My knees were shaking and my hands were cold.
The room was enormous, full of light and furniture and
staring people, magnified by panic into giants. These, as
sight refocused, were found to be Mr. Hope-Winter; a red-
faced stoutish man with a grizzled moustache and a glass in
his eye, both in evening dress; and a tall lady in mauve, very
low-necked, with a royal fringe and a dog-collar of pearls.
Geraldine, in a dress of some soft creamy stuff, lay on a
long wicker couch. They all appeared to be waiting for
somebody. Me? . . . I saw the lady glance at the clock and
heard Geraldine's lazy voice—so like her uncle's—"There
you are, at *last*. We were just about to send a search party
to find you."

I stayed rooted, lost, abandoned in a vast expanse of rugs
and polished parquet. Mr. Hope-Winter stood with his

back to the fire, his feet on a white polar bearskin complete with head and glassy staring eyes. Even that skin of a bear had to stare.

"Ah, Miss Flight." Mr. Hope-Winter came forward, gave me two fingers and dropped them, and turned. "Let me introduce you to my sister, Lady Stilton"—the lady in mauve. I said, "Pleased to meet you" and put out my hand. Ignoring it, she looked at me along her nose. "Sir Frederick Stilton," said Mr. Hope-Winter, with a smile in his voice. I stuck out my hand again. The red-faced man took it and shook it. "How d'ye do, Miss Flight?" I told him, "Quite well, thank you." From Geraldine came a little spurt of laughter and then the butler at the door, as if we were in church, said: "Dinner is served."

It was awful.

Never to my dying day shall I forget the agonies I suffered at dinner that first night. Mr. Hope-Winter sat at the top and Geraldine, carried down in the wicker chair by two footmen, sat at the end of a table large enough to seat three dozen. I was placed next to Sir Frederick with Lady Stilton opposite. The silver candelabra, the napery, the glass, the flower-filled epergne, thankfully concealing most of me from the ever-searching eye of the Aunt, were each and all part of a nightmare.

I think every one of us, at some time or another, has endured the horrors of a shaming dream, in which, among a crowd of strangers, fully clothed, one sees oneself in nothing but a much too inadequate vest. And on this occasion, seated at that table with Sir Frederick beside me making hearty conversation: "Have you been to any good plays lately?" or "Did you have a pleasant journey here, Miss Flight?" as if I had arrived from darkest Africa, I experienced that same unbearable embarrassment, the more appalling for the knowledge that from this I could not wake; it was no dream, but stark reality. So there I sat, while Geraldine, to increase my discomfiture, addressed herself exclusively to somebody invisible and to whom she made pretence of introducing me.

"Montmorency, this is Peridot. Isn't she sweet? Her father was French. She would have me believe he went to the guillotine sniffing a rose to keep away the smell of the

common people. Her dates are a trifle inaccurate. Peridot,
Montmorency says he knew your great-great-grandfather
who was apothecary-in-chief to poor Louis Seize and had
his head chopped off for supplying aristos with drugs to
dull their senses in the tumbrill on their way to the block.
He says he was in at the death and saw your great-great-
grand-père with his mouth wide open laughing to kill himself when his head was held up for the *hareng res* to see."
. . . "What? What's all this?" said, or rather roared Sir
Frederick. "Only a fairy tale, Uncle. Can you give me a
tip for the Grand National?"

The Aunt spoke. "Surely, Adrian, you don't allow that
child to make bets?"

"My dear Hilda," Mr. Hope-Winter's voice still held a
smiling edge to it, "there is never any question of allowing
that child, as you so mistakenly call her, to do or not to do.
She does as the spirit—or Montmorency—moves her. But
Larkin, I believe, supplies her with all necessary data relating
to the Turf. His judgment I am told is more reliable than
Freddie's who invariably backs the wrong horse. His own."

Everybody laughed except the Aunt and Larkin, at whom
I glanced to see how he would take it. He took it like a deaf-
mute, his face a wooden mask. The two footmen, Charles
and another, were both equally expressionless. Automatons.

Heaven only knows how I ploughed through seven
courses, I, whose knowledge of a dinner was limited to
Sunday joint, roast beef and Yorkshire pudding, cooked by
me; or those hot-one-day-cold-the-next meals submitted to
her pupils by Miss Genn. I luckily remembered how she
had dinned into us to drink soup from the side and never
from the point of a spoon. But I know that I used the wrong
things for the fish, and went hot all over when a footman
unobtrusively supplied me with another knife and fork for
the next course—a dark brown mess in a highly seasoned
gravy, full of mushrooms. This was followed by something
that might have been mutton and served with red jelly; and
then came roast fowl and after that ice-pudding. I thought
this *must* be the end of it; but no. There was every kind of
fruit in or out of season, and little glass bowls of water with
rose petals floating on the top. I watched how they removed these bowls, put them by their plates and dipped

their fingers in them, so of course I did the same. Grapes were passed, but I didn't care to tackle those on account of the pips. The pineapple appeared to be the easiest, cut in slices and eaten with a knife and fork; no mistaking which to use now, all the others had been taken off the table. Then coffee was served in the tiniest of cups, and chocolates and sweets in silver dishes. I thought they would never have done eating.

By this time my head was beginning to buzz because Larkin had filled all the glasses by my plate—five or six of them—with wines of different colours. I drank some of each in turn but found them all so nasty I left most of them unfinished. Nobody seemed to mind. Their manners were atrocious. There was no watching what you ate or drank or asking you to have a little more. They simply didn't care, and I noticed they never said thank you for anything offered; they just took or refused—with a wave of the hand—and went on talking. And now all the glasses except two were whisked away and port was handed round in a decanter from which we were supposed to help ourselves. I refused, and when Larkin muttered in my ear, "Will you take——" it sounded like 'liquor'—I was pretty sharp to tell him, "Not for me, thank you. I've done very well." And perhaps it was the unaccustomed wine that made me say with a silly sort of laugh, "If I have any more I'll be tipsy."

A moment's awful silence was broken by a blare from Sir Frederick: "Any news of——" I didn't catch the name —"Is he still as bad as ever? Why don't they bring him over here to see a brain specialist?" The Aunt said: "Why should they go to that expense? There must surely be good enough doctors in Dublin." And Mr. Hope-Winter: "How old is he—sixty?"

Geraldine, who was gobbling grapes, chimed in: "Garth saw him at Christmas and told me the poor old thing thinks he's Parnell and keeps on raging against the English wolves who are howling for his blood. He must have got that from the papers. Of course he's as mad as a hatter."

I began uneasily to wonder what sort of place was this; and the way they lapped up the drink, even Geraldine, had given me a shock. I'd seen quite enough of that at Tamar Street with Milly.

Strange how the mind registers unconsciously each and every detail, no matter how minute, of incidents forgotten in time's passing; for, as I recall it, I can hear again the play of words around that table, an echo of dead voices in the Eternal Now. . . .

Sir Frederick, addressing the company in general: "Did you see that cartoon in this week's Punch—'Dropping the Pilot'? Very good, I thought it."

Geraldine, with her mouth full of a sweet, said: "Poor Bismarck. How vile of the Kaiser to throw him out after all he's done for Germany."

Brandy was handed to the gentlemen.

Sir Frederick, lifting his glass to his nose—a monster of a glass—told her: "Bismarck has done so much for Germany, my dear, that Germany may one day do for us!"

The Aunt said, scornfully: "Freddie is spoiling for a European war."

And Mr. Hope-Winter: "Which none of us, except perhaps these two"—he glanced at me and then at Geraldine—"will likely live to see."

The Aunt said: "Adrian! Surely you don't think——"

Mr. Hope-Winter, tiredly, agreed: "You are right. I never think. But so long as war is looked upon as evil it will be sought, to appeal to the popular taste. Once war is vulgarized by hypocritical heroics it reverts to bestiality. There is nothing more savage than man fighting man for what is called a righteous cause."

Sir Frederick, setting down his glass, retorted: "Dammit! ——" "Frederick!" the Aunt interposed with a frown, "if you please!"

Sir Frederick said sheepishly: "Sorry, my dear," gulped brandy and continued: "But I must say it's pretty cool for a chap who has never fired a shot in his life, not even at a bird, to talk of war as vulgar. We didn't think it vulgar, only dam—dashed uncomfortable when we were chasing Fuzzy-wuzzies out in the desert, eaten alive by sand-flies. And I suppose," he glared at Mr. Hope-Winter, "that you would call Gordon's martyrdom vulgar?"

Mr. Hope-Winter, smiling, said: "Though I fear to offend you, I do."

The Aunt murmured: "Adrian, not before the——"

Geraldine finished softly: "—child? But my very dear Aunt, you forget. I am not a child. I have never been a child. Montmorency and I are elementals and as old as God."

Sir Frederick turned a laugh into a cough as he caught the Aunt's eye. She said: "That remark is not amusing, Geraldine," and rose from the table. The two gentlemen stood. Geraldine and I remained seated.

"Miss Flight." The Aunt called me sharply to attention. "Kindly ring the bell."

The bell! I looked wildly about me. "Behind you," said the Aunt with disapproval stiff in every joint of her. I found the bell and pulled it. The two footmen who had left the room with Larkin, came in to wheel forward the long wicker chair. Geraldine told them, "No, take it away and give me my stick. I will walk."

I tried not to see how she walked. That lovely young body distorted, the right hip painfully protruding, those dragging, faltering steps. She laughed round at me with her face full of warmth and her eyes full of light. "Come along, Peridot. You and I and Montmorency go together."

I went to her; her hand took mine and held it close. Such a narrow boneless hand. Mr. Hope-Winter opened the door. The Aunt passed through it. We followed. Slowly, step by step, we mounted the stairs, Geraldine chattering, joking, and asking: "Isn't Uncle Adrian a duck? Don't fall in love with him. Every woman does. But you're not a woman, you're a pixie." And she turned from me to whisper: "Wasn't she adorable at dinner, Montmorency? Her eyebrows are perpetually surprised. We shall have lots of things to teach her, you and I. . . . Peridot, tell me if I lean on you too heavily. You're such a little, *little* thing. But I hate to go upstairs with Charles or Albert. They smell." She sniffed at my neck like a puppy. "*You* smell delicious, of honey and apples." Her hair tickled my cheek. She slid an arm round my waist. I felt the warmth of her hand through the thin stuff of my bodice and I tingled with an aching queer excitement. She was so strange, and yet no more to me a stranger. . . .'

*　　　*　　　*

That first evening's ordeal, although it might well have dismayed, did not discourage Miss Flight. On the contrary it served to strengthen her resolve to overcome the disadvantages of earlier environment and profit by example of her present elevation.

We have it she was much relieved to find that Lady Stilton was not a member of the Brook Street household; but she lived inconveniently near enough to take an active interest in the management thereof, and the daily life of Geraldine.

That her brother's choice of a companion for her niece did not meet with her ladyship's approval was only too apparent to Miss Flight, who, shortly after her arrival, overheard a conversation—how or where is not recorded; yet there is every indication to presume that she, with an ear to a keyhole, decided it were best to be forewarned and thus forearmed.

It would therefore appear that Lady Stilton to her brother denounced Miss Flight as—'utterly impossible. How could a girl of Geraldine's intelligence and upbringing derive any benefit from one so inferior in birth and education, *and* so obviously Lower Middle Class?' She had hoped for and expected the daughter of a parson, or a country doctor—but this!

'This' meanwhile, having taken due precaution to arm herself against the Aunt's objections, strove to counteract them by strategic conquest of the niece.

Miss Curran, despite her intimacy with the finer arts and literature, and all such knowledgeable matters from which Miss Flight, by force of circumstance, had hitherto been barred, was found to be no less susceptible to admiration than any other of her age and sex; and perhaps the little more, consequent upon her isolated singularity.

On her young companion Geraldine bestowed the same affectionate indulgence she had formerly reserved for her personal pets, a white cat and a black and tan terrier, both recently deceased. But neither of these, while duly responsive to favour, could have sat at her feet, as did Miss Flight, in homage of her beauty, of her culture and her wit. To act Mentor to so willing a Telemachus was a unique and delightful experience. True, Miss Curran may have found equal delectation in criticism calculated carefully to sting, but borne by its recipient in humble gratitude.

With Mr. Hope-Winter the tactics of Miss Flight were of

necessity limited to those of a dependant, respectful, discreet, and conscientious in fulfilment of her duties. At her own suggestion she issued bi-weekly reports to her employer on Miss Curran's state of health. There were times when she suffered bouts of pain, assuaged by soothing draughts prescribed by the family doctor in consultation with that most eminent of orthopaedic surgeons, Sir Crispin Bellew, who visited Miss Curran twice a month. And in a notebook kept solely for that purpose Miss Flight would inscribe their medical instructions, implicitly obeyed. To this she would refer in those confidential sessions held in Mr. Hope-Winter's private sanctum.

The walls of that austere apartment exhibited the cream of his collection of early Tuscan art: triptyches, diptyches, altar pieces, fragments of frescoes; and, placed upon pedestals carefully posed against dark velvet curtains, terracotta figurines and statuettes in marble of the school of Donatello; but most prized of all was an earthenware rondel of various fruits, framed in garlands of flowers and wrought in bright colours, attributed to or after Della Robbia. . . . 'Made in Birmingham, *circa* four hundred years after,' was the Philistine remark of that hopeless ignoramus, Captain Curran of the Fifth Hussars.

On the death of his father, Adrian Hope-Winter having been left with ample means enough to indulge his extravagant tastes, was urged by his satellites to promote an art gallery in Bond Street, wherefrom he had lost a considerable portion of his capital. Money, however, so he was wont to say, held no interest for him more than as an aid of escape from mediocrity.

Adrian Hope-Winter has been described by that ·same Captain Curran—whose aesthetic sensibilities admittedly were wanting—as an 'art scavenger'. Yet if his connoisseurship was not entirely infallible, the pictures and *objets de vertu* with which he joyed to surround himself were, as his feminine admirers insisted, a collector's dream; a dream destined, alas, to go unshared by fluttering maidens whose mammas, as surely as season followed season, joined in the chase of this most eligible *parti*. But, as on his own accounting, 'marriage was too serious to be taken seriously', he was eligible still, at thirty-eight.

By dint of careful probing Perry learned that Geraldine's father, the late Major Dennis Curran of the 29th Lancers, killed at Khartoum, had appointed his brother-in-law her guardian, requesting that his daughter made her home with him—doubtless to save her from the Aunt. Geraldine's mother, who died in child-birth, had come in for a share of the Hope-Winter fortune, most of which, however, was dissipated by her husband on the Turf. The little that remained had been left in trust for Geraldine until such time as she should marry, or, should she die a spinster, it would revert to her father's next of kin.

Of these, her two uncles in Ireland, one, and the head of the family, was that unhappy gentleman whom Perry had heard discussed at dinner the first night of her arrival. His brother, who managed the estate for him, was a widower with two sons; the elder, a convert to Roman Catholicism, had entered a monastery, 'And so,' said Geraldine obscurely, 'is out of the running for Donaghmore which will eventually go to my cousin, Garth Curran. And if he doesn't marry and have children or should die before I do, it will come to me— and I am the last of our line. Not that any of us would want such a mouldering tomb of a place, full of ghosts. I stayed in it once. It stinks of death and is falling to pieces with no money to restore it. And now that the Land Leaguers have been on the rampage destroying the farms and the crops, it's worse than ever. My cousin Garth, who was born there, tells me the most frightful tales of the tenants' revolts against my uncle Brian——' retailed to a wide-eyed Perry. 'Only think! Once they brought a steam-engine—this was in the 'eighties— and deliberately ran down my uncle who was walking in the grounds, and he never walked again. His legs were squashed flat. He was always a trifle—odd, shall we say—and after that he went completely off his head. And just imagine that sanctimonious old horror, Gladstone, wanting to give those savages Home Rule. He'll probably get it for them, too. . . .'

Which was not yet to be, for, with victory in sight, a few months after Perry came to Brook Street, fell the thunderbolt.

Parnell, the Crusader, who had devoted his life to the cause of Irish oppression, he who had created a party in his name, and by systematic bludgeoning in and out of Parliament, had remade ministries, to break them, stood, in the blaze of his glory, eclipsed, disgraced . . . Divorced!

The momentous decree, pronounced in November 1890, proved the great Irish leader guilty of an adulterous associa-

tion with the wife of his friend, O'Shea. Like fire the news
flared through London, or at least the London that was
bounded on the north by the mansions of Lancaster Gate, on
the south by the Palace of the good shocked Queen.

Perry read the papers and Perry wondered why poor Mr.
Parnell should be held up to ridicule, pilloried, mocked, and
condemned as a monster of evil for loving another man's wife.
She, who knew nothing of love, believed it to be 'a kind of
madness that came upon you unawares, but if you were so
unlucky as to love where you must not, then surely God, not
man, should be your Judge. . . .'

The weeks, the months, flashed by in a series of impressions,
incongruous, bewildering, each day an eagerly awaited fresh
adventure; each night, in her room's solitude, a tireless self-
searching inquisition. She must learn to be as they are; to
think, to speak as they do, to understand their talk of things
entirely unknown to her; to guard against betrayal of her ignorance, to watch, and, in the fastness of her privacy, to search
through books purloined from shelves, and read, with ever
growing interest and wonder, of those great Italian masters so
fluently discussed by Geraldine. From Pater's *Renaissance* she
learned of Leonardo, Botticelli, and was stricken to remember
the first time that she had heard the name, so woefully mistaken for a 'bottled'—never mind! She would profit by trial
and error; but above all must she learn with equanimity to
suffer—Geraldine.

'. . . Her tempers, swift and sudden, unaccountable and
crazy; her spasmodic effervescence, and the childish caprice
of her that chattered nonsense by the hour—but not so often
now—to her familiar, "Montmorency". Her arrogance, her
cruelty and her courage, the heart-wrenching waste of all
that stranded beauty; and for every devil's mood of her that
made you want to wring her neck I loved her, yes, I loved
her, as I think that, in her fashion, she loved me.'

Daily in the Park they drove together, accompanied, but
mercifully not always, by the Aunt. She, as Perry was soon to
discover, availed herself of her brother's carriage and pair to
save the expense of keeping more than a modest one-horse
brougham in which to go shopping. For important occasions,

Court functions and dinners, she would commandeer the elegant Hope-Winter equipage. An admirable wife, Lady Stilton held to the belief that Sir Frederick's not insignificant income should be saved for a nebulous future. Having failed to present him with an heir, the future for which Lady Stilton far-seeingly provided must have been her own prospective widowhood, and this notwithstanding that she was her husband's senior by some seven or eight years. According to Geraldine he had been 'madly in love' with her mother and had married 'Aunt Hilda' on the rebound. 'And how any man,' Geraldine gracelessly added, 'could bring himself to sleep with her is past my understanding.'

Perry had not been an inmate of the Brook Street household for more than a week before Sir Frederick discovered she played the piano sufficiently well to accompany his songs. Having, until then, paid a professional accompanist, a German youth, at the fee of a shilling an hour, Sir Frederick, at his wife's suggestion, called upon the service of Miss Flight who—'of course,' said Lady Stilton, 'could not expect to be paid for her strumming. She is grossly overpaid already.'

And so it came about that Sir Frederick would go twice, or sometimes thrice a week, to his brother-in-law's house with a portfolio of songs for the amiable Miss Flight to 'strum'. Sir Frederick, whose singing may possibly have given greater pleasure to himself than to his audience, made a point of taking with him his repertoire whenever he dined out, and required little urging to oblige.

In his rollicking youth Sir Frederick's vocal achievements had been much in demand in the officers' Mess. There he would entertain the mellowed company with such popular favourites as 'Chichaleary Bloke', 'Champagne Charlie' and 'Rackety Jack', of which the refrain, bawled privately to Perry, who picked up the tune for his accompaniment, ran:

'Hey! Hi! Here! Stop! Waiter, waiter, fizz, pop!
I'm Rackety Jack, no money I lack,
And I'm the boy for a spree!'

It was unfortunate that Lady Stilton should have chosen that very moment to call upon her niece who had taken to her bed with one of her painful bouts. The Aunt, on her way to Geraldine's room, had paused at the drawing-room door to see her husband bending, while he bellowed, to turn a page of music, and Miss Flight, in fits of laughter, gleefully pounding out the chorus, when——

"Frederick!" His wife from the doorway gave voice like the cry of a wounded macaw. "What on earth do you think you are doing?"

What Sir Frederick thought he was doing might have appealed to the Aunt even less than did Rackety Jack.

We have it that on very short acquaintance with Miss Flight, Sir Frederick found her to be, and, in fact, assured her that she was 'a little puss'.

A stray sunbeam had alighted on Miss Flight's down-bent head, warming to honey-gold the ash blonde hair, coiled on a neck so surprisingly white as to have caused Sir Frederick some acute discomfort. 'Hey! Hi! Here! Stop——!' and Sir Frederick had barely stopped himself in time from diving his moustache to that tantalizing nape, before the entrance of his excellent good wife.

"Doing?" Sir Frederick's monocle dropped from his eye and dangled by its cord against the buttons of his frock-coat. "Just trying over a song, my dear."

Miss Flight apologetically rose from the piano-stool. The Aunt sat, and, with acerbity, bade her: "Please to leave the room, Miss Flight."

Miss Flight left the room, and outside the door she lingered awhile, highly diverted to hear:

"So this is the sort of thing you practise with that girl. Low music-hall ditties. You told me you were bringing 'Songs of Araby' for her to try."

"We have already tried it, my dear." And stentoriously Sir Frederick demonstrated that he would: 'Sing thee So-hongs of Araby and ta-hales of fairr Kashmirr, and—tum-dee—dee—dee—diddledee——' "

"You don't know a single word of it," rapped out the Aunt, "so why stand there and tell me lies?"

"If you'd rather I sat here and told you lies——" Sir Frederick had evidently sunk into a chair. This jocular attempt to pacify was followed by a silence and a hissing of silks, as if Lady Stilton nursed beneath her petticoats a colony of snakes. At last, in tones of restrained exasperation, she spoke.

"It is always the same. So soon as you are left alone with a girl of inferior class, you lose all sense of proportion. I can't employ a housemaid under sixty."

"Come, Hilda, come!" lamely protested Sir Frederick. "Wha—what *are* you talking about?"

"I am talking about you and that common little creature Adrian was fool enough to bring here. We shall have to get rid of her. She is not a fit associate for Geraldine, in whom I already see a marked change for the worse. She seems quite to have lost her head about Miss Flight, who, in my opinion, is a most pernicious influence. I don't like it at all."

"Whether you like it or whether you don't, I can tell you," Sir Frederick daringly ventured, "that since Peri—Miss Flight, took her in hand, Geraldine is fifty per cent more normal—not so highly strung and temperamental and—you know."

"I do not know. You seem *all* to have lost your heads about this little shop girl—or whatever she is. She came with no references, only a recommendation from Todd, who knew nothing about her more than that her father was a chemist in some sort of slum and that she served across the counter." Another pause, then, shudderingly: "I think it's dreadful." And Lady Stilton's silks rustled in serpentine agreement to the decision, "I shall have to speak to Adrian and persuade him that Miss Flight must go."

But Lady Stilton's persuasions may not have been sufficiently persuasive, for Miss Flight did not go. She stayed.

FOUR

Brook Street.
Nov. 3rd, 1890

'Went with G. this a.m. to Mr. Whistler's studio for the
last sitting. It's a lovely portrait. He has painted her lying
on a couch. He talked a lot about someone called Oscar.
Very sarcastic. Real American drawl. Said he would like to
paint me or rather what he called my "dim unforgettable
features". He's a funny old thing. Don't care for him much.
Too affected. The Aunt, Sir F. and Capt. C. to luncheon.
Capt. C. leaves for India next week to join General Lockhart
with reinforcements at Manipur. Sir F. full of all the old
tales of how he fought the Fuzzy-wuzzies in the Sudan.
Said Capt. C. was in for trouble on the frontier. Capt. C.
said he hoped so he wouldn't want to arrive when everything was over bar the shouting. After luncheon Sir F.
dragged me off to the piano with a Pair of Sparkling Eyes.
The Aunt at her cattiest. You'd think she'd be pleased
knowing how stingy she is that Sir F. has someone to play
his accompaniments that he doesn't have to pay. You can't
count a box of chocolates once in a while, but must say am
getting a bit sick of dreaming that I dwelt with Sir F. in
Marble Halls or galloping along with him on his Wedding
Morning.

Capt. C. stayed after Sir F. and Lady S. had gone. We
shan't see him again I don't suppose before he sails. G. says
he is bound to be caught by one of those garrison hacks out
there and did I think cousins should marry. Told her don't
ask me ask the Queen she married her cousin and did she
want to marry Capt. C. Can't think why she should fly out
at me for that but considering the spiteful things she says
of him behind his back I must say I was startled.

N.B. Captain C. still has my shoe. Don't like to keep on
reminding him.'

A MILD autumn had followed that glorious summer, when

85

every day and all day long the grassy spaces of Hyde Park lay
burning, parched, beneath a brazen sky; and, mingled with
London's own particular smell of melting tar and dung and
leather, always the scent of lime-blossom had drifted through
the scarcely stirring curtains and venetian blinds of Mayfair's
open windows. Boxed on the sills under gaily striped awnings,
calceolarias drooped and geraniums sent forth a faintly bitter
dying breath.

To Perry, for whom the warmth and glory of previous sum-
mers had been an endless torment of customers to serve, of
housework and cooking at the broiling inferno of a kitchen
range; of nights unbearable in a hot stuffy attic filling and
labelling jars, those Mayfair days of June were, by contrast,
paradisaical. For Geraldine, however, the height of the season
differed little from the customary routine of her gilded mono-
tonous life. Not for her the doubtful delights of the débu-
tante, the round of dinners, parties, balls, following a presentation to the Queen; not for her the fear of failure attached to
these frivolities, transmitted to their daughters by over-anxious
mammas, since every drawing-room in those stately mansions
north and south of the Park was as much a hunting-ground
as any jungle.

Equipped for the chase in froths of white tulle, satins or
rustling silks, excitement aglow in judiciously pearl-powdered
cheeks, eager young tyros marked and stalked their quarry,
urged on to the kill by perspiring matrons, each a past mistress
of the hunt. But time was short; a first, a second season, perhaps a third, and then the dread of empty years to come, un-
wooed, unwanted. Only a very few of these had stepped aside
to blaze for herself a new trail and respond to the clarion call
of the feminine careerist. For the rest, would their life's aim
and purpose be fulfilled at the altar of St. Margaret's, St.
George's, or were they doomed to fade, discarded wallflowers,
forgotten, on the shelf?

But neither Geraldine nor her young companion would be
called upon to suffer the hopes and fears and agonies of such
humiliations, nor yet the triumph of a capture. Spectators,
merely, of that tireless pursuit, they stood united in their
mutual observance: the one with a cynicism far beyond her
years, aped from her uncle. . . . 'See!' she would say, con-
temptuously reading from *The Times* the list of those who the

day before had struggled, half swooning, unrefreshed, through the crowded state apartments of the Palace to curtsy before that formidable little Old Lady, whose dumpy gloved hand, out-stretched for their kiss, would send them forth upon their quest acknowledged aspirants. 'See, the latest scroll of honour, Miss Thingmebob and Lady That—white martyrs prepared for the sacrifice. Thank God I am out of it. A pretty figure I would cut hobbling on two sticks to fall over my train before the Queen! And for what? To snatch a husband? I could name half a dozen who would marry me tomorrow and with*out* a presentation. . . .' While Perry, accustomed now to these pitiful boastings, laughed with her and hid the ache in her heart for all that 'stranded beauty'.

So much for Geraldine; as for the other, a concentrated watchfulness spurred determination to learn how this new world, into which she had been jettisoned, lived and had its being. But what *was* its being? Pleasure, wealth? To dress exquisitely, to stroll on the lawns of the Park accompanied by gentlemen, moulded to one pattern, moustached, clean-cut, square-shouldered, 'with voices coming out of the back of their throats'? What did they do with their lives? Did they work? Did they go to the City and make money or keep shops? No. Money, in this world of Hope-Winters, of Currans and Stiltons, and all of their kind was not made, it was inherited. Nor did the Ruling Class, to which such as these belonged, go to the City, nor did they, a race of shopkeepers, keep shops. Only three professions were open to a gentleman, the Army, the Navy and the Church, these the choice of younger sons; an elder son or immediate heir to expectations awaited the demise of him from whomsoever his prospects would descend. Meanwhile they enjoyed to the full the carefree leisure of an age when Income Tax was sixpence in the pound, and death duties a periodic bogy presented by scarifying Radicals at a minimum of one to a maximum of eight per cent; an age when it cost very little to live and nothing at all to die.

Perry, too, found it enjoyment enough to sit with Geraldine in the carriage, under the shade of drowsy trees, and watch the motley promenade of Fashion in the Park; the lace-frilled parasols guarding sensitive skins from sunburn and freckles; the pastel-tinted trailing gowns lifted daintily in one hand to avoid the dust; to hear the tinkle of laughter tuned to the

answering drawl of high-hatted escorts in lavender gloves;
the interchange of greetings, small-talk, bows, the distant
strains of a military band, and all the trivial importance of
those green and golden afternoon parades. Then, suddenly,
amid the sparkle of silver-pointed harness, of shining paint
and perfectly matched pairs of greys or bays, arch-necked,
champing, foam-bespattered in the torture of the bearing-rein,
a carriage, more splendid than any, would pass to a raising of
hats, a flutter of curtsies, a straining of eyes to see the graciously
smiling Princess of Wales in pale coloured chiffons and a
toque.

In the first week of July Sir Frederick and Lady Stilton had
gone, as was their custom, to their place in Sussex where they
entertained a small party for Goodwood. And, when the
season closed and London emptied, it was arranged that
Geraldine should spend a few weeks in Somerset with an
elderly cousin of her mother, a Miss Burbage; a bitter disappointment, this, for Geraldine, who had been promised a
month at Baden with her uncle.

He, who had left town in April for Florence and returned
to London the following June, was now deeply pre-occupied
with his latest venture, the promotion of a publishing firm to
be devoted to the production of books by recognized authori-
ties on art. Having discovered a *magnum opus* on the Primitive
Tuscans, he at once, and to the consternation of his sister,
realized a substantial portion of his capital, secured a long
lease of premises in Sackville Street and proceeded sump-
tuously to furnish them.

With these offices and the *magnum opus*, for which the
author had received a five-figure sum in advance of royalties
at fifteen per cent of the published price—a more than generous
percentage in those days—was founded the Odyssey Press.

A board of directors appointed by the chairman, Hope-
Winter, and drawn from a nucleus of friends, lent to the
enterprise their names if nothing else. The engaging of staff,
consultations with solicitors, and further hurried journeys
back and forth to Rome and Florence to secure photographic
reproductions of the Masters with which to illustrate the text
of the Great Work, claimed the chairman's time to the exclusion of social activities and Geraldine's holiday abroad.
To Perry was assigned the unwelcome task of breaking the

news of her uncle's change of plan. We have it that Mr. Hope-Winter summoned Miss Flight to his study and said:

"I have arranged with a cousin of mine, a Miss Burbage, that you accompany Geraldine to her charming sixteenth-century house in the Doone country. You have, of course, read *Lorna Doone*?"

"Yes, indeed," was Perry's mendacious reply, and her gaze that had been perseveringly fixed on the carpet went straight to the chandelier. "How I adore Laur—that book!"

He smiled his twisted closed smile and asked: "How long have you been with us now?"

"About"—she paused to calculate—"four months."

"Four months." His eyes, amazingly blue in the tan of his face, scrutinized the childish figure standing so modestly before him with downcast lids and hands folded and, always, he was reminded, she wore grey; a shadowy moth-like little creature, yet—"In so short a time," he said, "you have passed through a stage of transition as remarkable and curious to watch as that of the Lepidopteron, dreaming away the forma-tive pupa months of its life, from which it awakens to its magical winged metamorphosis. And when that moment comes to you, as sooner or later it must, will you, too, spread your wings and fly from us? I wonder."

Although accustomed now to the exaggerated mode of speech in which her employer indulged, this meditative utter-ance, barely understood, was more personal than any he had hitherto addressed to her. And with a twinge of apprehension she seized upon the imagined hint conveyed, that, at some future date, perhaps when she and Geraldine came back from—wherever it was—her service would no longer be required.

"I think"—deliberately she hedged, avoiding his pene-trating glance, that was, she admits, as if he could see right through her body to her bones—"I would never wish to leave Geraldine unless"—she paused and pinkened—"you are not satisfied with what I—am."

"But," he asked her quizzically, "what *are* you?" And with a swift turn of his hips he walked over to a picture on the wall. Standing before it, one hand caressing his short pointed beard, he called to her: "Peridot, come."

She came and stood beside him. Light from the window fell on the wondering shell-like face, portrayed against the background of a sunless dawn. "The wind," he mused, "has whipped her hair. Her eyes are coloured like the sea from which she rises. In her we may understand something of the Greek ideal, only sensed in Botticelli, for we know more than he had ever known of the Hellenic spirit. This is a copy of the head—a very good copy, too, and almost, I should say—contemporaneous—of Sandro's 'Venus'. I bought her in Pisa. It is interesting to note how precisely he repeats himself in this same face and figure. We see her dancing on a lawn dotted with daisies, or adoring her Child surrounded by young angels, but there is always that same remote, wistful look of surprise—which is yours."

"Oh," breathed Miss Flight, with a flutter of her eyelids. "Am I really like that? She's ever so pretty."

"Ever so!" He wheeled round on her, darkling. "Ever so—and—pretty! No, a thousand times, no! You are nothing like that. A cockney sparrow perking and pecking at the doves of Aphrodite. Go," he pointed to the door. "Away with you!"

"Why, what have I said?" Her cheeks flared to a sense of injustice; her eyes, an angry sea-green, met his squarely. "You knew what I was when I came here and"—that inflammable storm of resentment against the Aunt, and criticism overheard, ignited—"if I'm a cockney, is it my fault? I'm not used to high society"—she was lost now to decorum, her manners and her place, to rush on madly, shrilling at him—"and what I've seen of it doesn't make me very anxious to see more. If I were to tell you the truth about myself, for I'm not what you think but as good or better than any of you that pull me so to pieces——"

She stopped, dismayed, shame-covered. Yes, indeed! What *had* she said? She was done for, sacked, no question. To blaze out at him like that, and he her employer who paid her fifty pounds a year to be—genteel. She crushed a tooth upon her underlip, drooped her head and heard, but could not see his smile: "Do tell me the truth about yourself."

Control regained, she released her bitten lip to say composedly: "I must apologize. And"—she made up her mind in an instant, for how after this could she stay?—"please to take my notice, which, you may remember, can be given as one month on either side."

His eyebrows shot up.

"Dear, dear, this is very distressing."

"I am sorry, Mr. Hope-Winter, but it will have to be. I see I am not what you want. I make mistakes. Only yesterday, at luncheon, when I dropped my serviette——"

"Pray," he shuddered, interrupting, "*not* a serviette."

"You see?" She spread her hands; he noted with interest that slightly foreign gesture. There might be something in the tale Todd had told him of her birth; pure conjecture, certainly, yet was not heredity stronger than environment? Such exquisite frail-boned structure could surely not be accidental. . . . She was speaking, her tone clear, her enunciation careful, possibly too careful. "I find it not so easy to remember what words to say and not to say. I've had an education of a sort—but not your sort. You knew that when you engaged me. I've done my best, only it's so different to—from"—she hastily corrected—"your life and Geraldine's. I think it's best for all concerned for me to go."

He nodded, pursing his small mouth.

"You do, do you?"

And she was suddenly afraid. Having spoken her mind, which she knew was not her mind, it seemed that he would take her at her word. "Of course," she temporized, "I'll not leave you in the lurch. I can wait, if you wish it, till you're suited."

"Aha!" His dark, sardonic face relaxed. "The chrysalis emerges."

He strolled over to a lacquer cabinet, took from a drawer a box of cigars, selected one and held it to his nose. She watched him furtively.

"But if you want me to take Geraldine to—this—Laura Doone in August as you said, for I wouldn't like to upset your arrangements, and it's not as if you'll find someone else to replace me so soon—not at this time of the year—I'd be willing to oblige."

"Geraldine," he said, "will miss you. I, too, will miss you." He lighted his cigar. "You have been an interesting experiment."

Perry lowered her eyes.

"*N'importe que tu sois sage, sois belle. . . .*" The flame of the match flickered and died out. He tossed it into an ash-tray. "Yet in all fairness to Geraldine I cannot accept your notice.

If, when you return from your holiday, you are still determined to leave us—then so be it. I shall not allude to this again unless you do."

"Very well, Mr. Hope-Winter." Assumed indifference disguised her relief. She went to the door followed by him and a luxurious whiff of Havana.

"I had almost forgotten"—with his hand on the door-knob he stayed her exit—"in the agitation you have caused me"— she gave him a suspicious glance; his face was solemn as a crow's—"that I have two guests for dinner tonight. You and Geraldine will dine with me."

Not unless invited did she and Geraldine dine with Mr. Hope-Winter. Good! She could wear the new evening dress she had bought out of last month's salary. He opened the door. "And I leave it to you to tell Geraldine that I will not be taking her to Baden. There might," he cocked an eyebrow, "be a rumpus."

There was.

"You! You beast!" Raising herself on her pillows Geraldine pointed an accusing finger. "*You* have done this to me—you and he in league together to prevent me from having any sort of life beyond this prison!" Viciously she thumped the satin cushions, then seized one, and at Perry's head she flung it; but before its descent upon a table that held a Dresden lamp entwined with Cupids, it was dodged and deftly caught. "Snake!" screamed Geraldine, "sneaking your way into our house, upsetting me and everyone—Bowler hates the sight of you, and so do I. Do you think I can't see how you toady to my uncle and pander to his selfishness— creeping little toad! Why couldn't you have told him what Sir Crispin said, that it would do me all the good in the world to go abroad? You knew how I was longing for Baden—and even if I had to be wheeled around in a bath-chair it would have been heaven compared with staying at Cousin Lavinia's. You don't know what she's like. I do. She's an old witch. She brews nauseating medicines from herbs which she forces me to drink to make me sick—and she has a mania for tidiness. You have to change your shoes every time you go into or out of the house. Everyone loathes her and nobody comes near her except the vicar and the curate—and *that's* what I'm to be inflicted with instead of Baden. And I'd made Uncle

Adrian promise to take you with us, which I was keeping as a surprise and would have bought you some new clothes out of my own dress allowance—the sort of clothes you ought to wear and not those silly schoolgirl things—and now I'm to be dumped on Cousin Lavinia. Curse him!" Geraldine's voice rose to a shriek. "And you—you—*you*! I hate you—you beast, I do! You all want to make me wretched. You rejoice in my misery, pinned to this sofa, a cripple. Let me die!"

The blood rushed to her face; on her forehead a vein stood out like a whipcord. Frenziedly she hammered with her heels upon the couch, then uttered a yelp of pain.

"My hip! I've twisted it——"

Perry, who throughout this brainstorm had sat silent, less from choice than from necessity, took advantage of the momentary cessation of abuse, coldly to say: "Of course if you *will* bang about like that——" and rising she went over to the couch. "Don't play the fool, Geraldine. Have you really hurt yourself?"

"Get away!" was the shrieking reply. "Don't come near me. I loathe you—I wish you were dead!" And in a ferment of hysteria she raised her fist to her mouth, digging her teeth in the back of her hand. It was hideous to hear those animalistic sounds as she snarled at her flesh, biting to draw blood; to see that lovely face a writhing mask, transfigured, frightening. But in this—not her first experience of those 'hellish tempers' —Perry kept her head while Geraldine lost hers, and from screaming fell to crying, then to laughing, until Perry fetched her a box on the ear and put an end to it.

In outraged astonishment Geraldine stared, and—"What the devil," she gasped, "do you mean by—you hit me!"

"And I'll hit you again," threatened Perry, cool as the other was hot, "if you don't pull yourself together. Going on like a lunatic. Look what you've done to your hand."

Geraldine looked, and retorted, "I suppose I can bite my own hand if I like. Be thankful I didn't bite yours. And anyway it wasn't I who did it—Montmorency did it. He gets hold of me——" Tears welled and dribbled down her cheeks. "He makes me," she whispered, "do what I don't want to do."

"Listen, Geraldine," Perry sat down on a stool beside her, "if I have any more of this sort of thing I shall leave you. In fact I gave in my notice to Mr. Hope-Winter this morning'.

"Oh, no! *No!*" Imploringly Geraldine held out her hand bearing the imprint of two scarlet crescents. "I know I'm vile. I ought to be put away. There's madness in our family. Perhaps I'm mad. Am I mad?"

"No, you're not mad. You're spoilt—spoilt and pampered. You think you have only to kick and scream to get your own way, but you won't get your own way with me."

"You don't—you won't," blubbered Geraldine, "leave me? Say you won't, Peridot. You're only teasing, aren't you? You haven't really given in your notice, have you?"

"I have, but your uncle wants me to stay. Whether I do or not depends on your behaviour. Another repetition of a scene like this, and off I go. I mean it."

And on that immense admission Perry closed her lips.

Geraldine opened hers to moan: "Miserable wretch that I am—God help me!"

"God won't help you unless you help yourself and mend your ways."

"I wish He'd mend my hip," muttered Geraldine. "How would you like to go hobbling through life on a stick? Do you think I can't see how, when I walk in the Park or go to the play hanging on to your arm, people pretend not to stare? And then the pain of it—always a nagging sort of ache. I don't complain. You never hear me complain, do you?"

Perry shook her head.

"It's so cruel when I'm so beautiful," went on Geraldine, quick to perceive the unspoken pity in Perry's veiled eyes. "I am beautiful, aren't I—even though I am a cripple, a monster, a misery to myself and everybody else. I'd be much better dead, wouldn't I? *Wouldn't* I?"

Against that appeal Perry hardened her heart, rose abruptly and went to the door.

"Where are you going?"

"To fetch some carbolic and bathe your hand. It's bleeding. You had better wear gloves at dinner tonight."

"Why, what's happening tonight?"

"Mr. Hope-Winter has two guests, and you and I are asked to dine with him."

"Who are they?"

"I haven't the least idea."

Geraldine scowling, nodded her head. "I know. It will be

that fat slug, Lord Reginald—if you can imagine a slug in a wig—and Marcus Sankey. You've not met either of them yet, but I believe Uncle Adrian has roped them in for his board of directors. An odious couple. By your friends shall ye be judged. Did I make that up, or is it in the Bible? Tell Bowler I will wear my amber silk."

Thankful for this return to norm, Perry left her; and outside the door released a long-drawn breath. What a day of it! First her own exhibition with the uncle, and now *this* from the niece. No wonder the governesses left. But I, she determined, am not going to leave. I know how to manage her. They didn't. As for the uncle, him she dismissed as a 'posturing ass', yet she did not at all doubt that she could manage him as well. And with a satisfied small smile on her lips, she walked along the corridor to encounter Bowler on the way, who with a virulence scarcely conceivable, asked:

"What have you been doing of to upset Miss Geraldine? I heard her screeching."

In sedate silence Perry passed on to her room, but at the door she turned to say over her shoulder: "We are dining with Mr. Hope-Winter tonight. Kindly put out Miss Geraldine's amber silk."

"Ho!" ejaculated Bowler, arms akimbo. "So we're dining with the gentry, are we? And who's giving orders to me may I ask?"

Perry's chin lifted.

"I am."

For the second time that day, and from another employee, Mr. Hope-Winter received a month's notice.

"Sir, I wish to tell you," thus Bowler, without pause, disburdened, "that seeing as how Miss Flight has took upon herself to order me about I'm not one to stand for it. I know my place and duties and won't see them taken from me by a chit of a girl—beggin' your pardon, sir—what gives herself airs to lord it over one what has served Miss Geraldine loyal and faithful which as you know, sir, is more than what them governesses ever did and left within the month—and me putting up with her tempers and excusing them these two years knowing the poor young lady has her troubles and can't help it her not being quite—if you'll excuse me, sir—the way she talks to herself. And you'll never keep a lady's maid in this house, sir, while Miss Flight is here believe me."

And on Mr. Hope-Winter's assurance that indeed he did believe her, he suggested it were better she take a month's wages and leave the house at once, as, since Miss Flight was there, she would be likely to remain.

Miss Flight deserved her triumph. She had suffered much from Bowler, whose departure below stairs went equally unmourned.

"For to be quite truthful, Miss," confided Annie, while she hooked Miss Flight into the new evening dress of oyster coloured satin bought at Whiteley's July sale, "none of us liked her in the servants' hall and Mrs. Smith couldn't abide her, always complaining of the food, and as for the way she talked of you, Miss——"

Perry smiled.

"I can well imagine, but you needn't tell me. We'll forget her."

"Yes, Miss, willing and good riddance I should say. Will there," ventured Annie, "be another of them lady's maids coming, do you think?"

Not if I know it, Perry silently commented, and: "Rest easy in your mind," she said, "there won't be another. You and I will, in future, take care of Miss Geraldine's clothes."

"Oh, Miss, yes! But——" Annie's face that had brightened clouded to remind Miss Flight that she was only underhouse-maid. "The head-housemaid sees to Miss Geraldine on Bowler's evening out."

"Can you sew?"

"Yes, Miss. In my last place—nothing like as grand as this, only four in staff and me—I was tweenie and sewing-maid to the young ladies."

"Then," Perry told her as she pinned to the maidenly bosom of her gown a cluster of white roses taken from a vase in the drawing-room, "you shall be a sewing-maid again. Miss Geraldine can do without Bowler."

And down the stairs to the drawing-room she tripped.

Geraldine was down already, and, seated by her couch, a tall young gentleman, who, at Perry's entrance, rose briskly to his feet.

"Peridot!" Geraldine called to her. "Isn't this jolly!

Uncle Adrian met him by chance this afternoon coming out
of his tailor's as he was going in, and invited him to dinner.
He's off to Ireland tomorrow—and next month he goes to
Minehead, stag-hunting, so we shall see him at Cousin
Lavinia's. Her house is near Porlock—within easy riding distance for you, Garth, isn't it? Oh, I quite forget to introduce
you. Peridot, this is Cousin Garth—Captain Curran, of
whom you've often heard me speak."

She was deliciously animated. All trace of temper had
vanished, but she wore, it was noted, a pair of lace mittens;
and to herself Perry smiled, lifting her eyes to meet an answering smile on the face of 'Cousin Garth'.

"And in this past ten minutes I have heard Geraldine speak
of you," he said, "to the exclusion of all else. Do your ears
burn? Are they red?" He peered round as if to see.

"Isn't he," laughed Geraldine, "a caution, as they say?"

A careful glance aside assured Perry that he was. His close-
cropped hair had the same dark chestnut tinge as Geraldine's,
and under his moustache, frankly ginger, his broad smile disclosed remarkably white teeth, the only handsome feature in
his face. A plain young man, square-jawed, profusely freckled,
with a mouth too wide, a nose too short, an upper lip too
long, and small twinkling eyes the colour of old brandy. He
had the look about him of one more at ease in breeches on a
horse than in a drawing-room in tails and white tie.

"Your ears," he said, "are not red at all, although they
ought to be after Geraldine's hosanna to your charms, Miss—
is it Peridot? Surely an uncommon name, and you 'by any
other name'—— But he was wrong. If your name now, were
Gertie——"

"If it were," chimed in Geraldine, "I doubt she'd smell as
sweet. Each of us has our own personal smell, don't you
think? *She* smells of honey and apples, those little green
apples—more sour than sweet—that tempt you to taste and
spit out the first bite."

"For all that," said Captain Curran, "I'd be tempted to
taste—'where the apple reddens.' " And he laughed below his
breath.

"How full we are of quotations tonight!" mocked Geraldine.
"I had no idea you knew your Browning, Garth."

"Did you not? Well, now you do. Where will you sit,

4

Miss Peridot—here?" He drew forward the chair he had vacated and took another near it.

Perry was thankful to sit; if her ears did not burn her cheeks did. These cousins! What a way to talk—as if she were not there, discussing smells! Not very nice. None the less, the thought came to her swiftly, that for the first time since she had entered this house, she had met, as she put it, an 'ordinary person'. Even his voice, with its slight hint of a brogue, was different from, 'and so very much more natural than those lahdeedah accents which I tried so hard to copy and with such poor success.' But just as she arrived at that conclusion and was about to answer Captain Curran's question—would she be out with the hounds at Minehead?—an answer luckily spared to her who had never sat a horse in her life, the door opened to Larkin's announcement:

"Lord Reginald Tarrant."

"Ah! The Blessed Damozel!" He advanced to Geraldine's couch, bent over her hand, raised it to his lips, and: "How exquisite you are," he sighed, "in apricot. And how Rossetti, had he lived to see you, would have loved you!"

Geraldine, slightly wincing—it was her self-injured hand he clasped and kissed—withdrew it and presented: "Miss Flight, Lord Reginald Tarrant."

Bows were exchanged with a cursory glance at and away from Miss Flight, who, a trifle flustered at meeting a Lord, surveyed him from beneath her lowered lids and decided that Geraldine's description of a slug, Lord or nothing, was not inept; a white slug and a fat one. His large hairless face, glistening faintly as if impregnated with slime, was surmounted by suspiciously luxuriant curls of Neronian auburn. His hands, gesticulatory, small for his size, carried curious rings on each little finger. He wore 'one of those new-fangled dinner jackets with lapels of velvet, and he spoke in soft catarrhal tones that seemed, like his face, to have been greased'. . . . He had just returned from Fiesole. Such sun! And the glorious sky—pure cobalt! The golden light upon the olives and that rich purple scent of the vineyards. "Do you know Italy, Miss—ah——?"

No, Miss—ah—did not know Italy.

"See Naples and die, but I think Naples is much over-rated. The haunt of Germans, English *nouveaux riches* and

canned food importers from Chicago. No, never see Naples
and die. See Florence—and live! But where"—he had taken
his stance in front of the fireless hearth—"is our host? I am
famished."

He looked, remarked Perry, anything but famished; her
gaze, travelling up to that treble-chinned face, was intercepted
by a gleam in the eyes of Captain Curran. She caught back a
giggle, and Geraldine said: "Would a dish of hors-d'œuvres
brought to you here stay your pangs, Lord Reginald?"

"An hors-d'œuvre, like your beauty, Geraldine, makes
hungry," he waved his ringed hands, "where most it satisfies."

Captain Curran walked over to the window that opened
on a balcony. Drawing aside the curtains he stepped out.
Perry watched him. He was breathing in the cool fresh air as
if he needed it.

"Here, praise be," purred Lord Reginald, "is Adrian."

He came in leisurely, apologizing: "Reginald, forgive me.
I have been engrossed with Oscar's latest extravaganza in
this current issue of Lippincott's. It is trivial and wonderful
and terrible. Have you read it?"

"I," said Lord Reginald heavily, "have read it—in manuscript. Not Oscar at his best. He will never surpass his as yet
unpublished 'Sphinx'. I remember how, when we were together in Paris, he thrilled me when he read aloud in his lovely
mellifluous voice:

> " 'Who were your lovers? Who were they
>   who wrestled for you in the dust?
> Which was the vessel of your Lust? What
>   Leman had you every day?' "

Perry's eyes were spherical; Captain Curran, on the balcony,
inquiringly turned his head. Geraldine raised hers. "Do go
on reciting, Lord Reginald."

He came to her, murmuring:

> " 'How subtle secret is your smile! Did you
>   love none then? Nay, I know
> Great Ammon was your bedfellow! He lay with
>   you beside the Nile.'

But of course, nothing he has ever done or will do can compare to this youthful suppuration. In *Dorian Gray*, admittedly, there is some quite clever dialogue—*au reste*"—he shrugged— "melodrama, and as always with our Oscar, passages of un-adulterated plagiarism. You remember how Dorian revels in embroideries and tapestries? The original of that may be traced to Lefèbure."

"Mr. Sankey," was announced; and hurried in, saying: "Late? Adrian, am I inexcusably late? Pray forgive me."

"I," sepulchrally uttered Lord Reginald, "cannot forgive you. My stomach squeaks for food. We have waited half an hour."

"Then let us wait," said Adrian, "no longer. Miss Flight, Mr. Sankey—my niece, Geraldine, you know, and Captain Curran. Marcus, will you take Miss Flight?"

Mr. Sankey took Miss Flight, who sat at table between him and Captain Curran. If Lord Reginald were fat, Mr. Sankey was thin, black-haired, pale, with a long, inquisitive nose, small beady eyes and an anxious expression. A member of not the most exclusive club, he was often to be found in the waiting-room of Boodle's, White's or the Athenaeum, where, pending the arrival of the friends on whom he had unsuccessfully called, he would accept invitations on the club notepaper with the address erased and his own, in Bayswater, inserted. When not thus engaged he spent most of his time studying Debrett. He claimed acquaintance with all the British peerage, relationship with half of it, and lived on expectations from an aunt.

Having ascertained from Miss Flight that she was not connected with the Datchett-Flights of Worcestershire, and promptly losing interest in her, "Of whom," he wished to know, between spoonfuls of soup, "were you speaking, Reginald, when I burst in upon you?"

"Of Oscar, naturally," Lord Reginald replied; and nobody but Perry heard Captain Curran say: "Unnaturally, I should have thought."

"Too marvellous!" declared Mr. Sankey. "But isn't it quite too *mar*vellous—that thing of his in Lippincott's? And *did* you see those perfectly awful reviews in the *Pall Mall* and *Daily Chronicle*? I can quite understand Oscar's reaction— poor dear—but I think he's going rather far to keep up this futile protest."

"Good publicity," drawled Mr. Hope-Winter. "It should sell in thousands when it appears in book form."

"I can't be*lieve* it!" declared Mr. Sankey. "Those *too* awful criticisms have damned it to perdition."

"No true artist," said Lord Reginald, "should be disturbed by the vulgar cackle of critics who, for the most part, are unsuccessful and disgruntled authors."

"I *do* so agree, but—'leprous', 'poisonous', 'clumsy', 'corrupt', 'offensive', 'incurably silly'—the string of adjectives is inexhaustible, and finally summed up by the *Pall Mall* as 'only fit to be chucked in the fire'. Poor Oscar! They've cut it," Sankey concluded with relish, "to bits."

"From what I have read of it," said Captain Curran, "I'd have hanged and quartered it, rather than cut it."

"Have you," Lord Reginald sceptically stressed the pronoun, "read it?"

"I bought the magazine on the station at Dublin and skimmed through the hundred-page instalment coming over on the boat." Captain Curran helped himself to salted almonds. "I've never been seasick before."

There was something of a pause.

"Was it a very rough crossing?" Perry asked sympathetically.

"No. Smooth as silk. Have an almond."

She took one from the proffered dish. Captain Curran grinned sideways, and Lord Reginald, after one disdainful look, ignored him to lead the conversation, tossing the ball to Hope-Winter, who caught and flicked it to Sankey, touching on topics unknown to Miss Flight. The gist of these however, as recorded, revolved around the French impressionists.

"Monet," declared Lord Reginald, "accentuated atmospheric effects, exaggerating them as early art exaggerated colour."

"The exaggeration of Monet," said Mr. Hope-Winter, "is his attempt to reproduce visual sensation, always relative to human values as opposed to the esoteric strivings of the Primitives. Take Sisley, for instance——"

Sisley was taken, and by Mr. Sankey found to be, "profoundly exhilarating. He has that intense *sense* of pictorial architecture—even more brilliant than Monet's—which was the aim, but not always achieved, of the Pre-Raphaelites. Adrian, I must compliment you on your Chambertin. Not since I stayed with the Newburys—you know the Newburys? So sad to lose Buntington, the heir. The Duchess, poor dear, is quite prostrate. She was always *just* about to crumble, and now she's so utterly broken to pieces that she forgets to dye—I mean," tittered Sankey, "her hair, which more than ever looks like streaky bacon. I was saying that not since I last dined with the Newburys—my cousins on the distaff side—have I tasted anything like this vintage. There's only about a thousand dozen of it left in the country. Now, what were we talking of before I slid away? Ah, yes!" he sipped. "The Pre-Raphaelites."

Dismissed by Lord Reginald as—"Photographic, my dear. Frith, *par exemple*. My quarrel with Frith is," and he focused a fishy stare on the silent Captain Curran as if his quarrel were with him rather than the gentleman in question, "that he, although not of the Brethren, painted, as did they, a life history into each individual of his composite canvas, which I contend is not art." He swallowed wine. "It's literature."

"But, Lord Reginald," Geraldine reminded him, "you said just now that the Pre-Raphaelites were photographic, and I can't see how they can be literary as well. And though you may think it odd of me, I adore Frith's Derby Day."

"Youth," said Lord Reginald, indulgently, "adores a pantomime."

"I do so agree with you, Reginald," pronounced Mr. Sankey, with fervour, "the P.R.B.'s had not one idea between them other than precise and quite excellent coloured photography. The mechanical uniformity of masses was beyond them—they over*flowed* with extraneous trivia. Millais' 'Carpenter's Shop' is obscene, and Rossetti obsessed by women suffering from goitre——"

"Lord Reginald," interrupted Geraldine, "said Rossetti would have loved me, and I don't suffer from goitre—but I once had a governess who did."

"Every artist in the world," Sankey bowed to her, "would love you, Miss Geraldine. But *à propos* Rossetti, he couldn't draw, and Hunt can't paint, and Millais can't do either. So Adrian, for God's sake, or Art's sake, let us with our Odyssey revert to the pure essence"—he raised his glass—"of Cimabue."

Captain Curran turned to Perry. "Can you tell me what they're driving at, and who is Chimabooey?"

A dimple appeared in the cheek nearest his.

"I know no more than you, Captain Curran, but one wouldn't dare to say so."

His eyes met hers with that twinkle in them: "Do you not find the atmosphere just a trifle too *earn*estly precious?"

She glanced at Lord Reginald, then aside at Mr. Sankey, and back again at him; her eyes answered to that twinkle. " 'It seems to me,' " she quoted, " 'to be nonsense.' "

" 'Nonsense perhaps, but oh, what precious nonsense!' Did you see *Patience*? No, of course you were too young. It was first produced in '81 when I was a cadet. In those days Wilde astonished the bourgeois by wearing on his head a velvet beret—something like those worn by Basque onion sellers—and puce velveteen knickerbockers with black silk stockings and silver buckles to his shoes. One of our fellows had the supreme honour," said Captain Curran dryly, "of walking arm-in-arm with him down Piccadilly."

" 'With a lily in his——'?"

Geraldine caught her eye.

"Let us leave them to their port and their Pre-Raphaelites. My stick, Larkin. Come to us soon, Garth, and Peridot will play for you."

The gentlemen were on their feet; Perry rose to hers.

"What," murmured Captain Curran, "will you play for me?"

'. . . And what did I play for him—and Geraldine—when Mr. Hope-Winter and those two guests of his had left us to ourselves while they discussed their "precious nonsense"? I improvised, and never in my life so well. Geraldine and I had our coffee in the drawing-room where Captain Curran joined us before the other gentlemen came up. He talked to me—and Geraldine—of Ireland and the "arrowy rain" as he called it, "slanting down"; of the "sudden red of a peasant girl's cloak against the green", and "the sound of the hunter's horn ringing through those mist-grey mornings. . . ."

"I never knew you were a poet, Garth," said Geraldine. "A poet only when I think of home," he said. And to me, with the brogue in his voice, "You should come to my country where the women are fairies, though none," he whispered it, "so fair as you." And Geraldine on her couch was chattering away to Montmorency. "She has made an impression on our Garth, hasn't she? But he's so easily impressed and he doesn't mean a word of it."

I was certain sure he didn't mean a word of it, but I played to him—and Geraldine—as it came to me, of Ireland, his country. And he said when I had done, "Won't you give me more and more of it?" I gladly would have given him a little more of it, only that just then the gentlemen came in and it was time for Geraldine to go to bed.

"So you'll be off to Somerset in August?" Captain Curran said to me—and Geraldine, "I'll see you there, God willing. . . "'

                    *   *   *

Yet, although God appeared to be willing, two weeks elapsed before Captain Curran availed himself of the chance to ride over to Tarragon Cottage in the delightful old village of Luccombe, where dwelled Miss Lavinia Burbage.

Mr. Hope-Winter, having escorted his young ladies to Paddington, put them safely in the train and plied them with magazines and chocolates, watched them go, it is stated, 'with evident relief to be rid of us.'

Throughout the journey, Geraldine, who did not cease to bemoan her fate at being 'packed off to that godforsaken hole as if she were a parcel', arrived utterly exhausted at her journey's end where they were met at Minehead station by Miss Burbage.

She, a tall gaunt lady with iron grey hair brushed severely back from a determinedly chinny face, is described as 'mannish', in that, at Perry's first sight of her, she wore a hat of peculiar shape, 'spotlessly white and of the kind worn by officers in India in the *Illustrated London News*'—presumably a solar topee. Her dun-coloured dress, buttoned high to the throat, was finished by a stiff linen collar and cuffs.

"The train's late," was her brusque greeting, as Perry and an aged porter assisted Geraldine on to the platform. To Geraldine's cheek she offered a peck and to Perry three bony gloveless fingers. "Miss Flight," she said, "I take it," and to the porter: "Fetch the luggage from the van. Look sharp."

Looking as sharp as his years would allow, the porter

hobbled off to haul from the rear of the train three trunks, two of which, with two portmanteaux and a dressing-case, belonged to Geraldine. Eyeing them coldly Miss Burbage inquired: "What on earth do you want with such a quantity of stuff between the pair of you? One trunk would have been quite sufficient. We can't take all this on the brougham. A portmanteau, the dressing-case and that"—she pointed to Perry's modest box—"is as much as we can manage. The rest must be brought by the carrier. Hurry along now. Hurry along."

As Geraldine was in no fit state to hurry along, and, although supported by Perry, seemed unable to drag one foot after the other, Miss Burbage, striding on ahead, turned back to lend a hand, and together they got her into the antiquated brougham awaiting them outside the station. The luggage was hauled up, a window let down, and Miss Flight curtly ordered to "Hop in".

Miss Flight hopped in and sat with her back to the horse facing Miss Burbage and the greenly pale Geraldine. Leaning forward, Perry whispered: "Are you feeling bad? There's a flask of brandy in your dressing-case"—procured from Larkin as a last minute precaution, in view of Geraldine's insistence that she was always sick in trains. "Will you have a drop?"

"A drop?" Miss Burbage intervened awfully. "Of what?"

"Brandy, Miss Burbage," faltered Perry. "I think Geraldine is feeling sick."

"Then she must get out," said Miss Burbage. "She can't be sick here."

"I have no intention of being sick here," Geraldine retorted with a glare. "Don't fuss." And not another word between the three of them was passed throughout the drive.

Tarragon Cottage, that despite its name was nothing of a cottage, is presented as:

'A long rambling white house with a thatched roof and latticed rose-wreathed windows. A brick-paved path bordered with every kind of country flower led to an iron-studded oaken door which was opened by an elderly maid. All in that household were old with exception of the tweenie, and Miss Lavinia herself, the youngest woman for her years, which must have been then in the fifties, whom I have ever known.

4*

The maid, who had a face like a full red smiling moon, hoped, in broad Somerset, that "Miss Geraldine had a pleasant journey here".

"No," snapped Geraldine, "I didn't have a pleasant journey here. I didn't want to come and now I want to go."

I felt quite ashamed of her rudeness, but the maid still kept that comfortable smile as, in a loud aside, she said, "Poor dear. If you'll come up with her, Miss, I'll show you your rooms."

So upstairs we went, Geraldine halting at every step, complaining of her hip and desperately hanging on to me; but I managed to undress her and get her into bed. We had communicating rooms, oak-beamed, with crooked white-washed walls. All the furniture, too, was old, nothing modern, even the curtains were in keeping, chintzy and countrified. The only up-to-date thing in my room was the brass bedstead. Geraldine had a four-poster in hers, draped in old fashioned brocade with a canopy. I could see she was heading for a brainstorm, and so soon as the maid had left us, it broke in full blast. She couldn't stay here with that old horror—no she wouldn't and be damned to hell she wouldn't! She often came out with swear words in her tempers, and heaven only knows where she learnt them. I told her to be quiet. "Such language! Whatever will Miss Burbage think of you?" "I don't care what she thinks of me! And anyway she swears like a trooper herself. I hate her—and I hate Uncle Adrian for sending me here. I won't stay—I won't!" She began to scream, pummelling the pillows with her fists. "I loathe this house—beastly old house—and that devilish old woman! I'll kill myself sooner than stay—I'll take poison!"

I said, "You won't take poison. You'll take this." And I gave her a dose of the medicine that the doctor prescribed for her when I told him—for of course I had to tell him— of the awful scene I had with her when she bit her hand, and he said if she showed signs of an attack again I was to give her a dose of it every four hours. And then I bathed her forehead with Eau de Cologne and began to talk of the lovely scenery which she could see from the window as she lay in bed—— She interrupted to say: "You know I can't see a thing without my glasses." I said, "Then you must wear them. Here they are." She snatched the spectacle-case from my hand and flung it at my head. I caught it and went on to say as if nothing had happened, how interesting it was being in Lorna Doone's country—I had made it my business to read *Lorna Doone* before we left London—and how we would go for drives and see the Doone Valley and if it were not too far we could go to Lynton and Lynmouth and perhaps Miss Burbage would let us take a picnic basket and spend the day on Exmoor. "And if Captain Curran rides over to see you, as he promised," I said, "that will cheer you up."

But I seemed to have said the wrong thing. She flared out in a rage: "Don't talk to me of *him*! And don't *you* be taken in by his flattery, either. He's a hopeless philanderer and quite uneducated. He never went to a public school, he was taught by tutors and allowed to run wild at Donaghmore. I can't imagine how he passed into the Army—only that it's always the fools of the family who go into the Army or the Church. He can't even speak the Queen's English—that awful brogue."

"It isn't much of a brogue," I said, "and I thought it rather attractive." "You would!" she said, "as you're a cockney!" I let that pass and settled her down with a book, *The Egoist*, which I had just finished, but to tell the truth could not make head or tail of it. "This," I said, "is what your uncle calls a searching, remorseless study of selfishness. It would do you good to read it." She opened wide her eyes at me. "You don't mean to tell me you read Meredith?" "And why shouldn't I read Meredith? Even a cockney sparrow"—which is what Mr. Hope-Winter had been pleased to call me—"can peck at the crumbs of learning thrown to it from the rich man's table." "Clever-clever, aren't you?" sneered Geraldine. "No," I said, "not clever-clever. Only moderately bright." She looked up at me then, and those tawny gold eyes of hers shone with laughter —or tears.

"What a beast I am to you, darling—my darling!" Her hand came out to mine to take and kiss. I was well used to such sudden change of mood. "But you know I don't mean it, don't you? You know I love you, don't you?—

more than I ever thought it possible to love any mortal
being on this earth except myself. Why do I love you?
You're only a mouse. My little pet personal mouse——"
She sighed; and then she yawned. The medicine was taking
its effect. "If you love me," I said, and stroked her forehead
in the way that always soothed her, "you'll not talk any
more. Just go to sleep." And I waited there beside her till
she slept.

Yes, I had my trials, but I bore with them and her for
what she was, for what she might have been, and perhaps
because of all that she, so tragically, was not. . . .'

The mania for tidiness of which Perry had been warned
as one of Miss Burbage's idiosyncrasies, was manifest on that
day of arrival. Summoned by Ellen, the elderly maid, to take
tea with Miss Burbage in the parlour, Perry hastily washed,
changed her travelling dress and descended.

The 'parlour' she found to be L-shaped, long and, like the
bedrooms, white-washed and oak-beamed. The furniture,
an indiscriminate collection, included some Sheraton pieces, a
long-case marquetry clock, *circa* 1690, a Queen Anne com-
mode, and a Jacobean settle whereon, at a small Hepplewhite
table, was seated 'Miss Lavinia', as Perry came to call her.

To the profusion of home-made cakes, clotted cream, scones,
and Miss Lavinia's own special strawberry preserve, Perry
did full justice. The Exmoor air had given her an appetite—
"which," Miss Lavinia remarked, "I like to see. Those per-
nickety hashed-up messes they give you at Brook Street—no
good to you. Geraldine, and you, too, will drink a quart of
milk a day while you're under my roof." And when the tea
was cleared away she produced from her petticoat-pocket a
small silver box and took snuff—and took stock of her wondering guest. "For once," was her verdict, "Adrian has
shown some sense in his choice. In spite of your youth you
carry a head on your shoulders."

Perry glanced at her dumbly. Upon Miss Lavinia's determined chin sprouted a few grey prickly hairs; and, while
meditatively she plucked at these, Perry, fascinated, watched
her. So in mutual silence did they sit, Perry not daring to
speak until her formidable hostess spoke to her, when:

"At least," she allowed, "you're an improvement on the

thing Geraldine brought with her last year. Go up and change
your shoes and come into the garden." Rising from her chair
she stooped to retrieve from the carpet an infinitesimal fluff.
"What have we here?" demanded Miss Lavinia, and seizing
a hand-bell she vigorously rang it.

The elderly maid appeared.

"Yes'm?"

"Send Mary to me, Ellen. Dirt. Dustpan and brush." And
when presently Perry returned with the shoes in her hand and
a pair of buttoned boots on her feet, she saw, through the open
door of the parlour, a red-eyed chastened little maid sedulously
sweeping the speckless dustless carpet. Miss Lavinia, with the
solar topee on her head, gauntlet gloves on her hands and on
her arm a basket, asked: "Don't you feel the sun too strong
without a hat?"

"No—ma'am—Miss Burbage," stammered Perry. "I——"

"Go fetch your hat," commanded Miss Lavinia.

Perry went to her room again and fetched her hat. On the
way out through the hall she paused to look up at the portrait
of a bewhiskered young gentleman in the dress of the mid-
'sixties.

"My husband," Miss Lavinia said briefly.

"You——?" Perry closed her mouth and opened it again,
ineffectually to say: "Oh!"

"Not dead but gone," Miss Lavinia said, "after." And
from under the brim of the solar topee her eyes glinted with
grim humour. "I was born a Burbage and I shall die a Burbage
and a Miss—though not a maiden. Are you interested in
herbs?"

"I have not," Perry weakly replied, "had much experience
of country life, Miss—Mrs.——"

"Miss. Let us hope you will profit by acquaintance with it
here. Leave your shoes on the mat."

Perry left her shoes on the mat beside a pair that Miss
Lavinia had herself discarded, and hard upon the heels of her
who stalked ahead, she followed. Across a paved terrace, and
lawns green and smooth as baize, girt about with cedars, oaks
and yews, enclosed by trim box hedges and walls of mellowed
brick, was Perry led, to linger by and gaze upon and savour the
delicious smells and sight of an herbaceous border; but her
hostess would have none of that. She hastened her away with

a curt "Don't dawdle"; and so down a flight of stone steps, through a garden of roses they went.

Miss Lavinia, taking one gentlemanly stride to Perry's four, remarked, "Your heels are too high. Twist your ankle. You must buy yourself some sensible footgear in Porlock if you wish to go walking on the moor." And opening a wicket gate in a hedge: "Here," she announced, "are my herbs."

'A plain little flowerless garden,' to Perry's town-bred eyes did this appear, but in it grew a variety of plants giving forth a heady spicy scent. "Each of these," Miss Lavinia told her, "has a history. Named for the things they resemble. Most of them rare but some in common use in the kitchen—thyme, marjoram, mint—— Ha! Which reminds me—dose Geraldine with garlic. Those imbecile doctors see no further than the hip. Obviously pthisical."

"Do you mean——" Perry paused. What *did* Miss Lavinia mean? Something to do with this craze for table-turning and calling up of spirits?

"I mean——" Miss Lavinia stooped to a weed, saying: "Deadly nightshade. Gardener's boy. Clout his ears. *That* with the sage in the stuffing for the duck, and where would we be?"

Not at all sure where they would be nor, indeed, where they were at that moment in this maze of irrelevance, Perry feebly smiled.

"I mean," Miss Lavinia alarmingly resumed, "that Geraldine—or I'm a Dutchman—is consumptive."

"But," Perry caught her breath, "she has no cough."

"All the symptoms, none the less. In a fever when I met her at the station. The pallor you mistook for sickness was replaced by a high flush presently. Do you take her temperature every night and morning?"

"The—doctors," stammered Perry, "didn't tell me to, Miss—Burb——"

"Doctors! Jackasses!" said Miss Lavinia, profoundly. "Hip-disease, more often than not, develops into pthisis. Geraldine is predisposed. Her grandfather died of—Garlic." And bending, she pulled up a few small whitish onion-shaped bulbs and placed them in her basket.

"Doesn't garlic," ventured Perry, "make the breath—unpleasant?"

"What matter if it does? There's no man here," replied Miss Lavinia, obscurely. "This nice little creature," she pointed to something with glistening greyish leaves, "was named by Rabelais—ever heard of Rabelais?"

Perry admitted she had not. There was that in this masterful lady which insisted on the truth and nothing but.

"A bawdy old rip and a great physician," resumed Miss Lavinia, "was Rabelais—lived as near as dammit four hundred years ago. Named this herb Hippuris for its likeness to the tail of a horse."

Perry, who could see no likeness whatsoever to the tail of a horse, politely murmured, "Fancy!"

"And this is Psyllion, the flea-wort—shape of a flea, only some million times larger. Catch a flea—but you never will in my house—and compare the two. And this is Coronopus— you see?—like a crow's foot. And here is Artemisia Abrotanum or Armois—from Artemis. The old herbalists were given to lending the names of gods and goddesses to herbs. Artemisia was and—brewed by me—still is used in these parts as a cure for anemia and female pains. This little fellow," Miss Lavinia affectionately touched with her booted toe a small leafed low-growing plant, "is Mercuriali. Provides to this day a remedy for boils. Interesting, is it not?"

It was, since Perry had some knowledge of certain of the herbs that Miss Lavinia had mentioned; and, pricking her ears at the word Mercuriali, she summoned courage to say:

"Although I have not had to do with any of these in their natural form, I have seen drugs and essences distilled from— not all—but a few of them."

"Hey?" cried Miss Lavinia.

"I know a little something," Perry said, with diffidence, "of chemistry."

"What!"

Every expression save that of disbelief was obliterated from the countenance of Miss Lavinia as, searchingly, she gazed upon the blushful Perry.

"My fa—my step-father was a chemist, and I used to watch him mixing medicines, and," she brought it out bravely, "I served in his shop, so I learned quite a lot about ill-nesses, and what drugs to take for them from doctors' pre-scriptions."

"Oho!" ejaculated Miss Lavinia; and, so fiercely did she frown, that Perry much regretted she had spoken. "That then," declared Miss Lavinia, "accounts for it."

Hesitating to inquire what that might account for, and mesmerized beneath the gimlet eye of Miss Lavinia, Perry stared fixedly up at her who said: "The time will come—hope I live to see it, when women——" She bent to pick a bunch of mint, murmuring: "Cold lamb—who have gained their rights, will carve for themselves a career. You, having learned the rudiments of chemistry, would, if you had any gumption, have followed it up. Quite a few professions are open now to women. Voices calling from the desert. Olive Schreiner. Mint sauce and a salad. Come in."

They went in, Perry trailing after Miss Lavinia, who strode on ahead as before; nor did she speak again until, at the door of the house, Perry was bidden: "Take off your boots and put on your shoes. Supper at seven sharp. Geraldine will have hers in bed."

Had Miss Lavinia been born half a century later she might have represented a constituency or left her mark among the names of those who fought and won their way to women's freedom; as it is she leaves her mark nowhere save in these fragmentary records. But, despite her self-inflicted isolation, she took an interest, if inactive, in the embryonic cause of feminine enfranchisement; she subscribed to and was a member of the Women's Liberal Association, and, notwithstanding her regular attendance at the village church, she scandalized the vicar by declaring the Humanitarians to be the only true followers of Christ. She dabbled in Theosophy, and, to the dismay of the Reverend Mr. Price, expounded at her tea-table the effect of mind over matter—'For a state of consciousness,' thus Miss Lavinia, in a subsequent treatise, unpublished, expressed it, 'in which the intelligence is freed from the hampering of its physical limitations, is as yet but dimly understood by those accustomed to confine their ideas of life to preconceived doctrinal teaching.'

That night of their arrival when Perry was undressing, she came from her bedroom to ask Geraldine: "Why won't she call herself 'Mrs.' if she's married? And what did she mean when she told me her husband isn't dead but 'gone after'?"

Geraldine, now recovered from her brainstorm, retorted

with a giggle: "So he did go after—a girl from the Opera Comique. She didn't divorce him because she couldn't prove that he knocked her about. It has to be cruelty as well as the other thing. You should hear her inveighing against the divorce laws to the vicar. If he had any hair on his head it would stand up. But she lets him think, as does everyone else except the family who knows all about it, that she's an old maid. Of course she's quite dotty."

Those lazy August days were for Perry sheer enchantment. The quiet green of valleys ringed with rock-faced heights, veined by the silver streak of waters falling; the space and grandeur of rugged moorland solitude, the cheerful contrast of lush meadows and cornfields where reapers stacked the sheaves of that golden summer's harvest; the sunset change of russet hills from burnt green to glowing violet, and everywhere the ripened wealth of orchards—by all of these was she enraptured and enriched.

Often when Geraldine was resting she would wander out beyond the village to the edge of the moor. There, in some craggy hollow, she would sit among the heather and listen to the silence broken only by the plaint of sheep, the cry of plover or a lark's song, aware of a subtle change in herself described as 'outsideness'; a hesitant, half fearful perception, lending a warmer significance to things of sight and sound, and to her thoughts unuttered; to her dreams, wherein with one beside her, formless, nameless, she would stray in some such lonely, faery place as this. . . . Until a certain August day when came a rude awakening.

'. . . I had settled Geraldine in a hammock in the garden, for Miss Lavinia insisted she should rest out of doors whenever possible, "to breathe," she said, "the pure moorland air into her lungs". I waited with Geraldine until I saw her dozing, and then took the footpath through the valley to the moor below Dunkery Beacon. A little river—I forget its name—runs beside the path and widens to a sheltered pool with high rocks towering above it. I was hot after my walk and so heavenly cool was it there in the shade of the overhanging trees, that I shed my shoes and stockings and paddled in the stream. I was minded to shed more, all my clothes, and bathe, and might have done with not a soul to see, had I not heard the nearing sound of hooves half muffled on the sheep-cropped turf.

Even at that distance I recognized him who rode along the grassy track and hailed me: "Is this right for Luccombe? Can you tell me where I am?"

And there was I, in the middle of the stream, holding my petticoats and gingham dress knee-high. What I must have looked like!—I know what I felt like—never such a fool in all my life.

Lowering my petticoats and skirt for decency I splashed through the water in a scramble for the bank. My hat fell off and went bobbing down the river. I cut my foot on a sharp-edged flint and landed in a nettlebed. He had dismounted and was grinning wide.

I could have killed him.

"I knew you were not what you seemed to be," he said, "but I never took you for a water-nymph, although I might have guessed it from the colour of your eyes. Did you call to me across the moor for witchery, and lame my horse that I must turn him off the high road to ease him on the grass and lose myself to find myself—with you?"

My feet were stinging, and my face was too, but not from the nettles. The hems of my petticoats were soaking wet, my hair down my back in a tumble from my hurry, and I had lost my hat. A pretty tale this for him to tell to Miss Lavinia!

"What a surprise, Captain Curran," I said. "Geraldine is not expecting you today."

"Nor did I think to be here," said he; and went on to explain that he had been out with the stag-hounds when his horse had sprained a tendon. Seeing a signpost to Luccombe he thought to have his horse stabled for the night in the village with the farrier, and hire something else to take him back. And while he was talking I was standing barefoot with my wet skirts round my ankles and my shoes and stockings and my garters in a heap. He looked at them and grinning wider, said, "I'll turn my back." He did, and I sat down and bundled up my hair as best as I could. My foot was bleeding badly and hurting like the devil, so I bound it with my handkerchief not to risk the dye of my black stocking coming through. And then, of course, I couldn't get my shoe on, so I must do without the handkerchief and without my stocking, too. I stuffed it in the pocket of my petticoat. And all this time, while he stood with his back to me, he was singing "Clementine" to scare the birds. "Oh, my darling, oh my *darling*, oh my DARling Clementine, struck her *foot* a-gainst a *splin*ter, fell in*to*——" and so on till I told him: "Captain Curran, if you'll ride ahead along this track bearing left at the stile, you will come to the lane that leads to Luccombe."

"I will not," he said. "I'll only lose myself again if you don't guide me. Am I allowed to look round now?"

And round he looked just as I was slipping on my garter. I don't know what he saw. And so we started off, he leading his horse and now both of us—the horse and I—were lame. He noticed it at once and said, "You're limping." I said, "I'm not." He said, "You are," and was down on his knees in the grass and had my shoe off in a jiffy and my bare foot, dripping blood, in his hand. "You've gashed yourself properly, haven't you?" he said. "Wait. Sit you here and I'll bathe it." Then he took his handkerchief, tore it into strips, dipped it in the stream and bathed my foot and bandaged it as well as any doctor. "And now," he said, "I'll have to put you on my horse."

I had to tell him that I couldn't ride.

"Gil Blas," he said—his horse's name—"will take you sweet and gently." And with that he shoved my shoe into his pocket, lifted me and sat me in the saddle and held me with his arm to keep me there. And so we came to Luccombe and up the village street with all the yokels staring, the postmistress peeping through her bottle panes, and Captain Curran bursting into song again. "Light she *was* as any *fair*-y and her *shoes* were number NINE, herring *box*es without *top*ses sandals *were* for——"

"Captain Curran," I cried urgently, "pray don't sing so loud. Here's the vicar——" Coming at his brisk trot down the hill. He stopped, the horse stopped, and the sudden jerk of it sent me flying forward on his neck and there I clung, until Captain Curran hauled me back into my seat again.

"Dear me," said the vicar, peering from under his shovel-brim, "is it—can it be Miss Flight?" I stammered

that it was and that I'd hurt my foot and couldn't walk—
and then in my confusion I introduced him idiotically to
"Captain Cousin. Geraldine's Curran." Disgustedly the
vicar turned from me—as well he might—for most of my
hair was hanging down, my skirt rucked up and my bare leg
showing. "Been out with the stag-hounds, Captain Cousin?"
asked the vicar, who because he rode to hounds himself was
thought to be a sportsman, if sport it is to chase to its death
the lovely wild red deer. . . .

How often afterwards we used to argue, and the nearest
that we ever came to quarrelling, on that point.

Then, lifting his hat and with another awful look at me,
the vicar went his way and we went ours.'

It is regretfully recorded that Captain Curran appears to
have shown more concern for his hunter's game leg than for
Miss Flight's game foot. Having left her at the cottage he took
himself and Gil Blas to the farrier, nor would he accept Miss
Lavinia's curt invitation to return for supper—cold partridge
—at seven o'clock. Instead came the vicar to inquire if Miss
Flight had recovered from her unfortunate mishap, and what
had become of Captain Cousin, whose mellow baritone had
so entertained the villagers that they—the vicar facetiously
declared—had mistook the mounted lady and her songful
cavalier for the vanguard of a circus!

"Circus be damned!" retorted Miss Lavinia, unpardonably.
"Vicar, you are nothing but a gossiping old woman. Would
you have her walk three miles on a cut foot bleeding like a pig!
And if you want to chivvy Captain Curran—you could never
get a name right even at a christening—go look for him at
Porlock at the vet's."

The vicar, from long-suffering, immune to the acridity of
Miss Lavinia, did not look for Captain Curran at the vet's;
he stayed to supper and did such justice to cold partridge,
apple pie and Cheshire cheese, washed down with cider and a
potent brew of Miss Lavinia's elderberry wine, that:

"It is evident your housekeeper," was his hostess's remark,
"keeps you on starvation diet. I can see you losing weight.
You ought to take a wife. Cost you less and feed you better."

Said the vicar with a bow and the suspicion of a leer: "Like
Barkis, you should know that I"—he hiccupped—"I am willin'."

"Good heavens, man!" uttered Miss Lavinia, snatching at his glass to convulse Geraldine and put Perry in the chokes. "You've had more than enough and no head to carry it. Go home!"

And home he went in merriest humour with Miss Lavinia, himself, and all the world.

Later at her window Perry stood on one foot and watched the blossoming sky where a slip of a young moon lay on her back, caught between a tree-top and a star. Her room looked out upon the lane and the front garden where, guarding the gate, a pyramidal yew flung its shadow, black as a witch's shawl, across the silvered strip of lawn. No breath of air stirred the heavy-laden warmth, no sound save the hoot of an owl, the blind flurry of a bat, the rustle of some small wild creature in the hedge, and, somewhere in the distance, the eerie night-crow of a cock.

"D'you hear that now?" a voice called up to startle her. "Cross your thumbs to ward away the bad luck of it, and turn your money for a wish to the new young moon."

He was underneath her window, a shadow in the shadows of the dark.

"You're surely never walking back to Minehead, Captain Curran?"

"I am, since there's nothing in this village nor at Porlock fit to ride. How's your foot?"

"So kind of you to ask. No better than it ought to be, perhaps a little worse. How's your horse?"

"Lamed for a week or more."

"So that will stop your hunting."

"Not at all. I'll be up with the sun and the hounds in the morning."

"May I remind you, Captain Curran, that you have my shoe?"

"Yes," he slapped his pocket, "safe and sound."

"One shoe is not much use to me. I'd like to have the other."

"I'll be back sometime tomorrow and will give it to you then."

"Good night, Captain Curran. Don't lose your way again."

"I will not, for do you see?" He pointed upward, "there's a star for me to follow, so—good night."

But tomorrow and tomorrow, a succession of tomorrows brought no sign of Captain Curran, until the seventh day, when he came to fetch his horse, with the news that his regiment was ordered out to India. He hoped he would be sailing in November; in celebration of which, Miss Lavinia was moved to open a bottle and offer him a stirrup-cup. "And I'll leave," he said, "within it a kiss for each of you. Miss Lavinia, Geraldine, and"—he raised the glass—"but where's Miss Flight?"

Miss Flight, in bedroom slippers and limping still, a little, had gone about her business which was none of his. From behind the curtains of her bedroom window she watched him on the quite recovered Gil Blas ride away.

. . . 'And after all he never gave me back my shoe!'

FIVE

Geraldine Curran to Peridot Flight.

Nice
January 22nd, 1893

My Peridot,

I send you for your twenty-first this white coral necklace which I think is so very much you with its hint of
warmth beneath the whiteness. May it bring you all the
joy in your years to come that I have missed and many
many happy returns of your day. Oh, my darling, I am so
wretched here without you. It is barely two weeks since
we arrived and it seems like a century. If only Uncle Adrian
had not been in Spain when Sir Crispin ordered me to
winter in the S. of France he would have brought me here
and you would have come with us. Aunt Hilda, of course,
seized on the chance to give herself a free holiday in a sump-
tuous suite in the most expensive hotel on the Riviera, and
so instead of you I have *her* stuck over me morning, noon and
night. She has engaged a temporary French maid, ostensibly
for me, but you may be sure *she* makes full use of her. What
should I want with a maid more than to help me in and
out of the bath and dress me, who am only seen from my
head to my waist? Because—did I tell you in my last?—
that I have to be wheeled about in a bath chair. Which perhaps is just as well as I am not so conspicuous as when I
hobble on a crutch. The English Dr. here makes me drink
2 quarts of milk a day, but I empty them in the pot when
the maid isn't looking.

I've been practising my French on her and have read
that extraordinary book À Rebours which is supposed to
have influenced Dorian Gray. Wilde has cribbed whole
passages from it, particularly those about the jewels. Dorian
collects among other of his treasures 'the olive green
chrysoberyl and the pistachio coloured peridot'. (!!) Des
Esseintes, Dorian's counterpart, arranges in little bouquets
'les chrysoberyls vert asperges' 'les peridots vert poireau',
and they both, by some curious coincidence, collect precisely the same perfumes! The whole book reeks of beast-

liness and so does Dorian Gray. Wilde's 'shameless mimicry', you may remember, was one of the many grievances the critics had against him when Dorian appeared in Lippincott's. Will you ever forget the time he dined at Brook Street and brought with him that pretty blue-eyed boy whom he called 'Bosie'—Lord Alfred somebody or other—and how we both agreed that Oscar was insufferable—'intoxicated', as Disraeli would have said, 'with the hare-brained chatter of his irresponsible frivolities.'

I can't believe Wilde will live when he is dead and can no longer dominate a dinner table with his hashed up epigrams that you so aptly described in one of your cutting little remarks as 'gaudy' conversation. But if those who sit at his feet and adore could have heard Congreve or Addison talk, I wonder how Mr. Wilde would compare with them! He is at his best when he writes for the stage, being a born showman. We must go and see Lady Windermere's Fan again if it is still running when I come back. Oh how I long to come back! I loathe and detest it here. The hotel is full of the most obscene horrible people—women dressed to the nines with hard envious faces and claw-like greedy hands covered in jewels. Puppyish young men trying to look like Ouida's heroes with flowing moustaches and their waists pulled in. Paunchy old men lechering after costly cocottes (and don't ask me to tell you what *they* are, you little innocent!) and summing up the price of each. It's no distance from here by train to Monte Carlo. My God! The sights you see make you ashamed to be human. A man shot himself last night in the Casino gardens at Monte having lost his last franc on the tables. But my very dear Aunt is in her element. She has met several old friends and is busy making new ones. We go for drives but I can't enjoy anything, not even the scenery which is spoiled for me by "the wonderful blue of the Mediterranean and *do* look at our latest peeress! Rouged to the eyebrows and a hat like a coster's—but what can you expect, my dear, of a chorus girl?—and isn't this a pretty view? She's the third this year—dreadful to contemplate the future of Debrett—and those roses—just imagine—in January! And here comes Mrs. Flip-flap. I suppose one has to bow. Did you see her last night at the Casino? Her dress—*too* revealing—and her pearls! Yes, my dear, that awful Mr. Goldust from Johannesburg—so blatant—as if her husband could afford to pay the rent of that villa and how lovely the mimosa smells——" etcetera. Oh, I was almost forgetting to tell you. Garth landed at Marseilles last week on leave, and is staying at Cannes with some friends who have a villa there. I had a letter from him yesterday to say he is coming over to see me tomorrow. One of Aunt Hilda's hens who knew him in Quetta last autumn is clucking of his marked attention to the daughter of his Colonel, also one of the Cannes house-party, so we may expect to hear any day of his engagement—I suppose because he can't have me! I can tell you now in confidence that I have refused him three times. He is madly in love with me and always has been but I wouldn't have him if he were the last man on earth. He is so boorish and coarse and uncultured. I am much admired here and even that horrid little toad, Marcus Sankey—yes, he's here too with a quite unpresentable aunt—has had the impudence to propose to me. I wish I could fall in love but I haven't met a man who can compare with Montmorency—or with you! And don't believe a word I say. (I can see your funny little smile, for of course you don't believe me, and you're right!) What man who *is* a man would want to marry a cripple? Why wasn't I born ugly? I think I could bear to be what I am if my face matched the rest of me. I seem to mind it more here than in London. I suppose because the sea, the sky, the distant snow-capped Maritimes, the cypresses, the olive groves, the palms, the sun, the flowers and everything is perfect and only I am vile. No. Everybody's vile on the Riviera. Grabbing out of life their pounds of flesh-pot pleasure. Good night, my Peridot. I'm writing this in bed and I'm tired. I'm always tired lately. Kiss Phyllis for me on the wrinkle just above her nose. I saw a bulldog in the Jardins yesterday—a fawn waddly one in a muzzle! I hope the muzzling order won't come back again to England.

I hate to think of you all alone on your twenty-first but I have written to Uncle Freddie to tell him the date, so perhaps you *won't* be all alone!

Your ever loving
Geraldine.

Peridot Flight to Geraldine Curran.

Brook Street
January 26th, 1893
11.45 p.m. (so it is still
my birthday)

Dearest Geraldine,

What a lovely thing to give me! It came by the first
post today. A thousand thanks. I shall treasure it always.
I feel dreadfully old. Twenty-one and no longer a minor.
I've beaten you by nine months.

I'm so sorry, my dear, that you are not happy at Nice.
I too wish I could have gone with you but you know how
the Aunt whisked you off before I could get in touch with
your uncle to prevent it. Anyway it won't be for long. Only
a few more weeks, so try and bear it.

I agree with every word you say about O.W. I thought
him nauseating. It's funny you should mention him because
I have been reading his quite enchanting fairy tales 'The
House of Pomegranates'. It is incredible that he can be
such a mass of artificiality and yet produce 'The Star Child'
which might have been written by Hans Andersen. Yes, I
suppose he is a plagiarist—yet aren't we all? I remember
your uncle once saying that we are still so near the apes
that we must steal from and mimic each other until we are
angels—or words to that effect. But even angels, according
to the Primitives, are sickeningly similar, all exactly dressed
alike with identical gold wings and all worshipfully hymning
the same songs to the Omnipotence. I have yet to discover
which side I am on—the angels or the apes. I think for
preference the latter.

I was not alone today for my twenty-first because Sir
Frederick called this morning with an immense bouquet
of roses and carnations, three pairs of gloves—miles too
big for me but I didn't like to tell him so—and a quite
dreadful music-hall song which he surely will never dare
to sing before the Aunt. It is called "Ta-ra-ra-boom-de-ay".
and you can imagine how he *booms*-de-ay! The words are
too silly but it seems to be the rage. All the errand-boys
are whistling it. Sir F. also brought with him a niece,
Annabel, whom I have not seen before but expect you

know her. A horse-faced girl with a neighing laugh and a rather unfortunate nose. She was in Quetta last year when her father, Colonel Stilton, was stationed there. She, too, was full of Captain Curran's engagement which, she says, will shortly be announced, to a Miss Clara Bourne, I think that was the name. Her Papa I understand is very rich.

This evening Sir F. took Miss Stilton and myself to the first night of the new play at the Criterion, The Bauble Shop by Henry Arthur Jones with Charles Wyndham in the leading part. He was wonderful. At the end he came before the curtain and made a speech. It was a very fashionable audience. I wore the frock you gave me for Xmas and your necklace and so thanks to you, my dear, I had a lovely birthday.

Phyllis misses you as much as I do. She mourns by your couch and is quite off her feed. I'm sure she loves you more than she loves me. I try not to be jealous.

Always your loving
Peridot.

Telegram to Miss Flight from Mr. Hope-Winter, Jan. 27, 1893.

Just received letter from Geraldine forwarded from Paris reminding me of your 21st accept belated but sincere birthday greetings gift follows please call at office tell my secretary send duplicate cuttings of all reviews latest publication Simonetta last batch lost with portmanteau in train from Paris address pro tem Hotel Las Palmas Seville.
A.G. H.-W.

Miss Flight to Mr. Hope-Winter.

Brook Street
Feb. 2nd, 1893

Dear Mr. Hope-Winter,

Thank you very much indeed for your telegram of good wishes for my twenty-first birthday and for the beautiful white lace shawl—or is it a mantilla?—which arrived today. I greatly appreciate your kind thought.

I called at the office as requested but Miss Lane says she has no duplicate reviews of 'Simonetta' other than those kept in the files by the advertising manager, so I asked her to procure duplicates from all the most important papers and I hope you will soon receive them. I enclose these two taken from last week's Pall Mall Gazette and Daily Chronicle which I rescued from the boot cupboard. They are not very good are they? The critics do not seem to like what they call 'fictionized' biography.

I have long letters from Geraldine. I am afraid she is not very happy at Nice but I am sure she will benefit from the sun. I was rather worried about Sir Crispin's report which bears out what Miss Burbage suspected long ago, but we can only hope that the Riviera will help to cure her.

I have paid the tradesmen's bills for this month, and now have no money in hand for the servants' wages. May I again remind you that these are two months overdue, in consequence of which Charles and Mrs. Smith have left at a moment's notice. I have promoted the kitchen-maid in place of the cook and she is managing very well. I do not like to trouble you while you are on holiday, but I would be glad to have your cheque for £50 to pay the wages and avoid a general exodus of staff, all of whom with the exception of Larkin, Albert, the second footman, and Annie, the sewing-maid, are threatening to leave. Foster also tells me that there is a farrier's bill for one of the horses. I hope you will not think it presumptuous of me to suggest taking this opportunity of reducing the staff. Larkin says he is willing to do with one footman only, and the kitchen-maid tells me she can manage without extra help as you are away so much. It seems such a waste to have a houseful of servants doing nothing.

Your tailor called in person this morning with his account which I enclose and which you will see dates back to April 1890. He asked for your address which I refused to give him and he was most objectionable saying he would put the matter in the hands of his solicitors so perhaps you will see your way to satisfy him.

I send you also today's Times which gives the Queen's speech with the re-opening of Parliament. I thought you might like to see it, and the announcement of Captain Curran's engagement to a Miss Bourne which I have marked in case you wish to write and congratulate him.

There is no other news.

The weather is very mild for the time of year but there is a lot of influenza about.

Again many thanks for the lovely shawl.

Yours sincerely,
Peridot Flight.

P.S. I hope by now that you have recovered your port-manteau.

Adrian Hope-Winter to Miss Flight.

Hotel Las Palmas
Seville
(undated)

My dear Peridot,

I enclose herewith cheque for £50. Please to cash it at my bank and pay servants' and Foster's wages. Farrier can wait. Make such reductions in staff as you think fit but do not drive economy campaign too far. Reviews from Miss Lane received. Am shattered by the abusive criticisms of our first venture in fiction. The Odyssey's balance sheet for last year shows a disheartening deficit. Am likely to remain here for the next six weeks. Glutted with bull-fights, Murillos, and sun. Dined last night at house of famous matador. Extraordinarily interesting experience. Quite medieval. Dreadful food. Have bought a Goya, am sending it home. Hope it will arrive undamaged. Please instruct Curtis of Bond Street to hang it over mantelpiece in hall. Have sent cheque to tailor and rated him soundly for his impertinence in calling at the house.

I, too, have been anxious about Geraldine's condition but am informed by the doctor attending her at Nice that she is making marked improvement.

Have not written to Garth Curran. Consider marriage a case for condolence rather than congratulation.

It is a mantilla and you should wear it on your head sup-ported by a high tortoiseshell comb. I will bring you one on my return. You will look very piquante as a blonde Spaniard.

Adios.

Sincerely,
A.G. Hope-Winter.

P.S. No. Portmanteau not yet recovered from train. Set of pearl cuff-links and dress-studs, recently bought in Paris, lost with it and unfortunately uninsured.

A.G. H.-W.

So, it would seem that Miss Flight, in three years, has acquired not only poise and polish but a sense of responsibility toward her erratic employer to take upon herself the sole management of his domestic affairs. And although Lady Stilton could not be reconciled to her presence as a fixture in the house, she had come to accept her with something of the same unwilling resignation as one accepts a climate. Perhaps nothing could have indicated more the crux of Miss Flight's suzerainty than the introduction of Phyllis as a permanent inhabitant of the household.

It was in the autumn of 1891, that, shopping at Mantell's, Perry chanced upon Miss Hubbard in the Gloves. There had been previous encounters when an exchange of words was hampered by the all-pervasive watchfulness of Sign; but on this occasion, since Sign did not appear to be noticeably hovering, Perry was encouraged to inquire: "How is Mrs. P.?"

"Dead," Miss Hubbard, with shocking nonchalance, replied, and, in a whisper, she added: "Sign's looking. Be careful. Five and three quarters, modom, did you say?"

"Dead!" gasped Perry. "When?"

"Last week. . . . What colour, if you please, modom?"

"Grey. What did she die of?"

"Kids?" asked Miss Hubbard impassively.

"Anything—yes. Was it sudden?"

"Pneumonia. I've a nice line in kids."

Kids were produced and 'modom' provided with a small velvet cushion on which to rest her elbow while her fingers were squeezed into the glove.

"What's going to happen to Phyllis?"

"Put down. Her sister's there in charge. House to be sold. . . . These are a nice fit, modom. Two and eleven three."

"What do you mean—put down?"

"Sh! Not so loud. Or I have these in suède at three and elevenpence ha'penny."

"I must know," Perry urged in an agonized whisper, "what it was you said."

"Very chick. The latest thing from Paris. . . . Destroyed. The sister won't have her."

"Oh, *no*! They can't—she mustn't——"

"Miss Cheke," Miss Hubbard implored without moving her lips, "if you go on like this I'll be sacked."

"I'm dreadfully sorry—I forgot. I'll have this pair—and this," Perry said wildly. "When?"

"The vet's coming tomorrow to take her away. Will that be all, modom?"

"No!—yes—— It's too awful!"

"That will be six and elevenpence farthing, modom, if you please." Miss Hubbard tapped her pencil on the counter and called: "Sign!"

Sign, frock-coated, high-collared, majestic, approached to check the bill with a flourish of initials, while the customer, in a state of agitation, searched for her purse, flung down half a sovereign, and forgetful of her change and her purchase, fled the shop.

Across Oxford Street, under horses' heads, at imminent risk to her own, she ran, hailed a hansom and was driven back to Brook Street. Dashing past an astonished Charles and up the stairs, two at a time, she burst in on Geraldine to tell of the impending doom of Phyllis.

"But we can't," cried Geraldine, "let her be destroyed—the blessed heart! We'll have her here. Order the brougham and go and fetch her now—this very minute."

"I knew," sobbed Perry, "you'd say that. Only how shall we explain her to the Aunt?"

"I," Geraldine said grandly, "will explain her to the Aunt."

Yet neither she nor Perry gave a thought of explanation to the Uncle.

Thus Phyllis came to Brook Street and rapidly installed herself prime favourite of Larkin, and Geraldine's adored. Any objection the master of the house might have raised to her intrusion was circumvented by Miss Flight, who suggested that the dog, besides providing Geraldine with a new interest, would be an invaluable guard against burglars. "Only last week," was her apochryphal reminder, "the people opposite were burgled. And you know, Mr. Hope-Winter, that no thief will ever come near a house where there's a bulldog. They have the double lock, you see——" She prised open the massive jaws of Phyllis to insert a finger between the un-clenched teeth. "Once they get a grip they will never let go."

He shuddered. "Revolting. I'm covered in hairs. And why on earth they should call it the national breed, when it so much resembles some dreadful Chinese obscenity, I cannot con-ceive. All I beg is that you keep the creature away from me and on no account allow it in my rooms. But in view of recent burglaries, it might, as you say, be well to have a watch-dog in the house."

It had become his habit to depend upon Miss Flight to run his home, his staff, to present his cheques for signature, pay the tradesmen, attend to his correspondence, and generally to act as his confidential secretary. When he went abroad she bought his tickets, secured reservations in the trains and hotels, and, while strictly maintaining the relationship between them of employer and employed, had tacitly rendered her position in the household both secure and indispensable. To his tuition he attributed her metamorphosis from the 'pupa' stage to that of her fulfilled emergence. In these three years he had set himself, he said, 'to stimulate her motive and spiri-tual forces and to awaken her appreciative consciousness'.

She was not slow to learn.

Accompanied by Geraldine she would be taken on tours of the British Museum, the National Gallery, and Wallace Collection. Leaving his niece to rest on a settee, Mr. Hope-Winter would conduct his willing pupil through countless treasure-halls where she came to know and recognize the Masters, before whom she stood spellbound. He gave her Vasari to study. She steeped herself in Pater. Her quick ear for music responded to the mannered cadence of his prose. From a surfeit of this she turned to the poets, read Swinburne aloud to Geraldine, but confessed to a preference for Browning. The book-shelves of Mr. Hope-Winter pro-vided discovery of Congreve, Wycherley, Fielding, Sterne, and Thackeray. Yet Dickens, scorned by Geraldine and not by her patron encouraged, was 'my favourite of all, and meant more to me than any Imaginary Portrait'.

To the house in Brook Street came notable acquaintances of Mr. Hope-Winter whom Geraldine and Perry would, on rare occasions, be privileged to meet. Among lesser lights—

authors, then unknown, and artists not yet recognized—we hear of the young Beardsley.

'. . . uncouth, unkempt, and so frail one wondered if his bones were made of egg-shells. He was very gay and laughed a lot. He wore a velvet jacket—not evening dress —and had lank greasy hair falling over his forehead. He did a drawing of me, in about five minutes, on a pad that he carried in his pocket. I have it still. Very decorative, slit-eyed, heavy lidded with a full-lipped pursed-up mouth. I can't believe I ever looked like that. Lord Reginald, Beardsley, and one or two others, a Mr. Harland—Henry Harland—were discussing a new quarterly to be produced in the following year. There was some argument about its title. Beardsley was to draw the cover design and one of them said—I think it was Harland—that he wanted it bound in white with black lettering, but Beardsley said, "Let it be yellow, and call it The Yellow Book. . . ."

To be followed by the Yellow Press, that supplied to the man in the street his demand for sensational news. The urge for individual expression was no longer confined to those 'precious' few, whose pursuit of experience called for 'madder music, stronger wine'.

From the ashes of mid-Victorian restriction arose the flaming Phoenix of the mid-'nineties, crowing infective exuberant triumph to the chorus of *Ta-ra-ra-boom-de-ay*. It was the trumpet-cry of freedom calling to life-tasters, poetasters, those who worked and those who didn't, and to all the peoples of a nation that, for half a century, had been held in thrall by Mrs. Grundy. She, too, was dying, shocked to her death by the woman cyclist who rode tandem and in bloomers, to be immortalized in music-halls as 'Daisy'. . . .

Every barrel-organ played it, street urchins yelled it, Captain Curran presented Geraldine with an Edison-Bell record of it for the phonograph he gave her as a parting gift on his return to India in April '94.

With him, on that spring morning, came Miss Bourne.

Perry, home from airing Phyllis in the Park, was introduced by Geraldine to 'my future cousin, Clara'.

Miss Bourne we find to be 'tall, elegantly dressed, hand-

5

some more than pretty, with dark frizzy hair, a good figure, but something too much of a bust'.

"So you," Miss Bourne said brightly, "are Geraldine's little companion."

"My friend," Geraldine corrected, with her eyes on the ceiling. "My greatest friend. My *only* friend."

"Oh? I thought——" What Miss Bourne may have thought was not uttered, for Phyllis, after having boisterously greeted Captain Curran, sidled doubtfully up to his lady, who exclaimed: "What a villainous looking animal! Go away, you horrid dog!"

"Bitch," murmured Geraldine.

"Well, really!" cried Miss Bourne.

"I always think," said Geraldine, still staring at the ceiling, "that it is an insult to the canine species to apply the word 'bitch' as a term of opprobrium to the female of *homo sapiens*."

With a lift of her eyebrows Miss Bourne remarked: "A word only fit for the kennels. For my part I have no use for any breed other than hounds."

So she hunts, thought Perry; one might have guessed as much. Her hands were large and capable; her back was straight. She would look well on a horse. A well-matched pair, she and Captain Curran. . . . He, fondling Phyllis, expertly went over her points to pronounce her: "A grand-headed bitch——" "Please, Garth!" implored 'Cousin Clara', while heedless of interruption he continued to extol the bone and body-shape of Phyllis. "She's a beauty, Geraldine. Where did you get her?"

"She isn't mine. She's Peridot's."

"She's ours, Captain Curran," Perry said, "we share her. She belonged to an old lady whom I knew, and when she died and we heard that Phyllis was to be destroyed——"

"Phyllis!" interjected Miss Bourne, much amused. "What a ridiculous name to give a dog."

"I have a bull-bitch in India," said Garth, "but nothing like so good a one as yours. You ought to show her."

And now Miss Bourne's eyebrows were lowered to meet across her finely arched nose. "I didn't know you had a bull-dog, Garth."

"Did you not? Well, by the time you come out I may have half a dozen. She's been mated."

"How disgusting! I couldn't possibly live in a house full of bulldogs. Nasty slobbery things!"

A moment's hushed constraint fell upon the company; then, leaving Captain Curran, Phyllis leisurely advanced upon Miss Bourne, while from somewhere deep within her came a growl.

"Get away—you repulsive froglike creature! But isn't it exactly like some grotesque Titanic frog?" appealed Miss Bourne. "I don't want you. I don't *like* you. Oh, look, it's dribbling all over me. Miss Flight, please to take your dog away." And, as from under her flounces she kicked out at Phyllis a shapely if somewhat large foot, the hem of her white-spotted foulard was caught in the bulldog grip. There was a rending of silk; the lady screamed, Phyllis aggressively pulled, and Perry, forestalling Captain Curran, rushed to grab the collar of and drag the much offended Phyllis from Miss Bourne.

"I am so dreadfully sorry—she wouldn't have hurt you. It was only," Perry unconvincingly apologized, "her play."

"*Play!*" was the hysterical rejoinder. "If you call it play to ruin my gown—nasty savage brute!"

"Phyllis," said Geraldine, "is peculiarly sensitive. She is also, as a much-vaunted beauty, rather vain. She would naturally object—but wouldn't you?—to being likened to a frog, even a Titanic one. Come, my heart, come here."

Her 'heart' with wriggles of delight at the commotion she had caused, came there, to offer an ingratiating paw.

"Such a savage brute," cooed Geraldine, "is this." She slipped her fingers into the panting mouth of Phyllis. "Look how she mauls me, Cousin Clara."

"And look," Miss Bourne bitterly retorted, "how she has mauled my gown."

"Garth," Geraldine told her serenely, "will buy you a new one."

"It happens," snapped Miss Bourne, "to *be* a new one."

Geraldine turned her head.

"You surprise me! I bought the same model three years ago—but you are always behind with the fashions in India, aren't you?"

"This," was the freezing reply, "is Worth's latest creation, bought a month ago in Paris and never worn until today.

Garth, take me back to the hotel. I shall have to change my dress. I cannot possibly lunch with Lady Stilton in this state."

"If you're lunching with my very dear Aunt," Geraldine advised, "you should have something solid to eat before you go. You look as if you have a healthy appetite, and you won't get much to satisfy it there. Must you really leave us? Such a pity the wedding is to take place in India. I had hoped to see you well and truly married at St. George's after such a long engagement, Cousin Clara. You don't mind me anticipating our relationship by calling you Cousin Clara, do you?"

With every indication of minding very much, Miss Bourne replied: "I think we could dispense with the formality of 'Cousin' as there is so little difference in our ages, Geraldine."

"So *little* difference!" Geraldine echoed in highest amaze. "Oh, dear!" she clapped a hand to her mouth. "*Do* forgive me. I was under the impression—but being so short-sighted—and without my glasses——" She was in palpable confusion.

"Garth!" urged Miss Bourne in mild frenzy, "are you coming?" And she made, in some haste, for the door, followed by Perry, repeating apologies.

"Pray, Miss Flight, do not allude to the matter again. The damage is done. That ferocious dog of yours should be kept under proper control in a kennel—not in the drawing-room."

"It isn't," Geraldine called after her, "the drawing-room. It's my private sitting-room, my lair, my den—my *dar*ling!" This to Phyllis, who had got upon her feet, prepared to stalk the exit of Miss Bourne. "Of *course* we're not a frog. We're the loveliest thing God ever created—except me. Good-bye, dear Cousin Clara. You should keep rabbits."

Perry returned.

"Geraldine, you are naughty!"

"Am I, Garth, naughty? How silent you are, and how glum! Are you cross with me? But she needn't have been so beastly about Phyllis, and I'm sure she's years older than I—and older than you, too, I should think. Won't you kiss me good-bye? She can't grudge me a last farewell. God bless you. *Bon voyage*, and a happy one. I wish——"

He stooped and kissed her forehead.

"What," he asked her, "do you wish?"

"Only nothing. Only . . . something Montmorency and I

have often wished together. Just a joke between us, or a dream. But not a dream about ourselves, a dream for you." She smiled up at him, wet-eyed. "Go to your lady now. She's waiting."

Perry, too, was waiting at the open door to say: "Good-bye, Captain Curran. May I also wish you"—her throat closed—"a happy voyage."

He took her hand and held it fast, looking down into her eyes.

"Take care," he said, "of Geraldine."

"You know I will."

*   *   *

Spring blossomed into summer with some rejoicing at the birth, on June 23, of a Prince and future King, son of the Duke and Duchess of York.

If there were those who unfavourably compared the turgid congratulatory address of the Prime Minister, Lord Rosebery, with the dynamic thunderings of his predecessor, now retired to a life of literary leisure and the chopping down of trees, their voices went unheard in the almost unanimous applause of the majority. Only one inapposite protest, reported as 'airing republican views', was offered by Mr. Keir Hardie, who, with John Burns, and for the first time in Parliament's history, re-presented the 'New Socialism', self-styled 'Labour'.

On July 6, at White Lodge, Richmond, the child was baptized with an impressive string of names beginning with Edward and ending with David. His great-grandmother, the Queen, who attended the christening, was accorded an enthusiastic welcome as she drove through Richmond Town. That diminutive, silver-haired, and to her people, of late, so familiar a figure was, in her life's sunset, come into her own, the hearts of her subjects in whom imagination warmed to the reminder of a little girl saying at the age of twelve, 'I will be good.'

And what did she think of this shocking New Age superimposed on the shades of the past? What did she think of the New Social Consciousness, or of that swiftly approaching epochal reform, Women's Suffrage? . . . 'The Queen is most anxious to enlist every one who can speak or write, in checking this mad wicked folly of Women's Rights . . . with all its attendant horrors on which her poor feeble sex is bent. . . .

It is a subject that makes the Queen so furious that she cannot contain herself.'

Thus in 1870 was Majesty outraged; but in the 'nineties she had to contain herself, to shut her eyes to the awful sight of women riding bicycles in—knickerbockers! To shut her ears to the vulgar *vox populi* echo of *Ta-ra-ra-boom-de-ay*, while within her royal fortress she upheld her standard of inflexibility toward the smallest or greatest diversion from the rigid path of duty, thanking God in His Great Mercy for Mr. Gladstone's resignation. . . But still we had these dreadful strikes.

First, the coal strike when four hundred thousand men were out; and then the hansom cabmen who, on May 15, 1894, had ceased to drive. For a month London's streets were emptied of their hansoms, except for the few privately owned, until on June 14, the Home Secretary, Herbert Asquith, one of Gladstone's recent finds, settled the dispute—to the advantage of the drivers.

After the cab strike came another, and more disruptive, coal strike in Scotland, which lasted for seventeen weeks. It was a year of unrest, to close in disaster, when the North Western express from Manchester to Euston crashed into a goods train at Chelford. Thirteen were killed, sixty injured, some of whom died later, among them Father Curran, brother of Garth.

Visiting a monastery in Lancashire, he had taken the ill-fated train from Manchester to London *en route* for the Vatican. "So that," said Geraldine, "brings Garth one step nearer to the morgue—of Donaghmore."

She could only just remember her cousin John, she said, before he went into retreat. There had been a sister between him and Garth, killed out hunting at the age of seventeen. "Did I ever tell you? . . ." And with gusto she told of the legend in her family, how that some four hundred years ago one of her ancestors fell foul of a witch—'a beautiful young one'—who bore him a girl-child, and who, when he sickened of her and her evil works, was handed over to the priests, tried and found guilty of traffic with the devil, and burned for her sins at the stake. "And while she sizzled," Geraldine related to a doubting Perry, "she cursed the Curran, yelling out above the roar of flames that all the daughters of the

house of Donaghmore would henceforth be misfortuned. And
it worked! Our women have always been unlucky. One was
born a hunchback, another deaf and dumb; one drowned herself in the lake for unrequited love, and then there was Deirdre,
'the Desired', as they called her. *She* gave birth to a litter of
puppies——"

"Geraldine!"

"Well, it's true—and now there's me."

And, although accustomed to Geraldine's romancing,
Perry shivered. In these last months she had seen, and feared
to see, the fevered sunken brilliance of those eyes, the in-
exorable wasting of that fair young body. . . .

'She was so thin that one could count her ribs. Her hands,
more than ever restless, were almost transparent, her fingers
always plucking at her thumbs. Yet she seldom now had
brainstorms. She was growing up. "I have put away
childish things," she would say, "but I'll never desert
Montmorency. . . ." On her twenty-first birthday she was
in highest spirits. We had a cake with twenty-one candles,
and all the servants were invited to her sitting-room, each
to be given a slice, and Phyllis too, who gobbled hers whole
and was sick. In the evening Mr. Hope-Winter brought
Marcus Sankey, Lord Reginald, and one of the new poets,
Ernest Dowson, to see her, whom Mr. Hope-Winter introduced to us as "the Pierrot of the Minute". He was an
elderly young man with very dirty nails and, I think, a trifle
drunk. We had champagne and after his fifth glass Mr.
Dowson told Geraldine in a slightly slurred voice that he
was "desolate an' sick of an old passion, an' hungry for the
lips o' my desire. . . ." Mr. Hope-Winter's present to her
was a little gold watch with her initials in diamonds to pin
on her dress with a diamond bow. The next day she put me
in a fright by saying she had made her Will. "For you never
know," she said, and quoted Victor Hugo. "We are all
under sentence of death with an indefinite reprieve." She
said she had left me the watch and her pearls—and everything she had, except her income of which, now that she
was twenty-one, she had full control. but it was only hers
for life unless she married, and she made me and Annie
witness her signature. So then I felt I ought to make my

Will, and I did, and left her my peridot ring having nothing
else to leave; but I wouldn't let her witness it, for I knew
that no one named in a Will as beneficiary is legally allowed
to act as witness.

Mr. Hope-Winter had arranged to go to New York
that autumn, and we, with Miss Lavinia, were to be sent to
the South of France. "At any rate," said Geraldine, "she'll
be a slightly lesser evil than the Aunt. . . ." But a week or
two before we were due to leave, Geraldine had influenza.
It left her with a cough, and something worse. I thought her
nose was bleeding, but it wasn't from her nose. . . . Another doctor came in consultation with Sir Crispin and they
said she wasn't well enough to travel.

I had my bed moved into her dressing-room so that I
could hear her if she wanted me. Phyllis was her shadow.
Nothing, not even a bone, would budge her from the
couch by day, and she slept—and snored—in the bedroom
at night. And then, if I heard Geraldine tossing and turning
and talking away to herself, I would go in and light the
lamp and read to her until she went to sleep. She used to
love the stories in the Yellow Book—the first three volumes
were published that year. The art editor was Beardsley,
whom Wilde claimed to have discovered, but I am sure he
never did, for genius discovers itself. And what a galaxy of
rising stars supported him! The young Max Beerbohm,
just down from Oxford, with his "Defence of Cosmetics",
and his "Note on George the Fourth". Henry James was
a regular contributor, and John Davidson, whose "Ballad
of a Nun", in the October issue, she would have me read
to her over and over again.

"Poor little nun," she would say, repeating the lines—
she knew most of them by heart—"who, 'dug her nails
deep in her breast, sobbed, shrieked'—that's so like me—'a
fledgling flying from the nest'. And shall I too, 'life's dearest
meaning probe, and taste of love at last'? Perhaps some
day."

In her sitting-room above the mantelpiece was the Whistler
portrait. It used to be in Mr. Hope-Winter's study until
she asked to have it hung where she could always see herself. But the pictured face is nothing so lovely as hers. . . .'

Propped on her pillows in her cheerful room with the dusk outside, the warmth within, and the lamplight in a glory on her hair, she would sing, tunelessly, the latest songs that Perry played for her, breaking off with interruption: "Those damned doctors! It's idiotic to say I'm not well enough to travel. I'm perfectly well. They're only trying to make a case of me. . . ." While Perry, in silent agony, with sight love-sharpened, watched the remorseless pursuit of those micro-scopic death-hounds that hunted her by day, by night, and hoped, when hope was gone, that the doctors were mistaken. . . . 'She seemed to be so happy, full of plans for the future, always talking of the fun we would have together in the coming year. . . .'

Autumn drifted into winter and the last brittle leaves of the plane trees in the Park were torn from their branches to whirl in the mad joyous dance of the winds; and then came snow, the falling of a soft white shroud upon those lawns, bereft of Fashion now, and on the roof-tops of the city, and on a Mayfair street where straw was laid to dull the sound of hoofs and carriage-wheels.

"The air," said Geraldine, "is full of whispers. Do you remember. . . ?"

"Remember what, my darling?"

"That first time you came to me when I said we'd go to-gether you and I and Montmorency? You'll never leave me, will you? I won't be left alone."

"You'll not be left alone. I'll be with you . . . always."

And while shapes of shadows came and went unrecognized, and voice spoke, unheard; or when the sky, snow-driven, and the stars, the reeling universe, and time itself dissolved in the struggle for a single breath, so, in that darkened room beside the curtained bed, a girl and a dog kept faithful guard to the close of a short life's day.

*   *   *

"I was sure," said the Aunt, "that you would understand, and, of course, while Miss Burbage remains in the house, which she will certainly do until my brother arrives from New York, you are welcome to stay. I need hardly tell you, Miss

5*

Flight, how much we appreciate your service to my—to our—beloved niece."

And to her tearless eyes Lady Stilton carefully applied a black-edged handkerchief.

Perry's lips opened but they spoke no word; only the slightest movement of her head denoted stunned assent to her dismissal.

A bleak shaft of sunlight struggled through the three tall windows of the drawing-room where, for the first time in six days, the lowered blinds had been raised. The last of the snow had melted and the straw had been cleared from the road. Once again the sound of wheels and horses' hooves were heard, and in the house a stir of steps and muted voices as the servants went about their work. All was as it had been, and, for one, as it would never be again.

When, from that quiet death in the empty dawn, she had sought the haven of her solitude, and despite the dreaded knowledge that soon the end must come, it was as if by this most cruel annihilation her own life, too, was ended. To the very young five years is an eternity, and she, whose self-forgetful devotion had gained for her a fierce absorbing love, was now possessed by a turbulent revolt against those unseen forces that, with such merciless precision, had struck to deprive her of a friend—'My greatest friend, my only friend. . . .' So would she dwell upon those cool clear words that Geraldine had spoken before the hidden enemy advanced to take and slay.

Again and again, unbelieving, she returned to stand beside that strange unstirring form, dimly outlined beneath its stark white covering; to fix in memory those features, carved to a cameo fineness, on which still lingered the look of a smitten child, pale as the lilies she had laid between the hands. . . . And now she was gone. They had carried her away, to dig her deep in the ground and read over her, as earth was shovelled on the ghastly box, of Life and Resurrection.

To the small lonely figure in its brand new black, drawn apart from the others at the graveside, the grim horror of the moment passed before her eyes, uncomprehended, without substance. When, once before, she had encountered death, she had not been called upon to follow the last of Mr. Cheke to its finality, a dark worm-ridden hole in the ground. She had been ordered to stay behind and make ready the funeral feast; but now she must stand and watch, expecting, half hoping, that Geraldine would rise to share with her this agony, or mock at it. Could she see? Did she know? But of course she couldn't know—she was nothing—'dust into dust, and under dust to lie, sans song, sans'—what is it?—'sans singer and sans end'. . . . As through a suffocating haze she saw the solemnly fixed faces of the relatives, some known and some unknown to her. General Curran, father of Garth, hastily summoned from Ireland, florid, bewhiskered, a man of bulk and stature in a crape-bound topper and a suit of rusty black; Miss Lavinia, mannishly tailored, square-booted; Annabel Stilton—and why was she there?—looking like one of the funeral horses with black plumes springing from a silly little hat. Sir Frederick, surreptitiously wiping his monocle and blowing through his nose a trumpet blast to wake the—don't! The Aunt, discreetly sobbing behind black redundant veils. . . . And suddenly a paroxysm of hysteria attacked her and she writhed in convulsive silent laughter, while around her the dwarf forest of white monuments and crosses receded, revolved, pressed closer in a slow and awful jig, until the earth, yawning open, dragged her down and down and down . . . to Geraldine.

"Too great a strain for her," she heard. "I'll take her home."

And home, by Miss Lavinia in the brougham, she was taken, plied with salvolatile and put to bed.

That was yesterday; and today the Aunt had sent for her to offer, as reward for service rendered, a whole quarter's salary instead of the usual month's wages to be given in lieu of notice, and which her ladyship herself would undertake to pay Miss Flight in the absence of Mr. Hope-Winter. "For he cannot possibly return from New York until next week at the earliest," said Lady Stilton. "So that will give you time to make your arrangements to leave here before his arrival."

"I scarcely think so, Lady Stilton," was the soft-toned answer. "Mr. Hope-Winter will be here today."

"Today!" The Aunt's head jerked up as if pulled by a wire. "Oh, no, Miss Flight, you are mistaken. Mr. Hope-Winter did not receive my cable until the morning after my poor dear niece"—and again she mopped her eyes—"passed away."

"But he received my cable," Perry said distinctly, "a week before that."

"*Your* cable?" Lady Stilton's elevated eyebrows almost disappeared beneath the royal fringe. A stabbing glance accompanied the query: "Do you mean to say you cabled to my brother without first consulting me?"

"Not wishing to alarm you, Lady Stilton, I thought it best to prepare him for the worst. He wired me this morning from Southampton to say he would be here this afternoon."

"Southampton!" came the parrot-repetition. "Why was I not told of this? Show me," demanded her ladyship, "the telegram."

Perry left the room and returned with the pink slip of paper, snatched from her hand by Lady Stilton, who, at arm's length, read:

" 'Booked last minute cancellation cabin Campania morning your cable received landed Southampton this A.M. greatly distressed hope better news on arrival'— So he could not have *had* my cable," declared Lady Stilton. "He had already left. It takes at least ten days to get here even on the fastest boat. This puts us in a quandary. Miss Burbage intends to go back in a day or two. I don't want to hurry you away, Miss Flight, for I appreciate that you will have to find a lodging. Perhaps your relatives——?"

"I have no relatives, Lady Stilton."

"Indeed? Poor girl," was the brisk reply. "But nevertheless I cannot, in all justice to yourself, permit you to remain unchaperoned in a bachelor establishment. It would not be circumspect. You *must* see that, Miss Flight."

Miss Flight modestly lowered her eyes to the carpet.

"While in your capacity as companion to my niece," continued Lady Stilton, on a slightly higher note, "it was excusable, though never approved—I may tell you—by me."

"Of which," murmured Perry, still apparently engrossed with the pattern of the Aubusson, "I am perfectly aware."

"Solely on account of your youth, Miss Flight. In all other respects you have given every satisfaction, and should you desire a reference for future employment, I will be only too pleased to supply it. In fact," her ladyship graciously offered, "I will write you a reference now."

At a Louis Seize bureau she seated herself, penned a few hasty lines and read aloud:

"'To All Whom It May Concern: Miss Flight for the last three years,' or"—her ladyship asked, looking up—"is it four?"

"Almost-five, Lady Stilton."

"Dear me! So long as that? Five, then. I'll alter it—'years, has been employed as nurse companion to my niece, Miss Curran, now deceased, for which reason alone Miss Flight is leaving her present situation. I can thoroughly recommend her as scrupulously honest, sober, conscientious, and eminently suited to the care of the young or old.' I have purposely avoided bringing in my brother's name, for you will find it easier to obtain employment, coming as it were, from me. There!" With ineffable benevolence she bestowed upon Perry the sheet of tinted paper, and immediately withdrew it. "Oh! But I forgot. The address. I must head this reference with my own address. It would never do to apply to Mr. Hope-Winter, since I"—she gave a suitably hushed laugh—"have perjured myself in signing my name as your employer." She made the necessary alteration, slipped the note in an envelope, left it unsealed, and added: "Should any prospective employer wish for a *personal* reference I will most gladly give it."

Perry thanked her.

"That then," said Lady Stilton, "is settled. You will leave here, much to our regret—and I speak for my brother as well as for myself—when Miss Burbage returns to Somerset, which will, I think, be the day after tomorrow."

"Which you *hope*," rasped a voice at the door, "will be the day after tomorrow."

And Miss Lavinia, who unobserved had entered, sat firmly down in the nearest chair as if she never meant to rise from it again.

"I am here," she declared, "and here I stay until I wish to go. This," she pointed a finger at Perry, "needs attention. Nerves upset. On the edge of a collapse. Weeks of it. Night and day. Single-handed. Disgraceful. Why didn't you call in a nurse? Put upon and flog a willing horse—and there you are."

At this staccato volley, Lady Stilton, as if shot at by a catapult, recoiled, to recover and retort: "I must, Lavinia, ask you to restrain yourself. Miss Flight has already had enough to worry her without your——"

"Fiddle!" interjected Miss Lavinia. "Don't talk to me. I know."

What she may have known was by Lady Stilton's frigid silence disregarded, while Perry pacifically ventured: "Excuse me, Miss Lavinia, but would you be so good as to tell me when you *do* propose to go so that"—she glanced askance at Lady Stilton—"I can make arrangements to go too."

"Go?" demanded Miss Lavinia. "Go where?"

"I"—Perry swallowed a rock in her throat—"anywhere."

"I have explained to Miss Flight," Lady Stilton said, with icy patience, "that it is obvious she cannot stay here indefinitely. Adrian returns today, as I have only just this minute heard, and even you, Lavinia, with your advanced ideas," scathingly dismissed by Lady Stilton's shrug, "must see that it would be most improper for Miss Flight to remain alone in the house with him."

"And an army of servants?" rejoined Miss Lavinia. "Fudge! What's that," she asked sternly of Perry, "you have in your hand?"

That in her hand was her ladyship's reference, mutely passed in its open envelope to Miss Lavinia. She read it, plucking at her chin, keenly eyed the pale Perry, and demanded: "Have you handed in your notice?"

"No, Miss Lavinia. Lady Stilton——"

"I," struck in her ladyship, "suggested to Miss Flight——"

"Do you want to leave?" interposed Miss Lavinia, addressing herself exclusively to Perry, who falteringly said she hadn't thought about it—yet.

"Then don't think about it now. Off with you to bed. Fainting fits and what not. Valerian for you." Miss Lavinia pointed to the door. "Go on."

"But she can't," objected Lady Stilton, "go to bed in the middle of the day. Adrian comes home this afternoon and she must see that all is ready to receive him. His room has not been slept in for three months. I trust the bed has been well aired, Miss Flight?"

"Yes, Lady Stilton."

"And don't," insisted Miss Lavinia, as if stone deaf to these remarks, "get up."

Thankfully Perry escaped, to find an anxious Larkin on the landing.

"It's the dog, Miss. If you could get her out of that room. She won't let anyone but you go near her. Always so gentle as a rule, but she's showin' her teeth and growling something vicious at Albert and me. Not that she means any harm by it, only it's 'eartbreakin' to see her laid down by the bed and not touching a morsel of food."

"Yes, Larkin, I know. Perhaps if I give it her——"

"I've tried her with tripe," Larkin said mournfully. "She's a glutton for tripe as a rule, but she won't look at it now."

"Beat up a couple of raw eggs, Larkin, and—is there any rump steak in the house?"

"I think so, Miss. If not I'll send out for some."

"Yes, do. Cut it up in small pieces. Don't cook it."

"Very good, Miss."

In the bedroom, left at Perry's orders as it had always been, with fresh flowers by the bedside and magazines and books upon the table, Phyllis lay stretched, her head on her paws and her eyes, watchfully unwinking, on the door. A feeble wag of a tail greeted Perry's entrance and her whispered: "Come, my love, come and have your dinner."

With a long sigh of dejection and a backward glance at the empty bed, Phyllis suffered herself to be led away. Gingerly she inspected the bowl of beaten eggs served to her by Larkin in the servants' hall and which, coaxed by Perry, she was at last induced to lap.

"I put a dash of brandy in it, Miss," said Larkin, "for to tell the truth I had my fears the dog would go too, the way she's been pinin'. Worse than she did for the old lady when she first come here."

"Yes. Bring the raw steak to my room and I'll feed her with it later, a little at a time."

A hovering footman appeared.

"Did she take the eggs, Miss?"

"Yes, Albert, thank you. Will you please to see to the fire in your master's bedroom?"

"Very good, Miss."

As she went up the stairs, followed by Phyllis, she heard, in an undertone, from Albert: "She don't look up to much herself," and from Larkin: "Feelin' it more than the whole lot of 'em together—her and the dog." . . . Soon to be thrown out, friendless and alone again; and what of Phyllis? She couldn't leave her here. She must go with her wherever it was—the day after to-morrow.

She would have to find a lodging. She had enough money to keep her until she found the right sort of place, but it would have to be where they liked dogs. She could advertise. 'Young lady accustomed to care of dogs will accept nominal salary on condition that her own bulldog'—no, better not say bull-dog, they might jib—'own pet dog, docile, house-trained, would be allowed.' Yes, she would have that inserted in *The Times* and *Morning Post* and if nothing came of it she would try the country papers. . . . Mechanically she inspected the bed-room of Mr. Hope-Winter to assure herself that fresh paper had been sprayed with his favourite Fleur de Lys perfume to deodorize the smell of moth-balls; then to the linen room, where she took from the press a pair of damask towels for his hands, and bath sheets for his body. . . .

"Excuse me, Miss."

"Yes, Annie?"

"Her ladyship wishes to speak to you, Miss. She's in Miss Geraldine's—in the sitting-room, Miss."

"Thank you, Annie. Put these in your master's bathroom will you, please?"

"Aren't you going to get a lay down, Miss? You look done up."

"I'm all right, thank you, Annie. I've left Phyllis in my bedroom. Don't let her out, will you?"

"No, Miss."

At the bureau in Geraldine's sitting-room was seated Lady Stilton, who, at Perry's entrance and without looking at her said: "The maid told me you had not yet gone to rest, Miss Flight. In going through Miss Curran's papers, for she evidently kept nothing under lock and key, I have found—this."

'This' was a sheet of foolscap open on the desk before her. If the expression of those unwavering dark-circled eyes, so steadily fixed on her own, may have caused Lady Stilton the briefest embarrassment, her next remark, forensically delivered, gave no sign of it. "The last Will and Testament of my poor dear niece, which I see was made the very day after she attained her majority."

"Yes, Lady Stilton."

"You are aware, then, of the existence of this Will?"

"I am."

"And I presume you are also aware of its contents?"

A faint little smile on Perry's closed lips was her sole answer to that.

"Miss Flight," rapped out her ladyship, "do you or do you not know that this Will leaves to you, unconditionally, all that Miss Curran—poor misguided child—had in her power to leave, including her pearls—her mother's—my dead sister's pearls? And her jewels—my sister's jewels, never worn by Geraldine and which in all justice should be mine? Miss Flight, I feel bound to tell you that in this most unnatural procedure—for it *is*," excitedly declared Lady Stilton, "unnatural that a young girl should even *think* of anything so morbid as her Will and on the very day after she had become legally responsible, that I detect here some unwarrantable influence. I am confident that my brother will endorse my views and take immediate steps to have this ridiculous document disproved."

"Lady Stilton," and although her smile stayed, Perry's eyes held in each a danger spark, "that Will is already disproved. You may not know it, but I did—when Geraldine asked me to witness it having said she was leaving me all her personal possessions—that the Will with my signature to it, which if you look you will see," hurriedly Lady Stilton turned the foolscap page, "is not worth," said Perry softly, "the paper it is written on. If I had chosen to exert what you believe to be my influence over Geraldine, I would have asked her to call another witness instead of myself, but I did not, and so—the Will is null and void."

A silence followed, and a sigh from Lady Stilton that might have been relief, quickly changed into a sob. "The poor darling! Always so thoughtful of others. But to be on the safe side," her ladyship said blandly, "we shall have to take legal advice on this matter, for if the Will is indeed worthless—and I hope you are right—as none of us, yourself least of all, I am sure, would wish to be involved in any tiresome proceedings—*if*, as I say, there *is* no Will, then our dear one has died intestate and the next of kin are, I believe, entitled to——Yes, Larkin?"

"Mr. Hope-Winter, my lady," said Larkin at the door, "has arrived."

In the corridor Perry was waylaid by Miss Lavinia who took her temperature, pronounced her in a fever and marched her off to bed where she lay in a stupor induced, she believed:

'. . . by the variety of medicines prescribed by Miss Lavinia. The predominant flavour of these, I remember, was garlic when not overpowered by something too awfully bitter, that must, I think, have been distilled from poppy-seed. For three days she kept me in bed dosed with liberal glasses of Burgundy and a noxious something called valerian. On the third day I told her I positively must get up and pack. "Pack?" she said, as if the word were new to her. "Yes," I said. "I've been given notice and will have to go. At once." And I began to tell her of my plans and how I'd settled in my mind to take a situation with people who would not object to Phyllis. And then, whether it was due to all the wine and physic I had taken, or the climax of my misery endured in that last week—I fell to crying, turning over on my face and sobbing out my heart to shake the bed. "Now, now!" cried Miss Lavinia, "this will never do. Bear up." I was borne up with her arm round my shoulders and a pill that sent me off to sleep again, and when I woke much refreshed and ashamed of my lapse, I found myself quite ready for my tea. Then, having hustled me out of bed, Miss Lavinia put me on the ottoman and told Annie she could set the room to rights. There were masses of flowers, roses and carnations, all about that I had not remembered seeing there before.

"Adrian sent you these," said Miss Lavinia—she always spoke of him to me as 'Adrian'. "He wants to come and see you." "What, here?" I said. "Why not?" she said. "You're decent enough, aren't you?" Yes, I supposed I was decent enough, in the pink satin dressing-gown Geraldine had given me, but I can tell you I didn't much want to see *him*, and hear his confirmation of my notice to leave. Still, I thought it best to know the worst and be done with this suspense. So in he came and I thanked him for the flowers. I thought his face looked rather pinched, and he had lost the ruddy glow beneath his tan. So he was

feeling something too—I hoped. He took my hand, and
I remember thinking that never before had I felt that soft,
almost womanish touch of his hand for more than half a
second at a time. But now he held it, saying in that tired
drawl of his, "My poor little Peridot, what have they been
doing to you?" "Doing to her?" Miss Lavinia took him
up sharp, " *You* ought to know, and if that's all you have to
say to her——" "It's not all, nor half of all I have to say
to her," he interrupted with his crooked smile, "if I may
speak to her alone." "And a nice state she's in," said Miss
Lavinia, "for you to speak to her alone. Where's your
sense?"

His sense—and something more—was in his eyes that
seemed to pierce right through me. I wondered what he'd
heard from the Aunt and if he too believed I had used my
'unwarrantable influence' in the matter of Geraldine's
Will. But whatever he had heard had not, apparently, turned
him against me, for: "There's this I can say," and he said
it with a stare, "that unless you wish to leave me I refuse
to let you go."

From Miss Lavinia came a sound between a chuckle and
a snort. "You hear?" she said. "So now it rests with
you. . . ." '

An ambiguous position and one in which she felt herself
to be the guest of charity, for while nothing more of her departure was discussed by him or Miss Lavinia, she could not
help but think that they together had conspired to force on
her the option of handing in her notice.

Since Mr. Hope-Winter's return she had happily seen
nothing of his sister. Miss Lavinia accounted for her absence
as the result of 'words' between herself and 'Hilda', that took
place at a family conclave attended by General Curran. He,
jointly with his elder brother, were, as next of kin, entitled,
under Geraldine's intestacy, to all her personal effects. It
seemed there had been something of a 'tussle' on the part of
the Aunt, who, having hotly contested the General's claim,
was routed—"And in no mean terms," related Miss Lavinia,
"by me. So that's the way of it. Carrion. They bury their
young dead to dig it up and pick its bones. By the way, the
General has offered you her watch in token of his gratitude

for your care of her. The pearls will go to his son's wife. The jewels to be sold and the proceeds divided between the General and his poor devil of a brother. Not a bean to rub together among the whole lot of 'em. Barrack of a place. Should be pulled down."

"Did you say," Perry asked tonelessly, "to his son's—wife?"

And Miss Lavinia nodding said: "Beer. That young man's done well for himself. I'm told she'll have fifty thousand. You look peaked. Are you taking your tonic?"

"Yes, Miss Lavinia."

"Where are you off to?"

She was off to her room, where from a cupboard she took out a shoe; her eyes dwelled on it a moment, then, with a one-sided smile, she rang the bell.

"Yes, Miss?"

"Put this in the dustbin, Annie. It's one of a pair. I've lost the other."

"Yes, Miss—but what a pity. Are you sure you've not mislaid it? Perhaps it'll turn up."

"No, it will never turn up . . . now. It doesn't matter."

Nothing mattered any more. She had come to a dead end, must get away, out of here and start again. She saw herself, solitary, small, dwindling in a vacuum of nothingness, unwanted. This house! . . . But how without Geraldine could she endure this house? All very well for him and Miss Lavinia to shift responsibility on her—'unless you wish to leave'. Politely. As if he would care a brass farthing if she went—jolly glad to be rid of her. She had not been brought here to look after him—besides he was only at home six months in the year, and if he went on at this rate he wouldn't have a home at all, losing money hand over fist with that tomfool Odyssey, and overdrawn two thousand at the bank, as she had seen by his pass-book. Well, why not—if he left it lying about for anyone to see? Larkin and Albert too, she wouldn't wonder. And those two beauties of his, Lord Reginald and Sankey, always sponging on him. He would never be able to keep this place going if he went on spending money right and left. What did he want with such a huge house and all these servants, anyway? He ought to take one of those flats. But that was his look-out, not hers. She had her own life to live, such as it was.

'Dyzee Dyzee gimmeyeranswer do . . .'

From the street below rose up the shrill not untuneful
treble of a passing errand boy. She went to the window; the
lamps, just lighted, circled the pewter-coloured dusk like a
necklace of gold on grey velvet.

'I'm arfcryzy'

There shouldn't be much difficulty in finding another post,
if it were not for Phyllis. 'Scrupulously honest, sober'—but
after all, what was she but a sort of upper servant? Supposing
no one would take her with Phyllis? All right, my love, we'll
stick together, even if it's selling matches. She wondered what
had happened to Florrie . . .

'It won'be a stylish marriage
I can'terforder carriage'

Oh, shut up! . . . The curtain rings rattled noisily to her
impatient jerk as she pulled them close, enfolding the firelit
room in a warm flickering glow. She lit the gas, sat at her desk,
took up a pen and wrote:

Dear Mr. Hope-Winter,
    When you were kind enough to tell me. . . .

No, that wouldn't do. He had been kind enough to tell her
nothing more than she must tell to him. She crumpled the
sheet of paper and tossed it in the fire. Very well. Get it over.
Here goes. . . .
In his library Mr. Hope-Winter, scanning the pages of a
manuscript, was asked by Miss Flight if he could spare her a
moment?
"By all means." He got up to place a chair. "Won't you
sit down?"
"No, thank you." What she had to say was best said
standing.
"I have here," he told her, "a first novel sent me by Mr.
Sankey, who urges me to publish it. Admittedly trash, but, in
view of this deplorable financial year, we have decided to in-

clude in future lists a modicum of fiction. This would seem to supply all the required ingredients in the popular Ouida tradition. You are not, I believe, a voracious reader of the modern novel?"

"No. Geraldine and I——" She looked vaguely about her. The familiar room, its quiet opulence of well lined bookshelves and walls adorned with pictures, reflecting, not their owner's taste alone but something of his abstract, almost medieval impassivity, was, as she saw it now, like the setting for a play; herself the chief performer, foolishly smirking, eyes to the gallery, speaking her lines, unrehearsed . . . "When you came back a week ago you were kind enough to tell me—you remember?—that unless I wished to leave of my own accord, you would not want me to go—but I feel the time has come——" How awfully Gennish! 'Ai feel the taime has come'—a stumbling, lamentable, unconvincing bleat—"for me," she said, "to make a change."

He was watching her carefully, noting with aloof satisfaction the primrose pallor of her hair, the faintly tinted whiteness of her skin; those eyes, crystal green, provocatively hidden beneath the lowered lids.

"This seems," and he was smiling as if from out of a memory, "to be the repetition of something I have heard before. If you wish to go I have no right to prevent your going—no right," he repeated half to himself. "But if it is change you need, and that you want, and which, under the circumstances, is quite feasible"—she thought she detected relief in his tone—"you shall have it."

"Thank you, Mr. Hope-Winter." Her throat contracted. "When would it be convenient for me to——"

"When?" The ticking of a long-case clock was the only sound in a pause that drew her eyes warily to his. Their fixed intensity gave to the careless repetition of that monosyllable a disproportionate significance. "When? As soon as may possibly be. I will take you to Firenze." His words seemed automatically to follow the measured seconds of the clock. "I want above all things to take you to Firenze—your spiritual home. But if so—you understand?—I shall have to marry you."

Another leaden moment passed. Then:

"Marry," she whispered, out of breath. "Did you say——?"

"I did." And although his voice was cool, a show of colour tinged his face. "There is of course the disparity of age to be considered. I am twenty years older than you——" A whirr and six chiming strokes splintered, gratefully, a claustrophobic tension—"yet in some inexplicable way, God alone knows how, you have become of vital importance to me."

Her eyes, dilated, clung to his while she strove to tabulate clearly in her mind, and in a flash, the incalculable possibilities, beyond anticipation, beyond all comprehension, offered to her for her taking—here and now.

"I've done my best to——" Her very lips were white, uncontrollably trembling. She steadied them. No! Not to 'oblige'. A spasm of laughter, unmirthful, surged within her and was instantly repressed. Geraldine! What would Geraldine have said if she. . . ?

"It may be your unusual receptivity that appeals, allures, decides me." He had turned from her, was pacing the room and spoke as if he argued with two voices, one against the other. "Or just that something rare and epicene in you that defies your womanhood. For you are not a woman, Peridot." He came to her and took her hands and held them. His blue fastidious stare raked her top to toe. "You are half girl, half Ganymedes, but child though you are, you have managed to wind yourself into my life that I cannot do without you. I have carefully considered my case and yours. The advantages to be gained on both sides are fairly equal, yet again— and in all justice to yourself—I must insist on the difference in our ages."

"It is not"—her hands twisted convulsively in his—"not just the difference in our ages——" Her heart was hammering against her chest; she wondered could he hear it? "Not your age. That's the least of it—but how could I fulfil my position as your——?"

"Wife?" A smile edged his prompting. "I think—most admirably. For over twenty years I have avoided marriage. I am not what is called 'a marrying man', for the reason that no woman I have ever met could give me what I want, and think to find in you."

"Mr. Hope-Winter," she freed her hands and, in a flat little voice tuned to the dispassionate tone of his, "you speak," she said, "of advantages on both sides, but as far as I can see it the whole advantage would be mine.   What can I give you in exchange for—" her dazed glance travelled round the room —"all this?"

"What can you give me?"   He gathered her closely into his arms, "you can give me," he said, "all this."

SIX

'I have come to life again, appropriately, on St. Valentine's day, but I haven't had a Valentine from him. I bought
this journal in Paris as a Valentine from me to me. I shall
have lots to write in it now. When—is it only six weeks ago?
I wrote the last entry in my journal for 1894, "Geraldine
died today", something of me died with her. I seemed to
have lost my identity, if ever I had an identity. According
to Adrian—I shall never get used to calling him Adrian—we
have in each one of us hundreds of idiot voices, all shouting
"This is I", and not until we know ourselves to be the
masters of our Ego can we say "I am that I am". But what
am I? To all intent and purpose the wife of Mr. Hope-
Winter travelling with her husband in a reserved compartment of the Rome Express from Paris to Florence on her
honeymoon. Dash! It's almost impossible to write with
the train tearing along at about fifty miles an hour, and my
stylo jigging all over the place. He's asleep. Light from the
window falls full on his face, sunk in the sable collar of his
coat. I am wearing sables too, stole, muff, fur cap to match
and a mole velvet ensemble. Every stitch I have on, over
and under, has been bought by him in Paris. He chose
them—he and Worth together. I had no say in the
matter. "Mais, Madame must be dressed in a style tout
simplement. Madame a l'air ravissante d'une petite demie-
vierge." I've learned quite a lot of French in Paris. It seems
to come naturally, somehow. Of course G. and I used to
practise speaking French together. She was fluent having
had Mlles since she was a baby, and I had a fairly good
grounding myself at Miss Genn's. But Worth doesn't
happen to be French. He's a British born cockney and
speaks English with a perfect French accent, complete with
153

gestures. "La beauté de Madame is of a spring fleur."
"Crocus-limbed"—this from A. "Mais!" squeaked Monsieur, rolling his eyes at me, "parfaitement!"

A. has bought me a trousseau, a dozen of everything, trimmed with real lace and so flimsy you can see through them. Very suggestive. And three pairs of stays made for me by Worth for the new gowns. Half of them aren't ready yet, they'll have to be sent on to Florence. I have a half-hoop of diamonds, a ruby and diamond bracelet, and bottles of perfume enough to scent a harem. He has a passion for perfume. Our bathroom at the Meurice stank of scent. Not mine. Oh, yes, and the pearls. I was almost forgetting the pearls. A double row as large as peas. I daren't think what they must have cost. Such a waste and I much prefer my coral necklace.

As I watch him now asleep he is like one of those Elizabethan effigies one sees on tombs in old churches. His sable collar might almost be a ruff. He doesn't look his age. He is terribly sensitive about his age. He put it down as 35 on the marriage certificate but he's actually 43. It has just struck me that this is the first time I've seen him asleep. We had communicating rooms in Paris and after I behaved so disgracefully that first awful night at the hotel in Dover, he left me and slept in his dressing-room. Well, what could he expect? No one ever told me. Geraldine did sometimes hint at things when we read Poems and Ballads but I'm sure she didn't know much about it. How *could* we know, living such an isolated life and never meeting any men except those friends of his that aren't men but hybrids. All I knew was that we would have to share a bed. At least I went prepared for that. I think Miss Lavinia tried to tell me something the day before, when she spoke of my "marital duties. Intimate relationship. Butterflies. Flowers. Adam and Eve." (And a lot of help that was!) "Read the marriage service. With my body I thee worship." But I wasn't even given the enlightenment as offered by the Church, being married in front of the Registrar as it had to be kept from the Aunt. Sir F., sworn to secrecy, came to the wedding—if you can call it a wedding—"put the ring on your wife's finger" and there we were driving off in the brougham to the station. As I got into the carriage, Sir

F. slipped a cheque for a hundred pounds into my hand—
"to buy fal-lals". I banked it for a rainy day. You never
know, with A. spending money like water. He has no money
sense at all. I'll bet he's being rooked right and left over that
publishing concern of his.

Am trying to read Miss Lavinia's wedding present—
Mill's Logic—I ask you!—beautifully bound in red leather,
and a portable medicine chest as well. Left it at home.
Couldn't cart that about with me all over the Continent.
Poor Freddie, having to break the news to his dear wife.
He wrote us in Paris that she "cut up rough"—I can imagine
and that we'll probably be hearing from her soon. We did.
Four pages of it, forwarded from Br. St. telling A. he was
out of his mind, that I am a low cunning little adventuress
who from the first had set my cap at him, and *how* his poor
father would turn in his grave if he could know of the dis-
honour his son had brought on his name by marrying a nobody out of a slum (well, it wasn't quite a slum but very
nearly) and she ended up by saying that as long as she lived
she would never see or speak to him again. I wish I could
believe her—but can't help seeing her point. Let's be fair.
It's no use pretending that the advantages of which he
spoke when he proposed (never was so cool and calculating
a proposal—"I have considered both my case and yours"—)
are equal. They are not. The advantage is all on my side.
I'm not such a fool that I can't see I've made what is called
a good match. But what does he get out of it? I *am* a nobody. She's right. I had to tell him my legal name—and
other things—when he bought the licence. He said he had
known it all along. From Todd I expect. Last night I
showed him the photograph of Jean Marie. He looked at it
and said, "A star upon your birthday burned to make you as
you are." But even last night, when both of us were past
ourselves, half·crazed with Bernhardt and champagne—and
everything—even then he never said he was in love with me.
He has never said it. Am I in love with him? I don't know.
It's all so strange and wonderful and—well, I just don't
know. . . .'

THE pen slid from her fingers. She glanced across at him.
His eyes were closed. She put away the journal, locked it in

her dressing-bag, gold-fitted—another of his gifts—and leaned back in her corner to watch France speeding by. The last of the sun lay tenderly on mist-blurred harmonies of grey and green under a sky of luminous cloud shapes, like the Corots he had shown her in the Louvre.

Paris!

Disconnected fragments, emerging from a cloyed bewilderment of new impressions, recurred in repetitive pattern to cohere in one consecutive design. The elaborate movement of the streets, the tree-lined boulevards, the bright harsh colours of women's gowns in that restaurant in the Bois—their naked shoulders, their jewels, their hats—— Fancy! They wear hats with evening dress in Paris—shading eyes artificially darkened, staring, always staring at Adrian, who had eyes for none but her in palest green under layers of white filmy chiffon—'a white tulip bud', he had said, 'just coming into flower'.

Prismatic rays of light from crystal lustres shed their incandescence on immodestly bared arms and bosoms. "Those women," she had whispered, "how they paint!" And such amazing coiffeurs beneath the wide-brimmed hats. She wore no hat; her hair, at the order of Worth, was parted in wings on her forehead and coiled low in plaits on her nape. No frizz, no curl, dead straight, and so long she could sit on it. . . . A space in the centre of the floor had been cleared, a strip of red carpet rolled back from the parquet. The hurry of waiters, perilously bearing aloft the piled up dishes, was stilled as they stood apart to watch the *Can-Can* dancers; a sprig of a girl in a white froth of tulle whirling high above her knees, a tantalizing glimpse of garters and pink flesh—rather shocking! A pirouette on the tip of a toe, and a leap to the arm of her partner, attitudinizing and bedewed with perspiration, in black velvet, frilled shirt-front, and rouged to the nines. Then the *Grand Écart*, silk-stockinged legs stretched wide to split herself, and up again like thistledown to be borne away on that black velvet shoulder, blowing kisses to the shouts of laughter, clapping of hands and cries of '*Encore! Brava!*' . . . someone bowing at their table, a sickly blond young man with, she could have sworn it, powder on his face and affectedly bewhiskered—like a white cat—the Vicomte de something or other.

"*Enchanté* to meet Madame. *Mais!* What a surprise!"

He had only just heard from Corinne that Adrian was married. Would he be permitted to order wine and drink a health to the bridal pair? His English was meticulous; his r's rolled prettily off the tip of his tongue, much displayed between lips just a trifle too red. Champagne was brought, a toast declared: "*'À l'amour! Mais—à l'amour satisfait tout son charme est ôté.*"

The glasses clinked, the young gentleman drained his, flung it to the ground and set his heel upon it with the sound of elfin bones cracked.

"Madame," he bent to her gloved hand, "*mes félicitations! Ah, mon vieux*, you have all the luck! With any happy chance I shall see you in Florence. *Au 'voir*, Madame. *À bientôt!*" And he left them to join a party of three—all men—at another table.

So he would be in Florence, too.

"What," she asked, "did he say when he smashed the glass?"

"He drank to love," said Adrian, "unsatisfied."

"Oh . . ." She glanced at him sideways. He was smiling, close-lipped; his eyes had never looked so burning blue.

"Who is he?"

"One of a type. A young man of no importance. Does he interest you?"

"Not particularly." Her gaze absorbed the room. Mirrors reflected gilded columns, red velvet settees, crowded tables. The average Frenchmen were easy to caricature, so droll, with their imperials and pointed waxed moustaches, casting sentimental looks at her. Not one, or scarcely 'one of a type' such as he of the white cat-face.

"You are a *succès fou* with these *canaille*," murmured Adrian. "They strip you in a glance as no Englishman would dare to do, however much that he might want—to do. Are you bored? You don't look very happy."

She was not. The new corset made by Worth and too tightly laced, was mild torture. She had never in her life worn anything but schoolgirl stays, buttoned down the front, unboned, but: "I'm divinely happy," she assured him. "You are so good to me."

"Good!" He laughed shortly. "I'd show you how good I could be if——" And there he stopped, to leave her wondering.

They visited the Louvre, an hour snatched from shops and fitting-rooms, to stand before that golden loveliness attributed, he said, to Cimabue. Afterwards, luncheon in Montmartre at a restaurant where the food was marvellous, the atmosphere thick with tobacco smoke, and the clientèle composed of girlish looking boys in velveteen trousers, open throated shirts, flowing ties; and of boyish looking girls with straight fringed hair falling to their shoulders; shaggy bearded men, their clothes and fingers daubed with paint, noisily expounding their theories of Life and Art in every language, with American in highest-toned ascendant.

"Du Maurier," said Adrian, "has brought to the Quartier an influx of Trilbys, Svengalis and little Billees . . ." No time to see more than these hurried glimpses of Paris on that first visit, to be followed by a longer stay on their return in April, "when," Adrian said, "you will see Paris at her Springtime best."

But in those few days she had seen the Bernhardt.

'. . . Her voice! Like veils of gauze lifting, falling, to draw the heart out of your body, and no matter that I couldn't understand a word of it, I sat entranced, bewitched by the sorcery of that throbbing husky voice, those pantherish lithe movements, by the beauty, indescribable, of this most beautiful *belle laide*. . . . Then the curtain came down, the audience got up, a seething mass of heads, with mouths wide open roaring for her, while I, gone limp, flopped back in my fauteuil, tears rolling down my face, beating my hands together like a lunatic. . . . And that's what Sarah did to me and what she does to all of Paris—those men stamping, yelling for her, women sobbing, screaming for her. I saw one resplendent Jewess in a box tear a bracelet from her arm—("la Baronne de Rothschild," murmured Adrian, amused)—to throw at that thin bowing figure where she stood before the footlights, among the flowers at her feet. . . . The French!

How different was that frenzy from the politely restrained response of the English to an Ellen Terry or an Irving. I have attended first nights of both these two, but have never seen anything to equal the massed hysteria that greeted Sarah. At this distance in time I cannot now remember the name of the play—it may have been 'Phèdre'. With her the play is *not* the thing.

That night I knew myself one with these people of Paris, that beautiful crystalline city that looks as if washed in silver and where, each time, even after all these years when I return, it is with wonder renewed to see, to love, and to breathe in the air of the Paris that claims me, bred from a father unknown. . . .'

And in this state of ecstatic revelation she drove with her husband back to the Meurice, where supper had been ordered in their sitting-room.

"You have spent yourself," he said, "on Sarah."

"Yes." She returned him a beatific smile. "Excuse me, I must change my dress."

Released, with the chambermaid's assistance, from the whale-boned grip of her corset, she put on a tea-gown and joined him at table, ate oysters and drank rather too much of champagne. Ebullient with wine and emotion she sat speech-less while he spoke of this and that, their departure the next day, the time of their arrival at Florence in the evening.

"It will be full moon to-morrow. If you are not too tired after your journey you shall see Firenze for the first time under moonlight, as I did when I was your age. Which is something not to be forgotten. Let me peel you a peach."

She shook her head.

"Some grapes?" He cut a bunch for her, took a Henry Clay from an open box on the table, and asked: "Do you mind if I smoke?"

"No. I love it."

He cut the end of the cigar, held it an instant to his nose, laid it aside. "I'll have it later. The scent of you," he leaned to her, inhaling, "is too delicious to lose."

"I have," she told him suddenly, "a ring. I would like you to see it and tell me . . ." her voice trailed off. She got up. "I'll get it now."

"Presently. Why so restless?" He refilled her glass and in one draught she emptied it and asked for more. Like fire the wine fled through her veins; her head was feather-light, her eyes lambent, lost in his.

"My charming!" he reached for her hand.   "How you

burn." He crushed his lips into her palm. "Yes! You are quickening—have quickened to the Paris in your blood."

"So you know it, too!" she cried, exultant, and raised her glass and called a toast to "France! *Vive la France! Ma patrie!* . . . It can't be just imagination. Can it? Or," she brimmed with laughter, "am I tipsy? Adrian," a sighing breath escaped her, "why do you look at me so . . . Don't!"

That quivering appeal, red underlip drawn in as if half fearful of or half inviting passions unsuspected, unsurrendered, was too much for his self-imposed endurance; he gave way, sweeping her up with him into his arms, seeking appeasement in sight-blind touch, in broken words. "Is this imagination— or is this?" But at her instinctive recoil from the storm she had aroused, his arms slackened to release her. "What may I know of you," he whispered, "more than this? That you disturb me, frustrate me, torment me, but by God I'll make you want me," he said, "before I've done, as much as ever I have wanted you."

Then he loosened her hair and let it fall, long and shining, straight as rain, below her waist; he ran his fingers through the silken strands of it and marvelled—"A thing to wonder at. You are full of exquisite surprises," he said; and unfastened her gown and revealed her and knelt, to give, but not to take of love.

*　　　*　　　*

He had engaged a suite at an hotel on the Lung'Arno Acciaioli, looking out upon the river. They had dined and drank of *Lacrimae Christi*, and now, at the window, she watched for the moon. Facing her across the Arno she could see, reflected in its calm unhurried depths, the arched shadows of S. Trinita and the wrinkled pattern of that most beautiful of older bridges, Ponte Vecchio. A far off clock chimed ten, and from a boat at the river's edge a youthful tenor floated up in a song of love—"to his girl," smiled Adrian, "probably a chambermaid in this hotel, calling her out and away with him over the hills. The night is here, so let us go."

One by one the lights of the hotels along Lung'Arno died down; the streets were quiet. The clang of a distant tram, the voices of homeward bound townsfolk, the clatter of wheels on flags, the pistol-crack of a driver's whip, were stilled in the

hush that fell upon the city as the moon rode out from a
gossamer cloud in a sky of myriad stars.

Passing under the colonnaded gloom of the Uffizi she had
her first sight of the Palazzo Vecchio, towering high above
the moonlit grace of the Piazza; and in his casual, cool voice
he told her of those bitter feuds and endless hates and fiercer
loves whose secrets, for all eternity, are guarded in the stones
of that great fortress. There Savonarola was hunted to his
awful death; and there, too, Walter, usurping Duke of Athens,
saw his son hacked to pieces by the howling mob that drove
him, their tyrant, from the city; and there the Lily banner,
wrenched in rebel conflict from the Ghibellines, was hoisted,
red-stained emblem of mutiny triumphant.

Beside the sombre majesty of that ancient palace, the moon-
crowned statues of the Loggia de'Lanzi looked, in that fragile
eerie light, to have been carved from pearl, enduring symbols
of man's hopes, endeavours, aspirations—of his lusts, in Gian
da Bologna's Rape of the Sabines; of his heroism, in Cellini's
Perseus, who holds on high Medusa's head just severed from
the writhing body at his feet.

"The drip of blood," said Adrian carelessly, "is rather too
exaggerated, but it still remains his most important work—
an artist of infinite variety. As a goldsmith he excelled above
all others who have lived before or after him. In his biography
—brilliantly written, you must read it—he admits that the
casting of the Perseus gave him more trouble than anything
he had ever done. He chose for his model the son of the cele-
brated courtesan Giambetta, although there are some who
believe him to have been a peasant lad he brought, for his
pleasure, from the mountains. That, as likely as not. Come
along, there's more to see than this."

Sunk in beauty, she was led across the bridge where Dante
stood, and Beatrice passed; where Lippi, frocked and hooded,
humming jauntily, stole by tiptoe to slink down some dark
alleyway and through a door, left open. . . . But of all she
heard and saw that night, and in this labyrinth of images
evoked from passions mystical or murderous, it was the
Bridge, the oldest Bridge, that called her back again once
more to look, and lean her arms upon its parapet, and in this
very place where Macchiavelli may have schemed, while he
too watched the drowned stars, mirrored in the Arno, drift

with it on those waters to the sea. And there, between the
jewellers' shops, shuttered now but sparkling in the day time,
the young Lorenzo, not yet Magnificent, rode on his white
palfrey to pause and buy a ruby for his velvet cap. . . . All
this she heard from Adrian while his eyes dwelled always on
her face, pale as that of the enshrined Madonna, nursing her
Baby at the corner of a street in the dying flicker of a candle.

That night she dreamed a most strange dream . . .

'. . .that Geraldine and I were together in some half
familiar place of small houses, not quite but almost Tamar
Street, outside the shop where I was born. The carboys
were gloriously lit with shining colours, and Geraldine, not
crippled any more, walked strongly, striding on ahead so
fast I had to run to catch up with and tell her, "I thought
you were dead," and I heard her say, "We're none of us
dead, and how absurd it is that you're my aunt!" And she
laughed and laughed, and I laughed with her till I cried.
And then it seemed we stood at the foot of a tall tower and
its summit was the sword of Perseus thrusting up into the
sky, when, somehow, out of nowhere appeared a high ladder
and Geraldine was climbing it. Up and up she went, growing smaller as I watched. I tried to follow her but was held
back by one whom I could hardly see for it was growing
dark, and he kissed my mouth to madness and said, "For
this is as it should be now we're married." And when I
told him I was married to Mr. Hope-Winter he said, "Not
at all. You are married to me," and took a ruby from his
cap—which struck me as very odd for he was wearing evening dress and I was in my nightgown, but as he gave me the
ruby I dropped it, and when I stooped to pick it up I saw
there was blood on my shoe. The rest is just a muddle that
ended with Larkin leading Phyllis in a cowl—and looking
quite ridiculous—across the Ponte Vecchio to meet me.
Some dreams one remembers for ever. . . .'

Light was all about her when she woke to see, through the
slats of the Venetian blinds, what the night had hidden
from her: a clear white campanile, there, a stone's throw from
the window, pigeons clustered, bowing, preening in between
its small round arches. The sky was the blue of Madonna's

cloak and there were lilies by the bedside. Pinned to the tissue wrappings was a card bearing a pencilled message: 'Warmest greetings', above the copper-plate inscription.

Mrs. Theodore Vanduren,

Villa Rinaldo,

Florence.

And who the dickens was she? Through the half-open door to Adrian's room she heard his tread, the clink of keys, a muttered 'Damn! I must have left it in the train.'

"Left what in the train?"

"So you are awake—at last." He came to the door in a purple dressing-gown festooned with yellow dragons—what a thing! "You have overslept, exhausted with your ramblings through the past."

"What's the time?"

"Just on ten."

"Good heavens! Don't wait breakfast for me. Have you lost something?"

"My cigar-case."

"But you had it last night."

"That was another one. I have two—three. Anyway, it's gone. I must have left it in the train"

She said, automatically helpful, "I'll go to the station and inquire. Leave me now, please, I must get up."

And, as he closed the communicating door, it came to her suddenly that no fundamental change had occurred in their relationship. Theoretically she had been his wife before he married her, in that she had foreseen and carried out his requests, attended to domestic trivialities, searched for and usually succeeded in finding things he had mislaid. How many times had she called at railway stations or Scotland Yard to recover his lost property! The only present difference in their association was its emotional aspect—marriage in reverse, she reflected with wry humour. First his wife, and now his mistress.

At breakfast—delicious hot rolls, honey, curls of butter

crisped with ice—"You don't have to care for your figure,"
he said, watching her spoon a froth of cream from the top of
the chocolate she took in preference to coffee. "What a child
you are!"

But it was no child's dream that haunted her still, brushed
with magic.

"Who is this Mrs. Vanduren who sends me the flowers?
I didn't hear you come in with them."

"You were fast asleep. She's a woman I want you to meet
and who wants to meet you. We are invited to luncheon with
her."

"When?"

"When you wish."

"Is she Dutch?"

"No, French—twice widowed. Her most recent husband
is American and has one of the finest private collections of
Primitives in the world."

"Have you known her long?"

"About twenty years or so."

"Do they live in Florence?"

"Not all the year round. They are cosmopolitan. New
York, Chicago, Paris——"

"Is she beautiful?"

"Very."

"Were you"—she carefully buttered a roll—"in love with
her?"

"Of course."

"Oh . . ." Her heart gave a dive. "I see."

His eyes twinkled amusedly.

"What do you see?"

"At least that you're honest. Why didn't you marry her?"

"One can love without marriage, or wishing to marry.
The only happy end to a romance is to leave it unfinished."

"Does she know—did you tell her that you are—or were—
in love with her?"

"She is not the kind of woman to whom one tells the obvious."

His teasing look held hers an instant; then, averting her eyes
she said, sulky-mouthed: "Is that why you have never told
me?"

"What is it you want me to tell you?" He leaned across

the narrow table to take her by the chin and turn her face to
his. "That I love you to imbecility? And for my sins," his
voice thickened, "I love you. But I will never have you until
of your own accord you come to me. And there's cream all
over your lips."

He wiped them with his napkin; she pushed away his
hand and flared at him: "I don't believe a word you say. You're
glib. Too glib. To how many women have you said just
that?"

His eyebrows comically lifted. "And how many times—
and by how many—have I been asked just that? Don't let
us indulge in post-mortems. You are gradually unfolding, my
Peridot, but it would be a thousand pities if, in the process,
you became infected with the blight of curiosity that destroys
the charm of ninety per cent of your sex." He rose from the
table. "Go now and put on something warm—the Florentine
sun is deceptive at this time of the year—and I will show you
yourself as you were at the beginning, as you are, and as I
pray you ever will be. But I doubt it."

> ' "Candida è ella, e candida la vesta,
>   Ma pur di rose e fior dipinta e d'erba;
>   Lo innanellato crin dell' aurea testa
>   Scende in la fronte umilmente superba. . . ."

So sang Poliziano in praise of Simonetta, and if that is
how he saw me, in those shadowy dark woods—that beautiful dancing thing with her frock full of flowers, her eyes full
of light, for no man: or as that other, poised on a shell, on a
sunless shore, holding her wind-blown hair to hide her
nakedness—if that is how he saw me—well, no wonder he
believed himself in love! . . .'

*   *   *

Villa Rinaldo, newly built on a cypress-wooded hillside,
overlooked the city lying in the hollow of the mountains like
an ivory casket dropped there by some giant's hand. Far below, the scattered treasures of Florence were disclosed in a
sun-wreathed panorama of domes and slender towers intercepted by the topaz thread of Arno . . . "Here you have,"
announced Mr. Vanduren as if he offered it to Perry as a self-
imported gift, "one of the world's finest views."

They had lunched, and now, while his wife and Adrian walked in the gardens, laid out in dazzling parterres of daffodils, he conducted Perry on a tour of his domain.

"Daffodils in February! How wonderful!" She had almost exhausted her stock of adjectival gush. "Spring is at least six weeks earlier here than in England."

"Is that so?" His dark, monkeyish face radiated smiles exposing many teeth. "I just love your English spring. 'Oh to be in England now that April's there.' " He was the canned meat king of Chicago, tall, white-haired, immaculately groomed, with broad negroid lips, a button of a nose, and not an ounce of spare flesh on his body. "Your first visit to Florence, Mrs. Hope-Winter?"

Yes, her first, and she was overwhelmed with—

"A grand little town, I guess. Are you interested in art? Let me show you my collection."

She was shown his collection of pictures, altar pieces, frescoes, torn from their native churches to die a prisoned death behind glass, in precise catalogued order. Her head reeled with a surfeit of beauty interpreted by her host in a series of names unfamiliar to her with exception of Angelico—"Exquisite painter and dreamer," said Vanduren; and Fra Lippo Lippi—"this is a portrait of Lucrezia, the girl he loved who posed for the Virgin. Your husband has offered me twenty thousand dollars for this Baldovinetti in which you may recognize Angelico's influence, but I wouldn't let it go not for twenty times as much."

Twenty thousand dollars, thought Perry, doing sums, is— four twos—Good Lord! That's saved him something; but she said with bated breath: "Of course you couldn't sell anything so lovely. My husband has some—er—lovely pictures, but not to be compared with yours."

"Well," Vanduren complacently considered his, "maybe I've been at it longer. I'd like to have him see my latest acquisition. There's some controversial opinion as to its authenticity. If you'll come along here to the sculptures I'll show it to you."

She came along there to the sculptures, a ghostly company of statues, busts, and plaques exhibited against austere grey walls in a gallery paved in black and white marble.

"This," said Vanduren, halting before the bronze anatomical study of a horse, "is by Leonardo. Every bone, every muscle, every tendon is exact, a scientific miracle. And here we have"—he passed on to its neighbour, a laughing, dimpled baby with the hidden strength about it of an infant Hercules—"this Bambino which all of our first art critics including Aaronson and Gherkin have failed to place. Have you any idea, Mrs. Hope-Winter, whose it is? I'll give you a lead. It's not a typical example of this master's work—there's more grace and charm and lightness here than one usually associates with"—he flashed her a smile—"with whom? Take your time."

Blankly she took her time, to make a wild guess. "I'm no judge, Mr. Vanduren, but could it possibly be—Michael Angelo?"

"Well!" His smile reappeared, stretched to display his gold-tipped molars. "You surely have exceptional discernment, Mrs. Hope-Winter. It has baffled the best and it *is* by Michelangelo in sweetly gracious and informal mood. It gives us none of that harsh force and power that strikes an almost discordant note in some of his stronger work. You know the story of how in his youth he came to blows with a fellow-student and had his face bashed in to deprive him of his handsome looks and breed a kind of morose bitterness against life and man that Raphael so cunningly said of him, 'He went through the streets of Rome like an executioner'. I reckon this Bambino is an early youthful effort. I do congratulate you, Mrs. Hope-Winter, for a novice you show remarkable perception—and here is Mr. Hope-Winter——" Coming through the window that opened on the terrace, standing aside for his hostess to pass. "I was just telling your wife, Mr. Hope-Winter, that I'm astonished at her remarkable perception. She has actually placed me the Bambino which floored Aaronson and Gherkin and the whole bunch of them—see if you can place it for me—it's not typical. Did you show Mr. Hope-Winter the grotto, Corinne?"

"No, you may show him the grotto. I want to talk to his wife. You have kept her to yourself long enough. Come with me, Peridot—I insist to call you by your name. It is so pretty."

Less beautiful than Perry had been led to believe, Corinne Vanduren gave the impression, without the possession, of beauty.

'Her features were irregular, her nose too large, her lips too full, but the shape and colour of her eyes, dark amber flecked with gold, held a curious mesmeric quality that lent to her mobile face its enchantment. She spoke fluent English with the slightest trace of accent, and seemed to exude a vitality that made her appear much younger than her years, which I judged to be nearer fifty than forty. Her hair, just not black, was streaked with grey, her figure that of a girl. I could understand what Adrian meant when he said she was ageless and that one need not tell to her the obvious. . . . She took me to her salon that looked out on the garden and a vista of a long grassy avenue planted either side with cypresses and terminating in a pseudo-Gothic temple. The room was very French, crammed with gilded furniture, Rose du Barry curtains, and rather a predominance of Bouchers on the walls and painted Cupids on the ceiling. So there I sat, on guard, alert, attracted and repelled by her . . .'

And drawn to her against her will, to find herself confessed of intimacies that she had not dared to dwell upon, much less to disclose.

"You must forgive me," said Mrs. Vanduren in her low rippling voice, "if I intrude on the privilege of long acquaintance with your husband to offer one small little word of advice."

"Yes?" Perry stiffened. "Please do."

"Ah, now, you take offence! Regard me as your mother, which I am more than old enough to be." A pause, unfilled by contradiction from Perry, was followed by a shrug and a faint smile. "Adrian adores you. He is crazily in love with you—you do not know it? Do not care? How the young are cruel." Her smile faded; her eyes hardened; and the thought came to Perry swiftly: Yes, you're flint and roses.

"*Mon dieu*," the lady sighed, "*si jeunesse savait!* . . . You must be good to Adrian. You should not deny him. He is very patient, but do not try his patience too far."

Perry's face was burning.

"What," she heard herself ask, softly, "has he been telling you?"

Exchange of sexual confidences? Monstrous! Indignation

fused and flamed, while with lids downcast she sat, demure
recipient of this maternal tip. And, as if a shutter had slid
open, light was borne upon her to see, to know, this woman
as her husband's lover once, if not his lover still.

'. . . It seems extraordinary that I, so young, so gauche
and unsophisticated, could have calmly accepted a situation
that in all reason should have agonized me to a torment of
jealousy. Far from it. Intuition had already warned me of
this when first he spoke of her, and I was interested—intensely interested. And as I sat there in that over-ornate
room, scrutinized and cross-examined by her, my husband's
mistress—past or present—it made no odds to me, I wondered what it was she had that I had not. Experience?
That would come in its own time. Beauty? But she was
no more beautiful than I. What then? And suddenly I
realized that she was the lover, not of Adrian alone but
of all men, the eternal courtesan. I knew also, in that
moment of illumination, that I did not love, was not *in*
love, and never would be . . . with my husband.'

"But he has told me nothing," Perry heard her say, "nothing"—she spread her charming hands—"that I cannot guess.
You do not know how fortunate you are to have a man who is
—unselfish." And Perry saw those eyes like cold amber fixed
steadily on hers. "You are married," said Mrs. Vanduren,
"and are not yet his wife."
But how dared she—what right had she to expose her to this
searing inquisition!
"My little one," her voice was a caress; she rose from where
she sat to take Perry's face between her hands, forcing her
shamed eyes to meet her own. "You are so young," she said,
"so fresh. And so—we say no more. . . ."
But enough had already been said to shock her to a sense of
her deficiencies. Thanks to Corinne's well or ill-intentioned
innuendoes, 'I submitted unresisting,' we have her word for
it, 'to all my husband asked of me.'
Yet, while she gloried in the knowledge that she was now
no demi-virgin but the equal in experience of any other wife,
if not of a Mrs. Vanduren, she confesses that she found con-

6*

summated marriage 'disappointing'; and dwells somewhat
lengthily upon the reason why, which is of no concern to us.

*   *   *

Toward the end of March there arrived on a visit to his
step-mother, Corinne Vanduren, that same young Frenchman,
Philippe de Tournay, to whom Perry had been introduced in
Paris. Her first antipathy to him was nothing lessened by his
assiduous adhesion to Adrian, and, in minor degree to herself.
So surely did they stroll in the Boboli Gardens, de Tournay
would waylay them and refuse to be detached; or, when on a
tour of the galleries Perry dutifully listened to Adrian's dis-
sertation on the Masters, he was certain to be met as they went
in or they came out. At Doney's, fashionable rendezvous of
Florence, the ubiquitous de Tournay would be found at the
door, awaiting their entrance to plant himself between them
at a table and unceasingly to talk. None the less, Perry much
enjoyed these morning gatherings where the Florentine elect
met to sip apéritifs and pass the time of day and mutual scandal. Here, vivacious beautifully gowned women, officers in
blue and silver uniforms, strutting senile old roués, and always
a sprinkling of tourists, English, German, American—whose
wives and daughters looked to have been poured as molten
wax into their clothes, so perfectly they fitted—crowded to
overflowing the small rooms.

"If ever I will marry," declared de Tournay, "it shall be
with an American. They are *chic* and they have riches. For a
man there is only one excuse for marriage—that is money."

This on an occasion when Adrian had gone to inspect a
likely del Sarto, with a view to purchase. And God send,
prayed Perry, that it will prove *un*likely, or else anything from
two to five thousand down the drain. . . .

The day before she had taken the peridot ring to a jeweller
on the Ponte Vecchio to have it made small enough to wear on
her finger, and, as she came out of the shop the next morning,
she encountered a breathless de Tournay.

"Ah, madame! The happy chance! When I saw you pass
across the Bridge I gave the chase. Is Adrian not with you?"

"No, and I'm sorry, I can't stop. I have letters to write."
But as she turned he turned with her entreating:

"Only one little quarter of the hour for an *apéritif* at

Doney's. I have secured a table and I want you to meet a friend of mine who is visiting a few days at the Villa. He will go soon to Rome to join there his mother. He is a great friend with le Marquis de Morès—you remember?—he was intrigued with *l'affaire* Dreyfus, and the first to prove the handwriting of the *Bordereau* as that of the pig of a Jew. My friend has it all—as you say—from the mouth of the horse. You will find him very interesting. At dinner last night he gives us all as he heard it from de Morès. *Mais!* France owes an immense debt of honour to de Morès. Were you in Paris, madame, in January, when that abomination was expelled? No? Then you missed it all. That is a pity. It was magnificent. I attended it, myself."

"Quite a lot of people, in England, believe Dreyfus to be innocent," she said.

"Pah! Innocent! How can he be innocent when all the evidence proves him to be in the pay of Schwartzkoppen, the German military attaché? No, he is a villain, a traitor who sold his country's secrets to the enemy. Hell—or Devil's Island—is too good for that *cochon*."

They had by this time come to Doney's. The sun-dazzled Via Tuornabuoni, that beautiful street of ancient palaces and modern shops, swarmed with loungers exchanging greetings, buying buttonholes and posies from the smiling dark-skinned flower-women grouped about the foot of the Palazzo Strozzi. Thirsty, hot, and tempted by the thought of a long iced drink, Perry had succumbed to de Tournay's persuasions and was now seated at a table, half deafened by a din of voices and high pitched cachinnation. He ordered an orangeade for her, an absinthe for himself and continued—"À propos of money you have a proverb—is it not? that money is the base of all evil?"

"Root," corrected Perry, bored.

"Yes, but me—I say it is not money, it is the want of money that is evil. Corinne, *ma belle mère*, has married for money, having twice married for love, or for what with her may pass for love." De Tournay exposed his pointed teeth. "My father, he adored her. I remember how he say to me when I was quite a little boy—'I have a mistress, I adore her. I have a wife, and I adore her, and as they never meet they adore me.' But I think that is so charming! Ah, here is my friend. Allow me to present—Madame Hopvinter—Monsieur le Capitaine le Comte de Chantillon."

An effete, narrow-eyed, narrow-chested young gentleman was this, with hair sleek as a seal's, a moustache like an eyebrow, and carefully manicured hands on one of which he wore a signet ring—a square green stone, engraved. And to that ring as to a magnet, Perry's eyes were drawn.

The newcomer addressed her in execrable English; she answered him mechanically in French. More drinks were ordered; she was offered and dimly accepted, absinthe. She drank it, loathed it, and nibbled an olive to dispel the taste of aniseed, but still, unabashedly, her eyes were glued to the ring of the Comte de Chantillon. The arrival of more drinks interrupted the animated conversation of the two young men, when Perry seized the opportunity to say: "I am so fascinated by your ring, monsieur. May I see it closer? It looks almost exactly like mine."

She drew it from her finger and held it out to him.

Screwing a monocle into his eye he examined it, saying: "Ah! *Le coq!* This ring is French, madame?"

"Yes," her breath caught in her throat, "yours too—is yours a peridot and the crest a—chanticleer?"

"Pardon, madame—craiste?" de Chantillon glanced inquiringly at de Tournay. "What is craiste?"

De Tournay translated.

"*Ah, non,* madame," de Chantillon removed his ring and passed it to her. "*Ceci n'est pas un péridot; c'est une éméraude.*" Yes, a pale emerald, and the crest not a cock but an eagle perched on a royal crown. She returned it with a smile, thinned by disappointment.

"I thought for the moment that it was the facsimile of mine."

"But not possible, madame. This ring is a—how you say—give?—from *la Reine* Marie Antoinette to my—*alors,* Philippe?" he appealed to de Tournay to help him out.

"He is trying to tell you, madame, that his ring was a gift from Marie Antoinette to an ancestor of his who was the Queen's equerry. Are you then interested in the armorial of France?"

"Yes, I am, because this ring," she slipped it on her finger, "was given to my mother by one of her—her admirers, whose name I do not know. It came into my possession after her death when I was only four years old, and I am longing," she said lightly, "to find out to whom it belonged. I only know that he was French."

"So?" de Tournay's face was more than ever like a cat's; he stroked a whisker. "May I see again?"

She offered her hand with the ring on it for his inspection.

He shook his head. "The chanticleer is a not uncommon *emblème* of our *aristocratie*. I have seen many of such crests with some variation. This has a leaf in its mouth. Do you know it, Antoine?"

De Chantillon pursed a dubious lip with a shrug of negation. "*Mais non!* I cannot say, madame."

"I tell you who may know," suggested de Tournay. "Corinne. She has married two husbands of the *noblesse*, not to say," he added with smiling spite, "of her lovers. You would do well to ask her, madame. She is *au fait* with all the first families of France, and also with their—indiscretions."

Her fingers in an itch to tear that grin from off his face, Perry got up.

"Thanks, I will."

Both gentlemen were on their feet. "But you do not go!" exclaimed de Tournay. "Will you not wait for Adrian?"

"He won't be here. He is picture-hunting."

"Then, madame, permit me to escort you to your hotel."

'. . . "A strange coincidence, to coin a phrase, by which such things are settled nowadays." So said Byron, and so say I, for call it if you will coincidence, as I now look back upon my life I see how Destiny—and I cannot think if otherwise—has pre-ordained its pattern.

As Philippe de Tournay advised me I did ask Corinne, by proxy, through my husband. It was, I said, his duty to me and to any children I might bear him that he should make all possible effort to trace my paternal origin. I gave him my ring and the photograph, and insisted he should take them to Mrs. Vanduren. And this, briefly, is what inquiry elicited from her recognition of the photograph and crest.

My father was the younger brother of the Comte de Mélior-Fleury, who married the sister of Corinne Vanduren. With her husband, her six-year-old son and my father, then

about eighteen, they fled from France in 1870 at the fall of
the Napoleonic dynasty. The photograph may have been
taken shortly before they left Paris. A few months after they
arrived in England my uncle suddenly died of what must
have been appendicitis, diagnosed in those days as inflam-
mation of the bowels. His widow rented a house in Woodberry Down, Finsbury Park, where my mother was engaged
as governess and where she met my father. When the
affair between them was discovered—they were still little
more than children in their teens—my mother, as we know,
was dismissed, and my father sent back to France. He made
no effort to see her again. He may not have been aware of
her condition, but according to Mrs. Vanduren there is no
possible doubt that I am his daughter, for the likeness, she
said, is quite extraordinary. She had seen him on several
occasions when he was a boy, but never after they left
Paris. She told Adrian that she had been puzzled when first
she saw me by a resemblance to someone she had known
but could not place. His brother, several years older than
himself, was the head of the family which, already im-
poverished, was finally ruined by the war. Their mother,
who died giving birth to my father, was a de Tournay, and
I am a cousin, once removed, from Philippe, but have no
wish to acknowledge the relationship.

It appears that my father was a gifted violinist—he had
studied at the Conservatoire in Paris—and scraped a living
playing first fiddle in theatre orchestras. He died, unmarried, of consumption at the age of twenty-six, and was
buried at Père Lachaise.

I saw his grave. . . .'

*   *   *

On their return to London in April Perry found that the
exterior of the house had been repainted and the best bedroom,
adjoining Adrian's, hitherto kept for the use of visitors, was
now to be hers. A door had been built in the wall to allow
access from his to her privacy.

So began her married life, with no appreciable difference
from her former position in the house more than that she now
was mistress of it. Her five years' apprenticeship had taught
her to deal with the servants who accepted her promotion

with unqualified approval, conveyed in the gift of a silver [plated] salver inscribed to 'Mr. and Mrs. Hope-Winter on the occasion of their marriage, with the dutiful respects of the staff at 111, Brook Street.'

Contrary to hope and expectation, Lady Stilton was in waiting to meet them on their arrival.

"Her ladyship, madam," Larkin murmured apologetically, "is in the drawing-room."

"Thank you, Larkin, I'll—— Oh! my angel!" An hysterical Phyllis hurled herself at Perry, frothing with excitement. "How well she looks. I can't believe she pined for me."

"Not to notice, madam, after the first day or two. I kept on telling her you was coming back and I think she must have understood. Will you be taking tea with her ladyship, madam, or"—tactfully suggested Larkin—"will you be wishing to rest after your journey?"

"Yes, make my excuses to her ladyship. I am going straight to bed."

Where determinedly Lady Stilton sought her.

"My dear Peridot!" A kiss was implanted on her forehead. "As I have just been telling Adrian, one must—in Christian charity—forgive as we hope to be forgiven. You have both done me a grave injustice in keeping your marriage a secret. It was that, and that *alone*, which so immeasurably shocked and grieved me—his only sister. However, we'll forget it and let bygones be bygones. He is a free agent to marry whom he pleases, and from my heart I rejoice to see him happy. That is all I want and all I ask." Seating herself at the bedside, she raised to her eyes a lorgnette. "Those are beautiful pearls you are wearing." She leaned forward the closer to inspect. "I suppose they *are* real?"

"So I believe, Lady Stilton."

"No, no, no! Not," was the playful correction, "Lady Stilton any more. You must call me by my name. We are sisters now. I wish you joy of them, my dear."

Perry sat confounded. What might this astonishing change of front portend? She hazarded a guess, soon to be confirmed.

"You must, and I am sure you will allow me to advise from years of experience, how to sustain your position as Adrian's wife. You have certain obligations to fulfil. You will have to entertain. I can help you there by holding a reception—in this house, of course, not mine—when I can introduce you to all the *right* people. A young hostess suddenly raised to a sphere far—if I may say so—above her birth and upbringing, is almost bound to make mistakes, particularly as Adrian has no sense whatsoever of social distinctions. Those Bohemian friends of his, authors and artists and so on, are, for the most part," Lady Stilton shuddered, "quite beyond the pale."

Perry blinked; so the free entertainment of all the 'right people', at Adrian's expense, explained this gratuitous interest in her; and she said: "I much appreciate your kindness, but I don't quite feel inclined to hold receptions or give parties so soon after Geraldine's——"

"That," came the swift interruption, "is absurd. You were no relative of our poor darling. I, myself, am in half mourning now and will be out of it entirely next month. Oh, yes, and there's another thing. I have the Stilton girls staying with me for the Season—Annabel, whom I think you have already met —and her younger sister Marion, whom I am pledged to present. Too tiresome! How I've slaved for those motherless girls left on my hands while still in the nursery, and no thanks from their father for all I've done for them. I married off Edith, the second girl, last year, and should have no difficulty in settling Marion. She is very pretty. Annabel, poor dear, is a problem—with that nose. So if you *could* arrange for me to have the pair on the day of the Drawing-Room——"

"The pair?"

"The carriage," said Lady Stilton brightly. "I always have the pair for the Drawing-Rooms. This is just to let you know in good time. Otherwise you might be using it yourself."

"No," Perry shook her head. "I shan't be using it, nor, I fear, will you. I am so very sorry, but," she decided in a second's inspiration, "it is to be sold."

"Sold!" screamed Lady Stilton. "You are surely not selling the carriage and pair?"

"Adrian," said Perry, her voice hushed, "is in some—I hope and trust not serious—financial difficulty."

Lady Stilton paled.

"I might have guessed as much! Those pearls," she ran an expert eye over Perry's lace-embellished nightgown and the half-hoop of diamonds encircling her finger, "and heaven only knows what else besides, must have cost him a fortune."

"I am afraid so," Perry said in a tragic whisper, "and he has lost thousands with the Odyssey."

"I knew he would! I knew it!" cried her ladyship distractedly. "How I've begged and prayed him not to sink his capital in that foolhardy venture! He must get rid of it at once—it is only a white elephant—before he is involved in further losses."

But his losses had already involved him far enough. He needed no persuasion from his sister or his wife to abandon his Odyssey when it foundered to the verge of liquidation. After much advice from Mr. Todd the business was closed down, the creditors paid up, and clamorous authors gratified to receive quixotic compensation from the chairman, for books contracted and royalties unearned. The lease of the offices in Sackville Street was sold with the furniture to the incoming tenant, an olive-skinned gentleman, one Solomon McPherson, who described himself as a Company Promoter and conducted a side line in loans.

Perry's first step toward halting extravagance, the disposal of 'the pair', was followed by the suggestion, let fall to lie fallow, that—"this house is too large for just the two of us".

"Some time or other there may be more," said Adrian, "than just the two of us."

Nor after that could she harry him further, although no evidence of such eventuality, however much she may have longed for it, appeared to be forthcoming.

He had opened an account in her name at his bank, with a generous quarterly allowance, and her next move obtained his permission in a letter to the manager, prompted by herself, to examine periodically his pass-book. She was horrified to find his overdraft now stood at treble its original amount.

"You're six thousand overdrawn," she announced. "Why pay the bank all that interest? You have no right nor any need to owe. I've been watching the stock markets."

"Dear me," murmured Adrian, coldly.

"Yes." She lifted her chin. "I read *The Financial Times* every morning. One of us has to keep our heads above water. Look here"—she perched herself on the arm of his chair to wheedle: "Sell your Rands before they fall. They are standing just about as high as they're likely to go. There's a general slump in South African shares. The bank manager thinks there will be trouble in the Transvaal. He says Rands have risen twenty-five per cent on the price you originally paid for them, so if you sell out now you'll make profit enough to clear your overdraft and still keep a balance on the credit side. . . . And you needn't look at me like that. It's time someone took you in hand. You've no more business sense than Phyllis"— whom she collared to take for a walk in the Park, leaving Adrian sardonically smiling.

On a seat beneath a plane tree near the Serpentine she sat to consider and to brood upon her husband's lack of 'business sense'. Where would it end, in what disaster? She had no idea of his financial position more than that his outgoings in this last year had been, according to his pass-book, considerably above his income. No one, she decided, could go on spending capital and borrowing off banks without coming a cropper; and now that he was rid of his 'white elephant' he would almost certainly be taken with some other fad to break him. What to do with such a one, so hopelessly unstable—and what to do, she wondered, with herself. . . . She practised her music, took French and Italian conversation lessons, but neither these nor her household duties served to fill her time. The wheels of daily routine ran on clockwork, and although Adrian now dined at home three or four evenings a week, she saw nothing of him during the day. She entertained his guests at dinner, gave musical *soirées* with Freddie much in evidence, and the latest soprano, secured, at a price, to sing one song and no encores. She kept a good table, had a flair for devising enviable menus that within a year of her marriage had earned her the reputation of a hostess. She was At Home every fourth Thursday when a few women, more men, called to drink tea, and discuss the Jameson Raid and the Kaiser's telegram of sympathy to Kruger, subjects whose unflagging popularity had been equalled only by the catastrophic case of Oscar Wilde. But her At Home days, her musical evenings, and such-like trivialities could not absorb her energy or interest. Intuitively she recognized that Adrian's delight in the exploration of her mind had waned with possession of her body. In the first few months of their marriage he was slaked; her youth, her inexperience, her eager receptivity, had—she faced it squarely—ceased to stir him. Marriage, she saw with a start of dismay, was for him a calamitous folly, the impulsive swan-

song of his middle-age; for her an anchorage. She had therefore no right to demand of him more than he would wish to
give, or more than she would dare to claim. No question he
had been in love with her, but 'in-loveness', she reflected
wryly, 'is not love. . . .'

Long she sat there while the distant hum of London's
traffic mingled with the thin far-off voices of children at play,
until:

"It *is* Mrs. Hope-Winter! I thought it was. I recognized
your bulldog. May I sit down? Very warm, isn't it? Quite a
heat-wave."

Annabel Stilton, in pale blue pongée and a hat like a market
garden turned up at the back to display a wispy bun, sank
into the vacant chair at Perry's side and nursed on her lap a
brown paper parcel. "I've been shopping," she said, "for
Aunt Hilda. She always makes me carry this silly little parcel
when I go out alone. There's nothing in it—everything's sent,
but she says it isn't proper for an unmarried girl to walk alone
in the Park, even in the mornings, unless she carries a parcel.
Isn't it absurd"—she gave a whinnying laugh—"to be
chaperoned by a brown paper parcel? Oh, don't!" With-
drawing her foot from Phyllis's attention, she asked: "Does
he bite?"

"No." Perry rose. "She doesn't. I'm afraid I must be
going."

"Must you? So must I. Do you mind if I come with you?
We go the same way home."

They walked together.

"How your dog gasps and pants. Is he ill?"

"She's hot," said Perry briefly.

"I'm always terrified of bulldogs. They look so fierce.
They're very much a man's dog, aren't they? It was because
he kept bulldogs that Clara Bourne broke off her engagement
with Captain Curran."

Stooping to attach the lead to Phyllis's collar, Perry raised
a flushed face. "Did you say their engagement—I didn't know
it was broken off."

"It was announced in *The Times*."

"When?" inquired Perry, hurrying.

"Oh, ages ago. Don't walk so fast. You haven't a train to
catch, have you?"

Again that whinnying laugh.

"I'm sorry," she slackened her steps. "I didn't see any announcement. I thought they were married."

"Yes, she went out with that intention, but I heard in a letter from Edith, my sister, whose husband is in the same regiment as Captain Curran, that Miss Bourne fell in love with her latest fiancé whom she met on the boat going over— Porkie Lyndhurst, Lord Branscombe's son. Do you know him? He's *so* like a pig, but a much better match than Captain Curran—not that Porkie has any money either, but at least she'll be a Countess. Can't we sit down again? Here are two chairs. You're so energetic—I'm quite out of breath—and I'm wearing new stays. They pinch dreadfully. What's the time?"

Perry turned over the face of her watch, pinned to her dress.

"Half past twelve."

"G.C. How funny!" shrilled Annabel. "Garth Curran's initials."

"And Geraldine's," Perry said. "This watch was hers."

"Poor dear Geraldine." Annabel bent to her shoe. "I'd love to take it off for a minute, but I daren't. I'd never get it on again. I'm in the wars today—my shoes are new, too. Aunt Hilda came with me to buy them and insisted I should squeeze my feet into half a size too small because they're so big. Sheer agony. Do you have corns?"

"No."

"You are lucky—such tiny feet! What size shoes do you take?"

"Threes. Had your sister anything else to say about"— Perry was engrossed in poking holes in the ground with the ferrule of her parasol—"about Miss Bourne's broken engagement?"

"Oh, my dear, yes!" cried Annabel eagerly. "The bulldogs. I was going to tell you. Edith had it from her husband—she writes pages—you know they've nothing else to do but gossip out there. It seems Captain Curran has a lady bulldog too and it had puppies and Clara was furious. She said she loathed bulldogs and he must get rid of them all—the mother dog, whom he adored, as well. And then they had an awful row and she told him he must choose between herself and his dogs, and he chose the dogs. But everybody thinks that was only her excuse to be off with the old love and on with the new. After all, Porkie *is* the heir to an earldom, and she has all the money. They're Bourne's Brownie—the ale, you know. I always think it's so peculiar that beer is accepted and wine isn't, nor cigars, and they're nothing like so common. Oh, my corn does shoot! That means it's going to rain. Shall we go on? I shall have to find a hansom. I simply can't walk in these shoes."

They found a prowling hansom at Hyde Park Gate.

"Aunt Hilda will have a fit," neighed Annabel as she got in, "if she sees me drive up to the house alone in a hansom. I suppose you can't come with me because of the dog—oh, there's one thing I've forgotten to tell you"—and she leaned across the apron doors to say—"the Fifth Hussars are ordered out to Egypt and some of them are coming home on leave."

If some of the Fifth Hussars did come home on leave *en route* for Egypt, where Sir Herbert Kitchener was preparing to reconquer the Sudan, Garth Curran was not of them; nor did Perry hear news of him again.

The Diamond Jubilee, high light of that sixty years' reign, blazed in a glory of tumultuous rejoicing. Led by Field Marshal Lord Roberts, on an old grey charger, the procession swept through the shouting streets that roared deep-throated welcome to a frail little figure in widow's black whose simple message, 'from my heart I thank my beloved people. May God bless them', circled the four quarters of her Empire as she set forth upon her journey of Thanksgiving to St. Paul's.

From a Club window in St. James's Street, Perry, with her husband, watched her pass.

'. . . She was so homely, like anybody's grandmother, her white hair parted in the middle under her widow's bonnet, her wrinkled old face wreathed in smiles, and one black-gloved tremulous hand raised in response to the cheering. Before, behind her, went her troops, mounted or on foot. The Indian Princes, magnificently robed, glittering with jewels, were followed by the turbaned native officers, and then her own Bodyguard, the Cavalry, the Lancers, Dragoons and the Hussars. I looked for Garth, half expecting to see him riding at the head of a column, although I can't think why, for he was still supposed to be in Egypt. She had a marvellous day for it. The sun gleamed on breastplates, swords, and silver harness, and on her face as she passed in her open landau. But I could scarcely see her for a foolish rush of tears. She was so old, so very small, to be so great. . . .'

That was her last spectacular appearance before the storm clouds gathered in the Transvaal, to break in the thunder-clap of war.

SEVEN

Queen Anne's Mansions
Dec. 31*st*, 1899
11.45 p.m.

'I am waiting at my window to hear Big Ben strike the hour. Telegram from Adrian this a.m. saying he has gone on to Madrid from Paris with Philippe and won't be home until next month, which might mean anything. Apologizes for not being with me to see the New Year in. Have opened the window and am writing while I wait. The night is warm and muggy with some fog. I can hear drunken shouts and cheers floating up from Parliament Square, but there can be no jubilation with this ghastly news from the Front hanging over us. . . . The bells of St. Margaret's are ringing out the old year, ringing in the new, Big Ben is striking twelve, and . . .

This is the twentieth century!'

A DISMAL birth, overshadowed by that disastrous 'Black Week' of December. The simmering cauldron of Imperial demands and controversial ambitions in South Africa had risen to boiling pitch when the Uitlanders of Johannesburg sent a petition to the Queen demanding the assistance of Her Majesty's Government to obtain for them their franchise: a trivial enough demand, it was thought, and likely to be settled at the Bloemfontein Conference between the High Commissioner, Sir Alfred Milner, and President Kruger. But within a week of that meeting, Joseph Chamberlain stated to a packed house of Commons that the Conference had failed, Kruger insisting that the dispute should be decided by arbitration of a Foreign Power. With the rankling reminder of the Kaiser's telegram to Kruger at the time of the Jameson Raid there was little doubt which Foreign Power the wily old President had in mind.

Milner's refusal to permit the interference of any Power, unnamed, was received with loud cheers in the House. Mean-

183

while, Kruger, stubbornly resisting all proposals for a settle-
ment, was militarily mustering Boer farmers from the Veldt,
superb shots and first-class riders every man of them.

Ostrich-like and undismayed, Her Majesty's Government
ignored, not only this ludicrous threat from a handful of
Boers, but the psalm-singing President's warning, that 'in
the event of war the Orange Free State would be joined in
active alliance with the Transvaal'; and, 'though thousands
should attack them there was nothing to fear, for the Lord
would be the final Arbiter. He, and He only would decide.'

Upheld by his faith in the Almighty's jurisdiction, Kruger
proceeded to pillage half a million sterling from a mail van
at Veeringen, just within the frontier. This act of vandalism
was followed by the most audacious challenge ever flung from
a province to an Empire: 'All British troops must be removed
from the borders of the Republic, or failing such removal before October 11, 1899, the Transvaal Government would,
with regret, regard such defiance as a formal declaration of
war.'

To which there could be only one possible reply.

'The demands of the South African Republic were not to
be considered or discussed.'

Roused too late from her lethargy Britain rose up and,
despite all threats and warnings, unprepared, to meet that
'handful' of Boer farmers whose numbers, alarmingly, had
swelled from five to fifty thousand; and, while through the
streets of London red-uniformed ranks marched to the sound
of fife and drum on their way to the docks and embarkment,
our inadequately guarded frontiers fell to Boer invasion on
three sides. Mafeking, Ladysmith, Kimberley were in turn
besieged and gallantly defended; but for how long could that
defence hold out?

Before the outbreak of war in the previous October Adrian,
who was then in Paris, refused to return to London, because,
he said of 'a skirmish on the Veldt that would be over before
Christmas'. Perry might, had she wished, have joined him in
Madrid where, with Philippe de Tournay, he had decided to
spend the winter months, had not a certain experience on her
first visit to Spain, in the spring of '98, determined her 'never
again to set foot in that barbaric country' when, much against
her will, Adrian took her to a bull-fight.

'. . . Reginald Tarrant came with us to Seville. We crossed via Dieppe to stay a night or two at Berneval, where "Sebastian Melmoth", he who had once been Oscar Wilde, was in hiding. We called on him at his shabby little villa, and I could scarcely recognize, in that bloated shambles of a man, the once superlative dandy and brilliant *raconteur* who had been the playboy of the *fin-de-siècle*. But as soon as he spoke in that affected but extraordinarily charmful way of his as if his voice caressed each word, I knew him for himself. He told Adrian he had no desire to write any more—he was "undergoing the penance of enforced productivity, yet, as is said of torture, it helps a man to pass an hour or two". And then he spoke of Dowson who had died in poverty. "Much of what he has written," he said, "will remain, but nothing of mine—beyond my damaged reputation." This was the last time I ever saw that incalculable being who at the height of his fame had reigned monarch of all salons he surveyed, fawned on by theatrical managers, suspect of the bourgeoisie he loved to shock, and whose meteoric career came to such an abortive finale.

From Berneval we went to Paris, then to Madrid, and arrived in Seville in the Spring of the year. I was much impressed with this most beautiful malodorous city of narrow tortuous streets that still carry evidence of Moorish occupation. Only a few fragments of the former circular city wall, adorned, so Adrian informed me, with sixty-odd towers, remain. The cathedral and the splendid bell tower, called Giralda—two thirds of which, dating back to 1196, are definitely Moorish—has twenty-two of the sweetest-toned chimes of bells imaginable. All the houses are built round handsome courtyards, every villa has its garden, every garden its fountain, every wall is splashed with flowers, and every window holds its mystery of dark-eyed black-haired women peeping through the lattices that guard them from the touch but not the sight of men.

I had no wish to see a bull-fight, but Adrian, scornful of my "squeamishness", insisted I should sample this "quite unique" experience. "I cannot," he said, "understand why you, who profess disgust at what you are pleased to term barbaric cruelty to animals, can tolerate the brutal sport in which the Englishman delights——" I had often noticed that Adrian, when abroad, was inclined to ignore or disdain his nationality. Chameleon-like, he would take to himself the colour of his environment. His gestures would become more exaggerated, he would interpolate French, Italian, Spanish, as the case might be, for its English equivalent, snapping impatient fingers as if to recall the forgotten word. And so—"The Englishman," he said with a disparaging shrug, "will sit for hours yelling himself hoarse at a horde of his fellows kicking at a ball and each other on a mud-swamp, or go chasing after tame stags." "That," I agreed, "is revolting, but at least football, at which you scoff, and which I have never seen nor wish to see played, is a sport in which only men indulge. They don't victimize and torture helpless animals." To which he retorted: "A bull-fight is an emotional experience, that of all sports in the world calls for the highest skill and courage of man against beast. I insist that you come to the bull-fight."

So I went to the bull-fight with him and Reginald.

It was a saint's day and Seville *en fête*. The sun glared down on that vast sanded circus ringed with tier upon tier of seats to hold eighteen thousand spectators. Crowds swarmed at every entrance, and presently two military bands arrived to take their places at each end of the huge amphi-theatre. Their decorated uniforms, their brass and silver instruments, were sun-pointed in a shimmering trans-parency of heat that seemed to hold a brassy blue reflec-tion from the sky. There was no shade anywhere except for those, who like ourselves, sat in boxes under striped canopies, reserved for the grandees. Many of the women wore mantillas, cascades of black or white lace, framing their faces and supported by high tortoiseshell combs. Some of them had roses tucked behind an ear. There was a fine display of jewels and gloriously coloured gowns, but the majority were disappointingly plain—too fat, their dark oily skins too heavily painted, although here and there I saw remarkable breath-taking beauty, particularly among the peasants in their native dress. The men, on the whole, were better-looking than the women in their wide-brimmed sombreros with short side-whiskers, when not bearded like brigands. Where we sat, however, most of the men were in uniform, for Spain was on the brink of war with America and the whole country in a state of emergency. All about us there was a pungent smell of perfume, perspiration, oranges —and an indefinable sickly-sweet acrid odour as of stale blood coming up from the sand-covered arena. The bull-stalls were under the lowest tier of seats, and at these I kept looking and wondering how many bulls I would see tortured to their deaths that day. The noise was terrific, everyone shouting and laughing and talking; Adrian smiling, Reginald yawning, and I longing for a cool iced drink. Then one of the bands began to play and there was a sudden burst of cheering as into the arena rode a couple of horsemen dressed like medieval Spanish knights and each carrying a lance.

"The *picadores*," said Adrian, "principal performers of the first act," and he went on to explain how the bull-fight is a drama in three acts: in the second act the *chulos* take the stage, and the final act devolves solely on the skill of the matador—"victorious slayer of the bull". And then I offended him by saying I would like to go. He told me crossly not to be tedious, and, "Here come the *chulos*——" the toreadors, four of them, in short jackets, gay with ribbons, white breeches, white stockings, and absurd little shoes like a ballet dancer's. And, despite my "squeamishness", I felt a thrill of excitement when another burst of cheering greeted—as he rushed from his den—the bull.

He looked pitifully small in that enormous desert of sand, circled by mountainous cliffs of black and brightly coloured seated watchers. The bull, who had dashed out gladly enough to find himself released from his cage, stopped short and lowering his head moved it uncertainly from side to side as if bewildered at the noise and blaring music of the band. Then a toreador came dancingly up to him waving his red cloak fan-wise. Startled, the bull pranced, made a half-hearted charge at the cloak, and turned sharply, trotting off as if to seek exit from this terrifying unknown world in which he found himself.

A booing and a roaring from all sides of the arena halted him again—"a miserable bull," murmured Adrian, "no fight in him"—and there, with that same side to side blind movement of his head, he stood stock still while one of the picadors rode up on a bony decrepit old horse. "Now," whispered Reginald into my ear, "the fun begins."

The fun! . . . I tried to get up. I must go—get away—
but I found I couldn't move. I sat staring in hypnotic
horror-bound fascination at the picador who, having pulled
his horse to face the bull and bar its escape, now drove his
lance straight at its shoulder. With a bellow of pain and
astonishment the bull charged, head down, at the belly of
the horse. The picador leapt from the saddle and skipped
to the safety of the barriers, as the horse, with an agonized
shriek, reared on its hind legs, slowly tottered to its knees
and rolled over on its side with its hoofs pawing the air.
And, where it sank, the yellow sand was a dark steaming
red.

There were more shouts, of applause this time, and yells
of laughter at the inexpressibly comic sight of the fallen
horse waving its legs in spasmodic tortured jerks. The bull,
as if inflamed by the stench of blood and bowels and the
smart of its trickling wound, charged again, grinding its
horns deep into the upturned body of its victim. . . . And
what looked to be a slimy twisted mass of purplish snakes
oozing out: and a fearful smell: and the delighted audience
stamping, screaming, yelling. . . . I covered my eyes and
peered round through my fingers at Adrian. He was stooping forward, breathing fast, lips parted, eyes half closed,
and on his face was the look of one exalted. . . . Then a
coldness came upon me with a surge of nausea, and only by
a supreme effort of will did I save myself from being sick.

When I dared to look again at that carnage in the sand,
the horse was feebly kicking in its death throes.

How I got away, pushing past those seated, howling,
sweating, blood-maddened spectators, I do not know.

Reginald, not Adrian, followed me out. "Are you upset?
The novice always finds the beginning the worst part of it,
but you must wait to see the finale. The matador has yet to
appear and the bull to be killed. That is the great moment."

I told him to fetch me a carriage. He offered to accompany
me back to the hotel, but I said No, I wouldn't think of
spoiling his "fun". . . . Yet whenever I recall that hideous
experience and my horrified disgust of it I see engraved, like
a scar upon my memory, that look of exaltation, sensuous,
sadistic, on the face of him who was my husband. . . .'

*   *   *

It was on their return to England from Seville that Mr. Todd informed Adrian of an offer received from Mr. Solomon McPherson to buy certain of the Soho property held by him on behalf of the Hope-Winter Trust, 'with a view to erecting on the site thereof a hotel of vast dimensions.' Most earnestly Mr. Todd impressed upon Adrian that he, as sole trustee, would have been well within his rights to have disposed of the said property without consulting his client, but 'out of courtesy he felt in duty bound to obtain Mr. Hope-Winter's approval before proceeding further in the matter'.

The deal went through, and Mr. Todd reinvested the capital in divers industrials, to secure, as he said, the highest rate of interest.

The first intimation that all was not well with the Trust—and Mr. Todd—was conveyed to Perry in a headline of the *Morning Post*.

WELL KNOWN SOLICITOR FOUND GUILTY

From the report of the trial at the Old Bailey she learned that Mr. Todd had been sentenced to seven years' hard labour for misappropriation of Trust funds.

Before she confronted her husband with this devastating news, Perry cautiously approached the manager of Adrian's bank, who secured her the advice of a highly reputable firm of solicitors. Legal inquiry into the case proved that Mr. Todd had taken to himself the entire capital raised from the sale of the property, amounting to some forty thousand pounds. That the defalcation had been well covered by regular payment of dividends, so-called, did not, in Adrian's opinion, exempt his wife from what he termed 'unpardonable negligence', since, at her own request, she had undertaken to check his pass-book.

Appalled by this unfair accusation she retorted: "But how could I possibly have guessed him to be a double-dyed crook? You can't blame me for this."

He did blame her for that.

"You know perfectly well I am a very Skimpole where money is concerned. At your insistence I relinquished all such tedious business into your hands. Your early association with trade," he fastened a sting to his smile, "led me to believe you were equipped with common-sense enough to have kept a more careful watch on my finances."

"My French blood," she heatedly rejoined, "and not my association with what you are pleased to call trade has given me my common-sense. Although I have reason to believe my father was an artist——"

"Or," he interrupted meditatively, "a lackey. A ring, a chance resemblance to a faded photograph, is scarcely conclusive evidence enough to prove you an offspring of the Mélior-Fleurys. The pretty boy you declare was your father may have been a servant of the family you claim as your own, and the ring he gave your mother may as likely have been pilfered. *Quien sabe?*"

Her lips tightened and whitened.

"If you believe that——" But she knew he did not believe that. It amused him to chafe her to fury. She was not to be drawn.

"The alternative solution you offer me is even more romantic," she said softly, "than the truth."

He shrugged a shoulder.

"Keep your illusions if you will and let us return to our muttons—or our Todd. I am no worse off now than I was ten years ago before my aged relative left me a windfall."

This characteristic minimization served its excuse to release the kindled wrath his careless words had roused.

"A windfall! Disposed of for a fortune from which you have received no more than a year's bogus interest, paid out of Todd's pocket. And now we'll *have* to move. It is certain we can't afford to go on living here."

Useless for Adrian to argue that he still retained the bulk of his father's capital.

"Yes. You came into a quarter of a million and if you had a quarter of it left you could think yourself lucky. But you haven't *half* a quarter of it left. The rest has been sunk and lost in your worthless pictures and wild-goose schemes. You don't begin to understand what this house is costing you to run. I do. And however much I try to economize, your expenses will not meet your income—not at the rate you live— wintering abroad and staying in suites at the best hotels." Indignation mastered her. She seized an ash-tray and into the wastepaper basket disgustedly emptied its contents, the stubs of two half-smoked cigars. "And these! I paid the bill for these yesterday—a thousand Coronas, and another for five hundred Henry Clays, sent to Reginald Tarrant. I don't doubt you paid his expenses on that horrible trip to Seville. Make no mistake, those friends of yours—save the mark!—are no good to you and never will be."

"The greatest mistake of my life," he told her dryly, "has already been made."

"So now," with quiet enmity she answered him, "we know."

And, in that short duel of words, the stealthy undercurrent of mutual mistrust and hostility had risen like scum to the placid surface of their lives. No discernible severance, no parting of their ways, heralded the exodus from Brook Street. Yet every recurrence of some such niggling argument brought with it, as a breath on glass and as swift to fade, the widening between them of a breach. . . .

She had secured at a reasonable rent the lease of a flat in Queen Anne's Mansions. Of the staff at Brook Street, Larkin, now well over seventy, was pensioned off, and the remainder dismissed, with exception of Annie and Albert who had decided to marry—"Because, ma'am," said Annie, "we've been courting on and off these five years and it don't seem right to live in such close quarters, just the two of us together, unless we do the proper thing, like."

They did 'the proper thing, like', and were presented with a gift of twenty pounds from Adrian and a double bed from Perry, bought of Shoolbreds'.

Close quarters indeed was the fit found to be for Adrian's pictures. Those, that at Perry's persuasion he had decided to sell, fetched a lamentable price as copies bought and paid for as originals. Having sold the remainder of the ninety-nine years' lease of the Brook Street house with much of its furniture, Adrian approached the change to what he described as 'a tenement', with the fixed determination to make the worst of it.

He did.

More frequent, more prolonged were his absences abroad, while Perry stayed at home faced with the fact that not only had he ceased to find his marriage an exciting new experience, but that he heartily regretted it. Yet, although her hold upon him, never tenable, had waned, she was certain she had not been supplanted. The lure of the alcove and promiscuous adventure belonged to his youth, and, in his late forties, had ceased to attract. That he was still, contradictorily, insistent on his rights she regarded as one of those compulsions implicit to the squirearchy of ownership, inherent from a line of forebears whose wives were as much their sole monopoly as the lands they overlorded. This she accepted as inevitable of the age into which she had been born when woman, lesser half of man, must rest content within the limits of legalized concubinage.

Then came the South African War to crash in upon the even tenor of life, known, endured, and, without question, suffered by her and others of her kind. While from Mayfair to Whitechapel the City of London Volunteers—in their new dun-coloured uniforms, dubbed 'khaki', to camouflage them from Boer marksmen on the Veldt—answered the call to arms, so, roused from traditional lethargy, did women respond to the call for Red Cross nurses.

Men were dying like flies of enteric. Base hospitals, understaffed and overcrowded by the victims of disease, claimed a greater toll of British soldiers than did the deadly aim of Boer rifles.

The new century was scarcely a month old when Perry with Jasper, youthful successor to Phyllis who had died a peaceful death of ripe old age, walked across the Park to a Knightsbridge hotel. Leaving the bull-pup in charge of a page, she was taken up in the lift to the suite of Miss Lavinia.

The interview was brief and to the point.

"I hear," said Perry, "that Charters, the Stilton place, is to be turned into a hospital for wounded officers."

"Precisely so. And I," said Miss Lavinia, "am to be the Commandant."

She had changed little in these last five years; a trifle greyer, more chinny, more gaunt, and perhaps more consciously upright in bearing as befitting her status that, pending delivery of more orthodox uniform, was proclaimed by a white band decorated with a red cross upon her arm.

"I was wondering," suggested Perry, "if you could make use of me. I have had, as you know, some experience of nursing with Geraldine, but what I want most is to go to the Front. I thought," she offered winningly, "if I could train with you at the Stiltons' hospital——"

"At my hospital you mean," rasped Miss Lavinia.

Waving aside the interruption—"until," persisted Perry, "I could be considered experienced enough to go out as a fully-fledged nurse——"

"Not if I know it!" was the decisive reply. "Dead of enteric in a week. Never pass your medical and as for fully-fledged—takes three years to train a nurse. We don't want amateurs."

"I——" began Perry.

"Listen to me." Miss Lavinia rose from her desk, stuck her hands in the gentlemanly pockets of her skirt, and said sternly: "The base hospitals are cluttered up with young women who think it no end of a lark to go out to the Front. General nuisance. Chase from your mind all thought of *that*, my girl. If you want to be a nurse you can nurse here where you'll be an asset, not a liability. Need every woman I can get. Sign you on now as trainee if you like, but not for South Africa. Take it or leave it."

"Very well," said Perry meekly; and restrained herself from adding, "So you think!"

And: "Thank God," Lady Stilton to Perry confided, "that I am given this chance to serve my country by placing my house at the disposal of our gallant officers. I did, I must confess, stipulate for officers. They will be more appreciative, more careful, of my beautiful home than the dear Tommies. I could not bear to have the walls of my drawing-room riddled with darts, and the floors scraped by hobnailed boots."

"They are unlikely to wear boots," Perry reminded her, "in bed."

"They won't all be in bed. Most of them—I hope—will be convalescent. We are storing the furniture and pictures, and Freddie and I will have to pig it in Park Street. I shall superintend the catering department"—God help us! Perry voicelessly commented—"for which," continued Lady Stilton, "I ought to receive and will certainly demand from the Government a grant or subsidy of some sort. I only wish I were young enough—or strong enough," she amended hastily, "to nurse. However, I shall pay regular visits to the wards and bring them books and magazines."

Preparations went apace and within a few weeks Charters was ready to receive the first contingent of wounded. Miss Lavinia had collected some half dozen trained nurses, and numerous volunteer helpers drawn from neighbouring districts. Perry, not greatly to her liking, shared an attic bedroom with Annabel Stilton, who had eagerly offered her services to Miss Lavinia. Adrian, having extended his visit to Spain from three weeks to three months, returned at the end of February and was met, on the evening of his arrival at the flat, by his wife in nurse's uniform. She had twenty-four hours' leave and was taking the eight o'clock train back. They had an early dinner and he drove her to the station in a cab. At Perry's insistence he had given up his private hansom, but he still retained the brougham—"And that too," she told him, "you will have to sell. Foster and the groom have enlisted, and the horses—quite unnecessary to keep two for a brougham —are eating their heads off for want of exercise."

"Since," said Adrian, "you are determined to bring our standard of living down to the lowest common denominator, the best thing I can do is to take myself abroad again, where at least one may live like a gentleman."

Her lips closed on a smile.

The platform at Victoria teemed with men in khaki home on leave from or on their way to training camps. Newsboys were yelling, "British vic'tree—gryte British vic'tree—pyper, sir?"

Adrian bought an evening paper, scanned the headlines and handed it to Perry as he put her in the train, laconically remarking: "Cronje has surrendered. The war will be over in three months. Don't work too hard. You look quite charming in your nurse's bonnet, but I deplore the smell of disinfectant."

Depositing a kiss on her forehead, he stepped back and stood bareheaded as the train began to move, raised his hand for a second, and turned, walking swiftly away.

She had the compartment to herself and, in the dim light of its ceiling lamp, she read Lord Roberts' report.

'Paardeburg, 27th February, 7.45 a.m.

General Cronje and all his forces capitulated unconditionally at daylight this morning and is now a prisoner in my camp. I hope Her Majesty's Government will consider this event satisfactory, occurring as it does on the anniversary of Majuba.'

Cronje's capitulation turned the tide of war in Britain's

favour. The day after the battle of Paardeburg, Buller helio-
graphed to Ladysmith news of his victory at Pieter's Hill—a
prolonged and terrible holocaust terminating in Ladysmith's
relief.

It was the end of that hundred and nineteen days' siege.
For the last month the garrison had held out on starvation
rations, while hunger, disease, and bombardment decimated
their ranks of over ten thousand officers and men.

A few weeks later Charters received more than its quota of
casualties, those of the wounded considered fit enough to make
the voyage and ease the burden imposed on the crowded base
hospitals.

"And now we'll be worked off our feet," Annabel delightedly
declared. "Sixty more bed-pans came today and Sister has put
me on to scrub them up. I suppose you haven't time to help
me? I'll never get through before I go off duty."

No, Perry had no time to help her. She had a dozen extra
beds to prepare for the new arrivals. This done, she took
temperatures, carried round trays for mid-day meals, and sat
spoon-feeding a youngster who had lost his right arm and an
eye at Modder River.

"I say, Nurse," his one sound eye, the colour of a peri-
winkle, looked up at her with a laugh in it, "do you know this
is the third time in four days that you've stuffed me with
minced rabbit?"

"Chicken mousse," Perry told him demurely, "made from
Lady Stilton's own recipe. Come along now, eat it up. It's
delicious."

"*You* are, but *it* isn't, and if it's not rabbit it's hen—a particularly tough old hen. And talking of old hens——" He
slewed his eye round at Miss Lavinia who had stalked into the
ward accompanied by a paunchy bespectacled gentleman.

"We are not talking of old hens," Perry said firmly. "We
are talking of your smart new sleeping-suit. Is this the latest
thing?"

He nodded.

"Called pyjamas—a Yankee importation. Who's this old
johnnie with our excellent Burbage? Mr. Pickwick?"

"There's apple charlotte with cream to follow, but you must
eat this first," urged Perry, offering the spoon, neatly dodged
by Mr. Dickinson.

"If my eye does not deceive me," he murmured, "they are making for my bed."

"Good morning, Mr. Dickinson," Miss Lavinia bearing down upon him, presented: "Mr. Jordan—kindly come from London to give us an opinion on your eye. Take the patient's tray, Nurse."

"Good-bye, Dolly," muttered the patient from a corner of his mouth, "I'm sure your name is Dolly—must you leave me? It breaks my heart to let you go—and don't do me out of the charlotte."

"Nurse," Miss Lavinia commanded, "go to Ward Number Seven. You are wanted there."

Her tone implied she was not wanted here.

"Yes, Miss Burbage."

She carried out the tray and went off to Ward Number Seven. A harassed staff nurse met her. "Thank goodness you've come! I'm single-handed. Three nurses down with influenza. I want you to blanket-bath Numbers Four and Five."

Perry approached Number Four, one of those who had been delivered at the hospital within the last hour after a cross-country journey from Southampton. He had thigh and head wounds; his chin was adorned with a three days' growth of reddish stubble; his moustache, frankly ginger, needed clipping. His freckled hands lay inert upon the sheet.

"Sorry to disturb you," Perry said, professionally cheerful. "I'm just going to clean you up," and unwinding his bandages, she disclosed the face of him whom she had never thought to see again: Garth Curran.

He was too far gone to know her, for although the wound in his head appeared to be healthy enough, his thigh was turning septic. Suppressing a shudder at the angry sight of it, she signalled Sister.

"Will you have a look at this, please."

Sister, a wizened, pale, efficient little person, had a look, and pursed her lips.

"I'll get Doctor to him. Give me his chart."

Perry removed the chart from its hook above the bed. Sister examined it, handed it back, and lowered the bed-head.

"Just for a minute, Major Curran, for Nurse to blanket-bath you."

Nurse deftly blanket-bathed him, while with eyes closed, he lay unmoving.

"This is doing nicely," Sister told him as she redressed and bandaged his head. "Now I'm just going to put a temporary dressing on this thigh. Nurse! Don't stand there staring. Bring me a fresh bowl of disinfectant. Hurry up."

Nurse hurried up to hand the bowl of warm water and a bottle of carbolic.

"Pour it in, Nurse, pour it in!" And as she dipped a swab, Sister sniffed: "Probationers! More trouble than they're worth . . . Go on, Nurse, take these."

Nurse gathered up the dirty dressings and disposed of them. When she returned to Number Four, Sister was charting his temperature. "A hundred and two point eight. I'll fetch Doctor. Have you given him the bed-pan? Well then, *give* it. Must I have to tell you every mortal thing?"

She hastened, starchily, away.

After attending to the needs of Number Four, Perry went the round of the ward to relieve 'Staff' who had gone to dinner. When she came back to Garth his eyes, that held no shade of recognition in them, were open as, in a voice, hurtingly weak, he asked for a drink.

She raised him up and gave him barley-water. He sipped, grimaced, and said with the ghost of a grin: "D'you call this a drink? Can you not make it a whisky?"

"This is better for you than whisky."

"Not at all! There's nothing like a drop o' the boy for taking the ache out of me leg."

Controlling a tremor she asked, "Does it pain you?"

"Like hell it does." Then, with a puzzled look, he said: "Haven't I seen you somewhere before?"

Her heart gave a leap—and a dive. This was no time to jog his memory; and she answered coolly: "We all look alike in uniform. Now, you are not to talk any more. Try and get some sleep."

And with a heightened colour in her cheeks she passed on to Number Five.

That same evening Sister told her she had been put on night duty to replace another nurse down with influenza. "Report to Night Sister at eight o'clock."

A pleasant old party from Perth was Night Sister who informed her: "There's only the two of us, you and myself, and not much to be doing except for Number Fourr. You know where I am, Nurrse, if you want me."

Against the green and gilt panelled walls of the ward, once the dining-room, were ranged a double row of beds. Two incandescent burners gave barely sufficient light to read the charts, leaving a pool of darkness in the centre of the ward. In her felt slippers Perry went noiselessly about her duties. As Night Sister had said, there was nothing 'much to be doing'. The patients slept, on and off, with the exception of Four, whose temperature at midnight soared to a hundred and five. . . .

'Sister told me to bathe him in tepid water and that helped to bring him down. His thigh was a ghastly mess— and no wonder, after all those weeks in a hospital ship. I had an awful time with him that night. In his delirium he relived the charge at Kliptkraal Drift which I gathered from his ravings was on the way to Paardeburg. He was shouting to his men, cursing them, cheering them, leading them on. I learned quite a lot while I listened to his mutterings of names to be recognized again when I read them in the papers, but not until years after and under very different circumstances did I hear that he had won the D.S.O. for conspicuous courage in that charge. He had pursued his course for thirty miles to the capture of Kliptkraal Drift on the Modder River, cutting off Cronje's communications from Bloemfontein. In his fever he cried for water, not for himself, for his horse—shot under him. The sun was like a furnace and the veldt a red-hot oven. I lived it all again with him, was choked with dust and smelt the poisonous green fumes of the bursting lyddite shells from our howitzer batteries. And as his voice grew weaker and weaker so did his language grow stronger and stronger! It seemed to be hand to hand fighting. Afterwards, when he was convalescent, he told me that Cronje's resistance was magnificent.

"He had four thousand of the best with him," he said. "I'll say the Boers can fight." And so did he. I couldn't hold him down. He was tearing off his dressings. In the end I had to call Sister and we strapped him to the bed. Sister told me to fetch Doctor. Our house surgeon was a very up to date young man, just qualified. In those days there were none of these antibiotics. Doctor gave him some tablets of a new drug called something (unspellable) acid, known the world over today as aspirin. As he walked away with Sister I heard Doctor say there was an eighty to one chance against his living through the night.

He did live through the night, but only just. He must have had, the doctor said, the constitution of an ox.

I nursed him on night duty for a month. It was rather shattering to find he didn't know me.

Not until his convalescence when he was allowed to sit in the sun on the terrace—I was back on day duty by then— did he repeat, as if continuing the words he spoke on the day of his arrival—"You know, Nurse, I've seen you before but I can't think where."

Young Dickinson, who was working out a chess problem on the chair beside him, chimed in, "Sir, you've seen her every night for these last four weeks."

"I don't mean that." Garth wrinkled his forehead with a two-inch scar across it, nicely healed by this time, though he carried its mark for life. "Good God!" He sat up from his pillows to say, "If you're not Peridot Flight you're her double."

"I was, but I'm not," I said, "Peridot Flight." And into the house I carried his tray and left him to think it over.

He thought it over and told me that evening when he was back in bed and I was taking the six o'clock temperatures: "I suppose you mean you're married." And he looked at my left hand.

"How bright of you," I said, "Major Curran."

"Whom did you marry? Anyone I know?"

"One whom you used to know well," I said; and popped my thermometer under his tongue. "My name is Hope-Winter now."

"What!"

"Don't talk," I said, "with that in your mouth, or you'll break it." And I kept my eyes fixed on my watch while I felt his pulse. It was steadier than mine. I removed the thermometer and read it.

"I should think the shock of this," and he was grinning wide, "has bust the mercury."

I said coldly, "You're sub-normal." And taking my note-book from my apron pocket I asked him: "Will you have omelette or steamed fish for your supper?"

"How long have you been married?"

"Apples and baked custard or jam tart to follow. Which would you like?"

"I'd like a jolly good rump steak."

"You can't have rump steak at night. Please to give me your order, Major Curran. I have others to attend besides yourself."

"Sure, I don't care what I have, at all. Well, I'm——" I think he said damned. "So you married Hope-Winter. When?"

I passed on to the next bed.

"I say, Nurse!"

I turned a blank face to him. "Yes?"

"Do you ever have any time off?"

"Of course."

"Couldn't we——" "No," I said firmly, "we couldn't."

Miss Lavinia had made it a hard and fast rule which, needless to say, was seldom obeyed, forbidding the nurses to have, as she called it, "social intercourse" with any of the patients. However, what we chose to do in our off time and out of hospital, was our own affair.

On the following day I was moved to another ward and saw little or nothing of Major Curran until he received his discharge two weeks later, when I applied for and was given five days' leave. . . .'

On the morning Garth left Charters, Perry 'hung about' she shamelessly admits, 'on Lewes station', where he, who arrived at eleven-fifteen, found her at the bookstall. "I'll have this——" She bought the *Strand Magazine*, took a sidelong glance, saw him limping hurriedly toward her, turned her back and heard:

"Hullo! Are you going up by this train?"

"You!" She gave an admirable start of astonishment. "What are you doing here, Major Curran?"

"I'm discharged today. Didn't you know?"

She offered him a wide, limpid stare. "But how could I know? You are not in my ward."

"Here she comes." He grabbed her dressing-case. "I'll take this. We'll travel up together."

"First, sir?" The porter, trundling his luggage, wrenched open a door, hoisted Garth's bag on to the rack, received a tip and they were off.

Although she had nursed him for more than five weeks, she had never been alone with him for more than five minutes; nor on that journey to London did they have the carriage to themselves. The train was crowded, their compartment full. A little boy in a sailor suit gallantly gave up his seat to—'You, sir, a wounded soldier'; while Perry had upon her left an old gentleman asleep, and on her right a fat lady, reading *Home Chat* and smelling strongly of moth-balls. At Victoria, Garth put her in a hansom and apologized for not driving her home. He had an appointment with the War Office.

"If," she said carelessly, "you are free this afternoon do drop in for tea. There is so much I want to hear about—the war."

He would be delighted. "At the same address?"

"No, we have moved to a flat in Queen Anne's Mansions. At four o'clock, then?"

A letter from Adrian in Paris awaited her among a pile of his bills. She ran through them hurriedly, dismayed to find most of them outstanding and accompanied by threatening demands for wines, cigars, and a jeweller's account, two years overdue, for a gold cigarette case sent to Mrs. Vanduren at Villa Rinaldo, Florence. A return for hospitality, no doubt.

She folded her lips.

"If you please, ma'am——"

"Yes, Annie?"

"Mr. Hope-Winter came back last Friday, ma'am, and stayed two nights."

"Yes, I know. Your master wrote me he was coming."

She lied, he had not written for three weeks, and now:

'Paris is wonderful, London quite horrible. Nothing but hideous khaki, revolting posters, and drum and fife bands. I fled in horror to the Vandurens, who have a delightful new apartment on the Champs Elysées. You poor child! Why *will* you go on with this tedious nursing? Your trop de zèle appals me. If you feel inclined to tear yourself away from

7*

your unmentionable duties, come to me here. I shall be at
the Meurice till the end of the month. The Vandurens left
for the States today . . . .'

He signed himself devotedly hers.

She wondered if *l'affaire Corinne*, so to herself she named
that age-old friendship, had been resuscitated to become a
second blooming. She would never know, and the thought
flashed through her, with a shock of surprise, that if she did
know she wouldn't care. Nor did she take to herself any credit
for broad-minded generosity. Neither was to blame if their
marriage went awry for want of unity, shared comradeship,
the mutual surrender of heart and soul and body. Such was
not and never could be hers, with him. She had no right in nor
desire for possession, who had gone to him unloving and un-
loved.

Garth arrived on the stroke of four and was duly presented
to Jasper, a boisterous youngster, red-pied, with a most engaging wriggle and the white wrinkled face of a clown.

"I first saw him," Perry said, "staring at me from behind a
glass cage in Whiteley's live-stock department. He was very
small and very fat. When I tapped on the window he lay on
his side and kicked. I have never seen anything more like a
baby laughing—and I bought him on the spot."

Garth gave a tweak to Jasper's frantic tail, saying: "This is
too long."

"I know, and so is he—from head to stern—too long, and
too high on the leg and too houndish. In fact he's all wrong as
bulldogs go, but otherwise pure gold."

Tea was brought and over the tea-cups they spanned the
space of time—"since that day you came to Brook Street
with Miss Bourne."

She stole a look and caught a twinkle.

"What happened to Phyllis?"

"She lived to be ten."

"A good age for a bulldog."

"And a good end. She died in her sleep. I wouldn't have
wished her a more peaceful death. She simply adored Geraldine. It was pitiful to see her during that last illness. She never
left the bedside."

"Nor, as I heard from my father, did you."

"Geraldine," Perry's voice faltered, "was everything to me. I missed her terribly."

Garth nodded.

"I wonder what she would have made of her life, with that extraordinary beauty of hers, had she been—as others are."

"Do you believe," Perry handed him his third cup of tea, "that we *do* make our lives, or that life makes us?"

Slowly Garth swallowed a cucumber sandwich before he answered: "I am inclined to agree with Browning that 'life is only an insane dream we take for waking'."

"Yes." Her eyes shone greenly. "You quoted Browning the first time I met you."

"Did I?" He stayed his cup in mid-air. "And that's how long ago?"

"A whole life time ago."

He said: "You haven't changed at all, now I see you out of uniform. You still have that same young surprised look you had when I chanced on you standing in midstream on Exmoor with a gash in your foot. By the way, I came across a shoe of yours in a pocket of an old tweed suit when I first went out to India."

"A shoe of mine?" The uplift of her negligible eyebrows expressed nothing but a guileless amaze.

"I would hardly dare to hope that you'd remember." And watching her provocative smile, he said with curt inconsequence: "You've not yet told me how long you have been married."

She answered indirectly, gazing not at but beyond him and away: "When Geraldine died my life was very empty, and Adrian——"

Garth's voice broke the pause: "Filled a gap?" He uncrossed a knee and winced.

She said quickly: "Your wound—does it pain you?"

"Now and then—a twinge. Is Adrian in London?"

"No, in Paris."

He took a long look at her.

"After a year of nothing to see except khaki and dun-coloured veldt, the sight of you," he said, "is gladdening. Your eyes are like the sea and your hair is pale honey, and so—will you dine with me this evening, or would Adrian object?"

A moment of stillness passed, and then:

"Adrian objects to nothing that I choose to do or not to do," she told him coolly, "within reason."

"There won't be much reason in London tonight. Listen to that."

Through the open window could be heard, down in Parliament Square, a mighty humming as of Brobdingnagian bees. "They're on their toes, waiting for the news to come through on the tape."

"You mean"—she caught her breath—"Mafeking?"

Garth nodded.

"That's it. Two hundred days of suspense and now—any minute." He rose from his chair. "I'll be calling for you here at seven-thirty and I'll take you somewhere quiet if there's any quiet to be found."

The 'somewhere quiet' proved to be an exclusive little restaurant in a side-street off Piccadilly, noted for its cuisine and discerning clientèle. Garth, who appeared to be well known there, was greeted, nose to knees, by a bowing head-waiter and conducted to a corner table. The menu consulted, and the rainbow trout, recommended by the *maître d'hôtel*, consumed: "Strange," remarked Garth, "that we should come across each other again in that hospital."

"Not so very strange," she replied with elaborate indifference, "considering that Charters is my brother-in-law's house."

"Still, out of every hospital in England——"

"There aren't so many hospitals for officers in England. It was ten to one we should meet."

"And my luck." He raised his glass. "And my thanks for my life which the M.O. told me I owe to you—your good nursing."

"That," she said, flushing, "is his modesty. He worked a miracle that night. It was a near thing."

His glance lingered on her face, her lips, faintly smiling; on her throat, creamy white as the pearls that circled it. "I was always conscious of you there beside me—for my comfort."

Her eyes lifted to his; their glasses joined.

"To you," she whispered. "And to victory."

"It's on its way, but—by Jove! Those Boers can fight."

He told her how they fought, generous in praise of them.

"We were hell's target when we first went out in scarlet.

They knocked us down as fast as we came up, and not a man of them with any training more than pot-shots at wildebeest and lion, until we got into our khaki and our stride."

"Will they send you out again?"

But his answer to that was lost in a wild burst of cheering from the street, as, through the restaurant's revolving doors, surged a rowdy procession of youths. Arms linked and ignoring the protests of waiters, they stamped round the room singing:

> " 'All in a row
> Mind 'ow you go
> Fourteen jolly good boys
> All in a row——'

—Three cheers for Baden-Powell! 'Ip pip-pip——"

Decorous diners joined in the chorus of 'Hurrays!' Men flung napkins to the ceiling, women clattered cutlery, a table overturned, glasses crashed; and while an agitated *maître d'hôtel* made ineffectual attempts to re-establish order, Garth grabbed a grinning waiter, paid the bill.

"Come on." He wrapped Perry in her cloak. "I must get you out of this and home, if we can find a cab."

But they couldn't find a cab. What they did find, from Lady Mulvarnie's account of it, was:

'. . . All London gone stark staring mad. I have lived through two world wars but never have I seen anything to equal the saturnalian convulsion that attacked us all that night to celebrate the relief of a little town not half the size of Kensington Gardens and six thousand miles away! As we came out into the Circus we were caught up and dragged along by a screaming, dancing, singing, joy-demented mob that swarmed round Eros and went reeling, twenty abreast, down Piccadilly. Regardless of the efforts of the police to hold them back they climbed lamp-posts, waved Union Jacks, entwined themselves with paper streamers, let off squibs and crackers, flourished top-hats perched on walking sticks, laughed, cried—yes, I saw men positively crying maudlin tears. One may believe quite a number were considerably drunk. Garth, conspicuous in khaki, had his hand seized by an elderly party with mutton-chop whiskers and the crown of his topper bashed in, who solemnly assured him, between hiccups, that he was a jolly good fellow, and everyone took it up yelling, "And so say all of us!" We were surrounded. A coster in pearlies, shouting "Keep yer 'air on!" tore my hat from my head and replaced it with his cap. I pulled it off and threw it back at him, but I never saw my hat—a new one, too!—again. I was terrified lest Garth would suffer damage to his leg, and tried to tell those nearest us not to bang him about as he was only just out of hospital. But my voice in that hurricane had no more effect than the hum of a gnat.

"Hang on to me for God's sake!" shouted Garth. "And don't let go."

I hung on to him as best I could while he struck out right and left fighting a passage through that howling bedlam, where it was impossible to move one voluntary step.

The Victorian inhibitions that had held the Englishman imprisoned behind the fortress of his national reserve were swept aside in a torrent of primeval frenzy, uncivilized and unimaginable. I saw women, dowagers and débutantes, with their escorts—in false noses—elbowing a way for them as they emerged from the Criterion Theatre. Caught up in the maelstrom, they jigged along with the rest in a delirious farrago of penny whistles, ticklers, flags, and giant posters raised on poles, of Baden-Powell.

Garth with his arm round me was yelling in my ear, "Talk about democracy! Here it is—red-hot!"

It took us two hours to get from Piccadilly to Jermyn Street, where at last we found a hansom and were driven home with half a dozen rowdies clinging to the back of it.

"Sorry to have let you in for this," Garth said at the door of the flat.

"Sorry?" I took him up sharp. "Sorry that you and all of you out there have let us in for *this*—to win the war!"

"The war is a long way from won," he said. "I give it another two years. . . ."

And two years it was before the Spartan resistance of the many slow gave way to the too few swift. The strategic raid and ambush of the Boers, allied to a perfect knowledge of and acclimatization to a country where death-dealing enteric had depleted Roberts' armies, resulted in prolonged guerilla warfare.

Kruger's flight to Portugal in September decided the ultimate issue, and the 'Khaki Election' that returned the Unionists with a strong majority and Salisbury again as Prime Minister, brought to its head the Peace of Veeringen.

The struggle was over, but she, whose presence had upheld her subjects in their peril, and who, with them, had suffered a personal anguish in their losses and reverses during that first terrible year of the campaign, did not live to see the end of it.

A hush fell on the nation, of whom the great majority had never known life without her.

Watched by a mute black multitude on that drizzling February morning, 1901, passed the small white-shrouded coffin on which reposed the Orb and Sceptre of Majesty: and with it passed the glory of an epoch.

Five kings and forty ruling princes followed the cortège along the route to Paddington where, with crape swathed colours, heads bowed, and arms reversed, troops lined the sanded way.

It was hard to believe that those same silent thousands had, only a few months before, made of her capital a seething cauldron of rejoicing the like of which had never been nor never was to be again. And, as that great living throng stood in its awe-struck silence to see the passing of the gun-carriage that bore the royal bier, a universal sigh, as of dead leaves falling, shivered through the stillness. . . . Then, above the muffled beat of drums and toll of bells, was heard the National Anthem played by the slow marching bands, and a murmur went up from those many who voiced, for the first time, the words:

"God Save the King!"

EIGHT

'Saw procession from window of A.'s Club. Garth riding with Hussars. Spotted him at once. Wonderful display though nothing like so splendid as the Jubilee. The Queen perfectly beautiful. Very made-up. Had excellent view of them both. The King quite recovered. Looks rather old. Terrific ovation. Hilda rises to occasion with Coronation dinner. Exceedingly dull—and mock-turtle! Everyone shaking heads over Salisbury's resignation. No one seems to think much of Balfour. Made myself thoroughly unpopular by saying a good thing to see the last of the Queen's Grand Old Men. Talk veered hastily to King's operation. A. now convinced *he* has appendicitis. Came to my bedroom very worried because of a pain in his tummy. Told him no wonder after Hilda's awful fizz, but he insists on my making appointment for him to see Sir Frederick Treves. . . .'

So dawned the Edwardian era, and in his sixtieth year a King had come into his own, bringing with him a welcome release from the severe autocracy imposed on the Court by his mother. It was as if a fresh breeze had swept through the whole ill-ventilated social structure on which the Victorian tradition had been founded, and had thought to be indissoluble. And now, with the ghost of Grundy, it had vanished. In its stead stood a genial monarch, herald of change so rapid that even the young could scarcely keep pace with the amazing subversion from the dominant rigidity of morals, fashions, codes, that had held imprisoned the spirit of an age passed into history—or limbo.

The measure of the day was set to speed with one of those new motor-cars, a Daimler, for the King, and the Twopenny Tube for his people. Stuffy, dreary, afternoon Drawing-Rooms were at once abolished. The King announced that evening Courts only henceforth would be held: gay functions, these, with refreshments and music, and for débutantes a martyrdom no longer.

Self-assertive feminism, strident for the vote, formed the Women's Social and Political Union, calling to their ranks recruits from all classes. Church Parade in Hyde Park was depleted of Fashion, who spent its week-ends at house-parties.

With the re-establishment of Charters, Lady Stilton, determined to be in the swim, entertained frugally, Fridays to Mondays, in the hope of hospitality returned.

It was in September, 1903, that Perry resignedly accepted an urgent invitation.

My dear Peridot,

Do help me out next Friday. I am in a lamentable fix. The Lyndhursts—the Bourne girl as she was—were coming with his brother, Tommy Poole, for Annabel, and now they wire me today that Lord Branscombe, his father, has suddenly died and it has put out my numbers. We are few enough already, just the Vandurens and Reginald Tarrant and Valerie Croome, and I shall have to find another man for Annabel. I have written to Garth Curran, but I must have two more. It will greatly oblige me if you and Adrian can come and may I borrow Albert? My first footman has the measles, isn't it tiresome, I have had to send him off. I only hope to heaven he hasn't given it to any other of the staff and can you ask Adrian if he can let me have a dozen or more if he can spare it, of the port laid down by our dear father which you know he never touches so it only goes to waste, and I beg you not to bring that dog of yours. It ate me out of hearth and home last time. The servants actually gave him rump steak!

Come early if you can and help me with the flowers. We cannot afford a housekeeper with this awful income tax at one and twopence in the pound.

> Hastily,
> Hilda.

Perry passed the letter to Adrian at breakfast.

"There is none left of your father's port. You gave the last of it to Reginald. I suppose we'll have to go?"

"As you say—and if you wish, and as Curran will be there to amuse you——"

Leaving the rest of his sentence unfinished he unfurled *The Times* and disappeared behind it.

Perry allowed a moment's silence to follow his remark and the twisted smile that went with it; then, carefully buttering toast, she said:

"Adrian——"

" 'M?"

"Those Peruvian mines you bought on Sankey's advice have dropped alarmingly. You ought to sell."

With an exaggerated sigh he emerged from his paper to say:

"Always money, money, money. It becomes a trifle wearisome."

"Not so wearisome," she flashed, "as the loss of it will be. How could you let yourself be guided by Sankey? He knows nothing whatsoever of the stock markets. If you must speculate, why don't you consult a reputable broker?"

"As it happens I did consult a reputable broker."

"Yes." She nodded, wrinkling her nose. "Sankey's latest familiar, that mincing little ape, Tommy Poole, whose father put him on the Stock Exchange to keep him off the Turf. Those shares today aren't worth five shillings, and you bought them at top price."

Adrian passed his cup to be refilled.

"There is nothing," he drawled, "more distasteful to me and more unbecoming to you than this perpetual insistence on the state of my finances. My life seems to be haunted by women mercenarily obsessed. I married you as escape from my sister's bureaucracy——"

"So that was the reason," she interposed reflectively. "I have often wondered why."

"—only to find you are similarly tinctured with desire"—his small teeth, slightly stained from cigar smoke, were revealed as his smile reappeared—"for executive control of my affairs. It may be the merely atavistic instinct of the female for self-preservation, but that makes it none the less tedious to me."

"And this may be even more tedious to you." She tossed him a bill. "Last quarter's telephone account, long overdue. They are threatening to cut us off. I see there are several calls to Paris."

The telephone, a recently installed acquisition and not yet in general use, was enclosed in a boxy ungainly contrivance attached to the wall. Adrian glanced at it and said: "Which reminds me—you might ring through to the Vandurens at the Carlton and ask Corinne if they will drive me down to Charters. They are almost certain to go in their automobile, and if Hilda wants you there early——"

"Yes," Perry got up from the table. "I shall go by train."

She went by train, arriving at Charters in time for luncheon, cold mutton and pickles, served on the terrace to herself and Annabel.

"Uncle Freddie has been sent off to the golf club for his luncheon," snorted Annabel, "and Aunt Hilda is having hers in bed, where she will stay, with pads of cotton-wool soaked in witch-hazel on her eyes, so as to be fresh for the guests at tea-time. From the fuss she makes over her mingy week-ends you would think she was entertaining Royalty, and it won't be for want of effort on her part if she doesn't. We had one of the equerries here last week, and the chicken mousse was actually *not* rabbit! She has put you and Adrian in the bachelors' wing to save the electric light in the married suite intended for the Porkies. She refused to let Uncle have the house electrically wired throughout, although you would have thought it wouldn't have cost much more while she was about it. Valerie Croome has the single suite. She's a niece of the Lord Chamberlain, so you can't say that Aunt Hilda doesn't try. Next week she has Sir Albert Mendel. He's bosom friends, you know, with Someone Else. They call each other Bertie and they might be twins they're so alike. And, my dear, what *do* you think happened at Newmarket! I had this from Tommy Poole—such a shame he isn't coming, he's such fun. Well, according to him he went up to Sir Albert on the race-course, banged him on the back and said, 'Damn you, Bertie, I've lost my shirt on your filly'— And my dear, it was the King!"

Annabel's neighing laugh ended in a sneeze.

"I've hay-fever—so provoking! As if my nose wasn't big enough already without *this* to make it twice its size. There's only cheese to follow. I couldn't possibly, could you?"

No, Perry couldn't. "Hilda wants me to do the flowers. I had better find McGregor."

"You needn't. They are all cut and waiting for you in the

flower-room. I have to write the menus, and then dash off in the brougham to meet Valerie and Major Curran. They're coming by the two-forty-five."

It took Perry all the afternoon to 'do' the flowers, choosing tiger lilies for Corinne's suite, and carnations for Valerie Croome's.

Only two of the guests were assembled in the hall at five o'clock, when, having changed her travelling dress for a tea-gown, she descended.

"My dear Peridot!" Hilda's sisterly greeting suggested she had only that minute arrived. "Is Adrian not with you?"

Politely maintaining the illusion, Perry told her: "He is driving down with the Vandurens in their motor-car."

"Dear me! I trust they will get here safely. I am always so nervous of those nasty motor-cars. Let me see now—you know Lady Valerie, don't you?"

Yes, Perry knew Lady Valerie, a juvenile fifty with suspiciously blonde hair, forget-me-not-blue eyes, and a superfluous husband from whom she lived apart in greatest amity.

Tepid tea, that had stood for half an hour, was handed to Perry by Garth who, as he prepared to seat himself beside her, was girlishly recalled by Lady Valerie.

"Major Curran! Did I or did I not see you in Regent Street yesterday, driving a bright yellow automobile?"

"Yes, Lady Valerie, you did. And lucky for me that I didn't see you, or I might have lost my head"—he gave her a languishing look—"having long since lost my heart."

"What a compromising confession to make before witnesses! But your laboured gallantry is unconvincing. I am painfully reminded that you chose to take a smoker on the train when you might so easily have taken *me*!" She uttered a little scream of laughter. "Do give me one of those éclairs." And as he passed her the cake-stand she patted the sofa invitingly. "Sit here and tell me all about your wonderful new motor-car. *Is* it yours, and is it new?"

"It is new, and will be mine—when I have paid for it."

"I'm simply dying to go for a drive in a motor-car. But aren't you *brave* to drive yourself—and all alone! Have you run over anything yet?"

"Only a few hens."

"Oh!" Another little scream. "You blood-thirsty creature! Were they killed?"

From Sir Frederick, hitherto silent, came the query: "Are you insured against accidents?"

"Yes, at a fabulous rate."

"What does a motor-car cost to run?"

"Freddie!" cried his wife, "you surely don't contemplate buying one of those horrible machines. I should never have a moment's peace."

"Cheaper than horses, my dear, any day. Motor-cars eat nothing."

"Only petrol," said Garth.

"And hens," severely prompted Lady Stilton. "I suppose you had to pay the owners for the loss of them?"

"Yes, plus a fine from a bobby skulking in a ditch to have me up for scorching."

"How thrilling! I am quite determined," twittered Lady Valerie, "to buy a motor-car as soon as I go back to Town. Will you come with me to choose it on Monday, Major Curran?"

"On one condition only, Lady Valerie—that you engage me as your chauffeur."

"Most certainly I will, I should feel so *safe* with you at the steering-gear, or whatever they call the thing you guide it with—— Heavens! What on earth is that?"

'That' was the ear-scraping toot of a horn, a hideous scrunching of gravel, and a rattling as of tin cans tied to the tails of a hundred cats.

"It must be," said Lady Stilton rising, "the Vandurens." And as a footman flung open the door, three startling figures advanced. All wore goggles and shaggy bear-like coats. The foremost of these singular arrivals, whose sex was recognizable only by the veil attached to her wide peaked cap, unswathed herself, remarking:

"Please excuse, Lady Stilton, that we arrive so late, but something *dr-rreadful* happened! We were stuck half way in a lonely road, and our chauffeur spent hours underneath the automobile before he could make it to gò on. Poor man, he is black from head to foot."

"What an exceedingly unpleasant experience," commiserated Lady Stilton. "Let me take you to your rooms. I will have tea sent up to you—and you too, Mr. Vanduren. We don't dine till eight, so that will give you time to rest and recover. Adrian, you know your way, don't you?" And in a hissing whisper she added: "You're in the bachelors' wing. Have you brought Albert?"

Garth drifted out into the drive. Perry glimpsed him through the window in discussion with a uniformed and animated foreigner, whose face, decorated with an oily slime and waxed moustaches, expressed gratified delight at this interest displayed in his treasure.

Lady Valerie, exclaiming, "I *must* go and sit in it!" tripped to the door with a frou-frou of glacé silk frills.

"Did you ever see anything so blatant," Annabel surlily remarked, "as the way she hurls herself at every man she meets? I'm going up to dress."

At thirty, plus, and buoyed by the determined efforts of Aunt Hilda, Annabel had not yet abandoned all hope of attaining her Ultima Thule. In Perry's bedroom before dinner, she wished—"in strictest confidence, my dear——" that Garth Curran would come up to scratch. "We get on very well together, or we used to—in the hunting field, but now that he has gone mad on these beastly motors, we have nothing much in common. I suppose I shall end up by doing good works and sitting on committees—oh! I'm going to sneeze." She sneezed, and crossing to a heavy gilt-framed mirror that hung above the mantelpiece, examined, distastefully, her nose—"like an over-ripe plum. I ought to have worn anything but pink. It quite clashes. What do you think of my new dress?"

Perry thought it frightful but hastened to assure her it was charming. Poor Annabel. . . . She wondered if Garth *would* be persuaded to come up to scratch. Annabel would make him a good wife. He ought to marry. Once or twice she had suggested it, only to be told that he had missed his chance; which gave her to think he still hankered for Clara.

At table she found herself seated between Garth and Vanduren, who, recently returned from Paris, was full of the King's visit there in the previous May.

"A visit," he said, "that will proclaim your King Edward as a diplomat unparalleled in British monarchy. The enthusiastic welcome of the French indicates not only their appreciation of this cordial approach but a foresight of ramifications likely to bring about a lasting alliance with France, Britain's natural enemy. We had the honour—Corinne and I—of a presentation to His Majesty at the British Embassy reception. A thousand pities, Mrs. Hope-Winter, that you didn't accompany Adrian to Paris this Spring—you'd have enjoyed it but we'll be so glad to have you visit us this Fall at Monte Carlo. Pardon me." He turned to a footman whom Perry recognized as Albert, with his hair in powder and a livery several sizes too small, presumably his who had been taken with the measles. A nice thing if Albert were to catch it!— "A glass of iced water," commanded Vanduren. "As I was saying, Mrs. Hope-Winter, we have bought the cutest little villa at Monte just large enough to house a few of our most particular friends, it has its own private bathing beach and——"

"But how perfectly delightful," chimed in Lady Stilton. "May I hope to be included as one of your most particular friends?"

"Sure, Lady Stilton." He bowed. "Our guest of honour."

"So that," she replied with gay insistence, "is a promise?"

Perry turned hastily to Garth; their eyes met and shared a twinkle. "I was wondering," he said, "when you would detach yourself from the lure of Monte Carlo and condescend to me."

"I've never been to Monte Carlo. Have you?"

"Once, and had to borrow the money for my fare home." He lowered his voice. "What are we doing in this galley?"

"Making shift to oblige. The last—no, the first time we were here together in this room, I was holding you down in your bed."

"Was I fighting drunk?"

"No." Her eyelids fluttered. "Fighting mad—and very Irish. What's all this about?"

'All this' was Vanduren addressing the table at large.

"The internal combustion engine is an epoch-making advantage to civilization. I reckon that in twenty years' time the horse as a means of road transport will be as extinct as the dodo nor will progress stop at terrestrial speed. Why, right now in Dayton, Ohio, the brothers Orville and Wilbur Wright are experimenting with a heavier than air machine fitted with a petrol-driven motor that will enable man to put—as Shakespeare has it—a girdle round about the earth in forty minutes."

"Isn't it exciting," chirruped Lady Valerie, "to think that very soon we will all be flying in the air! We won't have to wait to be angels before we have wings."

"I would much prefer to wait," Lady Stilton said decisively; and rising, gave the signal to the ladies for departure.

Garth was at the door, and, as Perry passed, he whispered: "Are you going to play for me tonight?"

'. . . But I was not asked to play for him or anybody else that night. Bridge, just coming into fashion, claimed the company, to the exclusion of Freddie's repertoire. Even Adrian, who had always professed a superior disdain for cards, had succumbed to what he called "this revival of interest in the green baize, reminiscent of the Regency——" which was scarcely applicable to the limit of a ha'penny a hundred enforced by Hilda at Charters.

Annabel and I left them to it and sat talking together in my room till past eleven, when I sent her off and went to bed but not to sleep. I couldn't sleep on a mattress full of lumps, and after an hour of tossing and turning I got up and lit the gas intending to read. My room adjoined Adrian's with folding doors between, and was furnished in the worst mid-Victorian taste. Over the mantelpiece hung an enormous gilt-framed mirror, and under it a row of preposterous vases either side a hideous black marble clock. Then, as I turned to a shelf full of books that from their titles offered little hope of interest, a frightening thing happened. The light seemed to waver and the walls to bend, an optical delusion caused by that monstrous looking-glass, as slowly, to my horror, it leaned over. It was falling, was about to crash—on me!

I could, I suppose, have retreated to safety and allowed it to crash, but my first instinct was to save it, and I did, by rushing forward to push it back and hold it pressed against the wall. Once there, I had to stay, tiptoe, straining up with my hands glued to the glass. I dared not move to ring the bell for the thing would certainly have fallen on and possibly have killed me. I called for Adrian, but no sound came from his room. He could not yet have gone to bed. I called again and again at the top of my voice, hoping that the servants would hear me, but their quarters were too far away. My head was bursting, my arms aching, and I was screaming like a maniac for help, when the door to the corridor opened. "Thank God!" I gasped, thinking it was Adrian. "Ring the bell!"

"What the devil——"

It was Garth in pyjamas and his dressing-gown. Coming from the bathroom he had heard my yells. I didn't have to tell him what had happened. He could see. In a jiffy we changed places. I flew to the bell-rope and pulled it. I was barefoot and in my nightgown, but I gave no thought to that. Garth, standing spread-eagle, held the mirror flush with the wall while I pulled the bell again. "The servants," I said, "are a long time coming. This rings downstairs, and they must all have gone to bed. I'll go and find someone."

I was just about to put on a wrap and my slippers, when Adrian, hearing voices in my room on the way to his own, came in. I began in a hurry to explain. I admit it sounded thin. "Dear, dear," he said with his eyebrows up and his twitch of a smile turned down, "this is very distressing. You had better go to my room before the servants see you in your déshabillé, which might"—he looked at Garth, still standing in an attitude of crucifixion in reverse—"be misconstrued."

I went to his room, leaving the communicating door ajar, heard running steps along the corridor and Garth telling one of the men, who had at last answered the bell, to: "Clear that stuff off the mantelpiece and give me a hand." Together they lifted the mirror from the wall and that was the end of that. . . .'

Until the next morning when, having overslept, Perry came to breakfast half an hour late. Valerie Croome, who, the night before, had announced her intention of breakfasting in bed, arrived a moment later in a whirl of curiosity and kittenish blue bows.

Seating herself between Reginald Tarrant and Garth, both of whom she mustered to attend her—"*Very* weak tea and a morsel of toast. I simply *had* to disobey my doctor's orders," she informed them. "He forbids me to rise from my bed before noon, since I am in the fashion with a grumbling appendage—which sounds *so* like a husband—or is it an appendix?

—because I simply *couldn't* wait to hear all about Mrs. Hope-Winter's exciting adventure. Oh, thank you, Major Curran—and the marmalade, Lord Reginald—it seems so exactly like a scene from *The Gay Lord Quex*. My dear!" she trilled across the table to the silent Perry, "my maid is full of it, but one can't believe the gossip of the servants' hall. She has it firmly fixed that you *tore* the mirror from the wall in self-defence when Major Curran mistook your bedroom for his own, but that"—she screamed with laughter—"is really *too* Pinero!"

Garth, at the sideboard, called: "Devilled kidneys, Peridot, tea or coffee, bacon and eggs?"

"Cold ham, please, Garth, and coffee."

"There isn't any cold ham, only cold sausages."

"The sausages *were* hot," Lady Stilton said, significantly glancing at the clock. "But there's game-pie if you must have something cold."

"No thanks. I'll have bacon, Garth, no egg. The toast, please, Reginald."

Reginald passed her a toast-rack and took the vacant seat at her side. His face, rather yellow, was creased with an insinuating smile as he asked:

"What actually did happen last night? And where is Adrian?"

"In bed," said Perry shortly. "Suffering from shock."

"Poor man!" cried Lady Valerie, "and *how* it must have shocked him—but I *still* can't understand how it could have possibly occurred. Mirrors don't come tumbling down unless they're pulled—or do they?"

"They do," said Sir Frederick, "if the wall on which they hang is growing fungus."

"Oh, *no*! How disgusting! What kind of fungus? Mushrooms?"

"Dry rot. Bound to have happened sooner or later. The panelling is riddled with it. The whole lot will have to be replaced."

Lady Stilton paled. "Surely not! It will cost a fortune!"

"Cost more to have the house about our ears. I must send to Lewes for a builder and get an estimate. Well, shall we be off?" Rising from the table Sir Frederick gathered the male company beneath his eye. "The shoot is timed to start at half-past ten."

There was a general dispersal of the men. Vanduren, who had paid no heed to the discussion, laid aside a copy of *The New York Times* mailed him that morning, and said heartily: "I'll be glad to have a shot at your partridges, Sir Frederick. We don't have that kind of a bird in the States."

"I think," Lady Valerie sprang from her seat, "that I will change my mind and my clothes, and come with you. Do please wait for me—I'll not keep you a moment." She flitted to the door, and, to Garth, who opened it, she said: "I'll stand with the one whose birth month is nearest and most *sympatica* to mine, and bring him luck. In what month were *you* born, Major Curran?"

"September."

"September! *This* month! And *my* month—I'm Virgo, the virgin! So we're *both* virgins. How wonderful! This clearly indicates that I must stand with you!" And she ran, in peals of laughter, from the room.

Lady Stilton resignedly followed. Annabel looked across at Perry, sneezed and said: "Shall we go too?"

"Not I." Perry shook her head. "I can't bear to see birds shot."

"Hares are worse. They scream." Longingly Annabel's eyes watched Garth's exit. "I don't think I ought to go—with this hay-fever. I'd be sure to sneeze and put them off. I really must do something about my nose," she felt it tenderly. "It's turning purple."

"I can give you an ointment for that," Perry said, "made from my own prescription. You smear it on at nights and it sinks in and moves all 'blemishes, blackheads, pimples and spots, and is equally beneficial for the chaps'."

"The chaps?" giggled Annabel.

" 'And all discolorations of the skin.' "

"You talk like an advertisement. And what do you mean—your own prescription? Did you invent it?"

"No, not exactly, but I know quite a lot about face creams. Wait—wait a *min*ute!" She jerked up her head. "You're giving me ideas."

"Ideas of what?" stolidly persisted Annabel.

"Of something I have had tucked away in my mind as a means of livelihood should Adrian go broke."

"But," objected Annabel, "Adrian's not likely—is he?—to go broke. He's simply rolling."

"And has rolled," said Perry, making for the door, "too far."

Week-end parties at Charters differed little from others of their kind, save in that impeccable care for the proprieties with which they were conducted. No breath of scandal, no loosening of the fetters that bound Lady Stilton's generation to the rigid path of virtue laid down by the late Queen, were to be tolerated or condoned. Thus the mishap of the mirror and the resultant expense for repairs to the wall were, though deplorable, minor misfortunes compared with the circumstance of Major Curran's entry—in pyjamas—to her sister-in-law's bedroom. "Which," she told Perry, "has given rise to much doubtful conjecture from Valerie Croome, who reads into the incident her own—we hope, exaggerated—view of it. And now that we are on the subject, let me give you a word of advice."

The word of advice was given on the terrace after luncheon. Corinne Vanduren, having retired to her room to write letters, and Annabel to hers to write the menus, Hilda took the opportunity of suggesting—"And pray do not take it amiss if I tell you that you are seeing far too much of Major Curran."

"If you mean last night," was the simple rejoinder, "you are wrong. I couldn't see very much of him for he was in his dressing-gown. I'm afraid though, he saw rather much of me. But I shouldn't let that worry you. He stood with his back to me most of the time, holding up the mirror. Quite the officer and gentleman."

Lady Stilton froze.

"You know perfectly well what I mean, nor does your flippant evasion, which borders on the vulgar, amuse me in the least. I think you ought to know that you are getting yourself talked about."

"Am I? But that's better, surely," Perry said, wide-eyed, "than *not* being talked about?"

"You were seen," Lady Stilton said, studiously calm, "with Garth Curran at Hurlingham, Ascot and Lord's."

"Yes, wasn't it nice of him? He rescued me from Marcus Sankey's aunt. You know how he carts her about with him everywhere and always seems to plant her on me. She's stone

deaf, poor old thing, and half blind, and after Ascot my throat
was quite sore with having to shout through her ear-trumpet,
describing the colours, and screaming out the names, not only
of the horses but of everyone near us in the Enclosure—so
dreadfully embarrassing. I took it very kind of Garth to bear
me away for much needed refreshment."

"Mr. Sankey's aunt," Lady Stilton said inimically, "was not
with you at Hurlingham or Lord's."

"Oh, yes, she was, but Marcus had to take her home from
Hurlingham because she ate too many strawberries and came
out in a rash, and her face swelled up like a balloon. I admit
that at Lord's I left her rather too long in the Ladies to which
she inconsiderately found she had to go at the most exciting
moment when Sankey's cousin—or the boy he *told* me was his
cousin, Lord Somebody or other—had bowled the Harrow
captain for a duck, and when I went to fetch her——"

"At Lord's," Lady Stilton doggedly pursued, "you were
seen on the top of a coach shrieking with laughter and throwing things at Major Curran."

"Not," corrected Perry, "things. A bun. And I wasn't
throwing it at him, he was throwing it at me by way of demonstration how to take a middle stump. Here's Albert. He looks
worried."

So did Lady Stilton.

With something like relief she heard: "The builder, my
lady, has come to see about the wall——" which allowed her
to edge in a last word.

"I speak only for your good. Take it to heart."

"Too kind of you," Perry said. "I will."

A little malevolent smile touched her lips as she watched
Lady Stilton's departure. Then, luxuriously stretched in her
shaded deck chair, she gave herself up to the drowsy afternoon.

A flight of steps led from the terrace to a lawn where a
spreading cypress and two cedars cast their shadows. Bees
hummed in the parterre, colourful with zinnias, asters, and an
amethyst cloud of Michaelmas daisies. September sunlight
lay tawnily on stubble field and pasture, where, beyond the
yew hedge, cows grazed in a lingering stillness undisturbed by
the distant sound of shots. . . . And Perry lost her smile.

So they were talking—were they?—of herself and Garth.

Her lips tightened. Yes, but if only they had something tangible of which to talk!

Her mind went searching back along this year of their ripening friendship. After Mafeking night she had heard and seen little of him, for although his wound was healed it had left him with a limp sufficient for the Powers that Be in Whitehall to declare him unfit for active service and to appoint him Staff instructor at Sandhurst. Perry, who had given up all thought of nursing at the Front, stayed on at Charters until the signing of the Peace, when social activities resumed their normal course.

She had met Garth frequently at functions. She, too, must entertain, at Adrian's insistence. He allowed she was an admirable hostess. Unknown to him she had taken a course at a school of cookery and, with the aid of Annie, trained by her, she upheld her pre-war reputation for an irreproachable cuisine. 'I was greatly amused to receive a letter from Valerie Croome addressed to the cook of Mrs. Hope-Winter, offering her thirty-five pounds a year, a vast sum in those days, "if she would care to make a change"—and to which needless to say my "cook" did not reply.'

Adrian, who had become reconciled to his 'tenement', did not inquire to whom he was beholden for the delectable meals served to him and his guests. The rooms of the flat were large enough to accommodate a discreet number of his friends: not hers. She had no friends, other than Annabel, whose devotion to herself was returned with a similar—if not so great an affection—as that she bestowed upon Jasper. However, the grudging acceptance as one of themselves with which the women of Adrian's circle received her, was not maintained by their men folk. 'Had I wished to be à la mode and take a lover, I could have had my choice,' she says, 'of half a dozen. The woman who didn't had sunk out of sight, deposed by the "Woman who Did". But trivial intrigue held no appeal for me. . . .'

These insatiable pleasure-seeking Edwardians, their artificialities, deceits and petty lusts, and whose only moral code was the unwritten law, 'Thou shalt not be found out', both dismayed and repelled her. No question she had her opportunies; a peer of the realm, a Cabinet Minister, a German princeling and a famous actor-manager are named among those who sought her favour. 'But,' she naively confesses, 'they were all too old for me.'

To Adrian she recounted, with embellishments, her conquests, which, he said, did not surprise him. "Your peculiar charm that owes nothing to beauty, might secure you some advantage were it put to better use than the seduction of the elderly or impotent, though your lack of response to political, princely, or theatrical ardour is not, I see, extended to the younger generation. Garth Curran is your constant cavalier."

"When you," she said, "are not."

That was his first and, hitherto, only allusion to her association with Garth, on which she had come to rely as respite from the fatuous social world she despised, and, even more, from the anxiety caused by Adrian's extravagance and dwindling resources. Between Garth and herself existed a comradeship that had never once, however much she might have wished it otherwise, surpassed the bounds of bonhomie. Linked by the memory of Geraldine, his approach to her was nothing more than cousinly; he chaffed her, teased her, gave her chocolates at Christmas and flowers on her birthday, would send a hasty note on the plea of a spare ticket—could she come to a matinée? His 'lady-friend' had let him down. At Ascot, Hurlingham, Ranelagh, Lord's—which Adrian had sampled, 'to repletion,' he told her, 'at her age, and found all such perambulations tedious at his', Garth, with her husband's full cognizance, was her escort.

And now, as she brooded on Hilda's causeless innuendoes, the thought came to startle her that she would give all she possessed, which indeed was not much, if Garth's name and hers could be coupled with—truth.

It was out! Her cloistered secret, hidden, till that moment, from her inner self; unacceptable, dismaying. To love where love was not, and would never be returned—but what a thing to come to her, unsought and uncommanded! Love. What was it? A stealthy pastime, an ephemeral adventure with opportunity connived by obliging hostesses at house-parties? A seasonal infection, from which it was considered rather 'middle-class' to be immune. Every woman, were she passably attractive, had her lover; every man his mistress—for the flying moment, swift to come and go as the swoop and dart of swallows. Was that love? Or could it be a glowing heat to scorch

the heart of you as this late summer's sun scorched the green
out of the grass? Or was it merely nature's artifice to hide
beneath a pretty mask a grosser need? Adrian had taught her
the dark witchery of passion and all of passion's emptiness,
but he had not taught her love, this unaccountable obsession
that, as a fever, attacked without warning, and like a fever
must burn—to devour.

Her lips parted; her eyes closed, and raising her arms she
held them to the sun as if she were offering a gift.

"Hullo! Did I wake you from a snooze?"

Sir Frederick, unobserved, had come through the french
windows; his knickerbockered knees held traces of dried clay
and stubble. His face, a fierce brick-red, beamed down upon
her.

"No, I wasn't asleep. Have you had a good day?"

"So-so. Six brace and a hare. Tea ready?"

She looked at her watch. "Not yet. Freddie, I must ask you
something before the others come. Can you spare a minute?"

Lowering himself in the chair vacated by his wife, he adjusted his monocle, gazed his fill, and with unstinted admiration said: "You're sunburnt. Sort of goldy. Most women as
fair as you go the colour of a lobster in the sun. You don't
seem a day older than when I first saw you. How do you
manage to keep that little girl look when you must be——"

"Twenty-nine," she interrupted, adroitly razing off two
years. "Quite a hag. Freddie," she turned to him, dropping
her voice. "I'm dreadfully worried about Adrian's affairs.
He spends money at a most alarming rate—and it doesn't
seem to help a bit, having moved to that flat. His bills are excessive, he is always in debt and has a heavily increasing overdraft. What I want to know is whether he has any securities
in trust other than the Soho property which that vile Todd
embezzled."

"And for which," Freddie unhelpfully added, "he is now
doing time at Wormwood Scrubbs."

"Yes, we know all about that, but is there anything else?
Was any of his father's estate left in trust?"

Freddie shook his head. "No, the old man left it to the three
of them absolutely. Dennis Curran—Geraldine's father—ran
through his wife's lot like a dose o' salts. Hilda still has most of
hers invested in gilt-edged, and"—he grinned—"she doesn't

touch the interest. But Adrian came in for the bulk of the
Hope-Winter fortune. He may, though, have put some in
trust for himself—or you. Proutts', his bank, would know."

"Proutts'!" Perry sat up. "But he doesn't bank at Proutts'.
He banks at the Central London."

"Then he must have two banks. I had a cheque from him
only the other day drawn on Proutts'."

Perry, rather dazed, said: "I know nothing of a bank account
at Proutts'. Why did he send you a cheque?" And as Freddie
glanced uneasily away, she peremptorily insisted, "Why?
Have you been lending him money?"

The colour in Freddie's face deepened. "No. Nothing—
never—— Phew! Hot for September, isn't it?" Taking out
his handkerchief he wiped his forehead.

"Out with it, Freddie. How much?"

"Look here," he said desperately, "we can't—I mean—this
is just a private matter between Adrian and myself."

"I see," Perry drew a deep breath. "He must be in pretty
low water to go borrowing off you. And how many others
besides you, I wonder. I try to keep an eye on his account at
the Central, but heaven only knows what's going on at
Proutts'. Has he been speculating? If you know, you might
tell me."

"I don't know, so I can't tell you." Freddie moved his head
as if about to duck. "He has asked me once or twice to lend
him a few hundreds, but he always pays up in the end."

Perry looked at him. "Hundreds?"

"Well—a thousand or two. I say!" The monocle fell from
his eye. "It's not quite—is it?—playing the game to drag all
this out of me? What?"

"I haven't dragged anything out of you yet." She laid a
hand on his knee. "Come on, Freddie, let's hear the worst."

Turning if possible redder, "The damned fool," blurted
Freddie, "has been assing about on the Stock Exchange, and
dropped a packet in some ramshackle shares that——"

"Yes," she interposed calmly, "those Peruvian mines. I
made him sell. Freddie"—his eyes bulged at her hand on his
knee. Perry pressed it—"you did mean those Peruvians,
didn't you?"

"Maybe." He was breathing rather hard. "I forget now
what they were."

8

"You're a rotten liar, Freddie darling," she removed her hand. "And I suppose you stood the racket and gave him a few thousands more to 'ass about' with. Does Hilda know?"

"Is it likely? *Cave*, here she comes." He heaved himself out of his chair to greet his wife, who, in a trailing tea-gown, majestically approached along the terrace. "Ah! There you are, my dear! I was just telling Perry—Peridot—that we ought to have a little music tonight, and have asked her to try over a new song with me before——"

"Tea," Lady Stilton interrupted, "will be ready in five minutes. Go and change. And Peridot will not have time to strum over your songs with you. She has promised to help me with the flowers."

*　　*　　*

House-parties had a way of disintegrating rather than breaking up into one concerted exodus. Garth left by the afternoon train on the Sunday, and the Vandurens, with Adrian and Reginald, drove to Town that same evening. To avoid travelling up with Valerie Croome, Perry took an early train on Monday.

The knowledge, withheld from her throughout her married life, that Adrian kept a separate account at Proutts' bank relieved rather than enhanced her apprehensions concerning the state of his finances; but she could not approach him on the subject without betraying Freddie's confidence. Opportunity, however, to glean further information was presented by the Mayfair Branch of the Central London demanding repayment of Mr. Hope-Winter's overdraft, which, if not forthcoming within the time limit of one month, would leave them no alternative but to take possession of the securities lodged at the bank in his name.

Adrian handed the letter to his wife with the remark: "Infernal impudence. I will close my account."

"But," said Perry, swallowing shock, "you must have a bank."

"I have always," he told her, "had two. In future I shall deal solely with Proutts'."

She said, with careful composure, "I didn't know you had another bank."

"Dear child," he smiled, wearily patient, "that I gave you

a free hand to examine my pass-book at the Central, where I keep a current account for household expenses and your personal allowance, was a privilege you wrested from me, much against my will, but you cannot expect to take upon yourself entire control of my business."

She held her peace, doubtfully persuaded that her fears were groundless. She, who in her youth had learned to look at every penny, was not yet reconciled to Adrian's indifference to the pounds. He must still, by her standards, be a rich man with substantial securities lodged at Proutts'. He could not possibly have run through all his capital. . . . Not all, but very nearly.

That she stood in daily dread of and prepared to meet the blow did not lessen the severity of its fall when she learned that Adrian's losses, due to reckless speculation, had exceeded, in the last five years, the hundred thousand mark. From Proutts' bank a similar demand for repayment of his overdraft was followed by various writs from creditors and a suave letter from Reginald Tarrant—for she did not scruple to read any correspondence on which she could lay hands—reminding Adrian that he held his IOU to the amount of three thousand pounds.

In this extremis Adrian, characteristically, burdened his wife with his wreckage. . . . "Your passion for economy can now assert itself. Do your damnedest, sell my pictures for a song. We can live abroad on next to nothing, but we must have a *pied à terre* in Town. Find a hovel."

Methodically she set about to extricate him from his monetary tangles. After having settled with his creditors and Tarrant, and satisfied his banks, it was found that he still held a nucleus of gilt-edged investments totalling an income sufficient to stem the tide of immediate collapse. The lease of the flat was disposed of with much of its furniture to a wealthy American, and the pictures and *objets d'art*, sold at Christies', added another two thousand to Adrian's exchequer.

At a moderate rental she secured the monthly lease of a suite of furnished apartments at the Bayswater end of Lancaster Gate—'the wrong side of the Park'—deplored Lady Stilton, who, in a letter of several pages, declared Perry wholly to blame for what she termed Adrian's 'ruin'.

'. . . Knowing him to be a child where money is concerned which is only natural in one of his artistic temperament, you should have restrained him from extravagance.' She admitted the move from Brook Street to 'that flat' had been a step in the right direction—'but you made no attempt to curb his mania for buying worthless pictures, and those jewels of yours which must have cost him thousands'.

Yes, she had her jewels. In her early days of marriage he had been generous to folly, to shower her with rings and things. She stored them in the bank along with her pearls and the odd hundreds she had managed to save out of her dress allowance, placed on deposit to draw from in event of further disastrous developments.

'And I wish you to understand,' concluded Lady Stilton, 'that neither my husband nor myself is prepared to come to your assistance now or at any other time. By your crass mismanagement you have lowered my unhappy brother to the level of a pauper. You must now cut your coat according to your cloth and live within whatever means are left to you. . . .'

The means left to them were not enough to buy or even rent the *pied à terre* in Mayfair, on which Adrian insisted. After much persuasion he agreed to allow her to search for a 'hovel' further afield.

Annie and Albert, from whom she parted with the mutual assurance that so soon as Mr. Hope-Winter's 'affairs' were adjusted they would return to her service, had obtained a post as valet and housekeeper to bachelor chambers in Duke Street, St. James's.

Adrian, resigned with dispassionate fortuity to his change of circumstances, accepted an invitation from the Vandurens to spend the remainder of the summer at their newly acquired château in the Loire Valley, which Perry, on plea of house-hunting, refused.

During this interim, and between visits to various house-agents, she spent much of her time in the Reading Room of the British Museum. The result of her labours, deduced from reference to the *Lady's Magazine* and *Belle Assemblée*, are carefully noted in a penny exercise book. Among other eighteenth-century formulae, we are told of 'a wash to remove the vices of the skin distilled from the water of green pineapples'. Another recipe suggests, 'one dram of borax, four oz. of lump sugar well pounded, the same quantity of camphor and a pint of white wine'. A marginal comment suggests 'or a dash of gin. Much cheaper.'

The possibility of turning to advantage the concoctions devised by Mr. Cheke, had now materialized. Her observation of face creams displayed in chemists' shops, or those departments of West End emporiums that supplied ladies with toilet requisites, offered no originality nor indeed much inducement to buy. They differed little from the well-known proprietary brands upon which Mr. Cheke had attempted to improve.

'Mutton-fat,' she says, 'seemed to be the chief ingredient of the so-called "cold-creams" sold in unattractive pots, or squeezed out of tubes like horrible sticky white worms. I used to watch the customers who fingered them and heard, "But haven't you something more delicate for the face? This seems so thick and greasy."' She was confident she could, with ingenuity, devise a more acceptable commodity than these.

She searched among her files—she had always been methodical—and found, neatly copied, the name of the firm from whom Mr. Cheke had been wont to buy his jars; also the name of a wholesale chemist with whom he had been accustomed to deal; but that was almost fifteen years ago. Were they still in existence? The telephone directory assured her they were, and, on the strength of past custom, she wrote a reminder that they had been used to supply Roger Cheke, Pharmacist, deceased, of Tamar Street, Finsbury Park. As she, his former assistant, was now setting up in business for herself she would be obliged if they would send her—she placed an order for two gross of jars, and with the chemists, a quantum of ingredients.

In due course the packages arrived. She used the bathroom of her apartment for her experiments, and having provided herself with a pestle and mortar, filled four dozen jars, and scented them respectively with attar of roses, essence of lavender and Adrian's latest perfume. Her next move was to devise a set of decorative labels. She had often amused herself, as did other young ladies of her day, in painting flowers or imaginary landscapes on china, and in a few hours she had produced a series of designs from which to choose. She finally decided on grey stripes, giving a silvered effect, interwoven with a spray of staring pink blossom. Her second choice, striped green and white, was modestly sprinkled with snowdrops. These efforts she sent to a firm of printers and

received from them five hundred labels, colourfully repro-
duced.

About this time there appeared in the personal columns of
the *Morning Post* and *Daily Telegraph* the following announcements.

'Ladies! Do not fear the approach of middle age. Years
of research in chemical laboratories offer you the secret that
will totally exterminate those tell-tale lines and restore to
tired skins the bloom of youth.

Winter Blossom Cream, 2s. 6d. including postage. Apply
Box——'

'Young Ladies! Perhaps there is a reason why Mr. Right
has passed you by. Of what use your beautiful features if
your skin is (let us whisper it) disfigured with open pores,
blackheads or pimples? Guard nature's most precious gift,
your complexion, with my wonderful discovery distilled
from the flowers of spring.

Primavera Cream, 2s. 6d., including postage. Apply
Box——'

The result of this first venture surpassed all expectation.
Within a week her stock of jars was exhausted. She ordered
another two gross, a further supply of ingredients, and rein-
serted her advertisements, somewhat less sensationally worded
and with equally less result; but that did not disturb her. She
had satisfied herself that a market was ready and waiting to
swallow her bait; and her expenses had been covered with a
balance to the good. It was encouraging to find repeat orders
coming in, even though as she says, 'by dribs and drabs'. . . .
'Winter Blossom' for the not so young, seemed to be the more
popular of the two, and on this she determined to concentrate.
But first to find a temporary abode for herself and Adrian.
She decided on Brighton, where severed from all social con-
nexion, she could launch her enterprise. If at the end of a
year it should prove lucrative she would draw upon her
hoarded savings, sell her jewellery, and raise capital enough to
take premises in London. . . .

Meanwhile, here was Adrian returning, and still she had not
found him a home. She had obtained a list of 'desirable resi-
dences', furnished or unfurnished, in or near Brighton, where

she intended to put up at an hotel for a few days and allow herself time for inspection. While there she would apply to local
agents and secure further orders to view.

The day before she left Town, and while shopping in
Knightsbridge, she ran into Garth.

'The longer I live,' records Lady Mulvarnie, 'I realize
how much of human destiny is spun from trifles, chance
encounter, fate, or what you will. The smallest tokens mark
the greatest of events—a game of bowls, the blind eye of
a sailor, the necklace of a Queen—such as these have been
floated into legend and remembered when victories,
triumphs, dynastic upheavals, are forgotten. So, if I had not
thought to buy myself a hat in Knightsbridge on that Monday morning, and if Garth, coming from Wellington Bar-
racks, had not met me as I crossed into the Park—but why
speculate? The fact remains that we did meet, that I did
tell him I was off to Brighton the next day to hunt for houses,
and that he told me he was off to Pulborough that very
afternoon to stay with the Storringtons for Goodwood, and
would be returning to London on the following Saturday.
When he heard that I too would be in Brighton until Saturday, he offered to come over in his motor-car from Pulborough, meet me for luncheon at the Royal Hotel, and
drive me back to Town. I warned him I would have Jasper
with me, as I couldn't leave him alone for almost a week in
furnished apartments with no one I could trust to look after
him. He assured me that the dog would be perfectly safe
at the back of the car—and so it was arranged.'

Her search for a house proved fruitless. Those submitted
were either too large or too small—'suburban villas or Regency
mansions, and for the most part far too expensive'. She
stayed at an hotel in Kemp Town for a few days and left on
the Saturday morning to keep her appointment with Garth at
the Royal. She deposited Jasper, her portmanteau, and dressing-bag with the hall porter, and found Garth waiting for her
in the lounge. He told her he had come from Pulborough the
night before and stayed at the hotel to have the car overhauled
at a garage.

The enjoyment of the excellent luncheon he had ordered

at a reserved window table was somewhat marred, at its finish, by the unexpected visitation of Mr. Marcus Sankey.

"I was just coming in," he said, "when I saw you through the window, and what"—a fractional pause preceded the words—"are you two doing here?"

"I," smiled Perry, hiding hate, "have been house-hunting and Garth has come over in his motor-car from Pulborough to drive me back to Town."

"Pulborough?" Sankey turned his interrogative nose in Garth's direction. "For Goodwood? Did you come across my —ah—cousins, the Storringtons?"

"Yes," said Garth briefly, "I was staying with them."

"Oh, were you?" chattered Sankey. "I was, of course, invited, but alas! my poor old aunt, who has a suite in this hotel for a few weeks, has been very ill with something frightful called phlebitis, and I didn't like to leave her."

"Oh," said Perry, bored. "And is she better?"

"Marvellously better! A wonderful recovery considering her age. She's eighty-two."

"And may live for another ten years," was the disheartening assurance.

"I fervently hope so," declared Sankey with false cheer. "I have had my luncheon. May I sit down? If," he added archly, "I won't be butting in."

Garth curtly offered him coffee.

"Yes, thanks, I will. By the way I must congratulate you on your promotion."

Garth beckoned a waiter.

"Black or white?"

"Black, thanks. I saw in the Gazette," simpered Sankey, "that you are now Lieutenant-Colonel."

Perry looked across at Garth.

"Since when?"

"Last week."

"Then I must congratulate you, too."

"You don't have to." Garth glanced at his watch. "We ought to be making a start. I don't wish to hurry you——"

"Yes," she rose, very much in a hurry. "We certainly should."

Sankey leapt to his feet. "How long does it take to drive to Town?"

"About three and a half hours." Hooking a finger at the waiter, Garth asked for his bill.

Still standing, Sankey drained his coffee-cup. "I wish I could come with you, just for the drive, and back again by train. I *adore* motor-cars! The speed! So exhilarating."

"Sorry. No room." Garth snapped open a silver sovereign case. "We're loaded up with luggage."

"Luggage?" Sankey glanced from one to the other. "Oh, quite!" he said with haste, and followed Perry to the door. "Is Adrian back yet?"

"Tomorrow," she told him over her shoulder. "I must go and collect my things."

"I'll see you off."

He saw them off, planting himself on the steps of the hotel to watch Perry's bags, and Garth's, duly deposited, with Jasper, in the car.

"So you've brought your bulldog," tee-hee'd Sankey. "How frightfully funny!"

"Why is it," Perry asked, glowering, "funny?"

"Well, I mean—a terrifying chaperone. Allow me." He helped her on with her coat, and stood back waving both hands as the car screeched and rattled out of the drive, accompanied by excited barks from Jasper.

"Thank God!" shouted Perry above the engine's roar, "that you managed to get rid of him. For one ghastly moment I thought he intended to come with us."

"What?"

"Nothing."

A sudden gust of wind tore her hat from her head to send it curvetting to the railings of the promenade; but as Garth stopped the car, and prepared to go after it, two small boys forestalled him to chase and retrieve it from under a horse's hooves.

"New for this occasion," she mourned, "and squashed flat."

"You should have had a veil," he said unsympathetically.

"So like a man," she retorted, "not to have told me beforehand. You'd better take me to a draper's where I can buy a veil."

"And a motoring cap while you're about it." Garth pulled up at a hat shop in the King's Road; and while she made her purchases he sauntered along till he found an optician's where

8*

he bought a pair of goggles. These he handed to Perry as she came out of the shop. "You'll be needing them—and this." He took off his fur-lined leather coat and made her put it on. "That light thing you're wearing isn't warm enough."

"But what about you?"

"I'm all right. I have a mackintosh behind if I should want it."

He cranked up the engine and climbed into the driving seat beside her. "I'll take you over the Downs," he said, "we've loads of time."

Snorting, groaning, the car lurched up the steep road out of the town and into the high open country. Perry's ears were aching with the rush of wind; her eyes, despite the goggles, pricked with dust and streaming, received a blurred and darkened view of coastal Sussex, of the sea, the sky, the humped shoulders of the Downs, dotted with infinitesimal sheep, and below, in a hollow, a huddle of red roofs.

Garth slowed to a halt.

"She's hot. I'll have to cool her off. Would you like to get out and give the dog a run?"

Perry got out and released an hilarious Jasper. Removing her goggles she lifted her face to the glare of the sun. "It's glorious up here," she called to Garth, who was tinkering with the bonnet of the motor. His hands were black. He wiped them on a rag and looked at his watch.

"What about some tea? There's a village below. Shall we walk to it? We can leave the car. No one is likely to pinch her."

In the garden of a white-walled inn they lingered for an hour. Tea was served by an apple-cheeked girl in a sun-bonnet, and in her voice the Sussex burr. Bees were busy in the flower borders, massed with hollyhocks, marigolds and canterbury bells. A field of yellowing tree-belted corn stretched up to the burnt sunlit jade of the Downs.

"I can't think," said Perry suddenly, "why people live in towns unless they must. Although I am London bred and born, and," she smiled reminiscently, "in a neighbourhood unknown to you, which was not quite but almost a slum——" Her eyes with a glint of defiance, met his.

"And which," he said, returning that look to hold it, "has made you what you are."

A flush crept to her eyebrows. "Some day, perhaps, I will tell you what I am and of my beginnings, which were very different from yours. But I always knew," she added dreamily, "that I was never rooted there."

"Sometimes I wonder——" His gaze slipped past her and away. "I have lived in India, you know, where the secret things belong unto the lords their gods. One may believe we have a thousand lives to live, and live again—in this world and not in any other."

"That," she said, "is the belief of the Theosophists. I have heard Miss Lavinia discuss it."

"As good a belief as any."

"No." She shook her head. "I shouldn't like to come back and back again interminably. I want to go on and discover new worlds."

"So you may when you have finished with this. How can you account for life's indiscriminate injustices—the hideous poverty, disease, and hardship inflicted on certain individuals, while others, undeserving, are loaded with the best that life can offer? I'm not holding any brief for any theories, yet when one considers the meaningless chaos——"

"Man-made," she interposed softly.

"Ah, now! Don't be laying all the blame on us. The woman tempted me—remember?" A glimpse of Geraldine was in the face he turned to her; his teeth, very white in his gleam of a smile, his hair, rusty-red, and those high cheek-bones with their peppering of freckles. "The Lord," she heard him say, "had much to answer for when He performed that operation of manipulative surgery on Adam's fifth rib. Until then all the best of me and all the best of you," his voice warmed to its brogue, "were one. And now that we are torn apart we will never be at peace again until we're re-united."

Her heart lost a beat, but she said composedly: "That's a pretty way to clarify the origin of species. Darwin tells us we were apes——"

"More than likely." And then, abruptly, and vexatiously, he rose. "Time's getting on. We must be moving. I'll go and fetch the motor."

"On your way out," said Perry coldly, "will you ask that girl to bring a bowl of water for the dog."

The bowl of water was brought, and when Jasper had taken his fill of it, they followed leisurely along the village street and met Garth driving back.

"I'll have to put on speed," he said; and did. The car ate up the miles at the terrific average of fifteen to the hour. Fields, hedges, telegraph poles flew by in a whirl of dust; villagers, summoned to their cottage doors by the persistent hoot of the horn, stood agape and cowering, to watch the snorting, petrol-belching monster hurtle by. Scared fowls scattered, children screamed; their mothers snatched them to their bosoms, crying, "Road hogs!" Perry, glancing round at Jasper, saw him vomiting white froth.

"Hi! Garth, stop!" she shouted, "Jasper's being sick."

He halted the car, and she got out to tend the retching Jasper.

"He always does this when he's excited. I oughtn't to have let him drink so much. I'm afraid he has made rather a mess of the back seat—I'm awfully sorry—but it's only mucus. Is there time for me to take him for a run?"

Garth turned his head a very little.

"I shouldn't move him if I were you. Let him get it off his chest."

And when Jasper had got it off his chest Garth produced a clean rag and silently cleaned up the 'mess'.

"I think I'd better sit with him."

She climbed into the back.

"All right. I'll put up the hood." Garth put up the hood and took his place in the driving seat. The car raced on. Bumped, jolted, shaken to her bones, Perry clung to Jasper, wished to God she hadn't come, and heard from the engine a curious scraping and squeaking and wheezing. The wheels slackened. The car stopped dead.

"Damn!" said Garth feelingly. "That's torn it."

"Torn what?" inquired Perry.

Removing his goggles he told her briefly: "You'll have to get out again."

"Is anything wrong?"

"Don't know till I look."

"Come, my love," Perry hitched the lead to Jasper's collar, and walked him down the road through a gate into a field. The sun was lowering behind a bank of cloud, the blue had vanished

from the sky; a cool wind, blowing in from the sea, brought
with it a flight of gulls, skimming tree-tops. Jasper, now
wholly recovered from his indisposition, galloped off to investi-
gate delicious smells of cow-dung and other matters in the
hedge. Light rain began to fall; Perry consulted her watch.
A quarter to seven. She whistled for Jasper, she cajoled, she
called him to heel. He ignored her. He had found the deposit
of a picnic, an empty sardine tin from which he refused to be
parted. She walked away and hid behind a tree. The ruse
sufficed. He dropped his prize and went to seek her, tracked
her, was collared, and dragged, sourly protesting, to the car.

Nothing of Garth could be seen except his boot protruding
from under the chassis, but a vicious hammering accompanied
by an intermittent flow of questionable language could be
heard.

Perry sat with Jasper on the grass verge at the roadside,
hugged her knees, and waited . . . and she waited.

Half an hour passed before Garth, coatless, crawled from
his hide-hole, incomprehensibly to utter: "Big end."

"Big what?" she asked, shrinking from the horrid sight of
him. His face exuded a dark oily sweat, his hair, save where
grease had dropped to flatten it, stood wildly on end. His
hands, his arms, exposed in shirt-sleeves rolled to the elbow,
were equally befouled.

"We're sunk," he said. "Big end."

"You mean we can't go on?"

Deigning no reply to that superfluous remark, Garth produced his unspeakable rag, wiped his hands, and then his
forehead.

Perry giggled; and he glared.

"I'm sorry," she spluttered, "but I——" The giggles
welled up to an explosion of laughter, uncontrollable, inane.
"I can't—it's——" She was helpless—— "So funny—your
face!"

"My face," he said, scowling through its dirt, "may be, as
your friend, Mr. Sankey would say, frightfully funny, no
doubt. But you may not find it so frightfully funny if you have
to spend the night here."

"Where?" Perry pointed. "In that thing?"

"Unless there's a train back to Town."

"Where are we?"

He returned to the car and brought forth a map. Seating himself beside her on the grass he studied it while, she more conscious of his nearness than he was of hers, studied him.

"About thirty-five miles from London." His grimy finger traced a line. "Let's see—where's Lewes? The Stiltons' place would be—yes—twenty miles further back. I was thinking if we could hire a gig or something I could drive you there and——"

"No," Perry said with decision. "I would sooner stay the night in that"—again she pointed—"than descend upon Hilda with you."

He slipped her a grin. "As you say." And once more he referred to the map. "There should be a village about three miles on. Can you walk it?"

"I'll have to," Perry said mildly, "won't I?"

"No." Garth got upon his feet. "I think you'd better stay in the motor. I can sprint. You can't. The police station, if there is one, is almost sure to have a telephone. If there's no train I'll ring through to Brighton and order a car to come out and take us on. Are you sure you don't mind being left? You'll be quite safe with Jasper." He unrolled his sleeves, resumed his tweed jacket and belatedly apologized. "Sorry about this."

"Don't mention it," retorted Perry bitterly. "It's going to rain." She wriggled out of his motor-coat and handed it to him. "Take this or you'll be drenched."

"No, I have my mackintosh." He took it from the car, wiped the worst of the filth from his face, and told her: "If you care to smoke you'll find cigarettes and matches in my pocket. I'll be as quick as I can."

And, despite that he still limped a little from his wound, he made off as if starting for a marathon.

She watched him out of sight.

A rain-drop splashed on her nose; a chill breeze had sprung up. She hustled Jasper into the car. A hay-cart lumbered by. Partially screened from observation Perry submitted in digni-fied silence to jeers from the unseen driver, and the ambiguous remark: "What oh! She bumps!"

Rain fell drearily and dribbled through the canvas hood. A couple of oafs, sharing round their shoulders a protective sack, were the next to pass and stare. A raucous voice called, "Stuck in the mud?"

"No," replied Perry with quiet ferocity, "I'm here to admire the view."

No further interruption relieved a creeping hour. Dusk gathered the silence in a pall of grey. The sky turned a fiery red, massed with thick spongy clouds. Rain hissed in the puddles. Jasper sat and shivered. She wrapped him in a rug. He struggled free of it, jumped down from the seat, over-turning the portmanteaux, and scratched at the door of the car. She took him for a walk. He nosed about the hedge, to his satisfaction, and was brought back soaking. No sooner had she dried him with the rug than he asked to be let out again.

"Darling, not *again*! Well, you must wait."

The last of the light had faded; it had ceased to rain. Not a sound broke the silence, not a star in the murky darkness of the sky. She was beginning to feel hungry, searched for and smoked a cigarette, and heard the nearing approach of wheels and hooves. A gig, with Garth driving it, pulled up alongside.

"And about time, too!" said Perry.

'. . . Sunk we were indeed! He had telephoned from the local police station to half a dozen garages in Brighton, only one of which had a car for hire and that was out of order. His calls to the garage in Lewes brought no reply. The nearest station that connected with the main line to London was five miles distant and the last train gone. Garth had found, he said, "a sort of pub place" where we could stay the night. So with Jasper, who flatly refused to get into the gig and had to be hauled up by his scruff to sit between us on the box—and hating it—we eventually arrived at the "sort of pub place", grandiloquently named The Queen's Hotel. There were only two rooms vacant, and the landlord, a bald, sickly individual with a face like an egg, told us we were lucky to get those as being holiday time they were full up, but we could have a private parlour if we liked.

We did like, and when Garth had brought our luggage from the gig, the landlord said: "I expect you and your wife will want a wash." I looked at Garth, who didn't look at me but at the man to tell him crisply: "This lady is not my wife." "My mistake," said the man. He vanished through a glass panelled door marked Private, and presently emerged with a ledger. He laid it open on the hall table, produced an ink-well and a pen and asked me please to register. I wrote my name, Mrs. Adrian Hope-Winter, and our Bayswater address. Garth signed directly under it, G. D. Curran, Lt.-Colonel, White's Club. "I'll show you to your rooms," said the man. Jasper was suspiciously sniffing at his ankles. "Is he all right?" he asked, drawing back. "Perfectly all right," I said, "with the right people." "I'll have to charge you half a crown extra for the dog," he said, and taking two candles from the hall table he lit them and went up the stairs. I followed. Garth came after with the bags, put mine into the larger room and went into his own adjoining. Hot water was brought by a slovenly maid with her hair in wisps and her cap awry. She lighted the gas, gave one look at Jasper, said "Oee-er!" and bolted. I drew down the window-blinds. The curtains, of Nottingham lace, were full of holes. I washed, I did my hair, and examined the bed—a double-bed with a greyish white quilt and feather mattress. The sheets, approximately clean, were rough-dried. A large photograph of Queen Alexandra, obviously taken from an illustrated paper, hung above the mantelpiece between two texts framed in straw. "Be of good cheer, it is I, be not afraid," and "I need thee every hour." Over the chest of drawers hung a coloured print of Rebecca at the well in blue, offering her pitcher to Abraham's servant in yellow. We used to have a print of that at Tamar Street. The room smelt of beer, of mice, and, unpleasantly, of men. I opened the window. From somewhere below a gramophone was braying My Cosy Corner Girl. Loud voices bawled the chorus. Jasper was panting and blowing, and badly in need of a drink. The water-bottle on the wash-stand was empty. I pulled the bell-rope. Dust flew from it in clouds, and the tassel came off in my hand. The gramophone had done with the Cosy Corner Girl and was now entertaining what I guessed to be the Bar with the Honeysuckle and the Bee. I waited five minutes and pulled the bell again. Presently someone knocked at the door. I called "Come in."

She came in.

She was blowsy, she was bloated, she was fat. She had

two chins. Her hair, unmistakably dyed, was black as a boot. She wore a quantity of imitation jewellery and an ingratiating smile. Her teeth were very false.

I lost my breath.

"You rang, madam?"

"Yes." My heart was pounding at my ribs. "Would you be so good as to bring me a bowl of water for the dog?"

"Certainly, madam. Good doggie, then!" She made as if to pat him, and Jasper stood four-square to face her, folding in his upper lip to show his lower fangs. "Coo!" She edged away. "I wouldn't like to meet him in the dark. Will you be having your meal in the parlour, madam? There's only chops and chips it being late and the cook——" She broke off, staring.

I had moved across the room to take Jasper by the collar. He had his likes and dislikes. She was one of them.

"For God's sake!" I heard her say. Her eyes were popping. "Perry! After all these years—well, I'm jiggered! It's a small world, isn't it?"

I looked at her and smiled, and I offered her my hand.

"Yes," I said, "Milly, it is." '

NINE

Lancaster Square
Sunday, July 28th, 1904

"Back again in time for lunch. Adrian arrived last evening. Expected him today. Furious because I wasn't here to
meet him. Thanks to the breakdown I didn't get his wire.
What a night! And then to find Milly in possession there.
So that was the hotel on the Brighton road of which she
told me all those years ago, and that egg-faced man must
have been the "friend" of whom she spoke as "they". Most
unfortunate adventure. Still, it can't be helped. Pity I
signed my address in the visitors' book—hope to goodness
she won't look me up, when, as she said, she comes to London for the day. Jasper gave me the fright of my life. Garth
was right. It *was* his heart. Rudd gave him some pills,
says I mustn't let him walk up and down stairs for the next
week or two, but of course he has to go out to do his dog.
He's too much for me to carry, must get the German boy
to take him. Garth telephoned from Sandhurst, said the
motor had been towed back to Brighton. All Adrian had to
say about it was that motor-cars have a convenient way of
breaking down on the Brighton road.

And I wonder what he meant by that! . . .'

ON the night of the 'unfortunate adventure', and, for all her
exhaustion, Perry failed to sleep on a bed that might have been
stuffed with flint, not feathers. Jasper, equally ill at ease,
wandered about the room in evident distress. She groped for
and lighted a candle, saw his sides heaving, and froth on his
mouth, on the floor, on the rug. Then down he flopped with
his head between his paws, his tongue between his teeth—and
it was blue.

Garth, wakened by her voice shrill with alarm at his door,
came to inquire: "What's wrong?"

"Jasper—he's ill—collapsed. Have you any brandy?"

"Wait a minute." From the half open door she watched

him put on his dressing-gown. "Yes, I have a flask—it's in my other bag downstairs. I'll get it. Let's have a look at him."

One look sufficed.

"Heart," Garth said briefly. "You must massage it—like this. Now don't upset yourself. I've had them in this state before and pulled them through. Go on with the massage. I shan't be a jiffy."

She went on with the massage as Garth had shown her how. Very still, scarcely breathing, Jasper lay, with eyes half closed and lifeless, his teeth clenched on that faded blue shred of a tongue. . . .

In the Saloon Bar Milly told a circle of her gentlemen acquaintances how very small the world was. "To think that *she* what I mothered all those years ago, should have turned up here! As I was saying"—and over the rim of her tumbler Milly said it—"while they was in the parlour at their supper—see?—I tidied up her room." Milly winked. "She's not arf done herself proud. Got one of them fitted dressing-bags with gold-backed brushes, scent bottles and all, and real lace on her crape-dee-sheen night-gown. . . . Who? Me? Don't you be sersaucy! What d'you think I am? . . ." The laughter was uproarious, Milly's monumental bosoms shook; her bangles tinkled. "Well, I don't mind if I do. What's yours? . . . And a splash? Here's hoping!"

She clinked glasses with a large man in loud checks, a crimson waistcoat and a yellow tie. "Yes," said Milly, "double-barrelled name and all, and him what she's married to—or what she *says* she's married to's in Paris so she told me. We had quite a friendly little chat—between ourselves. Come 'ere!" Milly hushed her voice; and the grinning circle, specified to confidence, gathered close about the counter. "She isn't now nor never was no better than she ought be. What's bred in the bone comes out in the flesh I always say—not that there's much flesh about her . . . And that's quite enough from you, thanks! Anyway, better an armful than a bag o' bones any day in the week—or night—if you prefer it! . . . Yes, sir? Two mild and bitters? Right."

Milly's smile expanded; she pulled levers, filled and passed the tankards to a new-comer who retired with them to a table. "As I was saying"—she clicked coins into the till—"no, have this one on the house. I've backed the winner—arf crown each way—yes! Rank outsider, too—but what I'd like to know is, who's the toff? A pick-up in Brighton if you ask me—breaking down, that's *her* story—in his motor-car. And where's the motor-car? If Moon weren't such a poor fish he'd have asked them where's your motor-car? Not that I should worry! Custom's custom when all's said and done, and I'll bet my bottom dollar there'll be somethin' done tonight. . . . Go on with you! What a mind you have! Talk about a sink. Hullo, Jimmy! You're quite a stranger. What's yours? The usual? Right." Milly served her latest customer, wiped beer stains off the counter, and resumed, "Laugh! I thought I shoulda died, seein' her got up to the nines—all la-dee-dah—and doin' skivvy's work for me in the old days when I was married to me first what took another woman's by-blow out o' charity—that's all she is, a by-blow. And never so much as a word to me, mind, who brought her up and gave her all a mother's love and care." Milly's smile disappeared. "Never a word of her from that day to this, when she left me in me sorrow after old Cheke kicked the bucket. Some gets all the luck, and a darn sight more than they deserves. I always said she was a wrong 'un and I'm always right. Good night, sir—— Goo'night, Jimmy. Goo'night—goo'night! Mind your way out there—'old 'im up, Jack, 'old him up! Time, gentlemen, time, please. We're early birds in this 'ouse. It's past midnight."

And when the other 'early birds' had at last dispersed, Milly, having seen her 'poor fish' off to bed, sat awhile in the parlour, banefully squinting at and every now and then partaking of a bottle of Old Rye.

Footsteps in the hall roused her from a reverie. Peering through the panes of the glass-panelled door she saw 'that Perry's toff', in pyjamas and a dressing-gown, unlock a portmanteau and extract from it a flask. Her loose mouth opened. What the jooce! A dirty trick to bring in their drink and not call on the house. That'll be five bob extra on the bill, me lad, said Milly. Best see what they're up to. Making a night of it she wouldn't be surprised. She took another swig, and followed, at a distance, up the stairs.

Along the corridor, covered with a carpet—the throw-out of a sale, that still retained the velvet thickness of its pile—tiptoed Milly. For a heavy woman she trod uncommonly light in the wake of the hurrying Garth.

At the room adjacent to his own, which Milly had previously inspected and found much to ignite her curiosity, she saw him pause and enter.

Nimble, noiseless, spurred by Old Rye and heaven alone knows what of other latent fires re-kindled, Milly hastened to kneel on the mat with her ear at the keyhole, and heard:

"Darling—my darling! Don't leave me—you're not going to leave me! Oh God—I can't bear it! What shall I do?"

Milly grinned and nodded. He was giving her the chuck. There were murmurs inaudible, then soothingly: "That's better—that's the way."

Milly put her eye to the keyhole and disappointingly saw nothing; and now she could hear nothing more than a few sobbing breaths and a silence, prolonged.

Get on with it, said Milly, do. I can't stay here all night.

"Oh, Garth!" Promptly to the keyhole Milly's ear returned. "Thank God! Thank God—for you!"

Milly's leg had gone to sleep, and so, seemingly, had those two, for she heard, distinctly, snoring, and presently: "My precious! What a fright you gave me! You must never, never, never"—each repetition of the word was punctuated, unmistakably—"do this to me again."

Don't you be too sure, my girl, he will! chuckled Milly, and, quietly as she had come, she went.

*   *   *

When two or three weeks later, Adrian announced his intention of taking a room at his club while Perry continued her search for a house, she gladly agreed to the proposal. The furnished rooms in Bayswater had scarcely enough cupboard space to contain their clothes, and both Adrian and she objected to sharing a chest of drawers and wardrobe. Moreover, she was still receiving orders for her face creams, an encouragement to advertise again. In such cramped quarters it was difficult to conceal from her husband her activities, of which she knew he would greatly disapprove. True, since the Brighton episode he had been out for all his meals other than his breakfast, brought to his bedroom, yet she was never certain at what hour to expect him home. She must therefore conduct her 'business', as now she had come to regard it, in secret, and store in her trunks or in cardboard boxes under her bed any trace of the jars and their contents. So, "Yes," she said, "I certainly should take a room at your club. I know this place is awful but it's the best I could find, as you were so insistent on a house with a telephone——" Installed in the basement, and for which each tenant was more and adequately charged his share of outgoing calls. And, as her search for a house in the vicinity of Brighton had failed, "How," she suggested, "would you care for St. John's Wood?"

"The haunt of the demi-monde? Not a locality that commends itself to me, nor would I have considered it as suitable for you; but in view of recent circumstances——"

A shrug, a narrowed smile, terminated the discussion. Nor did she read in that elliptical reply a premonitory warning. She had told him all there was to tell of the mishap to the motor-car, and of Jasper's heart attack in that 'horrible inn' where they were compelled to stay the night. To her encounter with Milly she had made the least allusion. She had never dramatized her life at Tamar Street, and, out of loyalty to him who until a month before his death she believed to be her father, she had carefully avoided the part that Milly played as the woman who had warped her childhood.

So Adrian departed for his club. And Perry, having packed such clothes as he would need, saw him off in a four-wheeler, well content to see him go. She could now, between hours spent in house-hunting, conduct her 'business' undisturbed.

Orders poured in with increasing rapidity in response to repeat advertisements. She determined to follow these tentative beginnings, first, by taking out a patent for the Winter Blossom Cream—clearly the most profitable of her two preliminary ventures—and secondly, to find a house with ample attic space. There she would work upon her products single-handed, until such time when she hoped to be in a position to afford paid help.

Since Garth had telephoned her on the evening of July 28, she had heard nothing more of him until she received a letter from Ireland to say his father had died of what was possibly a coronary thrombosis.

'. . . the same thing that your Jasper had, but this was

the poor old chap's second attack—and a fatal one. I was only just in time. As you may imagine, there is much to settle here. My uncle is proving a bit of a problem. The doctors say he is not certifiable, but I can't leave him in this barrack of a place with only a male nurse, somewhat addicted to the bottle, to look after him, so I have decided to bring him to England. The doctor recommends a mental home for voluntary patients not far from Sandhurst, and I'm leaving for London tomorrow to arrange about placing him there. Any chance of seeing you? I shall only be in town a few days, then back again to fetch the old man and inter- view lawyers and so on. The Governor had power of attor- ney, which now devolves on me. It's a hell of a business!

Drop me a line at White's. Shall be there on Thursday.

Yours ever,

Garth.'

She dropped him a line, a short note of condolence, but ignored the 'chance' of seeing him, since his letter suggested no insistence to see her. He had her telephone number and could ring her if he wished. It had a little, but not unduly, surprised her that Adrian had not once called at their rooms, nor taken her to dine at his club or a restaurant. He had told her he would be much occupied for these next few weeks with his 'affairs'—indicative of further speculation. For her peace of mind she did not ask him to explain his ambiguity, aware that interference would not restrain him from, but well might spur him to imprudence. As in the past his buying and selling of pictures had in it always an element of hazard, so now did the buying and selling of stock induce the same provocative urge. From hard experience she had learned to know that when the gambling fever came upon him with a crave like a drunkard's thirst for drink, all argument was useless; and this deliberate avoidance of her only too surely implied that he was once more in the toils of the enemy. He had telephoned from time to time to hold a careless conversation, to inquire if she needed any ready money, if so he would send her a cheque; or to ask her to pack certain of his clothing, for which, he said, a servant from the club would call.

When, a day or two after she received Garth's letter, Adrian rang her up again, she heard him say, and could well imagine his pinched smile: "Sankey dined with me last evening, and told me he had seen you at Brighton with Curran—at the Royal. I understand you shared a quantity of luggage."

"What on earth are you talking about?"

"Your conduct, or misconduct—pray don't misunderstand me—in the sense of a gross disregard for the conventions——"

The vibration of the disc at her ear exaggerated his pomposity. She began to laugh, and through her laughter told him: "But I—the luggage was mine—yes, certainly it was and his too. I stayed—I told you I stayed—at an awful hotel in Kemp Town, the only one I could find that would take a dog."

"And yet you were seen at the Royal with Curran?"

And now she laughed no more.

"Garth came over from Pulborough the night before and put up at the Royal. He was staying with the Storringtons for Goodwood. What has that little beast Sankey been saying? What——? I can't hear you. The line's gone faint. What . . . ? No, I was *not* at the Royal on the Friday night. I brought my luggage that morning from—oh, but this is too ludicrous! We can't talk on the telephone. I must see you—yes, but you *must*. Now . . . Well, if you won't come here, I'll come to . . . Adrian . . . *Adrian!*"

He had rung off.

She went back to their suite. The bathroom was stacked with empty jars. She proceeded to fill them, her mind in a ferment. Sankey! Of course. He had made much of that quite innocuous luncheon, and of the luggage—yes! The luggage. . . . What a besotted fool she had been not to have realized that although this was the twentieth century, Sankey, and Adrian too, for all his alleged disregard for the conventions, were cemented by birth and tradition in the Victorian code. A couple of old spinsters, the pair of them. But how mean, how petty, how foul—she stayed her pestle an instant, then viciously pounded—to put the worst construction on a trivial luncheon and a motor-drive with Garth! Yet looking at it now—and she looked hard at the mixture in the mortar—that breakdown might appear suspicious, but not, surely, after she had given him chapter and verse of it. As she had nothing to conceal it had never for one moment occurred to her that Adrian egged on, no doubt, by the hateful innuendoes of Hilda and that little toad Sankey might suspect her of—Good

Lord! Impossible. Yet was it so impossible? Perhaps she *had* overstepped the bounds of what is 'done' or is 'not done', had laid herself open to suspicion—though the mere fact that she had been seen publicly with Garth must surely defy all suspicion. If he were in truth her lover, would she have flaunted him for Sankey and all the world to see?

She filled the last jar and took Jasper for a walk in the gardens of the square. The dusty plane trees stood unstirring in the humid August heat. On a bench she sat, unheedful of the few who passed along the path; a nurse wheeling a perambulator, an old lady with a pug, a child pulling a wooden horse on wheels. A yellow leaf fluttered down; the scent of wood-smoke, sure herald of autumn as the primrose is of spring, drifted like incense on the breezeless air. . . . Garth would be back from Ireland by now. She must telephone him at White's—but what to say? How hint at that which most certainly had never crossed his mind. Let it go! Adrian was in his moods. He swung always to extremes, had rung her up on an impulse having listened to and probably believed that little beast's insinuations—and by tomorrow, or tonight, he would have forgotten all about it. A pity it was August, London empty, and nothing else for him to do, when not plunging on the Stock Exchange, but to brood on his imaginary wrongs. Well, she must put him right, rid him once for all of these ridiculous assumptions. She would have to see him now. She would telephone him at his club this minute.

She called Jasper; he came bounding, his hind quarters in a wriggle, his tongue joyfully lolling, and, thankfully, pink. And as she crossed the square a burly figure in a bowler strolled by, paused to light a pipe, and then walked briskly away in the direction of the Bayswater Road. Perry turned her head to look after him. She had seen him before hanging about; a big man with noticeable feet. A follower of one of the servants most likely, in this, or some other house.

She telephoned Adrian's club. He was out. She left a message for him to ring her, but no call came from him that day.

The morning's post brought only three more orders. She would have to advertise again. She wrapped the jars, addressed them, and rang for the young German who waited on her suite.

"If Mr. Hope-Winter telephones, say I have gone out and will be back presently."

She posted the three parcels, changed the postal orders, received seven shillings and sixpence, bought, with the sixpence, a pound of stewing beef for Jasper's dinner, and returned to the house.

The German who answered the door-bell told her: "*Bitte, gnädige Frau*, Herr Hopp-Vinter mit von gentleman is come."

A gentleman? Sankey, no doubt. Good. She would have something to say to him—the sneak!

"This for Jasper, Karl." She handed him the beef. "Cut it and bring it to me raw."

Jasper had waddled on ahead up the stairs.

"I carry dog, *gnädige Frau*?"

"No. The vet said only for a week or two. He is perfectly well again. We mustn't make an invalid of him, must we?"

"*Nein, gnädige Frau*." A stiff little bow. "I'm am much pleasdt."

Their rooms were on the first floor. The door of the sitting-room stood open, and Jasper, ignoring Adrian, between whom and himself no love was lost, made straight for a ferret-faced, clerkly young gentleman who stood with his back to the window.

"Come here, Jasper. . . . He won't hurt you," was Perry's hasty assurance.

The young man came forward, offered her a pleasant smile, and an official looking document.

"Mrs. Hope-Winter?"

"Yes?"

Slightly bewildered, she glanced across at Adrian, standing with his back to the empty grate. The young man, smilingly, addressed him.

"Is this lady your wife, sir?"

"She is."

"Thank you, then I need detain you no further." And, in passing, the young man, very pleasantly indeed, stooped to pat Jasper, who wriggled delighted approval. "Friendly, isn't he? Good day to you, madam."

"Adrian!"

But he had followed the clerkly young gentleman, and as he went from the room he closed the door.

She rushed to the window, saw him hail a crawling hansom; and, with his escort, he entered the cab and drove away.

Greatly mystified, she glanced at the paper in her hand. Words, clearly spaced, stupefying, stared up from the black-lettered page.

In the High Court of Justice

PROBATE, DIVORCE, AND ADMIRALTY DIVISION
(Divorce)

Sight receded before her stunned mind registered . . .

'The Humble Petition of Adrian Godfrey Hope-Winter, sheweth' (How Biblical!) 'that she, Peridot Hope-Winter hereinafter called the Respondent) had committed adultery with Lieutenant-Colonel Garth Denis Curran, Fifth Hussars, on the night of July 27th, 1904, at the Queen's Hotel, Cowfold in the County of Sussex . . .'

The Thing dropped from her nerveless fingers. She sank limply into a chair . . . Garth! She must telephone him. Where would he be? Sandhurst, or his club? She must think, must think, must . . . But the one coherent thought that evolved from this whirlpool of seismic shock was that she had never known his second name was Denis. . . .

Jasper came to her, waggling his behind, raised himself on his hind legs, and nuzzled her chin. "Yes, my love . . ." She clasped him closely, then pushed him away and got up to retrieve the Thing from the floor. She put it in her desk and went down to the basement. Stark against the wall, outside the servants' quarters, reposed the telephone. Lifting the receiver from its rest she turned the handle and spoke into the mouth-piece protruding from the instrument's sloping wooden front.

"Number please?"

"National, St. James's, 010."

"You're through."

"Is Colonel Curran in the Club?"

Five dragging minutes passed, then:

"Colonel Curran is not in the Club, madam."

"If he comes in will you please ask him to ring Post Office, Bayswater, 050?"

"Yes, madam."

She went back to her apartment.

The second post brought four more demands for the Winter Blossom Cream. Having made up the parcels, she went into the bathroom to mix and pound ingredients for another dozen jars. Her hands performed mechanically the orders of her brain; her head felt as if an iron band had been clamped across it to prevent the exit of a hive of bees; and her thoughts, more than ever chaotic, hummed around the name of Milly. Yes! Milly. If she had seen Garth go into her room, yet even then . . . Had she—she couldn't remember—told anyone there about Jasper's heart attack? She certainly hadn't told Milly because she had not seen her again before she left. It was fantastic. What to do . . . to *do*? Defend it? How? Whichever way it went she would be disgraced. Divorce! Parnell. . . . The shame of it, and the world's disgust of it had killed him, but the world had changed in how long? Fourteen years. She must find Garth. Where was Garth? Why didn't he ring? If he were at Sandhurst he could hardly yet have received the ghastly . . .

"Yes?"

A knock at the bathroom door.

"Excuse, *gnädige Frau*, the telephone."

She raced downstairs.

It was Garth; his voice, dehumanized by metallic vibrations, said:

"I must see you at once."

"Have you"—her stiffened lips could scarcely frame the words—"had one too?"

"Yes, ten minutes ago, as I came in, just before I got your message. I'm coming to you straight away."

In a frenzy she waited, pacing up and down the room, reading and re-reading that she, Peridot Hope-Winter, had committed adultery with . . .

"Herr Kolonel Kerrone, *gnädige Frau*."

He was pale, his pallor enhanced by the tightly buttoned black frock coat and mourning tie.

"My poor . . . !" He took her small cold hands between his own and held them, gazing deep into her eyes. "That I should have dragged you into this."

"It's worse," she made her lips firm to tell him, "worse

for you. The Army. Your career . . . What are we going to do?"

"What do you want to do?"

"I don't know."

He released her hands, walked over to the window and with his back to her said: "You wish us to defend?"

"And what," her mouth was dry and tasted suddenly of lemons, "if we don't?"

He wheeled round. "You realize that if we *don't* defend, it will be an admission of—— Good God! But it's unthinkable. As if I would let you be a target for . . . I must get you out of it. I can't let you go through with this and not put up a fight." He came back to her. "It doesn't matter about me. You are all that matters."

Her eyes implored him. Now, she prayed, let him say it. Let him say . . .

But, misinterpreting that silent message, "You see," he told her slowly, and his face, his voice lost warmth, "there is only one course open. We *must* defend."

If then, and in that star-crossed second he had spoken, 'How gladly,' she confesses, 'I would have let it stand, to stand accused. But I believed he *wished* I should defend, not so much for my sake, as his own, his commission, his career, which was his life. . . .'

And so:

"I shall fight it," she said clearly, "come what may!"

*   *   *

It was Freddie who suggested that she consult the senior partner of Sewell and Sewell, Solicitors, of King's Bench Walk; Freddie, who took her to luncheon at his club and from whom she heard that Adrian had received an anonymous letter, 'to raise', Freddie said, 'a hornets' nest'.

So that was it. Milly! She might have known. But why had Adrian not come to her with this back-handed dirt, or chucked it in the fire? Or had he seized upon the opportunity to rid himself of an encumbrance? How often had she heard him say that marriage was too serious to be taken seriously. . . .

"Freddie," avoiding his unwinking stare, she negotiated carefully a lobster claw, "if Garth had not been so insistent on defence I might have——"

"Insistent!" interpolated Freddie, shocked. "Of course he was insistent, as any decent man would be." He squared himself, tipped hock into her glass, and said, "Would you have him sit down under it when both of you are blameless? The mere fact that you are prepared to fight it to the hilt proves your innocence—whichever way," he added paradoxically, "it goes."

"I see what you mean." Her eyes, green as the greenish glass she raised, held hidden laughter. "And I take your meaning kindly, but—suppose we lose?"

"We won't cross that bridge till we come to it. What will you have to follow. A Pêche Melba?"

"Nothing more."

"Sure? Well, then," he pulled out his watch, "I'll take you along to see Charlie Sewell. I know him pretty well and have already had a chat with him about you. He's a member of this Club."

"And so," she said dryly, "*sans peur et sans reproche*?"

"I don't know about that, but he's a brilliant lawyer and makes a speciality of this sort of thing."

"Definitely not," murmured Perry, "*sans reproche*."

Freddie's eyes goggled; he turned from her smile to a waiter: "The bill. I have made an appointment for you to see Charlie," he said, "at three o'clock this afternoon, if that's all right for you."

He paid the bill, piloted her out at the door of the dining-room set apart for lady guests, drove her in a hansom to King's Bench Walk, and left her in the waiting-room of Messrs. Sewells' office with an encouraging nod and the advice to—'tell him everything'. He would be back for her, he said, in half an hour.

Mr. Charles Sewell looked, Perry was dismayed to see, anything but brilliant; indeed, less like a lawyer than the village idiot. He had no chin, or what there was of it receded to imperceptibility inside the wings of his collar. To his face, long, bony, was attached a small, sharp, upward-tilted nose. He was lean, narrow-chested, remarkably tall, and his mouth was an inverted V.

"Good afternoon, Mrs. Hope-Winter." He bent from his height of six feet four to shake her hand. His clasp, firm and strong, at least was reassuring. "Pray be seated. Before we go any further," said Mr. Sewell, turning his swivel chair to face her across his desk, "I am bound to ask did you or did you not commit adultery with the co-respondent named in the petition?"

"But of course I didn't!" she retorted sharply. "Would I be defending if I had?"

Mr. Sewell allowed his peculiar features to relax into the semblance of a smile.

"Defence is not necessarily a proof of innocence. However——" He leaned back in his chair with his elbows on the arms of it, joined his finger-tips, and in tones of disconcerting weariness, said: "Now, tell me your story. Take your time."

She took her time and told her story, although, from his concentration on a point in vacancy, it was doubtful he had heard a word of it, until, lowering his gaze and his fingers, Mr. Sewell made vigorous notes on a pad.

"One moment," he darted her a glance like a two-edged sword. "Let us recapitulate. You left the hotel at Brighton on Saturday, July the twenty-seventh with Colonel Curran, his luggage and yours, and your dog, Colonel Curran having stayed the night at the Royal, and you for these few days at the Crown Hotel, Kemp Town. I presume you brought your luggage with you from this hotel when you met Colonel Curran for luncheon?"

"Yes, to save having to go back and fetch it."

He made another note.

"It was just a sequence of bad luck," continued Perry, "meeting Mr. Sankey at the Royal. But worst of all to choose the one hotel on the Brighton road kept by that woman I knew long ago, and who, when I was a child, made my life a misery. You see"—she spread her hands, and the gesture, slightly foreign, did not pass unobserved by Mr. Sewell—"it is just as if a spiteful fate had driven me to her. She was—I ought to tell you this—a sort of stepmother to me. Mr. Cheke, her first husband, whom I had always believed to be my father"—a vivid flush dyed her face—"was not really my father at all, though I was born in wedlock, if you know what I mean—and when he married this woman, Milly, she resented that I——"

"Exactly so," thoughtfully commented Mr. Sewell. "But the facts of your birth are immaterial to the case, other than that they show a motive why this woman should be so ill-disposed towards you as to write an anonymous letter to arouse your husband's suspicions. We cannot, of course, prove that she did write that letter, nor can we accuse her of it."

"Well, if she didn't," demanded Perry, "who did?"

"That again is immaterial. But let us presume that this woman saw Colonel Curran enter your room, that she overheard your conversation"—he turned his piercing look upon her—"can you recollect the words that passed between you and Colonel Curran while he was attending to your dog?"

"I hardly spoke to him at all. I was terribly upset. I thought my dog was dying. I may have called him 'darling'—not Colonel Curran," she added hastily, "Jasper."

"Jasper being the name of your dog?"

"Yes. And I talk to him as if he were a human."

"And usually in terms of endearment?" suggested Mr. Sewell.

"Yes. 'Darling'—'love', and nonsense of that sort. You know how it is."

"I know very well how it is." Again Mr. Sewell smiled. "My wife bestows on her dog words and caresses of warmer affection than she ever bestows upon me."

Which, Perry considered, stifling laughter, slightly hysterical, one can believe. . . .

"If," reflected Mr. Sewell reverting to his notes, "you have given me the true facts of your case——"

"Absolutely true!" she hotly interposed. "I have told you everything. I am not, and never have been guilty of—that beastly word. We are friends, nothing more. I have known him for years and we have never"—her voice trembled—"even kissed."

"I was about to say," proceeded Mr. Sewell, apparently unmoved by this admission, "that we appear to have a *prima facie* case for the defence. I propose we go for it, but I warn you it will be a tussle. Now, as to your witnesses. Did you consult a veterinary surgeon on the condition of your dog?"

"Yes. When I got back to London the next day I went straight from the station to his house with Jasper in a cab."

"And his name and address is——?"

"Mr. Rudd, 10, Porchester Road, Bayswater. He has always attended my dogs."

"Did he find anything seriously wrong with—ah—Jasper?"

"No, not really. He said bulldogs often get these attacks. It was his heart, exactly as Colonel Curran said. He has bred bulldogs out in India and is as good as any vet. He saved his life."

Mr. Sewell rose from his desk.

"Then that is all I shall require from you at this preliminary stage. You must, of course, file your answer to the petition and swear your affidavit in support. I shall also need a copy of your marriage certificate. And one thing more, Mrs. Hope-Winter. I advise you to avoid any further contact with the co-respondent."

"Don't," cried Perry, "call him that!"

"But, my dear young lady, in point of fact he *is* that, and it is not unlikely your husband has had, and will continue to have, your movements watched."

Perry's mouth fell open. "Watched? Do you mean——?"

"It is not unusual," said Mr. Sewell patiently, "to follow the service of a petition with supplementary evidence provided by a private inquiry agent."

"A detective!" She drew in a breath. "How disgusting! Yet now I come to think of it I have noticed in the square—once or twice—a big man, stoutish, with very big feet, who seemed to be waiting for someone."

Mr. Sewell nodded ruminatively. "Big feet are not uncommon to ex-members of the Police Force. Good-bye, Mrs. Hope-Winter." He held out his hand, and Perry, dwindled to a midget's size, reached up to find hers engulfed in that same warm reassuring clasp. He's really rather nice, she thought: he can't help his face. "I will keep you informed," he said, "of all latest developments and—beware of big men with big feet."

"Thank you, Mr. Sewell." She released her hand. "And when do you suppose I'll be brought up for trial?"

"For hearing," corrected Mr. Sewell. "Yours is not a criminal case."

"Not in the sight of God, perhaps, but in the sight of man—or woman, shall we say—it is." The white lids fluttered. "What a pity that the one witness who could clear me happens to be dumb!"

Yes, indeed a pity, and pity 'tis, 'tis true, reflected Mr.

9

Sewell as he closed the door upon her. Yet there was something to be said for it—a sick dog, the Court's sympathy, and
those green eyes—young-looking for her age, too—an attractive little piece. If it comes before old Watkinson, we're
home. He too breeds bulldogs. . . .

It did not come before old Watkinson. It came before old
Peabody, Mr. Justice Peabody, who in all his lengthy, distinguished career, his knowledge of Probate, Attestation, Naviga-
tion, of Salvage, of Marriage and the breaking of such, and
who in his not unsullied past had kept half a dozen mistresses,
never in his life had kept a dog.

                    *   *   *

During the interim before the Courts re-opened, Perry,
having notified Garth by telephone of Mr. Sewell's warning,
possessed her soul, but not in patience, for that which she,
despite correction, termed her 'Trial'.

Annabel, loyally adherent in the face of heated opposition
from 'the Aunt', had written to invite herself to stay with
Perry and see her through 'this Horror'. And from Annabel
did Perry hear—"Aunt Hilda's going mad. She talks of
nothing else, and is on the phone to Adrian all day and half
the night. Trunk calls too, regardless."

"A certain indication," agreed Perry, "of insanity." She
could well imagine the incessant trumpet-cry, 'I told you
so!'

"She's terrified," said Annabel, "that Adrian will tap
Uncle Freddie for the costs—if he should lose."

"Which he won't," replied Perry with cheerful conviction,
fathered by hope; for, if the case were decided in her favour,
nothing on earth, she declared, would induce her to return to
Adrian. Yet, she would still be his wife. What a coil! To stay
irrevocably tied to him who had sought these vile means to be
quit of her! She was grateful for, and not a little touched, by
the support of Annabel to whom 'this Horror', citing Garth as
co-respondent, spelled the abandonment of a forlorn last
hope.

"For Papa," she confided, "would never consent to my
marriage with a man who had been through the Divorce
Court. Not that Garth," she added dolefully, "has shown

himself the least inclined to marry me. I have always guessed, and now I'm sure that he's in love with you."

Shrill was Perry's laughter, fierce her denial, and her face on fire to dismiss that absurdity as "Rubbish! He loves no one in this world but himself, his career, and his damned motor that has landed us both in—the ditch!"

From another source, quite unexpected, came the assurance of partisanship in a typically inconsequential letter.

'. . . I don't believe a word of it.' Thus Miss Lavinia, 'You have far too much sense to run clear off the rails. Always knew him for a fool soon parted with his money, but never thought him fool enough to part with his wife. Bring matters to a head in any case. Wish I hadn't meddled as things turned out.' (Which recondite statement confirmed the stored suspicion that Miss Lavinia had brought some other matter to its head.) 'The Divorce laws are iniquitous. One more cog in the wheel of universal suffrage. While man obtains his freedom for an isolated act, woman must submit to black eyes and all the rest of it as well. Take self. Evidence in plenty but would not demean. Preferred to let him stew. Send herewith first number of Labour Record. Pethick Lawrence, editor. Not that I am politically in favour of the movement but he does devote a column to the W.S.P.U. Shaw is with us. Bernard. Knew him as a young man. Sandy beard. Expect to be in London in October. You must meet Mrs. Pankhurst. A lioness. What about the needful? Do not hesitate to call on me. And her two lion cubs Sylvia and Christabel. Grand girls both. Who's your Counsel? . . .'

Her Counsel was Evans, Mervyn Evans, K.C. "For since the other side," Mr. Sewell said, "has taken in a Silk——"

"A Silk?"

"A leader," Mr. Sewell indulgently explained. "King's Counsel."

"I see. And who pays for it all?"

"Your husband—we hope."

"But if it goes against us?"

"Colonel Curran has, I understand, some few thousands left him by his father."

"But I can't let *him* . . ." The shame of it! The beastliness. How could Adrian have sunk himself to this? Or could it be that his lust for new sensation had led him to a last dramatic climax—the Divorce Court? He would be at his best in the witness box—never at a loss for repartee, aphoristically glib, though that, from all accounts, would get him nowhere with Mr. Mervyn Evans, described by Mr. Sewell as a 'Welsh terrier with the devil of a bite behind his bark'.

For days before the dread event she rehearsed imaginary answers to the cross-examination by the 'Silk' the other side had 'taken in'—such curious expressions!—that most eminent and ruthless member of the Bar, Sir Eustace Mallaby. From him Mr. Sewell had prepared her to expect no quarter, but: "All you have to do is to speak the truth and let them hear you. Don't mumble, and remember to call the Judge 'my lord'."

His final injunction at a last conference was, "If the Judge questions you, look at and answer him fearlessly. Judges aren't ogres, you know. . . ." Mr. Sewell may have thought that Mr. Justice Peabody would not be found entirely immune from the lure of those green eyes when directed at him 'fearlessly'. . . . And so: "Good luck!"

*   *   *

An expectant public, piqued by Yellow Press allusions to 'Society Divorce Case, Colonel Cited', crowded the Court to capacity on that February morning, 1905.

Perry, pale, but determined, in the last and most treasured of her Worth creations, grey velvet and chinchilla complete with small fur cap, arrived early accompanied by Annabel and Miss Lavinia, up from Somerset to attend the hearing. With the fervent whisper, "You look lovely. Take this," Annabel thrust into Perry's hand a vinaigrette. "Smelling salts—in case."

Perry blinked, swallowed painfully, and received from Miss Lavinia a strong pat on the shoulder with the curt assurance: "Keep your pecker up. We'll win."

Mr. Sewell, who met her in the doorway of the Court, conducted her to a bench in the front row and sat himself beside her. She fixed her eyes on the Judge's empty chair, backed by dim red curtains under the royal coat of arms. The jury box, where twelve good men and true would presently hear her accused of misconduct—what revolting words they used!— was also empty. She felt sick, surreptitiously raised to her nose the vinaigrette, and glancing round saw Adrian take his place at the far end of the bench—immaculate in grey frock coat, a grey topper in his hand, and a white carnation in his button-hole. Did he believe it was a wedding? She stifled a giggle and thought: Both of us in grey, as if by mutual agreement. Would that be called collusion? . . . With him were Reginald and that viper Sankey, a chief witness. Milly would be an-other. Where was she? And where was Garth? Why so late? Suppose he didn't come? . . . Reginald and Sankey had retired to the back.

She closed her eyes.

There was a murmurous buzz, a shuffling and scraping of feet on boards, and a voice at her ear: "There's a restaurant downstairs. I'll fetch you for luncheon when they break." Freddie, bless him! Rather anxious, very red.

"Is Hilda here?"

"Not yet, but she's coming. Couldn't keep her off . . ." His hand slid down to hers. She gave it a convulsive squeeze. "I'm subpoenaed," he told her, "but may not be called. If I am——" He squared his shoulders.

"Yes, Freddie, I know. Thanks," she smiled up at him, "for—everything."

And here, at last was Garth—he still walked with a limp— looking neither right nor left, hitching up his trousers as he sat. Had he seen her? She was half hidden by Mr. Sewell's clerk. She leaned a little forward, glanced at him sideways, met his eyes as they slewed round to find her, and breathed a sigh of thankfulness. To have him there on this same bench with her, even though divided, brought comforting reality to this nightmarish scene. Now she could look about her, register externals. It might be a library in any country house, oak-panelled almost to the ceiling with bookshelves, none conspicuously bearing books. Mr. Sewell, seeming more than ever idiotic and so lean one might believe he had not had a round meal for a month, bent down to tell her: "Sir Eustace and your Counsel——" arriving together with their juniors, be-gowned, bewigged, and looking quite ridiculous. Why did they have to wear those wigs? She craned her neck to watch the two Silks take their seats in the row behind her. She had to search for Mr. Evans whom she had met twice in consultation. Mr. Sewell had been right. He *was* a terrier, with a crisp staccato voice, reminiscent of a yap. He was lantern-jawed, shock-headed, and, in his chambers, untidy, his fingers stained with nicotine; not at all impressive. But now, in that wig hiding his shaggy black hair, his sparse frame enveloped in that voluminous garment, he looked larger, more imposing, very frightening indeed . . . But not, oh, not so frightening as this great fat man, Sir Eustace. What a size! And what a face—like an owl's, with a small beakish nose, implanted in flesh the colour of suet. And now came another two, the foremost of them strutted, very pink and snoutish, accompanied by an eager dark young gentleman, both, of course, in wigs, and each carrying sheaves of documents.

"Colonel Curran's Counsel, Holbrook, K.C., and his junior," muttered Mr. Sewell. He had an awful breath. Turning her head to escape it she again encountered Garth's eyes, to jerk her heart; and from one of the Wigs behind her she heard, "The old boy's late as usual."

Sheepishly the jury filed in: young men, old men, seedy men and mashers, all come to judge the woman taken in adultery. Below the jury box were seated the Press, ready with their fountain pens and pads. She simply had to look round again, and saw Sir Eustace rubbing at his nose, frowning at his papers, plunging a hand beneath his gown to bring out a lozenge and pop it in his mouth. . . . Indigestion or sore throat? Her eyes travelled farther. Freddie, dodging heads to see the Wigs; Miss Lavinia beside him, plucking at her chin; Annabel, staring straight ahead at nothing—and, good heavens! Valerie Croome—in sables and a picture hat, there to see her pilloried and giving her the cut direct.

Perry looked hastily away. The atmosphere was becoming oppressive. She unfastened the flap of her chinchilla muff, contrived by Mr. Worth to hold accessories, took out her handkerchief, redolent of Chypre, and thankfully inhaled. . . . Really, Mr. Sewell!

A stir, a general uprising. His lordship made his entrance, was seated. . . . And:

". . . That, gentlemen of the jury is the case for the petitioner." Offered with damning detail and confidence supreme, to leave no possible doubt concerning the guilt of the respondent.

Having listened to as much as she could hear and interpret of that droning, incisive preamble, she began herself to believe that on the night of July the twenty-seventh, she and Garth—the 'co-respondent'—'had committed the act of adultery consistent with evidence of association, opportunity and desire.' Good God! Desire? What a mockery. Had either ever shown themselves the least desirous? Not she, and heaven knows, not he! . . . 'Over a period of . . .'

She went into a trance and came out of it to hear Sir Eustace call:

"Mr. Adrian Hope-Winter."

Into the box he stepped, very upright, his eyes very blue, his hair slightly grey at the temples, his beard neatly trimmed, his hand long and white, lifting the Book to swear in that familiar tired drawl, 'By Almighty God to speak the truth, the whole truth . . .' And which, under Counsel's guidance, revealed the respondent to be no more nor less than a designing little minx who had married him for money.

"Your wife, I understand, is some twenty years your junior?"

How, Perry thought, he must hate to admit it. And what was the point?

The point, carefully sharpened by Sir Eustace, gave a dig, at 'this marked disparity of age between the parties. A young girl-wife, a husband much her senior.' . . . Motive enough for infidelity. . . . "Before your marriage your wife was an employee in your service?"

"Yes."

"In what capacity?"

"As companion to my invalid niece who was also my ward."

"Your niece is dead?"

"Yes."

"How long after her death did you marry the respondent?"

"About six weeks afterwards."

"At that time you were a man of considerable wealth?"

"I was."

"And in these past few years you have suffered a succession of serious financial reverses?"

"Yes."

"You are now much reduced in circumstances compared with your former financial position?"

"Yes."

"Was it before or after you lost your money that you became suspicious of your wife's association with the co-respondent?"

"After."

"I see." Sir Eustace allowed a travelling glance to rest upon the jury as he repeated, "*After* you lost your money. While you could afford to do so did you make your wife a substantial yearly allowance?"

"Yes."

"And in addition to this allowance did you make her any gifts?"

"Yes, I spent," said Adrian with the deliberation of one who recites a lesson, "some twenty thousand pounds on her jewels, her furs and her gowns."

How vile! Perry paled. The picture so suavely presented to the gawping jury and that old tortoise of a judge, peering at her over his gold-rimmed spectacles as if she were something brought in by the cat, was of a heartless scheming wanton whose extravagance and greed had ruined her doting, middle-aged husband. And now the beast was off upon another tack.

"During the South African War did your wife nurse at a hospital for wounded officers?"

"Yes."

"And while there did she nurse the co-respondent?"

"Yes." A significant pause. "She did."

"Was that the beginning of their association?"

"No. He was a frequent visitor to my house in Brook Street while my niece was alive. He was her cousin."

"Your niece's cousin? No relative of yours?"

"No. But I have known Colonel Curran ever since he was a boy."

Perry glanced at Garth. The base betrayer of a long and trusted friendship sat, arms folded, eyes unswervingly fixed on the debonair figure in the box.

"Mr. Hope-Winter," how sympathetically caressing was

that voice, somewhat husky—from emotion or sore throat?—
"on what particular occasion did you confirm your suspicions
concerning your wife's relationship with the co-respondent?"

"One night in September, 1903, when we were staying the
week-end at a country house-party."

"Can you relate the circumstances that gave rise to this
suspicion?"

"The discovery of Colonel Curran—Major as he then was—
alone with my wife in her bedroom."

A stir swept through the Court, and, among the jurymen, a
movement as of water ruffled by a breeze.

"Will you tell his lordship and the jury what you saw on
that occasion?"

"I saw the co-respondent in his dressing-gown and pyjamas
and my wife in her nightdress and a state of perturbation."

"State of what?"

"Perturbation, my lord," replied Sir Eustace blandly.

Slowly the spectacles turned upon Adrian. "What exactly
do you mean by perturbation?"

The immaculate shoulders expressed the merest shrug.

"A state of emotional embarrassment, my lord."

"I see." The Judge lowered his head, put pen to paper and,
rapidly writing, said: "Proceed."

With exquisite satisfaction Sir Eustace did proceed.

"When you found your wife in these circumstances did you
demand an explanation?"

"No." Lifting his hand from the ledge of the box Adrian
remotely examined his nails. "She did not give me time to ask
for—she offered me an explanation."

"Which was?"

"That the mirror above the mantelpiece had detached itself
from the wall, that she saved it from falling by placing her
hands against it, and that the co-respondent had appeared in
answer to her cries for help."

"A very prompt and opportune appearance," commented
Sir Eustace, amused.

There were titters, and the whispered scream of a laugh.
Valerie? Of course!

"During this house-party did you," asked Sir Eustace, his
eyes sliding round to the jury box again, "sleep in your wife's
bedroom?"

"No. I slept in the room adjoining."

"Was the co-respondent's bedroom next to yours?"

"Yes."

"Did any lady other than your wife occupy a bedroom on this floor?"

"No. We were in the bachelors' wing."

"At what time did you make the discovery concerning your wife and the co-respondent?"

"When I went up to bed at about one o'clock. I had been playing Bridge."

"And at what time did your wife retire?"

"At ten o'clock as far as I remember."

It was like a game of battledore and shuttlecock; back and forth flew the questions, mellifluously poised, unhesitatingly answered.

"Did you go to bed before or after Colonel Curran?"

"After. Some time," added Adrian, "after. The one other occupant of the bachelors' wing stayed talking with my host downstairs."

"So that until you went to bed the co-respondent and your wife were alone together in the bachelors' wing?"

"Yes."

Perry writhed. How damnable of them to have dragged in this, knowing perfectly well that . . .

"Thank you, Mr. Hope-Winter."

With an air of ineffable content Sir Eustace sat down; Adrian prepared to step down, and Mr. Evans stood up.

"One moment, please."

Perry moistened her dry lips. What now?

What now was a salvo of questions delivered as, for all the world, in a series of staccato barks.

"There were two doors to the bedroom—you occupied—during this week-end?"

"I believe so."

"You believe so. Do you not—know—so?"

"Yes. There were two doors."

"Did one of these doors communicate with your wife's bedroom?"

"Yes."

"Did the other door—open—directly from the corridor?"

"Yes."

"By which of these doors did you enter your wife's room—on the occasion to which—my learned friend—refers?"

"I, really," said Adrian, bored, "cannot remember."

"May I refresh your memory? I put it to you that both the main door—and the door leading to your bedroom—were wide open when you entered your wife's room from—the corridor?"

"I have no recollection that either door was open."

"Have you not?" Good lord, what a bark! "Then perhaps you may recollect that you told your wife to go into your bedroom—at once."

"I did."

What the dickens, wondered Perry, is he driving at?

"Why?" insisted Mr. Evans.

"Because I did not wish the servants to see her in her déshabille."

"In her what?"

"Her déshabille, my lord," barked Mr. Evans.

As if emerging from a shell the tortoise head of Mr. Justice Peabody exploratively turned in the direction of the witness.

"Do you mean her nightgown?"

"Precisely, my lord," smiled Adrian.

"Then why don't you say what you mean? And had you any reason to suppose the servants *would* see her in her nightgown?"

Such a mumbly old voice, such a crumbly old hand, searching through the papers on his desk, those spectacles shining, rather fiercely, upon Adrian who very slightly bowed.

"My wife told me she had rung for the servants, my lord, but they had not yet answered the bell."

The Judge nodded. "Proceed, Mr. Evans."

"You say you were playing Bridge that night? With whom?"

"With two of the guests and my host."

"Was one of these guests—Colonel Curran?"

"Yes."

"At what time did Colonel Curran leave the Bridge table? . . . Well? I am waiting." As if at a rat-hole to pounce.

"I cannot quite recall the exact . . ."

The terrier pounced.

"Let me help you. I suggest that Colonel Curran left the Bridge table not more than fifteen minutes before—you—went to your room—which you have said was at one o'clock—in the morning?"

"I did not observe the time that Colonel Curran left the Bridge table."

"Did you not?"

And down went Mr. Evans and up went Mr. Holbrook.

"Mr. Hope-Winter"—cherubic, cheery, pouter-chested, affable, his voice inclined to the falsetto, was Garth's 'Silk'—"when you entered your wife's room was not Colonel Curran holding up the mirror with his arms stretched across it?"

"I did not look at Colonel Curran. I was looking at my wife."

"Exactly so." Very affable indeed! "But when your wife had left the room and a footman came in answer to the bell, did you see him and Colonel Curran together take the mirror from the wall?"

"Yes."

"And were the four supporting screws found to be so loose," the falsetto ascended almost to a squeak, "that they came *away* from the wall and fell to the ground?"

"I cannot swear to that."

"Then you can swear to *this*?" Not so affable. "That you were told by your host the next day, on the expert authority of a builder, who, with your host, Sir Frederick Stilton, is in the Court and can testify that the wall behind the mirror showed extensive evidence of dry rot?"

"I can swear to nothing," was the weary answer, "of the sort."

"Thank you."

With another little bow to the Judge, and a little smile dragging at his lips, Adrian left the box.

"Mr. Marcus Sankey," said Sir Eustace.

Pallid, very nervous, very sleek about the hair, very long about the nose and long about his answers, was Mr. Marcus Sankey. . . .

Yes, the witness had seen the respondent at luncheon with the co-respondent at the Royal Hotel, Brighton, on July the twenty-seventh. Yes, the respondent did tell witness she was driving up to London in the co-respondent's motor-car. . . .

Witness had asked co-respondent if he might be allowed to accompany them and was told there was no room in the car. Why? . . . Because it was loaded up with luggage. . . . Did witness see the parties leave the hotel ? Yes, witness had seen them off.

"And," Sir Eustace winningly inquired, "*was* there any luggage?"

"Quite."

"Quite?" From the Judge.

Witness turned, if possible, paler.

"Quite a quantity of—my lord."

"Can you describe this luggage?" urged Sir Eustace, honey-mouthed.

"Two or three portmanteaux, a lady's dressing-case and—so on."

"Two persons' luggage, in fact?"

"Yes, I think——"

Perry ground her molars. What a skunk was this Sir Eustace, and what a sneaking reptile this Sankey!

"And was the luggage in the motor-car when you saw it, Mr. Sankey?"

"No. It was—was in the hall. A porter put it in the—in the motor."

"Would you say this luggage was sufficient for a week?"

"Ker-quite . . ."

"Thank you, Mr. Sankey."

"One moment."

The terrier again, and to the ledge of the box witness clung in a pitiable fright.

"Were Mrs. Hope-Winter and Colonel Curran seated at a window table in the dining-room of this hotel—at Brighton—when you—accosted them?"

"I believe——"

"In a prominent position where they could be seen—not only by other visitors in the dining-room—but by promenaders on the front?"

"Ye-yes."

"Thank you."

Mr. Sankey was allowed to slink away.

"Mrs. Millicent Moon."

So that was her name now, and there she was—in black plush, a feather boa, and a toque adorned with a crimson rose precariously perched on a pyramid of curls. Removing her gloves she took the oath in a voice that could be heard in every corner of the Court, beamed upon the jury, smiled at the Judge, who returned her a stare. Her hands, red and puffy, sparkled with paste, her bangles tinkled, as, expectantly, she offered to Sir Eustace the full expanse of her polished white porcelain teeth.

Yes, before her second marriage she had been the widow of . . . No, not exactly the responder's father, although out of charity he had let her think he was, having married the responder's mother when she . . .

"My lord!" Up jumped the terrier, yapping. "I protest! This is utterly irrelevant."

Perry lifted her head to see the Judge looking down at her again; a wintry sunbeam slanting from an upper window, alighted on her hair under the chinchilla cap. Remembering Mr. Sewell's advice, she fastened her eyes on that old, cold face to receive a glance, surprisingly keen, from behind the spectacles.

"I cannot see," the old man rumbled, "where these questions are leading us, Sir Eustace."

"My lord, with great respect I was about to establish a former relationship between the respondent and the witness."

"Which," said the Judge, "is immaterial."

"With the utmost respect, not entirely, my lord. However——" His tone implied a tolerant indulgence for senility. "Now, Mrs. Moon, will you kindly tell his lordship and the jury what you saw on the night of July the twenty-seventh?"

"Well," determinedly grasping the ledge of the box, Milly deeply exhaled and told.

"I was coming from me room when I see the gentleman, that is to say the correspondent, slip into Mrs. Whatsername's—the responder's bedroom, so I says to meself that's funny they musta changed over, so I——"

"At what time would this be?" came the interruption, gentle as a sucking dove.

"Past midnight. H'past twelve, I should say. I'd been to bed and had to get up again to go down the passage, if you know what I mean."

Another whispered scream from Valerie, and from the Court concerted grins.

"Were you positive the co-respondent did enter the respondent's room and not his own?"

"Yes, because her shoes was outside of her door and his boots outside of his."

"And while you noted the position of the shoes and boots, did you overhear a conversation?"

"Not what you'd call a conversation, no. What I heard her—the responder say——" And with a great display of teeth, Milly said it—"was 'darlin', my darlin' don't leave me—you're never going to leave me, are you'—and all that kinda thing."

"What kind of thing?" asked the Judge.

"Well, kinda love-makin', your worship. I can't remember all I heard not bein' givin to listenin' at doors and that. Only she spokeser loud I couldn't help hearin'."

"Go on, Sir Eustace."

Sir Eustace went on.

"What else could you not help hearing?"

"Well, something about a bath."

A ripple of laughter ran through the Court. Up popped the Judge's head again. "A bath?"

"My lord," the face of Sir Eustace wreathed itself in smiles, "the co-respondent's Christian name, I understand, is Garth."

"I see."

"And was that all you heard, Mrs. Moon?"

"Oh, no." Encouraged by the titters Milly elaborated. "There was ever such a lot o' sobbin' and cryin' and him sayin' to quiet her down, 'you wait, now—everythin's going to be all right.' And after that I didn't hear no more for a bit and was just goin' to me room thinkin' well I'm sure I don't know what to make of this not liking to have such goings on in a respectable house which never before has had to do with——"

"Keep your witness to the point, Sir Eustace, please."

"His lordship, and the jury," said the dove-like Sir Eustace, "are only interested in what you overheard, Mrs. Moon, and not in your reaction to it. Do you recollect hearing anything else?"

"Well, there wasn't much else to hear except a lot o' kissin' and that—and 'oh, my precious, you must never do this to me again' and 'oh, whatever his name is—thank God'—she said it twice—'for *you*'. And then a snore."

"A snore?"

The Judge's head poked forward, the Court gasped, and explosive laughter now roared up to hit the ceiling. An usher called for 'Silence!' And Milly, smiling broadly, said, "That's right, your worship, just as if the gentleman had gone off to sleep."

"Thank you, Mrs. Moon."

And the Judge, with a glance at the clock, said: "At a quarter past two."

The underground restaurant was packed and indescribably stuffy. Seated opposite Sir Frederick and Miss Lavinia, with Annabel beside her, Perry concentrated on the sole, that in direct contradiction to her request for 'Nothing—just a cup of coffee', Miss Lavinia had ordered, and insisted she should eat. "You can't put up a fight on an empty stomach. Point steak, Frederick, for me."

Perry looked anxiously for Garth. "Has anyone seen Garth?" No one had seen Garth.

"That horrid smarmy fat man," snorted Annabel, "I hate him! The way he brought in all that stuff about the mirror when everybody knows how it happened."

"That's their job," her uncle said. "One builds up and the other pulls down. It's like a house of cards."

"Yes," said Annabel, eagerly. " 'Alice in Wonderland.' Those jurymen all look like the animals in the trial scene from 'Alice'. The foreman's like a lizard and there's another like a pig, and the Judge——"

"Is like a tortoise," said Perry, "or a turtle. And if I eat this sole I shall be sick."

"Here," Freddie poured her out a glass of wine. "Buck you up."

It did buck her up, to brace her for the coming ordeal with Sir Eustace. Clinging to Freddie's hand she was conducted to the more than ever crowded Court, aware that the eyes of every man were appraisingly upon her as the eyes of every woman, disdainfully, were not. Hands clasped inside her muff she saw Garth unconcernedly stroll in, and turn to speak low-voiced to Mr. Sewell's clerk. She caught a word or two . . . 'Police sergeant . . . Yes, and the garage proprietor. He's here. . . .'

And so was the Judge. The audience stood and a voice called:

"Mrs. Moon."

Mr. Sewell, now smelling gratefully of whisky, murmured into Perry's ear: "Taffy! He'll shake her."

Taffy? . . . Ah, Mr. Evans on his toes, and Milly in the box, her teeth much in evidence, her face a trifle redder, her toque a trifle slipping, and her voice a trifle slurred.

Yes, the correspondent did say when he arrived at the hotel that his motor-car had broken down—but that was *his* story. She never saw no motor. Yes, he did engage two single rooms, *and* a private sitting-room. Was this private sitting-room an office? Yes. And did witness's husband serve supper in this office and wait upon the parties at table? Witness didn't know. She wasn't there. Where was witness? In the saloon, having to help—it being a Saturday night.

"I see." The pause of a second for that to sink in. Then: "Did Mrs. Hope-Winter and Colonel Curran—sign the register?"

"I never bothered meself to look."

"Will you—bother yourself to look—now?"

An open ledger was passed up to witness who took it from the usher as if expecting it to bite, and returning it inquired:

"What about it?"

"That," barked Mr. Evans, "is what I am asking you. Do you recognize the signatures under—the date—July the twenty-seventh?"

"How should I reckernize what I've never seen before?"

"You have never seen these signatures—those of Mrs. Hope-Winter and Colonel Curran—in your hotel register before?"

"I thought they was husband and wife. It's not my place to——"

"You must answer yes or no," from the Judge.

A defiant "No!"

The Judge compressed his lips till he looked to have no mouth. "Proceed."

At what time did witness go to bed on the night of July the twenty-seventh?

"Lateish, about ha-past twelve. I was sittin' up doing the accounts——"

"You were sitting up—'doing the accounts'?" repeated Mr. Evans, in amaze. "And where were you—'doing'—these accounts?"

"In the office. The door has glass half-way so you can see what's going on and I see the correspondent come into the hall and take something from his bag and go upstairs again and into that Perry's—the responder's room. He was in his pyjamas and dressing-gown."

"And this you saw—as you came out of your own room— to go—as you told my learned friend—'down the passage'— having already been to bed?"

"I said so, didn't I?"

"Yes," barked Mr. Evans, "you *did* say so. Are you gifted, Mrs. Moon—with—second sight?"

The Court sniggered, and Milly retorted, bellicose: "There's nothing wrong with my sight, thank you."

"But apparently there is, for how—if you were coming from your bedroom—could you see Colonel Curran at the same time—in the hall?"

"Well," taken with the flushes, Milly gulped, and said: "I saw first—I saw'm first in the hall and then in the passage goin' to her room."

"So you had *not* been to bed?"

"I can't—it's—one can't remember everythink."

"You are on your oath," intoned the Judge, "to endeavour to remember everything. Correctly."

"I've told the truth, my lordship," said witness loudly, "and I'll stick"—she slightly swayed—"by what I've sworn, so'elp me."

And, Holy Moses! groaned Sir Eustace to his inner man, the woman's tight—and was saying: "I saw him go into her room and I heard them makin' love and that's the maing—the main thing, isn't it?"

"You are not here to question me," pronounced the Judge; and with a hitch to the tail of his gown as if he wagged it, the little Welshman said:

"I thank you—Mrs.—Moon."

The usher held her elbow as she stumbled from the box.

"So that, my lord and gentlemen of the jury," said the imperturbable Sir Eustace, "is the case for the petitioner."

The case for the defence as set forth by Mr. Evans, in accents miraculously changed, and charged with emotion, offered a very different head to the front of respondent's offending. The picture now presented a young and martyred wife, whose loyal devotion to a recklessly extravagant husband had led her to dispose not only of her home and all its priceless contents, her domestic staff, her carriages, her horses, but of her personal allowance, courageously sacrificed and without demur accepted by her husband to meet his mounting debts. As to the adulterous interpretation put upon a perfectly innocuous relationship between Counsel's client and the co-respondent, the evidence produced which might, at first appear to be incriminating, Counsel—categorically—could refute.

"We have already been told of suspicions based on the incident of a falling mirror that my learned friend thought fit to bring forward as indicative of both desire and opportunity, and which has proved to be"—the bark was uppermost again—"an entirely false scent. My client," vociferated Counsel, "does not *deny* association with the co-respondent. His close relationship with Miss Geraldine Curran, the young crippled girl"—a pause, and a lachrymose quaver—"whom my client loved, and, with what unceasing care, nursed through a long and painful illness terminating in an early death . . ." Overcome by the vision he had conjured of his client's broken heart at the loss of one dearer than a sister, Mr. Evans placed a hand across his heaving chest . . . "We have all heard of platonic friendship of which this association, so wilfully misunderstood, is a striking example. That young crippled girl, cut off from life in her blossoming youth, a sister in all but blood to my client, and beloved cousin of the co-respondent, served as a link in the memory of both to keep her presence evergreen." Mr. Evans shot a glance at the jury. The foreman, 'like a lizard,' blew his nose; another coughed. There was some eye-blinking, and, 'Struth! silently commented Mr. Evans, they've swallowed it! . . . "How cruel," his glance appealed to heaven, "that a friendship such as this, purely— but *pure*ly—platonic, should be, by the impure, mistaken.

Why, gentlemen, the very innocence of this wronged and gentle lady"—Perry bit back a giggle. She dared not look at Garth . . . Geraldine! If she could have heard all this! Perhaps she could, and would never have done laughing—"brought here to fight injustice and clear her stainless name, is proven in her total disregard for the conventions——"

Cripes! Mr. Sewell, who was yawning, pulled himself together. That's pretty close sailing—"in that she was seen—openly—with Colonel Curran in a window table at a fashionable Brighton hotel and in a full view of visitors within and without the dining-room. We have it that when Colonel Curran"—he debated at length on the offer made to drive her back from Brighton to London in his automobile—"an offer not to be refused by an"—he almost said 'adventurous', but deftly altered it to "an intrepid young woman who had never travelled in a motor-car before. What were the dangers attached to such an excursion compared with the excitement of it? Understandable indeed. But the Hand of Fate"—histrionically Counsel raised his own—"the Hand of Fate was at the wheel, the motor-car breaks down, there are no trains—and so—opportunity is given but *not taken*! Desire? Under the circumstances, which will be related, desire is conspicuously absent, and, gentlemen, adultery, remember, must be—proved! Mrs. Peridot Hope-Winter."

So here we go, thought Perry. But the Judge looked at the clock and said, "At ten o'clock tomorrow morning."

* * *

Perry's sleep that night, when sleep she did, was haunted by an interminable dream of Sir Eustace—in a toque and feather boa—explaining to the King's Bench on which were crowded a number of gentlemen in barristers' wigs and pyjamas, that the respondent was found guilty of Desire, Opportunity, Adultery, and of Extensive Dry Rot. And she must swear by Almighty God to speak the truth, the whole truth and nothing but the truth and tell his lordship—who was seated in a motor-car—exactly what she saw when she signed the marriage register—"which," said the Judge, "is entirely irrelevant". And Sir Eustace said, "With great respect there is a quantity of luggage in that motor-car, my lord, sufficient to establish an adulterous relationship between this wronged and gentle lady and the co-respondent with whom she was seen to take a bath." "Which," said the Judge, "remember, must be proved." And Mr. Sewell said: "He will lose his commission." And Perry heard herself retort: "The divorce laws are iniquitous. Black eyes and all the rest of it and his Christian name I'll have you know, is Garth." And the Judge said: "Don't confuse the issue—you may have a cup of tea, so drink it, drink it——"

"Drink it," Annabel said, at the bedside, "while it's hot."

Perry rubbed her eyes and began to laugh. "I've had such a silly dream about Sir Eustace and——"

"Drink your tea. I've told Karl to bring your breakfast to you here."

Perry drank her tea and asked for the morning papers.

"They've not come yet," lied Annabel.

But driving to the Court in a hansom, Perry saw, and averted her eyes from the screaming headlines of news placards.

SOCIETY DIVORCE CASE
Millionaire Art Collector in the Witness Box

"*The Evening Echo*," snorted Annabel, "gave it six columns. I put it on the fire. Uncle Freddie told me not to let you see the papers. Just imagine! Millionaire—Adrian was never that. I bet he's enjoying this publicity. He would! And those Press photographers swarming round him yesterday. I didn't think much of his answers, did you? I expected to hear him let forth a flood of epigrams, but he couldn't say boo to your Counsel. Aren't you dreading your turn? I am. I'm in a much greater funk than you are over this. I do so admire your courage."

"Born of despair," smiled Perry. "I expect the news placards will come out this evening with 'Bulldog cited'!"

"You are a scream!" neighed Annabel. "But what *will* you say to that horrible Sir Eustace?"

" 'To doubt my inspiration was regarded as heretical, until you cut me out with your placidity emetical—sing Booh to you, Pooh Pooh to you, and *that* is what I'll say'. . . . Oh, God!" sighed Perry, "here we are."

She was staggered to find an army of photographers ready with their cameras as she stepped out of the cab. The hateful

Press, who had blazoned up and down the country, news, un-expurgated, of the case, were already in their seats. Perry sat behind with Annabel and Miss Lavinia until Mr. Sewell came to fetch her to the front. "Cheer up, we're all hopeful. Evans wiped the floor with their chief witness yesterday. She was half-seas over."

"I could have warned them," Perry told him, "that she would be."

And there, once again, they all were, in their gowns and their wigs, standing to the entrance of the Judge.

"Mrs. Peridot Hope-Winter."

Chin up, head high, none to see her would have guessed her knees weak as sponges, her mouth a lime-kiln, and her heart in her high-heeled boots. . . . But what was this? Where the bark, the pounce, fierce nostrils flaring, lips drawn back, fangs exposed for the fray? Yes, but now he was fighting for and not against her and, as in his opening speech, the voice of Mr. Evans throbbed through the Court, dulcet as the notes of a Welsh harp. Step by step through the early days of marriage . . . Yes, a happy marriage (and Perry thought, it wasn't. Is that perjury?) and so to Adrian's debts, his writs, her courageous battle with adversity and her determination to adjust her life and his to their sadly altered conditions, did Counsel guide her, touching briefly on her voluntary service as nurse throughout the war, while her husband, despite his much reduced finances, travelled in luxury abroad. . . . And then to the hotel at Brighton, the interval for tea, and the head-long speed at the record-breaking average of fifteen miles an hour to make up for time lost, and—the disastrous halt.

"How long, Mrs. Hope-Winter, did you wait in the motor-car for Colonel Curran's return after he left you to walk to the nearest village?"

"About two hours."

"Were you alone in the motor-car?"

"No. I had my bulldog with me."

This, the first the Court had heard of any bulldog, stimulated interest that had a little flagged.

"Was your bulldog affected by the drive?"

"Yes, it made him sick."

Some faint but general amusement.

"Had he recovered from his sickness by the time you arrived at Cowfold?"

"Yes, but he was taken ill again in the night."

"At what time?"

"At half-past twelve."

"Please to tell his lordship and the jury the symptoms of your dog's illness."

"He seemed to be dying. His tongue was blue, and he was gasping for breath."

"And what did you do?"

"I went to Colonel Curran's room, knocked on his door, and told him that the dog was ill again, and asked if he had any brandy. He said he had a flask in his bag downstairs."

"Did he immediately fetch the flask?"

"No. He first examined the dog and said he was suffering from a heart attack. He showed me how to massage the heart and then he fetched the brandy."

"How long was he gone?"

"Not more than five minutes."

"And then?"

"Colonel Curran dosed him with the brandy."

"You were in some distress?"

"Yes."

"And in your distress did you speak to the dog?"

"Yes."

"And to Colonel Curran?"

She had been warned by Mr. Sewell that her own Counsel must not ask her leading questions, and he had explained what exactly *was* a leading question, which seemed to make no sense, since the other side in cross examination, and most unfairly, could put to her as many leading questions as it liked. So now, instead of asking her straight out, 'did you say this— or did you say that', to which it would have been so easy for her to answer 'yes', she must repeat word for word, as far as she remembered it, all that she had said to Garth, and to Jasper while he lay, apparently, for dead. However, even though her recitation, wheedled out of her by Mr. Evans, sounded like the burbling of one mentally deficient, she got through it somehow while the Court sat all ears and in the giggles. Beasts!

"And," continued Mr. Evans, "when the dog had responded to Colonel Curran's treatment, what did you do?"

All right, if I must, she thought, I must. "Well, then I . . . kissed him."

"Kissed whom?" asked the Judge, amid titters. The old fool! Whom did he think? "The dog, of course." Oh, dear, she should have said, 'my lord', with great respect—all this kow-towing! "And after that he went to sleep. I expect it was the brandy."

The Court held a laughing breath. Smiles appeared on the faces of the jury, and, fleetingly, upon the face of Perry, turned to catch the Judge's eye. Over the spectacles he looked at her, and, preternaturally solemn, he asked:

"Did he snore?"

"Yes, my lord." Perry answered simply. "Bulldogs always snore when they sleep. They can't help it. They have such short noses."

Again released laughter rocked the Court, even to the ushers, even to the Judge, who, controlling a spasm of his dry old lips, gazed down at the demurely smiling witness in the box. And watching the effect of those green eyes upon his lordship, Mr. Sewell thought: The little devil! We couldn't have done better with old Watkinson.

"Is there anything else, Mr. Evans?" asked old Peabody, and for all the Court to see he smiled straight into the respondent's upraised eyes.

"No, my lord, I am quite satisfied."

Not so Sir Eustace.

That elephantine man seemed visibly to swell as he brought the full weight of his batteries to bear upon her in whose mind, with Gilbertian insistence, ran the words: 'You stuff your conversation full of quibble and of quiddity, you dine on chops and roly-poly pudding with avidity . . .'

"Mrs. Hope-Winter, for how many days were you in Brighton before this episode of July the twenty-seventh?"

"From Tuesday afternoon of July the twenty-third, until Saturday the twenty-seventh—three full days."

"Your husband was in Paris at that time?"

"Yes, while I was house-hunting."

"And where," excessively bland was Sir Eustace, "did you stay for these three 'full' days at Brighton?"

"At the Crown Hotel, Kemp Town."

"And yet your luggage was seen in the entrance hall of the Royal Hotel at Brighton?"

"Yes." A little crease appeared between the negligible eyebrows. "I brought my luggage and my dog from my hotel on the Saturday morning and left them in the care of a porter at the Royal."

"Was the co-respondent staying at Brighton while you were there?"

"No. He stayed with friends at Pulborough for Goodwood week."

"Yet the co-respondent had arranged to drive you from Brighton to London in his motor-car?"

"Yes. That was arranged the day before I went to Brighton when I met Colonel Curran accidentally in Knightsbridge."

"Accidentally?"

"Yes."

"Mrs. Hope-Winter," boomed Sir Eustace, "you have just said that Colonel Curran did not stay at Brighton while you were there?"

"Yes, I did say so, and it is true, but——" And she thought, No, not quite true. I must get this right—"He told me when I met him at the hotel for luncheon that he had brought his motor-car from Pulborough the night before."

"Did he tell you also that he had stayed at the Royal Hotel the night before?"

"Yes—but only for that night."

"And did you meet the co-respondent 'only for that night'?"

The swine! Was he daring to insinuate that she and Garth had . . . She mustn't lose her head over this. But she had lost her breath and regained it, between a second and a second, to reply:

"I did not meet Colonel Curran during my stay at Brighton until the morning of July the twenty-seventh, when he told me he had brought his motor-car from Pulborough the night before to have it overhauled."

"In spite of which attention the motor-car broke down?"

"Yes." Perry looked at him, saw his lipless smile, and said coolly: "Big end."

"Big what?" From on high.

"Big end, my lord, so Colonel Curran said it was"—a lift of the eyelids—"but I don't know what it means."

"Nor," said the Judge, blinking through his spectacles, "do I."

Sir Eustace had now ceased fire on Brighton to turn his guns upon the inn at Cowfold . . ."where you say your dog was taken ill. Did it not occur to you to call in the assistance of a veterinary surgeon?"

"How could I—in the middle of the night? By the time I had roused the house and asked if there were a veterinary surgeon in the village and brought him there, the dog might have been dead."

That horrible face, like a balloon, swimming before her in a sea of staring faces, and, oh, lord! Hilda—in the back row with Valerie!

"So in the middle of the night you went to Colonel Curran's bedroom, woke him up and asked him to attend to your dog?"

"Yes, I did. I knew that Colonel Curran had bred bulldogs in India and is as good as any vet—veterinary surgeon."

"Mrs. Hope-Winter," those fishy eyes, embedded in flesh, gazing up at the ceiling, that hateful silky voice, trying to tie her into knots—"are you accustomed to address your dog as 'darling', and by other terms of passionate endearment?"

More sniggers; Perry glared.

"I seldom call him by his name, if that is what you mean."

And again the Judge was speaking.

"Sir Eustace, these terms of endearment, which witness was overheard to say, and, as we understand, in some distress, are they not often used by ladies when addressing their pet dogs?"

"That might be so, my lord, but with greatest respect, I submit that such terms are more commonly used between lovers."

"Mrs. Hope-Winter," the old head in its comical wig slowly turned to her; the old voice persuasively asked: "To whom did you address these words described by Counsel as of 'passionate endearment'?"

"To Jasper, my lord."

"Jasper?"

"My bulldog."

"Is that the dog's name?"

"Yes," she smiled up at him, "my lord."

And Sir Eustace, gnawing at his lip, thought: Be damned! who's conducting this case, he or I?

"Very well, Sir Eustace. Go on."

Like a battering ram he went on.

"Your dog's name, you say, is Jasper?"

"Yes."

"Are you asking his lordship and the jury to believe that you said to your dog, whose name is Jasper, 'Oh, Garth, thank God for you'?"

There were no titters now. The Court sat hushed, the jury attentive. They had heard this before, yet the words, as slowly and surely repeated by Counsel, held an ominous significance.

"I do not ask anyone to believe that those particular words were addressed to my dog. I thanked God—and Colonel Curran—for his successful treatment of my dog."

"Yes, Mrs. Hope-Winter, that is one construction that may be put upon those words, but may I also suggest that they could have been said as a conciliatory end to a lovers' tiff?"

"No!"

Her temper flared. She was pale but she boldly met his look, and his question poised to strike.

"Had you not previously said, 'My darling, don't leave me. You are not going to leave me?' And do you maintain that these words were addressed to your dog?"

"Yes I do. I thought my dog was dying and also——"

"Yes?"

She gathered strength to fling at him: "I also said—but your witness did not tell you that—'What a fright you gave me.' "

"Because you feared you had lost, or were about to lose, your lover?"

"It's a lie!"

Her mouth stayed open in the shock of her own vehemence, as, with weighty unction, Counsel capped it.

"Is it also a lie that the co-respondent was alone in your bedroom with you—and your dog—for an hour or more in the middle of the night?"

"No. That is the truth. He stayed with me until the dog was over his attack."

"Mrs. Hope-Winter," a shellburst this! "Can you say on your oath, that in such an opportune hour you did not commit adultery with the co-respondent?"

The jury were looking at her, the whole Court was looking at her, Garth was looking at her and to him she spoke.

"On my oath I did not commit adultery with Colonel Curran in that or any other hour of my life."

A stillness held the Court; furtively the jurymen glanced at the Judge, and at the small indomitable figure in the witness box. So colourless her face beneath the pale glint of hair, it was as if all blood in her veins had ceased to flow. A watchful usher sidled up with a tumbler of water in his hand, and:

"At five minutes past two," said the Judge.

"You were wonderful!" Annabel seized her arm as she forced her way out amid the general exodus. "The way you stood up to that detestable beast of a man! I'm certain you'll win. The Judge is all on your side. I could see by the way he——"

"Annabel," Perry cut her short, "don't let's have lunch in that stuffy place downstairs. Can't we find an A.B.C. or something?"

They found an A.B.C., dodging Miss Lavinia and Freddie, who had managed to detach himself from Hilda to say: "By Jove! You deserve a medal for the fight you put up. Mallaby is known to be the hardest nut to crack of the whole lot o' them." And then, as from somewhere behind him, a voice called fiercely, "Frederick!" he gave Perry's shoulder a squeeze, said: "I'll see you later," and to his wife, "So there you are m'dear! What a crowd. This way."

Over coffee and a sandwich, Perry asked: "How did Hilda take it?"

"We're not speaking, so I don't know. She has finished with me," Annabel said with her whinnying laugh, "for sticking to you. Shall we go? We mustn't be late. Who comes next? Is it Garth?"

It was Mr. Rudd, the veterinary surgeon, stepping gingerly into the witness box as they arrived.

"We *are* late!" whispered Annabel. "I'll have to stand."

As Perry slid into her seat, Mr. Rudd was taking, inaudibly, the oath. A precise, bald, timid little man, was Mr. Rudd, with a straggling moustache, pince-nez, and the air of one who owes the world a perpetual apology for his existence. To Mr. Evans' questions—no bark in them now—he answered in mild

self-effacing tones that scarcely rose above a whisper. . . .
Yes, he had attended Mrs. Hope-Winter's dogs for many
years. Yes, she had brought her bulldog to his surgery on
Sunday, July the twenty-eighth, at—as near as he could recollect it—twelve forty-five p.m. Yes, she had told witness the
dog had vomited during a journey in a motor-car the day before, and on that same night, so the lady said, the dog had been
taken seriously ill. . . . No, witness could not say his examination of the dog had discovered any marked symptoms of illness.

"What was your opinion of the dog's condition, Mr. Rudd?"

"I—a——" Mr. Rudd adjusted his pince-nez more firmly
on his nose—"I formed the opinion that there was nothing—a
—radically wrong with the dog more than a slight cardiac
murmur."

"I didn't hear that," said the Judge. "Will you please repeat
it."

In evident alarm, witness repeated it.

"Is this cardiac murmur more usual with bull dogs than with
other breeds?"

And Mr. Sewell thought: If only we had old Watkinson on
this!

"Yes—a——" witness was saying, "the bulldog's width of
chest——"

"Please speak up, Mr. Rudd," said Counsel kindly.

"The bulldog's width of chest"—with so terrific an effort
did Mr. Rudd speak up that he reddened even to his hairless
head—"causes a certain pressure on the heart and—a——"

"Have you known such cases to result in a fatal attack?"

"Yes, in the event of a—of a thrombosis——"

The Judge inclined an ear.

"Event of a what?"

"Thrombosis, my lord," prompted Mr. Evans.

The Judge opened his lips, and, with a glance at the timor-
ous witness, he closed them again.

"Did you prescribe for the dog," considerately Mr. Evans
modified his bark, "after having found this cardiac murmur?"

"I prescribed certain pills—and—a—advised as much rest
as possible."

"Did you hear Mrs. Hope-Winter address the dog by its
name?"

And Perry thought: So here we are again!

"A—no—no, I cannot say I did."

"How did she address him, Mr. Rudd?"

Witness took off and put on his pince-nez, and said mildly: "She addressed him as her angel and——"

A burst of laughter drowned the rest of it. An usher shouted "Silence!" and the Judge said sternly: "Quiet, please, or I must clear the Court."

Mr. Rudd cleared his throat to blurt: "She said 'My angel, do not be so naughty'."

Stifled giggles.

"And why," asked Mr. Evans, "did Mrs. Hope-Winter tell her 'angel' dog"—another roar of laughter, quelled by the usher—"not to be so naughty?"

"Because," said Mr. Rudd, "he appeared to be somewhat—a—obstreperous when I took his temperature."

The Judge stared down at him.

"How do you take a dog's temperature?"

"In the—er——" Witness cast a haunted look aloft—"in the—rectum, my lord."

The Court seemed to find this excessively amusing. Mr. Rudd and the Judge did not.

"Proceed, Mr. Evans."

"Can you recall any other terms of endearment addressed by Mrs. Hope-Winter to her dog?"

"I think—I—yes, I recollect that she called him her darling, but——"

"Please," encouragingly, "speak a little louder, Mr. Rudd."

Another fearful effort produced the words, amplified by terror to resound—"her darling, but as she dragged him from the room——"

"Dragged?" interrupted the Judge.

"Yes, my lord. With—with the obstinacy characteristic of the—a—breed, the dog refused to go and Mrs. Hope-Winter, she," despairingly ventured Mr. Rudd, "said to him, 'Come on, you devilish hound.'"

The Court held its aching sides as witness bolted to his hide-hole at the back, and:

"Colonel Curran," was called.

Below and past the Judge's throne, with the enviable unconcern of one who boards a bus, the co-respondent, slightly limping, stepped into the box, avidly watched by every woman in the Court. The feminine opinion of the gallery was 'not good-looking, rather plain but a nice face. Soldierly.'

Perry's hands, tightly clasped inside her muff, relaxed. How utterly at ease he was, nonchalant, unflustered. He wore one of those new lounge suits, the latest thing, in lightish brown. His hair, close-cut, receding from his forehead that still bore the two-inch scar of his wound, showed a hint of grey, as did also the gingery moustache. His eyes, deep-in, rested for one heart-wrenching moment on hers, and then away, as he militarily stood to attention, while his Counsel, Mr. Holbrook, in high-pitched, conversational tones, posed his questions, briefly answered.

Yes, he was born at Donaghmore in Ireland in 1863. Yes, his rank was that of Lieutenant-Colonel, his regiment the 5th Hussars. Yes, he had been on active service in India during the frontier risings and in the revolution at Manipur in 1891 . . . had served in the Transvaal War from October 1899 until February 1900. Yes, he had been wounded in the charge at Kliptkraal Drift . . .

"Where," said Counsel cheerfully, "you were awarded the Distinguished Service Order for your conspicuous courage and leadership despite that you had been severely wounded?"

"I hold the D.S.O."

Perry's lips quivered; her breath came fast. He had never told her—she had never heard that he had won the D.S.O.! The Judge turned to look at him and scribbled a note in his book, while Counsel asked: "After two weeks at a base hospital you were sent home to a hospital in England?"

"Yes."

"When was this, Colonel Curran?"

"In March, 1900."

"And in the following May you were discharged as unfit for active service and obtained an appointment on the staff of instructors at Sandhurst, which appointment you still hold?"

"Yes."

And having done with that, Counsel touched lightly on the meeting at Charters Hospital with the respondent—"whom you had not seen for several years?"

"That is so."

"Did you renew acquaintance with Mrs. Hope-Winter after your discharge from hospital?"

"Yes, and with her husband."

From which point Counsel casually led him over the same ground that had already been traversed, leaving no inch of it uncharted. Once again the Court was told of the luncheon at Brighton, of the breakdown of the motor-car—but here was something new, and the yawns were replaced by a general alertness.

Witness had stayed during Goodwood week, that is from Monday the twenty-second until Friday the twenty-sixth of July, at Lord Storrington's house at Pulborough? Yes. And at what time did witness leave Pulborough for Brighton on July the twenty-sixth? . . . After dinner at about half-past nine.

"Did you drive alone?"

"No. Lord Storrington came with me."

"Why?"

"He had left his motor-car at a garage in Brighton for repairs, and decided at the last minute to come over with me in mine and fetch his car back the next morning."

"At what time did Lord Storrington leave Brighton the next morning?"

"At eight-thirty."

"Did you see him before he left?"

"Yes, we had to share a room at the hotel as they were full up."

Why, wondered Perry, did he not tell her Lord Storrington had stayed with him at the Royal that night? But why should he have told? It was nothing to do with her. Besides how could he or she or anyone have guessed that they would be entangled in all this grubby business? . . . And what if Adrian should prove his case? Garth would be finished. He would not only have to resign his commission but be landed with costs and possible damages, so Mr. Sewell had said. Too awful to contemplate! We *must* win, she thought wildly, for if we don't . . . "At what time," Mr. Holbrook was asking, "did your motor-car break down?"

"At about six-thirty p.m."

There followed an incomprehensible discussion on the mechanism of motor-cars and the technicalities of 'Big End', in which the Judge joined with what seemed to be entirely futile questions. The audience began to fidget; there was nothing of amusement here. A few got up and went out. . . . And having ascertained that there were no trains to London until the next morning witness had telephoned from the police station at Cowfold to various garages in Brighton and Lewes. . . . And so on until the fatal arrival at the inn.

At what time did witness go to bed? At about eleven-thirty o'clock. At what time did Mrs. Hope-Winter retire? At about ten-thirty, immediately she had finished her supper, whereupon witness had returned to the police station to put through another call to the garage at Brighton and arrange for his motor-car to be fetched and towed back the next morning, after which he went to bed and to sleep and was awakened by Mrs. Hope-Winter at his bedroom door.

When witness went down to the hall to fetch the flask of brandy from his bag, did he observe a light in the office, described as a private sitting-room, where he and Mrs. Hope-Winter had been served with supper? . . . Yes. The door was glass-panelled? Yes. And did witness see anyone in the office? Yes, he had seen the hotel proprietress seated at a table.

"Did you observe anything on that table?" seraphically inquired Mr. Holbrook.

"I saw a bottle at her elbow."

Sniggers from the audience.

"As you went up the stairs to Mrs. Hope-Winter's room were you aware of being followed?"

"I thought I heard footsteps some distance behind me but I paid no attention to them at all."

"For how long," piped Mr. Holbrook, "did you remain in the room with Mrs. Hope-Winter while you attended to her dog?"

"Until I was sure that the heavy breathing and discomfort had subsided—about an hour I should think."

"Did you see Mrs. Hope-Winter again that night?"

"No."

"The next morning?"

"Yes."

"At what time?"

"Ten o'clock, when she came down to the hall ready to leave for the station to catch the ten-forty train to London."

"Did you take that train to London too?"

"No. I waited for the motor-car I had ordered from Brighton to tow my car back to the garage. I caught the twelve-forty train to town and went straight on to Sandhurst."

"When did you see Mrs. Hope-Winter again after this episode?"

"Not until the day the papers were served on her and on myself."

"Thank you."

"Colonel Curran," like a thundercloud Sir Eustace rose to cross-examine. "You say you did not see Mrs. Hope-Winter until the day the petition was served upon you both?"

"Yes."

"Are you asking us to believe that you made no attempt to see Mrs. Hope-Winter after this singular adventure?"

"I am stating a fact. I don't ask you to believe it but it happens to be true."

"Did you communicate with her?"

"Only by telephone to inquire about the dog."

"Is it not unusual, not to say ungallant, that you made no effort to see Mrs. Hope-Winter after having been involved with her in so equivocal a situation?"

"The situation, if equivocal, was the result of an unforeseen mishap and called for no gallantry from me, more than my apologies to Mrs. Hope-Winter for the inconvenience to which she had been put."

"Colonel Curran"—a howitzer boomed through the listening Court—"had you so little regard for this lady's good name that you did not immediately get in touch with her husband and apologize to him, not only for the inconvenience to which his wife had been put, but to allay all possible suspicion that must arise from this adventure?"

"As the adventure in itself was devoid of all suspicion, I left Mrs. Hope-Winter to explain it to her husband, which I understand she did."

"I take it then that the circumstances of your spending a night at an hotel with this lady, were accepted by you as the natural sequence of events between a man and woman conducting a clandestine association?"

"No!" Sir Eustace had drawn blood. To the watchful jury, to the peering Judge, to Perry, whose nails dug deep in her palms, it seemed that the witness, with fisted hand half-raised, would have struck, could he have reached it, the smile from that fleshy face, but—"I deny any such insinuation. It is untrue, and unjust—to her!"

"All justice to the respondent and yourself," was the serpentine rejoinder, "will be dealt with and decided—not by you." And Sir Eustace, relinquishing that point, returned to the bedroom scene.

". . . Where, despite your own admission that you and the respondent were alone together for an hour, always excepting" —Counsel, with icy emphasis, allowed—"the presence of a dog—you still maintain that the act of adultery did not occur between you and the respondent?"

"We did not," came the answer, cold and clear, "commit adultery."

The Court sat tense, expectant, while Sir Eustace struck again with heavy hammer blows.

"In all your long association and in that hour alone in a bedroom with another man's wife, can you solemnly declare that, despite the opportunity to commit the act of which you stand accused, you felt no desire for this woman?"

A long, long pause, and then:

"I have never shown for her the least desire."

And on that pause and substitution of a word, Sir Eustace seized.

"My question was not did you *show*, but did you *feel* desire for this woman. Can you say in all truth that you are not and never have been in love with her?"

"No." Garth's head went up. "I cannot say that."

"What then," smoothly urged Sir Eustace, "can you say?"

"I can say," and strongly did he say it, "that I love her—and have been in love with her for years, but she has never heard me tell her so until this minute."

And, in that beating second, her eyes uplifted, wonder-charged, were lost in his, while the Court froze to electrified silence, and Sir Eustace, serenely, sat.

Slowly the Judge turned his head to stare astonishment at him who, with audacity unprecedented, stood confessed. In all his long experience Mr. Justice Peabody had never yet been called upon to deal with such an untoward admission to damnify all hope of a favourable verdict, unless the jury,

which he doubted, would be swayed by that Welshman's
dramatics to believe . . .

And watching that probing look, the pulled down lips:
Hell! thought Mr. Sewell, now we're dished! But the cherubic
Mr. Holbrook dimpled into smiles as, rising to his feet,
effusively, he said:

"Thank you, Colonel Curran. . . . Lord Storrington."

A fleeting glance at him who, squat, short, monocled, dapper, stepped into the box to be sworn; and again to the front
row bench the Judge's eyes were drawn. . . . She! All
a-tremble colour coming, going, face like a picture, one of
those pale Florentine Madonnas. . . . No, she had never
heard him tell her so until that minute, but would the jury
stand for it? A decent fellow, too, a good witness, a good
record. D.S.O. Crack regiment. Pity he should land himself
in this. An Irishman, impulsive, touch of the brogue, but no
blarney. Gave his evidence straight from the shoulder. Steady
as a rock under Mallaby. And there was Storrington, used to
know his father, scarcely be a party to . . .

And there was Perry, very much 'a-tremble', in a daze, and
in her heart a prayer. Let us lose, we must lose, we can't win
now, don't let us, don't let us win! . . . But another witness
here for the defence to bear out word for word Garth's evidence until . . . No, he had not seen Mrs. Hope-Winter at
the Royal Hotel on the night of July the twenty-sixth, nor—he
was positive of this—had Colonel Curran seen her, as they had
been together all the time. . . . Nothing of advantage to be
gained from that.

And now the garage man to tell how he had fetched the
Colonel's motor on the morning of July the twenty-eighth. . . .
'Big end' again and more technicalities and more questions
from the Judge, who showed a greater interest in the works of a
motor-car than in the fate of two lives. . . . And now a uniformed wooden-faced police sergeant to tell how that at nine
thirty-eight o'clock on the night of July twenty-seventh co-
respondent had come to Cowfold Police Station to report the
breakdown of his motor-car. No, witness had not seen the
motor-car, but the co-respondent, whose face and hands
bore traces of oil and dirt, had asked if he could wash. Co-
respondent had then made use of the station telephone to ring

up a number of garages in Brighton. Co-respondent had also asked witness if he could tell him where a vehicle could be procured to fetch the lady who he said was waiting in the motor three miles up the road.

This, thought Perry, frantic, will kill all hope of any pre-arrangement to spend the night together! If they would only put Milly in the box again. God! please let them find us guilty. . . .

"At ten minutes past two," said the Judge.

A full report of the case taken from a leading London daily is pasted in the memoirs with little more than the marginal comments of Lady Mulvarnie. However, she gives us this glimpse of herself during the Judge's summing-up, when:

'I stayed outside the Court. I couldn't face it. I had deliberately avoided Garth although I knew he was hovering about me. Time enough to talk when all was over. I wondered if any other respondent defending a case had prayed as did I to be found guilty of an act she had never committed.

Downstairs in that dim gas-lit restaurant I sat with Annabel and Miss Lavinia, and ate sawdust but they said it was a chop, and drank ink which they told me was claret. I didn't know. I was in that degree of stupefaction, apprehension, exaltation, to deprive me of my senses. I think I was just a little mad. Annabel, believing me plunged in the depths of despair at what she thought to be my pending doom, was blithely chattering to cheer me till I could have screamed. She was convinced we couldn't lose. They had not a leg to stand on after what that policeman, the vet, and Lord Storrington had said. Miss Lavinia was not so sure. The circumstantial evidence was all against us, plus opportunity—you couldn't get away from that. And then Garth, like a fool, needs must put his foot in it to queer our pitch.

I took heart to ask her: "Do you really think that we shall lose?"

"I don't think twice about it," was the comforting reply. "The only one who could pull us out now is the dog and he can't talk." I said, "I saw you speaking to my Counsel. What does *he* think?" Miss Lavinia shook her head. "Refused to be drawn. Very cagey."

No, I couldn't face it.

I sat on a bench outside the crowded Court room at the end of that echoing wide corridor. I dared not go in to hear that old tortoise man pronounce a death sentence on my hopes, and my life to come. I knew the papers would have it all verbatim. Press photographers had swarmed round me when Annabel and I drove up in a hansom that morning. The Daily Mirror, in its infancy then, had made a front page feature of me, Adrian, and Garth, but no one could have recognized him with his hand up to his face. There was a full-length picture of Adrian—top-hat at just the least angle, white carnation, and that grey frock coat and trousers, bought (but not paid for) new for this—his great occasion. How he must have enjoyed his part as chief player, standing in the limelight to take his bow as the curtain fell on this comedy—or mockery—of marriage. Yes, and with his hangers-on around him at his club he would bring out his time-worn epigram, "The only happy end to a romance is to leave it unfinished"—with a new tag added—"and the only happy end to married life is a divorce. . . ." Poor Adrian. Such a sham idealist, and always such a glutton for sensation, gone awry.

So there I sat and waited for the verdict. I felt lifeless, numb, and deathly cold as if my heart had ceased to beat. I dared not dwell upon the meaning of Garth's words, nor why he should have waited until this twelfth hour to have spoken them before a Judge and jury. Unaccountable indeed was the way of a man with a . . . But I was not a maid. I was a married woman, and if luck went against me so must I remain until death do us part, who were already parted!

There was a hurrying back and forth, from other Courts, of barristers, solicitors, their clerks, and anxious-looking men and women, too, all intent on their lawful occasions and none concerned with mine.

I got up to peer through the glass door. The Judge was speaking now, on and on without stopping. So this was the finish. I wondered what last resource had been left to my Counsel. In his opening speech, playing up to the jury, he must have drained himself dry of pathos and bathos—too much of it, which might be all to the good to turn them against us. My hopes lay in that smooth-tongued snake,

Sir Eustace. How he must have rung the changes on my shame and Garth's shamelessness; the callous philanderer, who left his mistress—his friend's wife—to bear the brunt of it without a word, after having spent the night with her. That was black enough to damn us! . . . Pray God that it would damn us! I couldn't hear what the old man was saying. I could only see the movement of his lips.

I had to go in.

". . . The co-respondent has admitted," his voice was very mumbly, "that he is in love with this woman. If you believe such admission is commensurable with desire, you have been given ample proof of opportunity. You must ask yourselves was the act of adultery committed on this occasion . . . Evidence is brought to bear upon certain words that, the defence maintains, were spoken to a dog. Nevertheless, the parties were together at that time in circumstances which must give rise . . ."

It was a certainty! No jury, after this, could find us guiltless.

I sat down on the lowest of the steps leading to the crowded benches at the back. From a corner of my eye I saw Hilda, with a fearful fierce intensity, hanging on to every word the old tortoise-man was saying. What was he saying? . . . "Impressed with the honesty and integrity of both the respondent and co-respondent. . . ." He had swung right round, to present them with another angle of the case. . . . That fool of a vet! And his evidence about Jasper's 'murmur' brought up. Why did I have to tell Sewell of the vet? And why, oh why, did Garth make me defend? Why could he not have spoken of his love to *me*— and have spared us this? An undefended case would have had very little publicity but now we were the talk, not only of the town but of the whole country. . . .

By this time I was almost unconscious and came to myself to see the jury file out, felt an ooze of blood on my bitten lip and heard everyone suddenly whispering. A woman near me said gloatingly, "There are no two questions about it. Of course she's guilty. How could it be otherwise? Everything points . . ."

I closed my eyes, and opened them again to see those twelve shuffle back into their seats. All sat except the foreman—very like a lizard. I saw his mouth open, heard the words that came from it—shall I ever forget them?—spoken in jerks.

"We find the respondent . . . and the co-respondent did *not* commit adultery."

And, "The petition," said the Judge, "is dismissed. . . ." '

A surging exodus of satiated onlookers carried Perry with them to the door of the Court. Once outside she found herself surrounded. A voice tickled her ear. "Congratulations, bless you! I knew you'd win hands down. Those chappies on the jury were with you to a man." Freddie removed his slightly misted monocle, wiped it, muttered: "See you later", and hastened in the wake of his wife's cold-shouldered back. She turned to beckon Adrian, calling him, with emphasized compassion: "Come, dear. Come with us."

Separated by a protective wall of Annabel and Miss Lavinia, he passed by her whom 'those twelve' had judged unimpeachable, deserving still to be his wife. He slanted her a look, a pinched smile; his hand went up in greeting. "You have my sympathy," he said, mock gallantly bowed, and, his sister's arm in his, was walked away.

"What," asked Miss Lavinia, "are you girls going to do? I am due at Mrs. Pankhurst's for a meeting. Annabel, you had better take her home and pack her off to bed. I'll drop in after dinner to see how——"

Perry had sighted Garth, almost the last to leave the Court, in confabulation with Mr. Sewell, who was heard to say: "Somewhat irregular and unnecessarily quixotic, but if you insist——"

"I do," was the answer. "I wish to pay both mine and hers."

Costs?

Sir Eustace came out briskly, pausing to exchange a few words with his junior, a hearty laugh, and, his gown ballooning after him like the sail of a ship, he also went upon his way. Garth, with a handshake, was leaving Mr. Sewell and coming toward her, elbowing aside the staring stragglers who crowded round for a near glimpse of the successful respondent.

"Let's go," said Annabel. "I'm dying for my tea."

"I don't want any tea."

"But you must have——"

"Will you *please*——" Perry's fingers nipped her arm.

"Don't!" neighed Annabel. "That hurts. Oh!" She too had sighted Garth. "I see. But do you think you ought? I mean—isn't there something or somebody called King's Proctor, so Uncle Freddie says—or would that apply now if you've won it?"

"I'll meet you," panted Perry, "in the Ladies. . . ."

She was standing on the steps of the main entrance in the grey dusk of the winter's afternoon. Annabel, bearing no grudge against the nip, had tactfully disappeared. Garth, who without a word had led her there, was gone to find a hansom.

"Mrs. Hope-Winter"—vaguely familiar were those ripe silky tones—"pray allow me to congratulate you." That enormous fat face, seen as in a nightmare, but wigless and bereft of Milly's toque, with a suspicion of side-whisker under his high hat. "You were admirable"—beaming, urbane and positively fatherly—"although the case was yours from the moment we put our chief witness in the box. Good-bye, and—good luck to you." A lift of the hat, and Sir Eustace stepped into his carriage drawn up at the kerb.

Garth was at her side.

"Can't find a hansom, they're all bagged. I've managed to get a four-wheeler. Do you mind?"

Mind!

He handed her in, gave her address to the driver, and: "Sir Eustace," her voice was a strangled bleat, "congratulated me. He's——" Her breath expired.

"So it seems," Garth said slowly, "that if I hadn't spoken as I did we would have lost."

She was in greatest trouble now, past all belief, past bearing. Could it be his pleasure to torment her? Had he truly spoken in the hope that they might lose—or win? What did he mean, or did he mean—nothing?

The cab jerked and jolted on its way. He sat beside her dimly, his face a blur in the darkening dusk, fitfully revealed in the glaring electric lights of Trafalgar Square; and as they passed along Pall Mall, he broke the weighted silence that enwrapped them, casually to ask: "Would you care to have tea at my club?"

"No, I think——"

She must stop the cab, get out, hide herself from him and from her misery. *Why* had he spoken? To shield her, or to win the case and save her name—and his commission? A sob, unchecked, tore from her. Frantically she fumbled for the window strap and was dragged back and into his arms. "My dear . . . My lovely dear." His broken words were on her lips. "You see I had to speak in one last hope that we might lose . . . to win. And is it so with you? Is it? Tell me, is it? Is this love between us?"

She was lost, dissolved, surrendered to the sweet surprise of touch, while her lips answered his with gentle madness till sense perished, and she slackened and lay still. She heard him sigh. "You have me utterly. But," he drew his mouth from hers to say, "what's now to do? We're as we were. I've trapped you where I thought to free you. No hope for us, at all."

"Beloved idiot!" she whispered. "Why couldn't you have told me this before—on that ghastly day when they served us with the papers? I gave you every chance."

"Woman! You are lying in your teeth." He crushed her lips against them with his kisses. "Sure, I thought you had no heart for me." His hand strayed to her breast. "And here it is. . . . How fast it beats."

"For you. Were you so blind?"

"I was. And I was dumb. An oaf, tongue-tied to think myself was nowhere in the running and that you were all for him. How could I know?"

"Heavenly grace!" she appealed. "Will you hear him?" Was such silliness to be believed? Her laughter bubbled over till tears came. The mastering elation of such joy as hers was enough, she thought, to kill her. Time stood still. A miracle had happened, was happening. The eternal cause had singled out two very ordinary persons, lifting them to transcendental heights to endow them with magic, to make them gods. All heaven was theirs, the dingy cab Olympus . . . Until a raucous voice at the opening door brought the universe about their ears.

" 'Ere y'are, sir. Lancaster Square. Are yer gettin' out or goin' on?"

* * *

Short lived was Elysium for those two whose stars in their courses fought so bitterly against them. Their plans were laid, their day was in its dawning, while back and forth between Sandhurst and the War Office went Garth to deal with his resignation, which the Powers at Whitehall were unwilling to accept. They had little time together in those two last weeks before their final departure, snatched hours the sweeter for brevity, with promise of joys suspended and fulfilment yet to come.

'. . . We intended to travel by motor-car from Calais to the south of France. Garth had arranged with a firm in Paris to send a car to meet the boat. He knew the representative of this particular make—a Renault—and had fixed it all in less than a fortnight, heaven alone knows how. We were to halt at hotels along the route and so to Provence and the sun, where, if luck went with us, we might find a villa, and then, when we were free to marry, or if Adrian refused to go through with it again. . . . But beyond that we dared not think.

I insisted on taking Jasper, for from him who had joined us together, I refused to be parted. There was much to be done before our break-away. Orders were still coming in for my face creams, although I had stopped all advertisements. I had finished with that, as with everything else to do with my life that was past.

I had a monthly tenancy of the Bayswater apartments and had already given in my notice. Annabel—dear Annabel—was to stay with me to the end. Under Miss Lavinia's persuasion she had become an ardent member of the W.S.P.U. I remember how astonished I was during those last few days, when I heard her declare herself with me, "heart and soul in my bid for freedom". And she went on to say that spinsterhood held no "inhibitions" for her. . . . The word was new to me—the first inception, surely, of the Freudian theory that in those early years of the century had reached no farther than the platforms of medical societies and the meeting-rooms of women who clamoured for their rights. They were swift enough to seize on the apostasies, expounded by this Viennese Jew, which were to revolutionize all pre-conceived accepted lines of thought

for good—or ill. So there was Annabel up to the neck in it,
flinging down the gauntlet in challenge to her maidenly
preserves. She too had made her break-away, disowned by
her Papa, "dishonoured", as he called it, and "disgraced".
She had a little money of her own, left her by her mother,
and on that she would live, she told me, in three furnished
rooms near Hampstead Heath with another "girl", an old
school-friend and equally enthralled initiate, whom she had
met at a meeting at Mrs. Pankhurst's house. Annabel's
world, as well as mine, was topsy turvy.

In almost the last talk I had with her, two days before
Garth and I were to leave England, she spoke of what she
called her "release from suppression and the dominance of
Man". She had it pat. She was taking elocution lessons
so that she might learn to speak and voice her message to
others like herself, unwanted women, who having missed
their chance of marriage were condemned, despised and
spurned as failures in their sole excuse for being. "In the
eyes of Man," said Annabel, "we are nothing more than
mammals. But you wait!" Looking more than ever like a
horse about to take a jump, she whinnied, "Wait until we
who have stood by to serve are called upon to show our
mettle. As for you . . ." and she expounded at length on
the shameful inequality of the divorce laws—the subject,
as I understood it, of a recent debate instigated by Miss
Lavinia. I had only half an ear for this while I knelt to
pack my portmanteau. Garth had told me to bring as little
as possible—he would buy me all I wanted in the south of
France. "Why," demanded Annabel, standing over me,
"should men have it all their own way? A woman must
prove cruelty, desertion, bruises and black eyes"—here I
detected Miss Lavinia again—"*and* misconduct. But all
that will be changed when we are represented in Parliament."

I sat back on my heels and looked at her. She was
flushed, inspired, trembling in a sort of ecstasy. . . . And
just at that moment as I heard the clock strike five, in came
the German boy to say a gentleman was here to speak with
with me. I asked who? He didn't know, so it couldn't have
been Adrian or Garth. Annabel said she would go and see.
She went and came back with Albert.

I knew that shortly after Adrian had started proceedings

against me he had been staying in those Duke Street chambers where Annie and Albert were employed. And there in the doorway stood my ex-footman to tell me, pronouncing his words with care for his aspirates, that Adrian had been "taken" with a stroke the night before. . . . "I was laying out his dress suit for the hopera," said Albert, "and had just put the studs in his shirt when the master was sat down in a chair sudden like, and hearing him make peculiar sounds, I looked round and I see his face hall twisted——" Albert's face was slightly twisted too.

I said, "Yes?"

He said, "Yes, madam. Well, it give me quite a turn so to speak and I hasked him was he feeling queer? He tried to hanswer me but could only make those sounds like he was struck dumb——"

"Yes?" I said again.

"Well, then I rang for Annie, madam, and sent her for the doctor and he come along at once and we got him into bed. And today the doctor brought a specialist what says it is a stroke, but he can't speak nothing, madam, only just your name, as we managed to make out."

"Is he," I heard myself ask calmly, "in danger of his life?"

"The doctors didn't say, madam, only it seemed like he was telling them he wanted you to come, and the specialist he said I should fetch you to him, madam, so I come here right away."

"Thank you," I said, "Albert. Will you please to call a hansom? I will go with you at once. . . ." '

And there in those Duke Street chambers she found him. He lay as if in living death, an awful death. Only his eyes spoke for him, looking out from a distorted mask. His lips were screwed awry in an exaggerated travesty of his pinched smile; and to those crooked lips she laid her own, felt something warm and wet drop on her cheek. Slow painful tears oozed from his eyes that had never surely been so staring blue; and, as she lifted her head, she saw he was making a desperate struggle to frame words, grotesque in utterance, "Don' go. Wan' you . . . Stay. Forgive."

TEN

. . . The specialist came again this morning. Says he
may live like this for years, but there is hope of some par-
tial recovery of speech. Albert has had a bed made up for
me here in the sitting-room. Yesterday went to fetch some
clothes from Lancaster Square. Renewed monthly tenancy.
Albert has given notice to the Chambers and will come
daily to attend on A. Shall have to go house-hunting again.
When I find something permanent, he and Annie have
promised to come back to me.

Telephoned Garth to tell him what has happened. He
wanted to see me at once. I refused. Can't trust myself.
Should never have strength to go through with it if I saw
him, so I wrote what must be said.'

The following extracts from that letter are, with her permission, quoted.

'. . . so you see, my dear one, it was not to be. Let us
look at it this way. Suppose we had never found each other
we should not have known even this much promise of loveliness together . . . I don't ask you to forget me. I know
you never can, any more than I can ever forget you. But I
do ask you not to see me, because if you were within sight
and touch I should never be strong enough to carry on with
what I know I have to do . . . If you could see him as he
is now, you would understand that we *can't* do this to him.
We simply can't. . . .

In this short two weeks you have given me all the happiness that I have ever known, and in that I am luckier than I
had ever dreamed or hoped to be. Don't write. Don't
come to me. Help me as I know you will.'

But he did write to her.

'. . . I have seen him. I telephoned his man to ascertain a time when you would not be there. I saw him while he slept. It was enough. You are right. We can't do this to him.

'I love you. While I live and till I die and afterwards, if there is an afterwards, I shall be behind you always—till you turn and come to me.'

*   *   *

So, as April frost may blight an orchard rich with promise, did she accept the wreckage of her life deprived of 'all the happiness that she had ever known'. But she was not of the stuff that finds a masochistic solace from the probing of a wound. In the years that followed her renunciation she had gained an added dignity as of one who has looked upon the death of her illusions; and if her eyes held shadows, and the faint indelible markings spread fanwise about them to tell of inward hurt, these might be but the outward and visible tokens of time's passing. Or if, as she went about her 'business', self-imposed to meet her ends, she carried in her heart a scar and in her spirit, lost and lonely, the gnawing ache of it, she gave no sign.

Those were the days when the whole structure of social evolution, speeding the steady growth of industrialism, had consolidated that sense of security inherited from the carefree Victorians.

True, there were mutters of internal eruption from the inheritors who threaded the economic fabric with capitalist gold. Gloomy prophecies, voiced by the fattened turtles of St. James's, were heard in Clubland to tell of approaching legions who upheld the red banner of 'Labour'. Bad enough to have the Liberals in power with Campbell-Bannerman to lead them and a stalwart army at his back to stand united, and win the confidence of wavering Tory recruits with the bait of 'Reform', that song their grandfathers used to sing; but now it carried a more sinister portent. For the first time in history the working-class was represented in the Cabinet by John Burns, instigator of revolutionary demands!

With a pursing of lips and pessimistic head-shakings, names recurred as indicative of 'Left Wing' influence: a term newly coined to be brayed by this rabid mutineer Welshman,

Lloyd George, clamouring for Old Age Pensions; and the young Winston Churchill—but no one paid much heed to him, a gas-bag—all talk and high-falutin'. And now this Yorkshireman, Asquith, yes, he was a menace—in the running to succeed the Scot, 'C.B.', with his eye on the gallery, those greedy hordes of Olivers who fell upon to gobble every juicy morsel flung to them, and then to ask for more: Workmen's Compensation, Miners' Eight Hours, Health Insurance— that damned Welshman again—preaching even distribution of the National income to over-tax the wicked money-grubbing Rich, who bled the hard pressed Poor!

Yet, with this universal gestation resultant on the mating of the Old Age with the New to bring forth from its Labour pains a lusty infant, Perry, who read nothing in the papers more than her own advertisements, was the least concerned. But although she knew it not, she also was a pioneer: a woman engaged in commercial enterprise, surreptitiously conducted in the attics of a house she had secured in Maida Vale, built in the time of the Regent.

It was mildewed, damp, and all but derelict; it faced the canal, that 'River in the Street', posthumously famed by Concord, who not until after his death in the First World War, was acclaimed and acknowledged by his fellows as a Master.

So, with Annie and Albert to help her, she set herself to put her house in order and, aided by a local builder, to transform her 'rat-hole', as she called it, into a habitable home. She was fortunate in those two loyal souls, to whom, hard upon their installation, was born a daughter, gladly accepted by their mistress, and by Jasper, long past middle-age, most greatly loved.

Under power of attorney she had paid comparatively little, and much less than she had feared in respect of Adrian's costs for the divorce suit, since Mr. Sewell had told her the 'co-respondent' had insisted on paying his own, and had placed with him a sum at her disposal for Counsel's and solicitor's fees. This she refused to accept and, to meet expenses, sold her pearls, which realized but half their worth; yet she still retained sufficient to tide her over the removal to the house in Maida Vale with two thousand left for investment in gilt-edged. Her diamonds she held at the bank in reserve.

To that Regency villa, gracefully restored at a minimum

cost, she brought her helpless, almost speechless husband. The deadly seizure, which had mercifully dulled his brain, now made of him a child, retrogressed, to care for, work for, and in his stricken state, to cherish and, perhaps for the first time in her life, to love.

He knew no more than that he wished her always near to feed and tend him. The hemiplegia had affected his right side only; he could still use his left hand. She bought him toys, a miniature *petits chevaux* was his pet. He joyed to spin the wheel and watch the little horses whirl and stop and win for him a pile of gold paper-covered sovereigns. She procured from Florence a set of coloured reproductions of the Tuscan Masters in the hope they might illuminate that shuttered mind; but all his past existence and its interests were forgotten. He knew only that it pleasured him to lie upon his couch and gaze out at or be wheeled along the tow-path of the 'River in the Street'; to watch the slow-moving barges reflected in the water under a sky of almost Italian blue. Once she heard him say, "Ven'ce . . . Gon'd'la." And she rejoiced, to ask the doctor: "Isn't that an association of ideas—a sign of memory returning? Will the mind right itself eventually?"

While the doctor could offer her no hope of that, he found her husband's health considerably improved. He had stoutened, he enjoyed his food; he liked to hear her sing nursery rhymes at the piano, to bring a crow of laughter to those twisted lips; but most of all did he delight in the Eton Boating Song of which he could never have enough—a hopeful sign—to tell the doctor: "His old school song. Surely that must mean he can remember?" And the answer, non-committal, "Time will show."

Freddie was a constant and welcome visitor, but the mere sight of Hilda would put him in a state. And once when left alone with her he took a glass of milk left by Albert at his bedside table and flung it in her face.

For her brother's tragedy she held Perry solely culpable. 'The shame of the divorce case and the disgraceful verdict of the jury, led by that obviously biased judge, had brought him,' she insisted, 'to this pass.' Yet Hilda may have had her private reasons to thank God for that 'disgraceful' verdict, since 'otherwise', she told her husband, *'we* would have had him on our hands for life'.

Not until Perry saw her way to a safe launching did she confide to Freddie that she had 'gone into business'.

From his first shocked recoil he turned to offer a substantial loan—'or call it a gift'—towards its promotion. She would have none of that. "I shall build it up," she said, "entirely off my own bat." And in modification of what might have been thought an ungracious refusal, she added, "But if in the future I find I shall need some financial support, then——"

"Call on me," Freddie said.

Meanwhile her bi-weekly advertisements were bringing in more orders than she could deal with unaided. Annie gave her such little time as she could spare from her household duties and her baby, but that was not enough. She engaged two 'hands'—their joint ages were a year short of thirty—to fill and label the jars at a wage of fourpence an hour. After three months they demanded a rise of a penny a day. She made it twopence. Then came to her a brain-wave, when Freddie took her, with Annabel, to a matinée of 'The Merry Widow'. A rare event for her now was a seat in the stalls of a theatre. She went home with the Waltz in her ears, and an itch in her fingers to play it. And while Adrian beat time, out of time, to the tune, her thoughts were busy with her Great Idea. . . . She would circulate free samples of her face creams in the dressing-rooms of Daly's, the Gaiety, and all musical comedy theatres.

The next day she put in an order for a gross of two-ounce jars, and walked the length and breadth of theatreland to distribute her samples at stage doors.

Results were nil. She crushed her disappointment with her pestle, tried again, and joined the queues at matinées, waiting at those same stage doors for the exit of the star. She learned to know by sight the dressers of all the leading ladies, and stood in wait for her who attended . . .

"Will you please give this to Miss Lily Elsie with my compliments?" Into the dresser's hand she slipped half a sovereign and a pamphlet, one of a hundred, specially printed to extol the 'Preparations of Peridot Flight'. "Do ask Miss Elsie to try this excellent cream prepared by me in my chemical laboratories for the care of the skin after the removal of grease-paint. It is used in all theatres with quite wonderful results."

The dresser took the pamphlet and the sample jar, wrapped in pink tissue paper and tied with silver cord, and with the half a sovereign she departed, full of promises . . . And Perry heard no more of her.

Nothing daunted, she delivered her free samples in the ladies' cloakrooms of West End hotels. The latest of these, recently erected in Regent Street, to mutilate the uniformity of Nash's superb crescent, was the first to respond with an order for two gross.

Less than two years later, every ladies' cloakroom and almost all theatres, flaunted on their dressing-tables a choice of 'Peridot Flight's Preparations' with tinted face powders to match. And the attic rooms of the Regency house accommodated fifteen 'hands'.

*   *   *

She does not stress those early days of struggle. Hers was 'a one-man business', she would say, and added mostly, 'luck was on my side'.

Not luck but acumen, and just that touch of shrewd perception complementary to the opportunist. She was nothing if not that. So, with fierce determination to overcome all obstacles, she pounded her glutinous messes, and the white powder she mixed into what she was hopefully persuaded would be turned, with her Midas touch, to gold. Resolutely did she disregard the yearning emptiness that came with bitter-sweet reminder of all she had missed of love and hope. Poor substitute for these was her 'one-man business' and the mushroom growth of its success.

From Annabel, who had it from her uncle through Lord Storrington, she learned that Garth was in Canada, and then in San Francisco, to torture her with fear lest he had hit the earthquake; and then he was in Africa, vaguely big game shooting. But as, with snail-sure persistence, Perry exploited her pestle, so swiftly did the tide of events beyond her cramped four walls exploit the giant stride of progress.

On July 25, 1909, a French aviator, Blériot, flew across the Channel in a machine of his own invention. The elders of St. James's, in their saddle-back chairs, sat aghast. If in the future this flying were accepted as a natural form of transit—God forbid!—Britain would no longer be an island. Why, even here, in Blackpool of all places, another of these Frenchmen, with an English name—fellow called Latham—has ascended in a gale to beat the record with the wind against him, too, at ninety miles in one hour! There were some who opined that these portentous happenings presaged the end of this civilization—or worse. If men could command the elements and fly in the air, what if other countries, fired by example, should go one better? Over there in Germany that Count what's his name—Zeppelin—had turned out four of those damned airships—whacking great things, shaped like cigars, and himself had flown one of them two hundred and seventeen miles in *twelve* hours! . . . And now it was this wireless telegraphy. Yes, but that might prove to be a boon in the tracking down of criminals. That murderer, Crippen, had been nabbed by wireless telegraphy on board a liner in his attempt to flee the country with his typist disguised as a boy, which was all to the good, and the world owed a debt to Marconi, but . . .

More head-shakings. Progress was all very well if you could keep the women out of it and in their rightful places, instead of shrieking like maniacs up and down the country for the vote; creating disturbances, chaining themselves to the railings of Number Ten, shouting through megaphones, hurling abuse at the Prime Minister . . . The Suffragettes!

"I'd have them all in quod if I had my way," said old Peabody to old Watkinson over their port in the smoking-room of the Athenaeum. "They're nothing more than a lot o' sex-starved spinsters."

"What most of 'em need to quiet 'em down," growled old Watkinson, "is a jolly good—well, and there it is."

Yes, and there were they, militant and marching in their thousands to meet at the Albert Hall. And Annabel—'dear Annabel'—had got herself in 'quod' for hammering to splinters a shop window in Regent Street, and serving her heels to the shins of the policeman who took her.

Perry went to visit her in Holloway and saw:

'. . . A narrow cell, a bed with a bolster, no pillow, sheets and blankets not wide enough for cover, a dustpan, a slop-pail, a scrubbing brush and gas-jet. Of this delectable apartment I was permitted a glimpse on the bribe of half a crown to the wardress. Annabel and I sat opposite each other at a table in the visitors' room, guarded by a female Cerberus. Annabel was in her glory and a frightful prison dress marked with broad arrows, black on mustard colour. Her thick woollen stockings were ringed with red and she wore a sort of Dutch cap tied under her chin. Miss Lavinia had much to answer for—and Annabel was easy prey.

She had been in fourteen days, "A very reasonable sentence," she called it, to give me the impression that she would have gladly suffered fourteen years for the good of the Cause. But she was in again before six months were out. . . .'

From all these diversions, excursions and alarms Perry stood apart. Work was her narcotic to dull the persistent ache of her loss, yet of this she makes no heroics, no harping on self-sacrifice. There were times, no doubt, when she may have rebelled against her 'non-conformist conscience' inherited from her missionary grandfather, forbidding her to take love where it was offered and still remain her husband's wife, his nurse, and now—his mother. And in her solitude she may have railed at and cursed her 'middle-class' respectability, 'that hair-shirt of the hypocrite' she calls it, which forced her to accept her 'cruel fate' when only cruel necessity kept her to the grindstone. Doctors' bills, wages, the upkeep of the house by the Canal must be paid for. Night after weary night she sat, adding, subtracting, counting to a ha'penny how much she dared take from the business to meet all these endless demands, and how much would be left with which to carry on. That, in the first three years, but by 1909 the worst of it was over. . . .

And in that year she opened her factory at Harlesden, a monstrous brick-built edifice, recently vacated by a firm of pickle manufacturers. Within its walls, newly decorated on the proceeds of her jewels and the last of her capital reserves, she now commanded not fifteen, but fifty 'hands'. She must, however, still go cautiously with one eye on her balance sheet. Yet if all went well, that fifty might be multiplied by ten. The factory was large enough to hold a legion. She shut off the major part of it and concentrated on the renovation of departments immediately required. She engaged a forewoman, a sparrow-like, busy little person, oddly reminiscent of Miss Genn, particular of speech and needle-sharp. To her was consigned the care of those fifty 'hands', all exactly dressed alike in grey overalls, provided by the 'firm', and bearing on the breast pockets of each the device P.F., pink-embroidered: this, her one excusable extravagance. A step in advance of her time, she installed in the mixing room a set of wash-basins served with constant hot water. She insisted on maintaining the highest standard of cleanliness among her workers. A fine of threepence was deducted from the wages of any girl who failed to wash her hands before taking her seat at the benches. She also provided them with a canteen where they could buy a sandwich luncheon, with tea or coffee for fourpence, or for ninepence 'a cut off the joint and two veg'. The fractional profits therefrom covered little more than expenses, but: 'I knew', she said, 'that I must feed them well and treat them fairly if I wanted good work in return.'

Their hours were from eight to six, at a minimum wage of thirty shillings a week. 'I was determined that no girl employed by me should be driven to do as poor Florrie had done—I often wondered what became of her—to earn in her spare time "a bit of extra".'

She had her office, Turkey-carpeted, imposing, managerial, where she interviewed travellers from wholesale chemists, Frenchmen from Grasse with samples of perfume to be prepared, it was suggested, for her sole monopoly. She took the samples, approached an English firm to match them, well diluted, and added to her list of preparations, 'Scents'—not perfumes—at half the price demanded by the French importers.

She had become a force to be reckoned with among transatlantic competitors who flooded the market with their luxurious and equally more expensive products, and whom she wisely did not attempt to rival. 'But the French and American firms,' she admits, 'had me marked. I was approached by more than one to combine, be bought in, or bought out . . .' All such advances were flatly refused; and—this, a gesture of defiance—she splashed her advertisements on the new motor-buses, on hoardings and in the weekly illustrated papers. Since photographers' models were rarely used in those days, chorus girls posed for her 'Preparations' with the addition of

one or two 'Stars'. Her advertising campaign sank her profits
for that year down to half, but she made good her losses in
results.

The death of King Edward brought about a slump, followed by a Coronation boom. In those galloping years of the
new reign before the world plunged to disaster, it was easier
to make than to lose money; when the greater industries were
no longer entirely controlled by a one-man employer but by
joint stock companies. Yet she, who directed the mammoth
growth of her own Proprietary Brands, stayed immune from
usurpation to reap unshared her harvest. She stood fast, un-
affected, and wholly undisturbed, as indeed were a myriad
others, by the approaching cloud in Europe's sky, no bigger
than the Kaiser's hand.

What though Germany was building battleships and casting
covetous eyes on our Dreadnoughts? We were an island, our
Navy was invincible, and the Kaiser, whose hysterical threats
vacillated from moods of highest elation to darkest
despair, was behaving like a lunatic. How could you take
seriously one who had commanded Haldane to dinner, and
then invited him to be a member of his Cabinet for that one
night?

In 1912 Miss Flight, as she was named by those commer-
cially concerned with her, bought a Daimler to drive her to
and from her office and take Adrian for outings. His condition showed no change beyond a slow insidious atrophy of
his befogged senses. The doctors had warned her that a
second stroke would almost certainly be fatal, yet his physical
health showed little evidence of deterioration. He ate, he
slept, was excessively fidgety when awake, an elementary
organism, the limits of whose world were confined to a couch,
a window and infantile games. Tears came readily if thwarted.
He had a passion for liqueur chocolates doled out to him by
Albert, two at a time, as a *bonne bouche* after taking his medicine; and when he signed for more, to be refused, he would
fly into tempers and scream. "Very bad for him," said Perry.
"Sooner let him eat the whole boxful."

And one day he did eat the whole boxful, crammed into his
mouth when the male nurse, engaged to relieve Albert, had
been called to the telephone and left him, who was never left
for more than ten minutes, alone. On that day his wife, as was

her habit, came home at five o'clock to sit with him while he
had his tea.

She let herself in with her latchkey, ran upstairs to his room,
and, on the threshold, halted. His couch was drawn up to the
window in its accustomed place, with the small table beside it
overturned. His head had fallen sideways and his mouth had
fallen open; his face was dark, the eyes bolting, dreadfully up-
rolled to show the whites; and on his swollen blackened tongue
were the remnants of the chocolates he had grabbed with his
left hand to choke, and to strike him down. . . .

*   *   *

It was as if she had been bereft of a loved and fractious child.
The house, fraught with macabre memories, had become in-
supportable now. She must move on again. This time her
search took her northward out of London into Hertfordshire,
to find a seventeenth-century manor house securely islanded
in its timbered grounds, ringed with wooded hills and meadow-
land and farmsteads; a bare fifteen miles from her factory by
crow and under twenty by car.

There with Annie and Albert, their small daughter, a sub-
sidiary staff, and James, successor to Jasper, who had died in
a third heart attack, she found peace and contentment. She
asked for nothing more.

In June, 1914, Miss Lavinia, white-haired and, latterly
white-bearded, more abrupt, more gaunt, and more incon-
sequent than ever, but still endowed with superabundant
energy, came to stay at Fairgrove Manor on her bi-yearly visit.
Despite her age, she still maintained her ardent support of
Women's Suffrage. Militancy then was at its height, and on
May 21, Mrs. Pankhurst, with two hundred supporters, besieged Buckingham Palace with the intention of forcing a
Petition on the King. A cordon of police intercepted their
arrival, and, amid the jeers of a hostile crowd, Mrs. Pankhurst
was arrested and carried off in a motor-cab to Holloway.

Miss Lavinia, who herself had attended the deputation,
'holding', as she said, 'a watching brief for the Cause', gave
Perry, on the night of her arrival, a first hand, if garbled,
account of it.

"The police—like the Assyrian—came down. Not on the
fold. They were scattered. Our women—magnificent! You

should have seen how they stood up to those wolves—chucked about like sacks of potatoes. Not me. I kept my distance." And sipping after-dinner coffee, "That dog of yours," said Miss Lavinia, "he's scratching. Fleas or ezcema?"

"Nerves," Perry told her. "Go on."

"Don't," Miss Lavinia was tetchy, "interrupt. I lose my line of thought. Ah! The woman on the tricycle."

Perry blinked. "The tricycle?"

Miss Lavinia nodded. "Paralysed. Nothing like so bad as your poor Adrian. Brain not affected. Legs. Mrs. Billinghurst. Worked her tricycle with arms. Pushed it in and out the crowd. Terrific! Those devils threw her back—upset her bicycle—tricycle. I coshed one of them with my umbrella."

"Dear Miss Lavinia!" chorused Perry, gleaming. "Did you lay him out?"

"Hope so. Knocked off his helmet—then ducked. I was spry or he'd have had me. *She* was with Drake. Charlotte. Left an orphan. Charlotte—not the Billinghurst. Four young brothers and sisters dependent. Manual toil. Sewing machinist. Most vigorous of all our speakers. Those swine manhandled Billinghurst. Didn't grab her. No. Too much of an outcry had they collared a cripple."

On Perry's face was the look, half quizzical, wholly affectionate, specially reserved for Miss Lavinia, who returned it with a chuckle.

"What a to-do! That'll set 'em thinking. Asquith will have to pull his socks up. Cat and Mouse be damned. Thought to save their faces, but they won't. And then," Miss Lavinia said with a crack in her voice, "then—they got at Emmeline. Just out of Holloway. Weak as a rat and looking like death—been on hunger-strike. But they took her. Yes!" Miss Lavinia's fist crashed on the spindle-legged Sheraton table between them and upset her coffee cup—"they took her—they did—our Pankhurst, our leader. Hauled her off. Put her in jug again. Better get a cloth and wipe it up or it'll stain."

And as Perry on her knees swabbed the coffee with her handkerchief, she heard: ". . . On my way to Whitehall, after it was over—and God alone knows how I got there—fairly shaken I can tell you. No joke at seventy-six—I'll have another cup. No milk. As I passed up Parliament Street to call on old Price—you remember our vicar? He's eighty. Retired.

Lives with a niece in a flat round there. Whitehall Court.
Plenty o' money. Not his. Hers. Jenny Price. One of us.
Well, there was I in Parliament Street—and there was that
young man of yours coming out of the War Office. Barged
right into him."

"Who?" weak-voiced and pale, Perry asked, to know before
the answer came.

"That young feller—that Curran—who messed up your
life and his own. Not so young now, though. Grey. Thin as a
rail. Brown as a nut. Just back from Timbuctoo or somewhere. Malay. Head hunting. His uncle's dead and he was
off to Ireland. Selling up the place. Asked after you. Wanted
your address. Gave it and your telephone number. Got it out
of me. Best be quit of him. No good to you. Rolling stone.
Madness in the family. Don't snore." Miss Lavinia tipped a
toe at the somnolent James.

"Is he—did you say he is going to Ireland?" Perry kept her
voice firm. She had learned the hard way and in a hard school,
how to screen superfluous emotion; but her eyes, with that
faint surprised lift of the brows, evaded the gimlet glance of
Miss Lavinia, who, watchfully shrewd, grinned aslant and
said: "It's half-past ten. I'm for bed."

Perry took her to her room, left her there, and went to her
own.

Long she sat at her window, gazing out at the moon-tinted
sweetness of the night. So! Back again, full circle. But this
meeting between himself and Miss Lavinia was more than a
week ago. He had her address and had done nothing about it.
Almost ten years! So resolutely had she banished from her
consciousness the thought of him, that the pain of her awakening was as if she had touched a glowing ember in the wintered
ashes of remembrance. I am too old, she said, for this. . .
And she too went to bed, and took a little pill prescribed by
her doctor, for since Adrian's death she had suffered from
bouts of insomnia.

She slept dreamlessly and woke refreshed to find, with the
morning's post, a letter. It was brief, precise and cool, as from
any old acquaintance returned after long absence abroad. He
would 'so much like to see her again. Could they meet when
he came back from Ireland at the end of June?' He dwelled
lightly on conditions 'here at home', was much occupied in

settling affairs to do with his uncle's estate, and was hers, 'as ever', Garth.

History repeated! And his letter an echo of that other written from Ireland after the death of his father, a decade ago, guarded, deliberately casual; yet might not this guardedness now be but the natural acceptance of hope too long deferred? She had passed the age of miracles; self-discipline had developed a callous, as shield to the Achilles heel of her woman's defences. And dispassionately she wondered at her cynical detachment—or indifference? Another life had claimed her. Material success had destroyed her fantasies, to obliterate a dream within a dream. So in her heart she insisted, and would brook no mutiny from sources uncontrolled, those treacherous complexities of nature crying havoc to her self-ordained vocation. That monster factory reaching out octopus tentacles to encompass invading competitors was her domain, inviolate. Would she be prepared to renounce her kingdom? Never. It was too much to ask of love, cast out and resurrected, come to tempt her, a sweetly tantalizing ghost. . . . Not now. And not again, and never more.

So may she have reasoned; and so may she have fought against her weakness as she went about her work for those few weeks, and heard nothing of him, not a word . . . until a month after she received and had pigeon-holed his letter in her bureau.

During Miss Lavinia's visit, she had taken a fortnight's holiday at home, but was still in daily contact with her office. And on her breakfast tray that morning of June 28, was brought certain correspondence forwarded from her general manager claiming her instant attention. She read, and, with a flush of annoyance, summoned her secretary.

"Take down these letters, Miss Blade."

To a chair, discreetly at a distance from the bedside, Miss Blade, pad and pencil poised, betook herself. Bespectacled, with shoulders stooping, nose dyspeptically pink-tipped, she awaited her orders.

Although for the last five years Miss Blade had acted as her employer's staff and prop at home, and her right hand in the office, Perry knew no more of her than that she spent her Sundays in Brondesbury with a widowed mother. From Miss Blade's loves, her hates, despairs, her joys and relaxations, her employer was severely barred. An early effort to penetrate these guarded defences had been, with an almost Chinese impassivity, rebuffed, to discourage further trespass.

Her correspondence dealt with, and a telephone call to her export manager demanding explanation of a delayed shipment to Australia, for which his lame excuse brought forth a rating from Miss Flight, she was reminded by Miss Blade of an appointment for a fitting with Lucile that afternoon at three o'clock.

"Then order the car to be here at a quarter to two."

But as Miss Blade went to the door the telephone, shrill at the bedside, called her back to it.

"Yes? . . . What name, please? . . . One moment." A tactful hand was closed on the receiver and in carefully hushed tones, "Can you speak to Colonel Curran?" asked Miss Blade.

For an instant Perry's eyelids closed; she heard her voice say: "No. Take a message."

"Mrs. Hope-Winter is engaged just now. Can you give me a message? . . . He says," again that covering hand, "are you likely to be in town today? If so, can you meet him for luncheon?"

Perry lay back against her pillows. Today! . . . I can't, she thought frantically. No . . . "Yes, I will meet him. Ask where."

Miss Blade asked where, and what time, and calmly delivered the message.

"I shall want the car here at a quarter to twelve. Cancel my appointment with Lucile."

And, while she dressed and cared for her face, she flayed herself. Was ever woman so great a fool as this, to fling open a closed door and come running to his call, who had shown no haste to revive between them that which had been so irrevocably lost? Closely, remorselessly, she examined her reflection in the mirror and decided that the years had left their mark, but not too deeply . . . 'Nor did I,' she frankly confesses, 'owe the preservation of such looks as I possessed to my own products, for I never used them, nor anything more on my face than soap and water.'

However, she did, on that day use judicious powder and a touch of lip salve, and went to meet him secure in the knowledge that her clothes, at least, were faultless, but—she was forty-two, and if he cared to reckon he would know it.

She was driven to London in her Daimler and told the chauffeur not to wait. She would return home by train.

Garth met her in the entrance to that same small exclusive restaurant where they had dined on Mafeking night. The years slid away as she faced him across the narrow table. Their talk was evasive as their eyes, that stealthily searched. Hers were veiled, yet he saw her now as she had ever been, with just that about her as if her youth, arrested in its flight, held captive the young delicious look as of one destined to fade before the bud has turned to blossom. "You are unchanged," he said.

Could she say the same of him? His hair was grizzled, tropic suns had burned him; time had engrafted deep lines from nose to mouth, and his cheeks were hollowed beneath their moulded bones. Both were stirred; each a little doubtful of the other, to take, as two prepared for duel, careful measure.

What passed between them there, while they ate of luncheon and surveyed their broken years, is not recorded. But one may believe them constrained to avoid a vista of entrancing possibilities. It flashed through her mind that this meeting of a couple of fogies, lovers once, who for so joyous short an interlude had been handfasted, sealed, was like the wooing of the Mint by the Butterfly in the lovely story of Hans Andersen . . . 'Friendship, if you please, but nothing more. I am old, and you are old; do not, at our ages, let us appear ridiculous.' It was on her tongue to tell him so, when:

"How strangely you smile to or at yourself," he stayed her words to say; and her heart quickened. Sedately she strove to lead the talk away from her to him; yet after his first embarrassed allusion to Adrian's death, gleaned from that meeting with Miss Lavinia, she could not withhold the reminder, "You were in no hurry to see me again."

No, not that. His uncle's death and the selling up of Donaghmore had claimed him. "We're in the devil of a mess over there. The Sinn Feiners are fighting like Kilkenny cats. I'm getting out of it while the going's good. Better cut my losses while I may." And then suddenly, disturbingly, deeply flushed, he said: "I've nothing to offer you now—not even a home, but I want you, and so . . . Will you take me or, or let me down?"

The shock of this singular announcement, and the joy of it, for all her determined self-deception, brought a swift uprush of ghostly rapture. She was wanted, and he—God bless him! —never mind how clumsily, was telling her: "I'm broke. When everything's paid up I shan't have five hundred a year."

She smiled happily, and stopped herself in time from saying she could beat him by ten times as much. She stretched her hand across the table. His closed upon it. "We could live well enough," she said, "on half of that."

"Then you will? Can I believe it?" He was incredulous, a simpleton, a boy, and—fifty-one!

"Oh, love," she sighed, tears springing, "what tricks it plays with us! I've waited twenty years for this, and you ask me—will I?"

To others lunching there about them, intent upon their appetites, these two whom life had harried and had parted, and who received each other now to know that they would never part again, were but one more commonplace middle-aged couple enjoying *Sole à Bonne Femme, Escalopes de Veau* soaked in Marsala and laced with a vintage superb of *Liebfraumilch*. None to see them could have guessed that all their outlived youth was revitalized, submerged in a radiant contentment beyond words. Their words were few. She let him talk and tell of his travels; she told him none of hers, her voyaging in fields far from and alien to his. Time enough for that. He touched on world conditions, spoke of Europe at strife as 'a powder magazine that could at any moment be ignited by a spark', and—he had rejoined his regiment.

She came down from seventh heaven to a sixth, to ask him shakily: "Does that mean . . . war?"

He nodded. "We're not prepared. We never are. It may be this year or it may be next, but sometime it will be. That's sure."

She stayed unshattered. What though a mad Emperor in Germany played with squibs to set the world alight? . . . "And perhaps," she said blissfully, "it will be never."

But as they came out of the restaurant and into that narrow street, the luncheon editions of the evening papers placarded the double murder of the Archduke Franz Ferdinand and his wife in the obscure Bosnian town of Sarajevo.

"The game's a-foot," said Garth. "And now . . . where shall we go from here?"

THEY went from there to her Hertfordshire home, and were married by special licence a week later. The register in the village church dated July 5, 1914, records it as between, 'Peridot Hope-Winter, widow, and Garth Denis Curran, bachelor, Lieutenant-Colonel, D.S.O., seventh Baron Mulvarnie.'

Thirty years they had together. There was no issue of the marriage. The peerage, inherited from his uncle, became extinct with the death of Major-General Lord Mulvarnie in 1944.

She lived long enough to see the first draft of this book completed in manuscript and to give me her aid and advice in the compilation of the narrative.

She died in October, 1955, at the age of eighty-three.